Frances Paige has made herself one of the most popular writers of the decade with the publication of her ongoing saga about the McGraths of Sholton, but she has always had a large following for her many novels, written under a number of pseudonyms. Under the name Frances Paige she published two novels before embarking on her saga: *Three Girls* and *Lost Time*. The first book about the McGraths, *The Sholtie Burn*, was published in 1986, to be followed a year later by *Maeve's Daughter*. A fourth volume is now in preparation.

Born in Scotland, Frances Paige is married to a psychiatrist whose thinking, she admits, has greatly influenced her approach to characterization. She and her husband live in Lancashire and travel regularly to southwest France, her second love.

By the same author

Three Girls
Lost Time
The Sholtie Burn
Maeve's Daughter

FRANCES PAIGE

The Distaff Side

This edition published for Diamond Books, 2000

Diamond Books is an imprint of
HarperCollins*Publishers*
77-85 Fulham Palace Road,
Hammersmith, London W6 8JB

This paperback edition first published in 1990

First published in Great Britain by
Souvenir Press Ltd 1988

ISBN 0 26 167343 2

Printed and bound in Great Britain by
Caledonian International Book Manufacturing Ltd, Glasgow

Set in Times

To Maisie

Acknowledgements

I would like to thank the following for permission to quote from copyright material: Unwin Hyman for the verse on p. 216, from *The Scottish Carter* by Angela Tuckett, published by George Allen & Unwin; Elspeth King, The People's Palace, Glasgow Green, for the lines on p. 375, from *Holloway Jingles* by A. A. Wilson; Messrs A. P. Watt Ltd on behalf of Michael B. Yeats and Macmillan London Ltd. for the lines from the poem 'They went forth to battle . . .' by W. B. Yeats, on p. 382, taken from *The Collected Poems of W. B. Yeats*.

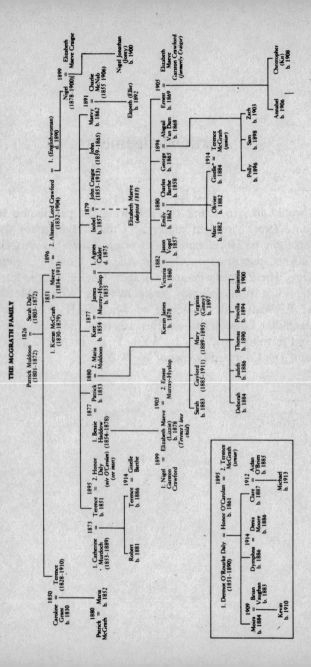

THE MCGRATH FAMILY

BOOK ONE
War, War . . .
1900–1906

1

The snow under the cedar tree, dappled gold by the wintry sunlight, was seemingly pierced by black spears whose tiny flower-heads were invisible except when they were shaken by a gust of wind. But Lizzie saw them in her mind's eye, delicate white bells, green-veined with frilled anthers.

She turned from the window of the Hall drawing-room, liking the trim feel of her waist in her wool morning gown after having slopped about in negligées for so long. 'The snowdrops are out,' she said.

'Do you tell me that now?' Her Grandmother's eyes were teasing behind the steel-rimmed spectacles she was forced to wear if she wanted to peruse the Glasgow Herald. 'And haven't they been before your very eyes this last month?'

'Ah, but today's different.' She had felt the load lift from her heart last night when Aunt Maevy, with Ellie dancing at her heels, had called with the news, welcome envoys if ever there were. 'Ladysmith relieved at last, Grandma! The world's beautiful, the snowdrops, everything! I woke up with no morning sickness for the first time.'

'Good news is better than Jim Geddes' medicine. Or was it Dr Belle you saw? She wants to specialize in women's troubles, doesn't she?'

'Yes. She's all right.' Lizzie thought of the doctor's daughter laying hands on her, the light grey eyes, almost silver they'd seemed under the dark brows, cool . . . why had they made her feel uncomfortable? 'But I'd rather have Charlie than either of them.' She laughed. 'Aunt

Maevy used to say, "Run to Uncle Charlie and he'll make it better." Anything. Grazed knees, even fishing out the elastic from my doll's body to anchor an arm or a leg. Did you see the joy on her face last night? "He'll find the War over when the *Carthaginian* docks," she said. But I'm relying on him getting there and finding Nigel. He promised.'

'Nigel's not lost, Lizzie. It's just that letters take such a time. He'll be marching in this very minute with General Buller.'

'Do you think so?' There had been Colenso and the terrible anxiety she had felt when she had read about all the men who had been killed escorting the guns. Nigel's regiment, the Royal Scottish Fusiliers. She had retched her heart out, nausea compounding the anguish. But she would have heard long ago . . . 'Where was it Uncle Charlie said he thought he'd be sent once he arrives at Capetown?' She spoke calmly.

'Natal. Maybe Pietermaritzburg. There's a big hospital there.' Hospital . . . supposing he had not been killed at Colenso but had been injured and was lying in some hospital, dying . . .?

'Read me what it says in the *Herald*, Grandma.' She turned to look again at the snowy carpet under the cedar. And the drifts of snowdrops. They were swaying gaily, a symbol of hope, not despair. Hold on to that.

'Let me see, then. Ah, here it is.' Her grandmother's colourful voice came to her, colourful like its owner with her red hair and blue eyes at sixty-six. Still a beauty. 'Mother's indestructible,' her daughter, Maevy, had said the other day. Aunt Maevy would be the last to believe she was the inheritor of her mother's beauty along with her name, but she was, together with the stalwartness of character. Maybe some day *she* would have it . . .' "Great crowds stopped the traffic in London last night around the Mansion House . . ."'

'They'd be dancing.' Lizzie spoke to the snow-covered garden. She and Nigel had danced here in this house when he had given her the ring. She looked down at the sparkling circle enclosing the ruby, red as blood . . .

'They'd be dancing all right, all over the country.' Her grandmother looked down again at the newspaper. '"All the clubs in Pall Mall lit their gas flambeaux . . ." what a sight that must have been . . . "The streets were blocked from end to end by a cheering, swirling multitude . . ."'

'What a grand word that is. "Multitude", not "crowd".'

'Worthy of the occasion. ". . . and carrying banners and flags. Even soldiers were carried aloft."' Lizzie turned to listen, excited at the picture in her mind's eye. '"Art students marched from South Kensington to cheer Chamberlain at Princes Gate."' She lowered the paper and looked with her bright eyes at her grand-daughter. 'What do you think of that, the Honourable Mrs Nigel Garston Crawford?'

Lizzie laughed. 'That it will be nothing to the fun we'll have in Sholton tonight, my lady!' Her mind was cleared of misgivings, happy. 'I'm going to the parish hall to help, and all the children have been excused school so that they can build the bonfire. Ellie will be organizing that, if I know her.'

'Alastair's been asked to set it alight.'

'That's right and proper since he's the laird. He'll have to wrap up warmly. You know what the cold and damp does to that leg of his.' Since she had lived at the Hall she had grown to care deeply for her father-in-law, Grandma's husband. They talked of Nigel together, about when he was a schoolboy, and how like his grandmother he was in his interest in nature. 'Creatures of the woods, both of them,' he had said to her, his amber eyes reminding her of Nigel's . . . 'Oh, Grandma, I'm suddenly living again!' She clapped her hands.

'The seige is over, my body seems to be my own again,

13

so *that* seige is over too, and Uncle Charlie will soon meet Nigel!' She picked up her skirts and whirled about the room, feeling her hair lift from her shoulders, then suddenly stopped. She must be careful not to harm the baby.

That evening she stood with the others round the bonfire in the football park. It flared and spat as it soared to the wintry sky. 'That must have been a magic torch I used.' Lord Crawford turned smilingly to her.

'We threw some cans of paraffin on the wood this afternoon,' she laughed up at him. 'You're not omnipotent after all.'

'Don't destroy my illusions.' His face looked pinched with the cold. 'What did you say, my dear?' Now he was bending his head to his wife, dressed to kill as usual in a fur cape and a cloud of veiling round her face and head. What an elegant couple they still were, she with that indestructible "something", a *je ne sais quoi*, Lizzie thought, remembering her step-cousin, Emily, in France, Madame Barthe. Maeve would always be *du monde* to Emily since her visit to Paris.

She saw Ellie darting about with some of her playmates, her plaits flying, and thought the girl looked like an embodiment of her young self except for her fair hair. She turned to Maevy on her other side. 'Ellie thinks this has been laid on for her special benefit.'

'Ellie and the Queen.' Her aunt laughed. 'But she won't go too near. I've warned her and she's biddable.'

'Look at John and Isobel.' She could speak easily now about her aunt and uncle who for so long had been her adoptive parents. 'I think he'd rather have been asked to say a few prayers first.'

'We got plenty of that this morning. A full complement.' They smiled into each other's eyes. Of course, Aunt Maevy was her soulmate, always knew what she was

14

thinking. Her eyes strayed again to her Aunt Isobel, her frail, faded prettiness. She had her arm through her husband's as she smiled dutifully from time to time at passers-by. She would rather be tucked up in bed, poor soul. She felt a great rush of love for her.

But that part of her life was over. She was a married woman, pregnant, her husband fighting in South Africa. But he'd soon be home, soon be home . . . she felt tears running down her face and surreptitiously wiped them. How selfish she was, with Maevy standing so straight and tall beside her, like Grandma. 'You'll be wearying to hear from Charlie,' she said.

'Aye, wearying, my lovely.' She felt Maevy's arm go round her shoulders. Oh, she was lucky with this family of hers, her real father, Terence, with his second wife, Honor, in Ireland, her Uncle Patrick and Aunt Maria in America, Aunt Kate and Uncle James. And Nigel marching triumphantly into Ladysmith behind General Buller, not to mention this baby safe inside her. She could not understand why the tears continued to flow . . .

2

He was lying with Lizzie on the grassy hill beside the ruined monastery. The autumn sun played down on them, that beguiling, golden sun which people had begun to call ominous, the calm before the storm. 'Dear Lizzie,' he said, turning to her, 'I have this longing . . .' his throat had become narrow with desire . . . 'I've had it since the first day when you told me your sad story . . .' The deep blueness of her eyes, the almost black blueness ('I blush with my eyes,' she'd said once), were engulfing him, it seemed; he felt the soft melting body against his, the warmth of the sun, and the silence. It became a waiting silence, and then, as he pressed her to him, it slowly filled with dread.

Now the warmth was a coldness, her body in his arms a wraith, a nothingness, the light dark, the silence suddenly shattered by the sound of battle all round him. Men were shouting, there was the loud screaming of bursting shells . . . He struggled to see in the darkness, calling her name, 'Lizzie, Lizzie . . .'

It was daylight and the air seemed to be singing with heat, burning the grass, the stunted bushes, causing the rocks to cast black shadows on the ground. He was at the head of his men as they tramped across a pontoon bridge, encouraging them as they scrambled down the great gorge of the Tugela. 'Come on, the Fusiliers!' He waved his sword. 'Follow me!' Ahead of him through the trees he could just see the tip of the first kopje.

Now they were hacking their way through the jungle growth of aloes, the huge red cliffs towering round them, making caverns of heat in which they sweated and cursed.

Butterflies flitted in the dusty sunlight, brilliantly-coloured, foreign-looking butterflies, much bigger than the pale yellow ones in the Hall gardens. They're happy, he thought, war or no war, it's all the same to them. Inconsequential. Not like those damned insects – he had felt a vicious sting on his cheek. Allies of Botha. He saw one on a broad leaf, fat-bodied, wicked wings quivering, and neatly hacked it in two. Lizzie wouldn't have liked that . . .

They were out of the gorge now and climbing towards the kopje. A hundred yards ahead of them the hillside seemed to erupt in their faces. Lyddite shells were smashing the boulders like giant hammers, and flying steel was making the earth rear up in fountains. He waved on his platoon. 'Our artillery's covering us. Come on! Not far now!'

The next advance took them beyond the cover, and heavy enemy fire coming from the direction of Railway Hill pushed them back again to the rocks. He rallied the men again. 'We're nearly at the plateau!' He was looking through his glasses and saw the creeping brown dots on the horizon. 'Buller's thrown in some reserves. Come on, lads!' They rushed forward at his bidding, reassured.

He did not know fear in the bayonet charge which followed. He had feared fear, but had not thought of the agony he would feel when the screams of the dying men seemed to shatter his eardrums, had not reckoned on the sickness which overcame him when he saw horses rolling on the ground, their intestines trailing. But there was also the strange kind of satisfaction, elation, rather, in hacking his way towards the target he had set the platoon, the neck of ground between Railway Hill and Hart's Hill to the west. He saw the raised hands, the terrified bearded face of a Boer as he plunged his bayonet downwards, tried to forget his eyes.

He was swimming in a dream. 'Up, run!' 'Take cover!'

'Up, run!' 'Take cover!' It had a kind of pattern, reminding him of snatching runs at cricket, but those green playing fields of his youth had been quiet except for the occasional ripple of clapping, not like this inferno. By God, those Boers were tough, and looked twice his age; farmers mostly, with all the fierceness of men defending their land. Did they never give in?

'Up, run!' Shrieking gun-fire. 'Take cover, men!' The feel of the hot earth under his body, the continual buzzing in his ears as if a bee were trapped there. 'Up, run!' And this time a great lift of spirits. They were almost there, the fire from Railway Hill was less now, was no longer there, they had reached the plateau. Old Buller's reserves had swung the balance. Good old Buller!

He turned, elated, to Forbes at his side. 'We've done it!' The words were out before he saw that half of the sergeant-major's face was blown away. One eye swung on a thread of bloody skin, the other was staring at him. He moaned, tried to hide it. 'I'm sorry . . .' he spoke to the eye, 'sorry . . .'

'I wish they were all as polite as you.' He heard a brisk female voice.

He put his hand out, his fingers slid on the shiny celluloid surface of a cuff. 'I was with Lizzie . . . and then I lost her. I had to fight, lead the men . . . where is she? She was in my arms . . .'

'Poor boy . . .' Who were they talking about? He wasn't poor, was he? He was the son of Lord Crawford of Sholton, and he had been with Lizzie on that grassy hillside . . . but *that* had been before they were married, before this war . . .

'Lizzie . . .!' he shouted, holding out his arms, but his voice was drowned, not by the noise of battle this time, but by cheers and bagpipes and marching feet. He looked down and saw his own, the worn boots caked with veldt mud, his legs in a pair of strange trousers, blue . . .

'Found them somewhere.' It was Captain Gilchrist speaking now. 'Probably came off a dead Boer, but all the better for that! Got to be decent for the parade, old man.'

'Got to cover my backside, you mean.' He heard the cackle of his own laughter. Always there was this relief of tension after a battle. The men played childish tricks on each other, or sat in their bivouacs writing letters, living the battle at second-hand with their wives or sweethearts. His English schooling did not approve of that. 'A slight skirmish, my darling. Nothing to worry about . . .'

Food was uppermost in the soldiers' minds. Even now on this triumphal march some of them were carrying dry bunches of tinder for firewood. They thought of only one thing at a time, which was good. Occasionally they cheered and waved to the tatterdemalion crowd lining the dirt road, soldiers off duty, officers, their wives and children, townsfolk, Zulus, doolie-bearers.

The spectators looked half-starved, poor devils, and was it his imagination that their welcome was half-hearted? Who could blame them after what they'd been through? They had probably been dragooned by White into standing there. 'Lo, the conquering heroes come . . .' And not before time, they would be thinking.

It was rather poor taste to have fit men walking past, swaggering past, this scarecrow lot. Not in keeping with old Buller. Maybe *he* had been dragooned into it as well. Gough's cavalry, fit horses, fit men, jogging over the Klip River bridge, should have been enough, rather than twenty thousand men marching past this emaciated-looking bunch. The sight of a woman's stony face turning away from them made him feel sick, a dull familiar nausea. And that flesh wound in his leg was aching. He had not felt like reporting it, not after Forbes, nor all those others they had spent half the night bringing in, men crying like babies, men with their limbs smashed, or missing altogether . . .

The lines of onlookers wavered in the heat. He must fight this nausea, the persistent headache, the occasional shivering. He was on his feet at least. He straightened himself up as he marched, had to be a credit to the Fusiliers, and to Lizzie. Dear Lizzie, her red hair, darker than her grandmother's but as abundant, those blue eyes which deepened with emotion and were darkest of all when they made love. His whole being ached for her, was submerged in the duller ache which never seemed to leave him.

It was like rubbing salt in a wound to march in front of those wan-faced people with the dead eyes. Captain Gilchrist had told him of the siege mentality, how one became apathetic, despairing. The poor rations did not help. Still, the siege was over now. It was a thing of the past. He thought of General Buller's words.

'Soldiers of Natal! The Relief of Ladysmith unites two forces, both of which have, during the last few months, striven with conspicuous gallantry and splendid determination to maintain the honour of their Queen and Country.' He drew himself up as they swung past, and this time a man in a torn shirt called out, 'Glad to see you! Glad . . .'

Later, when they broke ranks and shared rations with the men inside, he felt better. They fell in with some soldiers of the Thirteenth Battery who seemed friendly enough. 'Here, try a bit of this steak!' An officer, who had introduced himself as Peter Tait, held out a tin plate with some black-looking meat on it. 'Best horse. Better than trek ox any day.' He took it, trying not to think of the horses with their guts spilling out on the veldt. Beggars couldn't be choosers, he reminded himself. Tait was telling him that their diet had been meagre, a kind of soup-paste called Chevril, 'mystery' sausages, bread made from maize with the gluten from laundry starch. The death rate had been seventy a week. 'But it's all over, thanks to you. I'll soon be going home. Care to see some pictures of my wife and baby?'

'I'm not long married,' he said, 'no family, as yet . . .'

'It gives you something to fight for.' Lieutenant Tait was moist-eyed as he handed over the photographs. 'Here, try another piece of steak. Keeps you out of Intombi.'

'Intombi?' he asked. 'What's that?'

'A hospital camp outside the defences. They say if you go there you never come back.'

It was when he was chewing at the tough, stringy meat that the ache in his bones came back, the headache, but this time accompanied by a nausea so violent that he had to jump up and say to Tait, 'Where are your latrines?' Tait pointed and he ran across the pitted ground. The stench directed him.

He did not leave them for a long time, and on his way back to the tent the ground rose up and whacked him in the middle of the forehead. He lay under the burning sun unable to move, until another man making for the latrines discovered him. After that it was a confused, dreaming muddle, being lifted on to a stretcher, the tetchy voice of an older man who was prodding him, asking him to put out his tongue, sticking a thermometer in his mouth. 'Is that you, Charlie?' he said hopefully, knowing it wasn't.

'Enteric', 'virulent,' 'We've got enough of them here . . .' The words came to him in between the jolting of wagon wheels and he knew he had not died. 'Is it typhoid?' he asked, surprised that his voice was still there in the miasma of pain and shivering and sickness which was disintegrating his body. 'Yes,' someone said, 'we're taking you to Intombi.'

3

The heat struck Charlie like a blow as they marched off the *Carthaginian* on to the harbour at Capetown on the twenty-first of March. It had taken them all of three days to unload. The weather had been rough as far as Las Palmas, and there had been quite a few deaths amongst the horses. The veterinary surgeons had been kept busy. One of them, Bob Richards, now drew alongside him. 'It's going to be dark before we pitch our tents at Maitland Camp, I'm afraid.'

'Yes, but it's grand to feel solid earth under our feet again. You had the worst job.'

Richards nodded. 'There's a lot of horse when you're in confined quarters in a rolling ship. Especially as we may be on our way back before long and have to go through it all again.'

'You mean because of Ladysmith being relieved? I don't think the war's over by a long chalk. The Natal hospitals are full of casualties, not to mention typhoid. Even if we never fought another day there would be plenty of mopping up to do.'

'Might be easier to shoot the buggers the way we do horses.' The man cackled, then sobered. 'No, I didn't mean that, McNab. Just a joke.'

I don't like your taste in jokes, Charlie thought, but did not take the remark too seriously. A long voyage such as they had had caused tension. Even he had felt it. 'I'm hoping I'll be sent up near Ladysmith. I have a young relative by marriage there. I've promised his wife I'll try to seek him out. They're not long married.' He thought of Lizzie's anxious, lovely face when he had been saying good-bye. 'Promise, Uncle Charlie . . .'

'If he has enteric you'll be unlikely to find him alive. The death-rate's terrible up there.'

'So I've heard, but can you wonder at it? How often have we to learn that cleanliness is next to godliness? And there's the bad management. They haven't even enough mattresses! They're lying packed close together, the dying and dead amongst the living. Sorry, I'm riding my hobby-horse again. My wife's a nurse. She would have liked to come out too but one of us had to stay at home. We have a daughter.'

Richards looked thoughtful. 'Scutari all over again, eh? Endless form-filling, endless red tape, not enough health precautions. My father died in the Crimea. I say, McNab, why don't you put in a request to be sent to one of the hospital camps in Natal, or even a cushier billet, to an officers' Rest Home? Rehabilitation, they call it now. Getting them fit enough to be picked off by those damned Boers, eh, what? It's taking a hell of a time to show them who's master.'

'You think it's a question of who's to doff the hat?'

'Well, don't you?' He was a fresh-faced youngster. Everything was black and white to him.

'Maybe it's more complex than that. Greed for the Rand gold. Or politics.'

'We are all Imperialists now,' Joe Chamberlain had said. Waste of time to mention Darwin, Huxley or Unwin to this lad, or for that matter, Ruskin, who had pro-pounded what he called the palpable inevitable fact that what one person has, another cannot have. And what would young Richards think if he said out loud his own belief that this was a more unnecessary war than most?

'Where do you come from?' he asked. 'Town or country?' He only half-listened as the lieutenant enlarged on the joys of fox-hunting in Rutland. He was busy with

23

thoughts of home, of Maevy, and thinking that as soon as they were settled in camp he would write a letter to her and tell her he was safe and well.

'My dearest love to you and Ellie,' he would say. 'I think of you constantly in this new world of burning sun and milling khaki figures. Has the snow gone from Braidholme, and are the snowdrops making way for the primroses on the banks of the Sholtie?'

He was not long at Maitland Camp. Very soon they were transported from Capetown and installed in a hospital at Pietermaritzburg where the soldiers were brought by hospital train from further up the line as far as Pretoria. He had no time to think of home during the day but each night he managed to scribble a few words to Maevy.

'Our lifeline will be letters,' she had said. 'I've always depended on you.' The thought of her sweet and resolute face on the quayside when they embarked was always with him. Maeve, her mother, had once said to him that she was the best of the bunch. He could vouch for that. He put everything of himself and his love for her into his letters, at the same time making light of the trials and tribulations.

The long hours spent in the operating theatre did not worry him. He was tireless. What distressed him was the lack of equipment, the difficulty under the circumstances in practising his strict rules of hygiene. Many who died could have been saved if their wounds had not become badly infected before they reached him. He looked back ruefully to his time at the Royal Infirmary in Glasgow. There all he had had to combat as a disciple of Lister had been prejudice; here it was the simple fact that the conditions necessary to practise Lister's precepts were totally absent.

He kept a constant lookout for Nigel, asked every soldier who came under his care, especially if they were from Ladysmith. None had heard of him. Either they were too ill to think coherently, or they were elated at the thought of being invalided home and could talk of nothing else.

Their opinion of the Boers had changed from the euphoria at the outbreak of the war, when they had been led to believe that they were a half-educated, ill-equipped lot of men. The Boers' expertise in the saddle had come as a shock, their supply of musketry, but principally their resolution. This was their land and they would fight to the death to keep it. Their Calvinistic zeal gave them backbones of steel.

After he had been at the camp for a week he was sent to Mooi River to a Rest Camp for officers and men. One of the officers was suffering from an undiagnosed pain in his abdomen. A surgeon's opinion was needed. He went with lightened heart, hoping that he might hear something of Nigel. The man he had been sent to see had a fulminating appendix.

There was no heart-searching such as there had been in Maevy's case when he had been forced to stand back helplessly and see Mr Wilcox dithering over her. Those awful days came back to him as he dealt swiftly with the diseased appendix. 'When in doubt whip it out,' he said to the astonished young doctor who had been detailed to assist him. The invalid was well enough to sit up in bed and talk in a couple of days.

Lieutenant Tait of the Sixtieth Rifles was voluble in his thanks. 'I'll get back now, won't I?' he asked Charlie. 'I'd like to do some fighting instead of being shut up in Ladysmith.'

'At least you were safe there,' Charlie said.

'Yes, but at what a price. The boredom! Day after day seeing the men becoming discontented and often ill because of poor rations. Not to mention the humiliation. Do you know, we outnumbered the Boers by as much as two to one if not more! And yet White never made a move. My father was a Lieutenant Colonel in my regiment. I could never go back without having vindicated myself. My people have always been in the Army.'

Charlie kept quiet. Had not he himself joined the Volunteers when he was a young man?

'Don't rush it at least,' he contented himself with saying. 'You're in a run-down condition. Your strength needs to be built up.'

'It's not as bad as if I'd been in Intombi. Walking skeletons there, they say. Hardly any of them come out alive.'

'So I've heard. By the way, did you meet any of the relieving troops? My young nephew was with General Buller, I think. Lieutenant Nigel Crawford, Scottish Fusiliers.'

'We shared our rations with a bunch of them, come to think of it. There was a young officer, dark, very thin. But he didn't talk Scottish.'

'He was educated in England. Can you remember anything else about him?'

'Nothing except that he looked as if he was pegging out. He spent most of his time in the latrines. And his eyes looked strange, wandering . . .' Charlie's heart felt as if it were being squeezed.

'Did it look like enteric?'

'It could have been. I noticed his hand was trembling when he was holding his mess tin. He was very polite. That's what I most remember. Kept trying to force down the stinking horsemeat which was all we could offer them . . . "Thanks most awfully. It's delicious."' Somewhere there was a faint echo of Nigel's speech. He saw the young man was tiring, and arranged his pillows.

'Lie back now and have a rest. Could you tell me, if it were enteric, would he be sent to Intombi?'

'It's likely. It was the nearest place and they'd want to

26

dump him out of the way as soon as possible. We all dreaded the thing.'

By the time Charlie got back to Pietermaritzburg he had made up his mind. He saw his Major, and asked if he could be sent to Intombi. The man was non-committal. 'I've no power to chop and change, Captain McNab. We've all got enough to do here.'

'I know that, sir. But if we were sending supplies up the line, or additional surgeons were required for emergency work . . .'

'If, if . . .' The man looked like a fussy bank clerk. His desk was strewn with papers. Charlie remembered Leiutenant Richards' remark: 'Endless form-filling, endless red tape, as bad as Scutari.'

A week later he had a message brought to him by his orderly. 'Proceed to Intombi at once. Possible amputation required.' He packed his valise hurriedly, but with a sick kind of premonition.

It had been right. Nigel lay on the bed he was led to. The face on the dirty mattress matched its colour, a dingy grey; the brown of his hair had dulled to a no-colour; his face was so emaciated that his nose was beak-like. But the aquiline features, with the same look of nobility as his father's, were clearly recognizable, the distinctive curve of the mouth although the lips were cracked and peeling, the fine setting of the eyes.

'Nigel,' he knelt on the floor to make himself level with his eyes. 'It's Charlie.' He made himself smile. 'Do you know me?'

'Charlie?' The eyes wandered.

'Lizzie's uncle . . .'

'Charlie!' His voice became stronger. 'I've been dreaming, of home . . . now you're here. Sorry, old chap . . .' He struggled to raise his head from the pillow. 'Didn't want you to find me like this . . .'

'I've found you, that's the main thing.' Charlie pushed him gently back. 'I'm here to get you well.'

'Oh, good.' It was a breath of a voice again. 'When did you arrive?'

'You mean at Capetown? On the 21st March. I'm based at Pietermaritzburg. I've been sent to see you.'

'Sent . . . I've been here a long time . . . stupid. Tell me . . . tell me about Lizzie.' Her name seemed to rally him. 'How was she when you left?'

'Blooming. She's pregnant. Did you know?'

'Did you say . . . pregnant?' The amber eyes filled, and Nigel turned his head away from him. There was a silence.

'So we've got to get you well again.' He saw the head nod. When he turned again to Charlie he was composed.

'We'd hoped. My little Lizzie. I wish . . . I wish . . .'

'I promised her I'd find you.'

'Did you? She always had . . . great faith in her Uncle Charlie.'

'Now that you're a prospective father . . .' he said, but he could not go on. The boy's face was like death, what he could see of him merely skin and bone. 'How did you get to Intombi?' He changed the subject.

'I was brought here after the Relief . . . stupid of me. Felt sick. I thought it was just that damned horsemeat but that was just . . . the finishing touch.'

'I expect this was the nearest place.' Charlie saw that Nigel's eyes had closed. He was like a skeleton. The typhoid was responsible for that, of course, but there was the other thing, the reason why he had been asked to come. He put his hand on the emaciated one lying outside the sheet. 'I've been told you've a leg which is giving you a little bother . . .' He saw Nigel's eyelids flicker. 'Maybe you'll let me have a look.'

'So long as you don't chop it off.' The mouth moved.

'Who said anything like that? I just want to look at it. You lie quietly.'

'It's nothing. I got a little flesh wound at Pieters Hill . . . nothing . . .' his voice trailed away.

'I won't even touch it. Just a glance.' The thin sheet was the same dingy colour as the mattress. Flies were buzzing. Lister would have a heart attack if he saw the conditions here. He had to force himself to take hold of a corner of the sheet, lift it.

The leg had a bandage round the calf, none too clean. Beneath that and extending to the foot it was discoloured, the skin tight – no point in beating about the bush, it was totally black. His heart filled with tears as he looked at it. That was the sensation, a swelling, as if it touched his rib cage. This was too deep a sorrow for ordinary tears. The lad had gas gangrene in his leg.

'I'll see you tomorrow, Nigel,' he said. 'No need to worry. I'll take care of you.'

'So long as you don't . . . chop . . .' His eyes were still closed. Lizzie would die if she could see her handsome young husband in this state, he thought, die . . . There was no choice. The leg had to be amputated, and in the middle of the thigh if there was to be any hope at all.

The following morning he told Nigel, and thought for a moment that he had killed him then and there. He stood beside him as he lay on the trestle table and held his hand unashamedly. 'I had to tell you, Nigel. I couldn't operate without your permission.'

He was grey-faced. His eyes were smudged black underneath. 'And if I don't give it?' It was a whisper.

'It's gas gangrene. You'd lose it in any case. You'd die.'

'Is there morphia?'

'Yes, enough.'

'It's not for the pain, Charlie. It's for blocking out the thinking . . . knowing . . . what was happening . . . what . . . it meant. Oh, what d'you think Lizzie would say? She wouldn't want me . . . like that.'

'She loves you. She'd want you back. You know that as

well as I do. And there's more reason than ever now. The baby.'

'I'd . . . forgotten about the baby. It would never have known me any different . . . but there's . . . father.'

'He'd be proud of you. We all would.' This swollen heart of his pressing against his ribs made it difficult for him to speak. He'd go to the Major, say he could not perform this operation, that he was too emotionally involved. But there was no other surgeon in Intombi, and by the time a replacement was sent for, Nigel would have died. You volunteered, he reminded himself. He remembered once long ago, in another world, it seemed, he had said to Ellie about some small remark of hers, 'Hoist by your own petard,' and she had said in her bright enquiring way, 'What's that, Daddy?'

'With or without a leg.' Nigel's voice was bitter.

'You know everyone would.' He spoke sharply. Choices. It was the same in surgery as in everything else, only more urgent.

If the leg was left, Nigel would die, if it was amputated the shock might kill him. The dangerous time was always at the moment the tourniquet was removed and the body was suddenly flooded with histamine from the operation site. Especially with someone as weak as Nigel. He had sat up half the night thinking about the possibilities, even although the Major had reassured him.

'One step at a time, McNab. You've confirmed my opinion although I'm not a surgeon. We both know he'll die if it isn't done, perhaps if it is, but at least there's a chance. Eight o'clock tomorrow morning. Lieutenant Baird will be the anaesthetist and an orderly will be there to help you . . .'

He turned, saw the two men coming into the room, the young lieutenant and an even younger orderly, mere boys. He nodded at them, said to Nigel, 'We're ready now, but it's for you to say.'

30

The boy's eyes opened, those strange, attractive amber eyes which must be so attractive to Lizzie. The look was direct. He stopped thinking of him as a boy. 'If it's got to be done I'd rather have you than anyone else. Go ahead.'

He had stood beside him until the morphia began to take effect, listened to the rambling voice talking about Lizzie, always Lizzie. 'Do you remember that first time, Lizzie, at the ruined monastery? That wonderful summer before the War? The short grass, burnt . . . "You're daring me to be shocked," you said. You loved to be teased. But you liked the feeling that . . . they . . . had been there before . . . There were no birds singing . . . when I kissed you. The ring, Lizzie!' He was suddenly distressed. 'Do you still wear it, my darling? You hid it at first . . . on a chain . . .' Lieutenant Baird nodded to Charlie.

'He's out.'

The leg was painted with iodine. He had sterilized the towels himself, arranged his knives and saw. The tourniquet, a black rubber elastic band. 'Circular amputation,' he said, taking up one of the knives. He pointed it downwards and then cut into the leg. Work quickly but accurately. One clean sweep to divide all the skin around the limb. 'We'll need local anaesthesia to deal with the shock,' he said. His concentration was complete. He no longer thought of Nigel as a person, lying unconscious beneath his flying fingers.

4

Ernest Murray-Hyslop, being driven in the Crawford carriage from Sholton Station, thought of the note he had received from Kate's mother – at thirty-one it seemed ridiculous to think of her as 'Grandma', or for that matter, Kate as 'step-mother'. Each had that rare quality of treating you as yourself, unlabelled.

He had been busy enough since he had left America to spend a year or so in the Glasgow office of McGrath and Company, Haulage Contractors, the firm started by Lady Crawford with her first husband, Kieran McGrath. It had been his own idea to come here, and Kate's brother, Patrick, had been in favour of it. It was strange that while Patrick had pulled up his roots from Scotland and gone to live in America with his wife, Maria, and family, he had done the reverse. But, then, he had always been restless. Maybe that was why he had reached this great age and remained single.

But he who travels alone travels fastest, he consoled himself. Not that he needed any consolation. He had always been able to enjoy himself, and in the short time he had been here he had found the Glasgow ladies more than willing to help him.

Now the coachman was passing through the large wrought-iron gates with an imposing crest picked out on them in gold – he craned his neck to see it. An eagle with outspread wings and some lettering beneath it, Latin probably. Strange to think of Kate's mother living here in such style, when she had started her married life in a small cottage in the same village, a miner's wife.

The carriage had stopped in front of the house, the

coachman was getting down. When would Lord Crawford decide to have a motor car? he wondered. *He* had his eye on a Panhard when he could afford it. That would impress the Scottish girls with their bright eyes and their long vowels, 'Oh, Er . . . nest!'

It was an imposing house without a doubt, quite different from Wolf House, his parents' home in Wanapeake, or even Springhill, Great-Uncle Terence's house across the Hudson, that jolly brother of Lady Crawford who had made his and his brother George's childhood so bright. He and Great-Aunt Caroline would be glad they had their one ewe lamb, Maria, back beside them once more.

Gothic Revival, Charlie McNab had told him before he went overseas; a knowledgeable man, Charlie. And he liked Maevy, his wife, Kate's youngest sister. He hoped she would be here tonight. He liked the cresselated towers at each corner, like a castle, and the three-storied centre part, vaguely reminding him of a cathedral. It was not unlike some of the grand mansions on the Hudson with its tall decorated chimneys, or were they copies of this? And that front door under the massive stone porch with the butler standing beside it was certainly imposing. Yes, he was amongst the swells tonight.

But nothing could have been simpler and less ostentatious. Lord Crawford was formal, of course, as befitted his age, but his wife was as he remembered her when she had visited them at Wanapeake, with that wonderful air of vitality scarcely diminished.

'Come away in, Ernest, and warm yourself at the fire. It's a raw evening, but a "braw bricht nicht the nicht", eh?' She laughed. 'Has Kate taught you any of the Scots language, or have you picked up any in the office?' She did not give him time to answer. 'And here's your Aunt Maevy and cousin Lizzie just dying to meet you!'

Maevy was like a younger edition of Kate although fairhaired, but with that same sweetness of character; as

33

for Lizzie, he was lost in admiration. What a lovely young woman she had become. He kissed them both, especially Lizzie.

'Wee Lizzie,' he said, holding her hands, 'after all those years! Do you remember our bicycle ride round Wanapeake Point? What fun it was.'

'I was there, too,' Maevy laughed. 'Don't leave me out. Or have you eyes only for Lizzie?'

'Eyes for both of you! Don't you know that's what brought me to Scotland, to see if there were any more like you?'

'Come and sit down beside me, you flatterer,' Lady Crawford said. 'And have you had time to notice any other Glasgow girls?' She was teasing him. She and Lizzie had the same dark blue eyes. 'I'm sure you've been far too busy to look up from your ledger.'

'I'm never too busy for beautiful ladies of all ages.' He beamed at her, highly pleased at the attention he was receiving. She was still a beauty, and her draped dress of *écru* lace with its wide lace collar revealing her white shoulders was highly becoming, as were her jade earrings, echoing the green velvet ribbon threaded through the waist. 'Thank you.' The butler had handed him a glass of sherry. Lord Crawford, elegant though stooped, a bit of a dandy yet in his white tie and frilled front to his shirt, was saying pleasantly:

'I hope it's to your taste. I fancy myself a judge of Spanish wines. I used to go there often to buy pig-iron for my firm. It was always cheaper than we could produce.'

'It's fine,' he said. The rich darkness of the sherry was in his throat, the firelight and the golden shaded lamps were making everything beautiful to him. 'Mother lights up a room,' Kate had once said. 'That will only go when she goes.' She had looked sad. 'The world without her isn't to be imagined.'

'Are you coping with the work at McGraths?' Lord

Crawford asked him. 'You must find it all very strange after New York.'

'The language is strange to me,' he laughed, 'but I expect they'd say the same about my American twang. I like the city, and I've made one or two expeditions to your ocean, the Firth of Clyde.' He looked around at the laughing faces. 'Have I said anything amusing?'

'We don't call the Firth of Clyde an *ocean*,' Lizzie said, 'and if we did we'd call it the sea.'

'Now, that's Irish enough,' her grandmother said.

Ernest smiled. 'I haven't had much time for pleasure, to tell you the truth. The Boer War has depleted the staff badly, as you know, Lady Crawford.'

'Yes, I understand so. Now that I'm retired, and with Patrick in New York State and Terence in Ireland, you're the only member of the family to bring me news of the business.'

'A poor representative. The head lady in the typists' department was saying to me how much you were missed. "Mrs McGrath held it together," were her words, so there's a compliment for you.'

She looked pleased. 'Sometimes I think it held *me* together. But, there, I'm an old lady now, or so everyone tells me.' She looked absurdly young for her age, sixty-six, wasn't it? 'But I'm sorry to hear the staff is affected.'

'Three men went from the Accounts Department last week, and one of our best sales representatives as well. And with the death of Mr Carter, the accountant, not to mention Mr Johnson being struck down with a serious complaint – though fortunately Dan, his son, has stepped into his place – we're in sore straits.'

'Bob and Tom helped to build the firm with my first husband and myself. "The two stalwarts", we used to call them. I can't bear to think that one of them is no more and the other so ill. Maevy wanted to go overseas as a nurse, but I tell her she should go into the firm. It would help her to pass the time while Charlie's away.'

'She's mentioned it before, Ernest.' His aunt smiled at him. '"Something for yourself", you always said, Mother, didn't you? But when he comes back, would you want me to drop it? A busy doctor needs a wife at his side. And there's Ellie.'

'If you want to do a thing badly enough you'll always find a way. Well, the offer's open.'

'What about Robert, Terence's son? Isn't he supposed to be a business type?'

'How about me?' Lizzie said, laughing.

'You'll have plenty to do, my lovely, in the next few months.' Her grandmother smiled fondly at her.

She's going to have a child, Ernest thought. That would account for the extra bloom. And yet there was a darkness under her eyes as if she did not sleep well. She would worry about her husband. He felt a vague twinge of envy which he smothered. 'Have you heard from your husband recently?' he asked her.

'Very little.' The anxiety was there in her eyes. 'I've had one letter, but there was little . . . news in it.' He saw the eyes deepen, as if in remembrance of the words of the letter. 'I don't know if he's incarcerated in Ladysmith or still fighting.'

'Well, now that Ladysmith's relieved, so must you be.'

'Yes, I am. But, oh, I long to know if he's all right! I'm depending on Uncle Charlie. He's promised to look out for him.'

'If Charlie says he'll do a thing, you can depend on him,' Maevy said. 'I expect the first letter I get will be telling me about their meeting.' How reassuring her aunt sounds, Ernest thought. You could depend on her, too.

They went in to dinner, and Lord Crawford turned again to the subject of the War. Perhaps it was the only way he could express his anxiety about his son. Nigel was his only child. Will he perhaps bear a grudge against me? Ernest wondered. He had no desire to volunteer, and being an American citizen there was no compulsion on him. It had been a remote issue to him until he came here, and his concern at the moment was only because Nigel and Charlie were involved in it. Besides, they were relying on him at McGraths, especially with a depleted staff. He had no intention of feeling guilty.

'We can begin to see the end of the tunnel at last,' Lord Crawford was saying. 'Kimberley, Ladysmith, and now the splendid news that General Roberts has gone into Bloemfontein. That's a significant loss considering it's the capital of the Orange Free State.'

'Yes, indeed, sir,' he said. As an outsider and without what he thought of as the 'peculiarities' of the British, he believed it would be a long struggle even if there were no more pitched battles. Both sides seemed to him to have passed beyond reason to a state of blind faith in the right of their cause. It was as if Lord Crawford was reading his thoughts.

'What is your opinion, Ernest? The outsider often sees most of the game.' That was it in a nutshell. Everything was a 'game' to the British.

'I think Great Britain will win eventually.' He decided to be truthful. 'She'll pour in more troops, more generals, till they get the mixture right, at whatever cost. But the Boers have one great advantage: they know their terrain.'

'How long is "eventually"?' Lizzie appealed to him. 'I want Nigel home soon.'

'I'm sure you shall,' he said, smiling at her. He was captivated by her this evening. The sapphire blue of her velvet gown set off her eyes, and her rich copper-coloured hair was abundant, dressed low on her neck. Her skin had a warmth and a duskiness which the older woman's did not have. Hers was the true fairness of the red-haired. He had thought Lizzie an engaging young girl when she had visited them in Wanapeake, and so had Kieran, he remembered, his young step-brother. But this was a beautiful woman – married, he reminded himself. 'Especially,' he said, 'if Lord Crawford is right and it degenerates into guerilla fighting.' He turned to him. 'Was your son employed on the estate?'

'He had no time to be employed in anything, but I made him a director of our Iron and Steel Works before he left. It gives him even more to fight for . . .' He was interrupted by a loud knocking on the outside door. He looked at his wife, his eyebrows raised. 'Who can that be at this hour? It's most unusual.'

'Some little crisis,' she said reassuringly. 'Do you remember that time of the storm when the tree fell across this window?'

'And the next day Nigel left for Oxford,' Lizzie added, 'but he was soon back for your ball, Grandma, and we got engaged . . .'

'The knocking's stopped,' her grandmother said, looking at her husband.

'Redfern will have attended to it.'

'Oh, the dancing that night!' Lizzie's eyes shone. 'Do you like dancing, Ernest?'

'I've been told I'm a very fine dancer.' He kept his face straight.

'The Eightsome Reel, and the Schottische, and the Quadrilles?'

'I'm not so sure about those,' he laughed at her, 'but I can manage a very passable Polka.'

'I don't believe you! Well, I tell you what. When dinner's over you and I will dance the Polka together. We have a phonograph . . .' There was a discreet knock at the door. The elderly butler entered, face impassive. He was bearing a silver tray with an orange envelope on it.

'This has just arrived, your lordship.'

'Thank you, Redfern.'

The man coughed behind a white gloved hand. 'Er . . . it's addressed to the Honourable Mrs Nigel Garston Crawford, your lordship.'

'Oh . . .!' He looked across the table to Lizzie. She was holding her napkin to her mouth. It was no whiter than her face.

Ernest watched Maevy rise. Of course she had been a Sister in that huge Infirmary beside the Cathedral. Competent, everyone said. More than that, he thought, looking at her, prepared . . . She went round the table to where Lizzie was sitting, rigid, put an arm round her.

'Don't anticipate, Lizzie. Maybe they've let him home because Ladysmith's been relieved.' Lizzie did not answer. Ernest had never seen anyone sit so still. He saw the raised cords of her neck, the wide open eyes. She was trying to prevent herself from screaming . . .

'Would you like me to open it for you, Lizzie?' Lord Crawford said. 'Maevy's probably right.'

'No, don't open it! I can't . . . bear it!' She shrugged off Maevy's protective arm fiercely.

'Open it, Alastair.' It was Lady Crawford's voice. He was surprised at the harshness of it. 'She likes to get things done, Mrs McGrath,' the head of the Typists' Department had said. They still thought of her as Mrs McGrath.

He slit the envelope with his thumb, opened it, glanced at its contents. Ernest, watching him, thought he suddenly became an old man. His shoulders slumped forward. His head remained bowed over the paper.

'You must tell us, Alastair.' Again the harsh voice. 'Get it over with.'

'Yes. Yes . . .' The face he raised was grey, the eyes anguished. Without looking down again he said, as if in a dream, 'We regret . . . to report that . . . Lieutenant Nigel Crawford has died . . . of his wounds . . .'

'Oh . . .!' The sound which came from Lizzie was

39

scarcely human, a long, keening wail, which went on and on. Ernest jumped to his feet, stood uncertainly looking from her to Lord Crawford whose head was still bowed, feeling more distressed than he had ever felt in his life. And more useless. He saw Lady Crawford had risen also and was going towards her husband. Her arms were round him. She was speaking softly. 'My poor Alastair. Come, my dearest, don't give in. You know how we all depend on you . . .' She looked towards Ernest. 'Help Maevy,' she said.

'Yes, yes . . .' Maevy was trying to raise Lizzie from the table where her head and shoulders had collapsed. Her arms were spread out. One hand had knocked over her wine. The red stain was spreading on the white damask.

'I think she's fainted,' she said to Ernest. She was calm. She was not weeping. No one was weeping.

'I can manage her. You show me where to go.' He bent down and lifted Lizzie in his arms. She was light, but then she had always been slender. The child inside her did not make much difference as yet. Why should he think about the child at this time? he wondered, as Maevy opened the door for him.

A group of servants stood in the hall. Maevy spoke to the butler. 'There's bad news about Master Nigel, Redfern. Jessie, will you get hot bottles and bring them up to Mrs Crawford's room, and you, Cathy, see if the fire's burning well. And ask Cook for a hot drink. This way, Ernest.' She led him up the great staircase, calling out over her shoulder, 'And send for Dr Geddes right away, please.'

He took the stairs slowly. Lizzie did not stir. Her face was like marble; the copper hair, parted in the middle, gave her a Burne-Jonesian look. He had always been interested in art . . . This is what war does, he thought. I hardly believed in it up till now. But nothing's worth this agony dealt to a family, surely, and especially to a pregnant wife.

5

Maevy could scarcely believe it was the Maevy McNab she had been for so many years who was being carried swiftly in the train from Sholton to Glasgow to begin her first day at McGraths. She looked out of the window as it passed the wooded valley of the Sholtie to convince herself of the reality.

How much that river was entwined with the McGrath family, she thought – the drowning of John, her brother, then the fight between Patrick and Terence over Bessie Haddow, Lizzie's mother, when they had both ended up in its waters. And that terrible time when Lizzie had discovered her real parentage and had come stumbling up its steep bank to accuse her of keeping the fact from her.

Ah, well, like most things it had been sorted out in the end. Lizzie had become reconciled to Isobel and John who had brought her up in deliberate ignorance of Terence being her real father, and had fallen in love with Nigel . . . and lost him before their baby was born. What a terrible five months it had been since that evening when Ernest had come for dinner and carried her up to her room senseless with shock.

Lizzie ill, apathetic, at one time likely to lose the baby – Belle Geddes was a good enough doctor although a strange young woman whom Maevy had never warmed to; Lord Crawford looking like a ghost and limping more than ever, 'all the stuffing knocked out of him' – that was an expression of her mother's. *She* had been the mainstay, caring tenderly for Lizzie and her husband, maintaining a cheerfulness which somehow they had all grown to expect from her.

41

She herself went every day in her professional capacity as a nurse, and also as an aunt, trying to comfort Lizzie and persuade her to eat the delicacies she or Susan had prepared. Susan put her heart and soul into the making of beef tea, pieces of tender chicken set in their own jelly, individual egg custards. There was nothing she liked better than a bit of drama in the family, and goodness knows she had had plenty of that.

Even Ellie had been a help, picking fresh nosegays of flowers every day and taking them to Lizzie, or labouring over little notes, with drawings painstakingly coloured at the top of them. 'Dearest Lizzie, Today the sun's shining and when my homework's finished I'm going to take you a little walk along the banks of the Sholtie . . .' 'Dearest Lizzie, Pansies for thoughts. I hope they're pleasant ones of the little baby on its way.'

It was as much as Maevy could do to keep from weeping each morning when she saw the girl, the dark-eyed sadness, the swollen belly, and yet looking even more slender because of the gauntness of her face, the thin arms and legs. She did not use the platitude that it was necessary for Lizzie to get well for the sake of her baby. She knew the girl would far rather have died of the aching grief for Nigel which never left her, and which looked out of her eyes like a spectre.

In one sense Maevy longed for the immediacy of the birth, something which would bring the grieving girl back to the present instead of living in a dark well of loneliness, or a make-believe world where Nigel was with her and where they walked and rode and made love.

And even that when it came seemed to have no immediacy. When Lizzie went into labour that September morning, Maevy, at the Hall on the first message from her mother, found a white-faced but calm girl. 'I've started, Aunt Maevy,' she said. She was in pain, but there was no joy in her pain.

The day wore on, Maevy encouraging her to walk about, rallying her, telling her she would soon have a beautiful baby to love. 'Cry out, my pet,' she said, 'let yourself go. There's nobody to hear us up here.'

'It's not the pain I can't thole,' she said, her face as white as the pillow.

By nine at night Maevy was worried and had asked Belle Geddes to call. The young woman had been abrupt when they had spoken outside the door. 'It's a first baby. Twelve hours is nothing.' Nothing, Maevy thought. How would *you* feel if you were putting up with it husbandless . . .

'But the waters haven't broken yet, Dr Belle.' She spoke as calmly as she could.

'I know, I know. And that the cervix isn't dilated.' She was being put in her place by a girl fifteen years younger; she, a former Sister at the Royal, was being reminded that she was speaking to a *doctor*, one of the first women doctors to come out of that Infirmary, with *honours*, as her father was never tired of saying. Once she too had longed to qualify in medicine . . . 'She's tense, young, inexperienced. The village women could show her a thing or two.'

'As long as there's no mal-presentation.' She could be haughty, too.

'Everything's in order, I assure you, Maevy,' Belle Geddes said. What strange eyes she had, a lovely face and yet not a 'taking' face. Why was that? she wondered. Even her smile was, to her, unappealing, and yet she was well-regarded in the village. Or was it mostly by the men? 'I know you took your midwifery exams.' That sliding smile, not mirrored in the eyes.

'Oh, I'm not querying anything, doctor, just . . . well, she's . . . Lizzie.' She had known herself that all was well, that Belle Geddes was competent as she watched her hands, sure, efficient. Maybe it was better not to let sentiment interfere. 'I was just reassuring myself that everything was in order.'

'The position of the child in the uterus couldn't be better, as you well know. Nature will take its course.'

And, of course, she was right, as Maevy had known. The pains grew longer and stronger, and at last Lizzie was roused from her apathy. She seemed to welcome them, her face grew as red as a turkey-cock's (the first colour in it for months), and her eyes seemed to stare out of her head.

'This is it now, Lizzie,' she said. 'You'll have to work. You're as right as rain. We don't need Belle Geddes.'

'You don't . . . like her . . . either?' She was panting in a brief respite.

'Did I say a word?'

'It's in your face. I'm glad she isn't here. I don't like her eyes.'

'Come on, then.' Maevy was twisting a towel for her to hold on to. 'We'll surprise her. We'll get this baby born between us before you can say Jack Robinson! That's right, push, yell your head off, the walls are thick . . .'

If there had been ugliness in the girl's face during the hard-fought labour, it made the serenity of her expression the more beautiful when she held the child in her arms. And afterwards she slept peacefully for the first time since Nigel had died.

Her mother and Lord Alastair had been at the door, and she had summoned them quietly to come in and look at the sleeping girl with the infant in her arms. Her mother had her arm round her husband's shoulders. He was an old man now. His eyes were wet. Hers were not, but they were luminous. It was as if in becoming a great-grandmother the years had fallen away from her.

The child's arrival had been a watershed. The terrible grief went in the daily care of the infant; it was a quieter, sadder Lizzie, but one who could be safely left without the anxiety that living might prove too much for her and she would slip away.

It was then that Maevy's mother approached the subject of McGraths again. They were sitting at the fire in the Hall drawing-room at the beginning of October. Lizzie was upstairs in the nursery feeding 'Jonty' as she had begun to call the baby, Alastair was resting before dinner. 'We've had a lot of visitors today. Isobel and John – he did most of the talking. Anxious to know when the baby is being christened. Isobel looks *shilpit*. Winter's her worst time. Then Ernest came straight from work. He still hasn't managed to get someone to take charge of the office. He's out a lot, taking Terence's place more or less – like him, he gets on with people – and Dan Johnson has been appointed as accountant. He's always wanted that.'

'I'm glad we still have a Johnson in the firm.'

'So am I. If we'd been depending on Bob Carter's girls it would have been a poor lookout.'

'They try hard, poor souls.'

'Yes, to catch husbands, though how they expect to with all that silly giggling and them past their first youth . . .'

'My, you're getting quite nippy in your old age.' Maevy laughed.

'I feel old enough at times without you rubbing it in.' She thought her mother's face looked thinner, the sprightliness subdued. She deserved to be free of worries now.

'Now that the baby's here and Lizzie's better, do what your husband does. Have a rest some time every day. You've had a hard time these last few months.'

'I could devote my time to Alastair if I didn't worry about McGraths. It's like my own flesh and blood. If it weren't for this war taking away so many good men . . . Oh, I'm sorry, Maevy,' she put her hand on hers, 'that was thoughtless. As if it could be compared to Charlie out there. But Ernest was saying there's a general slackness

45

in the office because there's no one to hold the reins. That was always my job. Your father and I worked hard to build up McGraths. I'd hate to see it go down. A good ship needs a good captain.' She's set her mind on my going into the business, Maevy thought, ever since Charlie went away . . .

'I had a letter from Charlie this morning,' she said. 'He told me about Nigel's death. It was terrible for him. You see,' – she didn't know how to put it – 'he was there.'

'You mean as a doctor? In that place? What was it called?'

'Intombi. It was for typhoid cases near Ladysmith. Charlie had found out from someone that Nigel was a patient there, and he asked if he could be sent when they needed a surgeon. He was, but it turned out to be Nigel.'

'John would say the Lord directed him. But what a shock to find Nigel in sore need of him.'

'He had to amputate his leg, Mother. Gas gangrene from a wound. It was a terrible decision for him to take. Leaving him meant he would die in any case, taking off the leg was a grave risk . . .'

'Oh, poor Charlie! He would suffer as much as Nigel. But there's one good thing.'

'It's difficult to see.'

'There's only one man in a million who could stand up to something like that, and that's Charlie. He's the salt of the earth. He'll not burden you with this sorrow, Maevy. He had to tell you, of course, but he's as true as steel. Did he say anything about telling Lizzie?'

'No, I expect he left that to me.'

'Well, take my advice and don't. She's making a brave try at getting back to normal. I actually heard her laughing with Ernest today. He's a good tonic for her.'

'Yes, he's a bright lad . . . Charlie said Nigel's talk when he was dying was all of Lizzie. His last words were, "I'm coming to you, my dearest . . ." I told her that bit.

46

She cried in my arms. I thought she would never stop.'
Her eyes filled. 'This bloody war!'

'Mind your language.'

'You feel the same. I know you. You look tired,
Mother. Maybe I shouldn't have burdened you . . .'

'It's not a burden if there's any way I can help you to
thole it. Yes, I'm surprised how tired I get recently. Oh,
if I were only ten years younger I'd be away into that
office and get them on their toes again! There was no
slacking when *I* was master of the ship, I can tell you!
Kieran used to say that I sailed in every morning like a
ship dressed overall.' Maevy smiled. She never gave up.

She said, her face bland, 'I wrote to Charlie about
McGraths and about helping you out.'

'What did he say?' Her mother's eyes deepened, she
straightened her back.

'He doesn't see himself getting home soon. The injuries
of the men are terrible. And the conditions. "If only you
could come out too," he says, "but one of us has got to
be at home with Ellie."' She saw the look of impatience
on her mother's face.

'On the other hand,' she said, enjoying herself, 'he says
there's no point in smothering Ellie with motherliness.
Susan can give her her midday dinner and as long as I'm
back early in the evening . . .'

'Just as I did!' Her mother's eyes were bright.

'"We've only got one egg in our basket," he said, "but
that's no reason for keeping it wrapped in cotton wool."'
She looked straight at her mother. 'I'm thirty-eight . . .'

'Nothing . . .' Maeve waved her hand.

'And there's very little chance of adding to our family
now. I'll confess it: there was envy in my heart when I
saw Lizzie with that baby in her arms. You know how we
wanted a son.'

'We all want. But don't forget, you have a husband,
Lizzie hasn't. Children grow up and leave you, husbands

47

don't . . .' She met Maevy's eyes. 'That was tactless. But Charlie will come back. I was never surer of anything than that. Nigel was a different kettle of fish. It seemed . . . right. He was a bit like his mother, Annabel . . . my one woman friend.' She looked away. 'Other-worldly.' She turned again. 'Now, don't ask me what I mean.'

'You're like an old Irish soothsayer,' Maevy said, laughing to hide her emotion. They'd always been able to tease each other, the closest of relationships. She hoped she would have the same with Ellie.

'Yes, I believe I have a bit of the second sight in me,' her mother nodded almost smugly.

'So,' she said, 'I'll start at McGraths whenever you want me.'

'Well, if you insist, Maevy.' The voice was prim. They looked at each other then burst out laughing.

'Mother, you're the limit!' She fell into her mother's arms to hide her tears.

She had been to the York Street premises only for Board meetings. Her mother had appointed her a director when she became twenty-one. Sometimes, when she had been nursing, and walking through the Glasgow streets in the middle of the night to attend a confinement, she had thought wryly, 'A fine thing for a director of McGraths *this* is,' especially when she passed the offices and stables in the Gallowgate and heard through the great wooden doors the muffled kicking of the tired horses. 'Only they and me awake . . .'

But those new offices were very splendid in comparison, red sandstone with a flight of marble steps, a commission-aire at the front door who saluted and said, 'Good morning, Mrs McNab,' and a lift with wrought-iron gates to take her up to the first floor.

Ernest and Dan Johnson were waiting for her and she hoped her appearance pleased them. She had deliberated over a business dress and a dust coat to cover it, or a grey suit, and had plumped for the suit worn with a crisp white blouse with a bow tie and a shiny black sailor hat perched on her fair hair. Her mirror had told her she looked the part. Charlie would have praised her . . . but that was silly: if Charlie had been there she would never have gone to work in McGraths in the first place.

They shook hands with her, Ernest's brown eyes merry. He had the same wry expression as his father, James, although he was not as tall, and his sandy hair was straight compared with his father's grizzled locks. But the urbanity was there. 'You know Dan,' he said.

'Yes, indeed. I was sorry to hear about your father, Dan. How is he keeping?'

'The same, I'm afraid, Mrs McNab. But at least he isn't suffering any pain.' He's a grand young man, she thought, and his three years in the firm had given him confidence. At least here were two people who could be relied on.

'You're still losing a lot of men?' she asked Ernest when thy had seated her and asked a girl to bring in tea.

'Yes, it's a worry. Mostly clerks from the main office. They're all desperate to go and fight. I think their girl friends urge them on.' She wondered about Dan. He could not be more than twenty-seven. He seemed to read her thoughts.

'I volunteered, too,' he said, 'but I was failed because of bad eyesight. Hence these.' He touched the steel frames of his spectacles. 'Maybe if they get really desperate they'll be prepared to take me.'

'I hope it's over before they think of it.'

'How is Dr McNab? Sholton will miss him sorely.'

'He's fine. I heard from him not so long ago. There's plenty of work for him to do.' She had a moment of unreality. What was she doing in this place, preparing to change her whole mode of life, Ellie left to the tender mercies of Susan? She wanted to stand up and say, 'I'm sorry, it's all a mistake . . .'

'Mother seems to think I can help here a little,' she smiled, '*my* War work. Of course it would only be to fill in time until Charlie comes home . . . or until my brother's son, Robert, comes.'

'That won't be for three years yet,' Ernest said. The girl had come in with a tea-tray. 'See if it's all right for you, Maevy.' She sipped and had the feeling that the brown eyes were looking through her. Ridiculous, she thought, and rushed into speech again.

'It's fine, thank you. Terence says he'll be good at business. He cheats his brother at cards with the greatest regularity.' They all laughed. 'That's a typical remark of Terence's. *He*'s no wish to come back to McGraths, anyhow.' And why should he, she thought, and he so happy with Honor in Ireland. Glasgow would only remind him of Catherine's suicide and all that misery . . . Dan was speaking to her.

'What about the younger son? I don't remember his name.'

'He's called Terence, too. Honor, my brother's wife, seems to think he has an artistic temperament. She should know. She's a published author. He wants to be a painter.'

Ernest had risen to his feet. 'I'm sorry, but I have an appointment with a client at ten o'clock, Maevy. I waited to see you but I'll have to go now. Dan will show you round the office and introduce you. And your mother's room is waiting for you.'

'I hope I can do justice to it.' She smiled at him, feeling like an untried girl.

'Oh, you can, don't have any doubts about that. She's just the same as her mother, isn't she, Dan?'

'Different but the same.' Dan grinned at her. 'Your head's screwed on the right way, like hers.' He's coming on, she thought, remembering the shy lad at her mother's retiral ball.

'Right, Dan,' she said, getting up. 'Come and we'll find out.'

Dan gave up a day to 'show her the ropes', as he put it. First there were the introductions to be made in the various departments, and where she seemed to be warmly welcomed. The older members enquired about her mother, saying more than once, 'Well, if you're anything like your mother, you'll do.'

The young men were polite and in some cases she saw a flicker in an eye which gave her feminine gratification. She felt like a new person, neither Sister McGrath of the Royal nor Mrs McNab, the doctor's wife, but someone to be considered in authority, simply by having been one of the McGraths.

Some spoke of Patrick and asked how he was faring in America, others even more warmly about Terence when later on Dan took her to the Gallowgate to see the stables.

There, with the strong and not unpleasing smell of dung in her nostrils, she saw the heart of the business which her mother and father had founded so long ago. She met the job masters who were responsible for the hiring of horses for carriage and commercial work. 'How's Mr Terence?' one of them asked. 'By Jove, no one knew horses better than he did, except his father. They tell me he's breeding race horses in Ireland now, lucky man. He should do well in that.'

She saw the cob boys in ragged clothes, who brought round the horses, and wondered why, with all the money they made, they couldn't provide overalls for them. Maybe she could raise the matter at a board meeting.

Old Mick, who remembered Kieran, her father, held her up, but not unwillingly. She had never been fond of

51

riding, like her mother or Lizzie, but she was surprised how interesting it was to learn about the buying of horses. 'If they turn out to be a bad buy we sell them to the Tramways,' he told her. 'The best ones come from Holland, a crossed Cleveland Bay with a good Dutch stallion is maybe the best. Quiet as lambs, they are. When they slow up after ten years or so we sell them off to commercial delivery vans. Young Mr Ernest's a dab hand at that. Got more cheek than Patrick ever had. Even when they're eighteen years old farmers are still prepared to buy them for slower work. Aye, they're used right doon the line, puir beasts, till they drap deid,' he finished.

'A sad end, Mick,' she said, but he wouldn't have it.

'That's how I'd like to go, better than being shot to pieces in that bloody War. My, it was a tragedy aboot your niece's husband, and they jist married! It'll make you anxious about yours, Miss Maevy.'

'Oh, he's not fighting,' she assured him. 'He's working in a hospital. A non-combatant.'

At the end of the day she thanked Dan. 'It's been an eye-opener to me,' she said, 'how the firm's grown.'

'Do you think you'll like it?'

'I think I will.' Her mind was teeming with ideas, as if she'd been waiting for a challenge like this. 'One thing that struck me, Dan. What's wrong with filling those vacant jobs with women? They're easily trained. I've always thought women had a natural flair for office work.'

'We've found that in the typing department, certainly. But, clerical . . . it's a man's domain.'

'There's no reason why not. When the firm was in its infancy it was all hands to the plough and Isobel and I did all the paper work in the wee office we had in Sholton. Isobel was especially good at it.'

'Things are changing, that's true enough. Do you think *they*'d be interested?'

'I'm sure they would. Some need the money with their

men away fighting for us. And they're beginning to think of careers in offices now. They don't all want to type. The world's opening out for them. When we were young about the only thing a girl could do was to go into service or nursing. Some aren't suited for that but are good with figures. We could train them, Dan. And the technical colleges will soon be starting to do that if they're not already. This is going to be the century for women branching out, believe me.'

Dan looked at her with scarcely-concealed admiration. 'Well, you take the biscuit, Mrs McNab! You'll be wanting votes for women next.'

'And why not?' she said. 'It's high time.'

Going home in the train she was surprised at the feeling of excitement which still remained with her. She surreptitiously touched a cheek. It was hot. She saw a man in the opposite seat looking at her. He smiled and she turned away to look out of the window in case he thought she was encouraging him. There was an indescribable lightness in her heart, and she thought, with a shock, 'This is the first day since Charlie went away that he hasn't been constantly in my thoughts.' She concentrated on the panorama in front of her, the ugly disused coal bings, the winding wheels, the distant view of Crawford's new Iron and Steel Works, the rearing chimneys of the blast furnaces, the corrugated roofs, remembered Lord Crawford saying, 'Steel's the thing now.'

Everyone had to think ahead, just as they in McGraths had to think ahead. Soon, or perhaps not so soon, Patrick's prediction would come true, that the horses would be scrapped in favour of motor transport. But she would also think of the welfare of the workers. 'Fair do's'. Who had said that? She remembered. It was Arthur Cranston, that schoolfriend of her brothers, who had fought for the welfare of the miners and was still doing it, no doubt, or something similar. Arthur would be lost without a cause.

The landscape was uncluttered now, just the green fields running down to the banks of the Sholtie, the trim hedges and trees, russet-touched, the landscape of her childhood, of Patrick's and Terence's and Arthur's. Soon even this verdant pocket would go too, swallowed up by industry, maybe the Crawford Estate also, and what would Lord Crawford and her mother do then, and for that matter Lizzie and her baby?

You will be aiding and abetting that transition, she told herself, by working in McGraths, by trying to improve it . . . her spirits plummeted at the same time as she heard the porter calling out, 'Sholton . . . Sholton Station . . .!' What was she doing, dressed like this, carrying a brief case? This wasn't the Maevy McGrath who'd worked so hard for people in the Royal Infirmary, or been wife and lover to Charlie.

A strange feeling came over her as she walked up the drive to Braidholme. Mother had done this, tirelessly, for years. Lizzie had come running to meet her when she'd lived here after Bessie's death. 'Mammy! Mammy!' Was she imagining that voice? And then it broke strongly into her consciousness, shattering her introspection. 'Mammy! Mammy!' It was Ellie running to meet her and she held out her arms. Mother had said that that had been the best part of the day.

6

Lizzie stood at her mirror putting on her cloak over her black velvet gown. She noticed how the depth of its blackness set off the pallor of her skin and the auburn of her hair, absently – but at least I'm noticing, she thought, bending forward to adjust her earrings. Her father-in-law had given them to her at Christmas, pearl-encrusted on the silver shanks and with diamond drops. She had begun to call Lord Crawford 'father' after Nigel's death. It seemed to her that it might be what he wished. On that terrible evening when the news came he had become an old man in one stroke. 'It would be a small comfort to him,' her grandmother had said.

The chief comfort to her was Jonty. She crossed the room to his cradle to bend over it and look lovingly at her sleeping son; a true Crawford, she thought, tracing with a finger his nose and chin, fine-honed. The baby stirred and opened his eyes, not amber like those of his father and grandfather, but a brilliant blue – McGrath eyes, she thought. She longed to lift him and hold him, but instead she stroked his cheek softly till the eyes grew heavy and fell shut.

'The Lord giveth and the Lord taketh away,' John had said. He had grown more platitudinous as he grew older, and Isobel more submissive. She saw that objectively now, and was only thankful she did not have to live with them. They had reared her, and for that she was grateful, but at the same time she realized it had been for their own benefit. She did not now blame them for keeping her in ignorance of her parentage, nor grudge them the part of her life they had had.

But there was no doubt that in her almost inconsolable grief since Nigel died, the best people to have around had been Grandma and Aunt Maevy. It was Maevy who had helped her through her confinement and out of the terrible slough of despair she had been in. And Grandma had always been there in the background. There was no softness in her love. 'Nigel is dead, my lovely, dead. But you have your son to care for. Don't use him as something to weep over – even a small baby can be aware of tears – but something to live for.'

It was a household which suited her, and in her father-in-law she had a man with a fine mind who did not dwell on his own sorrow but was especially tender towards her because of hers. 'Sleep tight, wee one,' she said and went from the room quickly.

Lord Crawford made to rise when she went into the drawing room. 'Oh, please don't,' she said, going towards him.

'I want to do homage to this vision of beauty. Don't you agree, Maeve?'

'She hasn't lost her figure, that's for sure. I doubt if mine was ever as slender as that.'

'Shall I send to the kitchen for a measuring tape?' Alastair asked jauntily.

'Now, I won't have you shaming me! Isn't he a terrible man, Lizzie? Have you told Cathy to keep an eye on the bairn?'

'Yes, she's taking up her sewing to sit with him. And Thomas has the coach ready at the front.'

'Well, you be off, then, and not keep the others waiting. Thomas will bring you and Maevy back and we'll be waiting up to hear all about it.'

'You should have been going too since it's a McGrath outing.'

'No, no. Alastair and I prefer the comfort of a fire these cold evenings.' She knew by the bright interest in

56

her grandmother's eyes that she would have liked to go. All her life she had enjoyed 'occasions' and had planned many.

But this one was Maevy's own doing, a trip to the Theatre Royal to see that fine pantomime, *Aladdin*. All the office staff had been invited, and Maevy had hit on the idea that it would be good for Lizzie to come along, too. 'You're a McGrath by birth and you've been confined to the house long enough. You're only twenty-three, for goodness' sake! It will be good for you.' Maybe John and Isobel would not have approved since she was still in mourning, but grandmother and father-in-law had applauded the idea, saying it was eminently sensible.

Maevy was standing in the foyer welcoming her guests when she arrived. How dignified and lovely she looks, Lizzie thought, going towards her. Since she had started working at McGraths she had acquired an extra dimension. She was made for positions of authority. A house to run had never been enough for her. And her gown was smarter than usual, made in Wilson's, perhaps, Grandma's favourite shop, and not run up herself as she had been in the habit of doing when she was at home all the time. Her fair hair was shimmering with vitality.

'Lizzie!' She came towards her. 'So Thomas got you here all right. Now, I want you to meet Mr Donaldson, our head clerk, and his assistant, Mr Cross, and this is Miss Boyes from the typing department, and this is . . .'

'Dan Johnson,' Lizzie said, smiling. 'It's a long time since I saw *you*.'

'Yes, indeed. I was sorry to hear about your sad loss, Lizzie.' She had steeled herself to be ready to accept this kind of remark.

'Thank you.' Don't look at him . . .

'How is your baby?'

'The apple of my grandmother's eye.'

'I wish you'd persuaded her to come, too. They all have such grand memories of her in McGraths.'

'She would have enjoyed it, but Lord Crawford doesn't keep so well now. She doesn't like to leave him. Oh, Ernest, I didn't see you!' He was standing at her side, spruce in his white tie and tails, the straight lock of sandy hair falling over his brow. He'd never been able to control it.

He kissed her on the cheek, then Maevy. 'I was wondering if you'd heard the latest news about the Queen. She's sinking fast.'

'Oh, no!' Maevy's face showed concern. 'I've been too busy all day to think about it. Oh, that's sad.'

'I've been out and about. Every customer I visited gave me the latest bulletin. There's the warning bell! I think you'd better gather up your flock, Maevy. What a grand idea this is of yours! Is it an innovation?'

'Yes, I wanted to show my appreciation to the staff for putting up with me. A Ne'erday celebration.'

'I hope it becomes an annual occurrence. Shall I lead the way with you?'

'Thanks, Ernest. We're going in now!' She raised her voice. 'Follow us, everyone, please.' There was much talking and laughter as they trooped into the theatre, Lizzie following with Dan at her side.

The curtain was taking a long time to rise. After the scuffling and talking while people settled into their seats, and the subsequent rustling of chocolate papers, the audience had fallen silent, strangely silent. Lizzie herself had run out of small talk with Dan.

'I hope there hasn't been a hitch behind the scenes,' he said to her.

'I hope not.' She looked along the row to Maevy. She was sitting straight in her seat, the Muldoon back, Grandma called it. They caught each other's eyes and

Maevy shrugged her shoulders, looking perplexed. She would hate her party to be ruined. A slow murmuring began to spread throughout the theatre, there was no laughter, just a sonorous rumbling like distant thunder. They're apprehensive, Lizzie thought. It was in the air.

A man appeared from behind the curtains, a rotund magpie of a man, important-looking, possibly the manager. He held up his hand for silence. 'Ladies and gentlemen, I have sad news for you. What we have feared has come to pass. Our great and noble Queen has departed from this life.' The rumbling swelled and seemed to split into hundreds of voices. Someone sobbed, loudly. He held up his white-gloved hand once more. 'The management feels it should show due respect on this mournful occasion, and to this end we have regretfully decided to close the theatre forthwith. There will be no performance tonight. We are sure this would be in accordance with your wishes.' He bowed and withdrew behind the curtains.

'I'm not surprised,' Dan said. Everyone was talking as they gathered their possessions together and stood up. Bang goes Maevy's 'do'! And mine, Lizzie thought.

But it was the right thing to do, of course. Everyone should be circumspect and sober at the news that the old Queen was no longer with them, an awesome thought. She had been the background of all their lives, but they were into a new century now. It was fitting perhaps that they should start with a new king. Goodness knows, he had waited long enough.

In the foyer Ernest was busy going round their group. She saw the nods, the pleased exprssions. 'Ernest has a ploy on,' she said to Dan.

'Aye, he would.' Was his tone ever so slightly grudging?

Now Ernest was beside them, his bright brown eyes like the robin's she fed every morning in the Hall garden. 'It's sad about the Queen, but for Maevy's sake I think

59

we shouldn't let the outing fall apart. Would you like to join us for a bite of supper at the American Bar before you go home?'

'Oh, no, really,' she said instinctively. It had been an effort to come. Now all she wanted was to get home. The brief flicker of excitement she had felt when she had been dressing had evaporated. She wanted to creep into bed and retreat from the world, to dream and fantasize about Nigel, to relive their love and passion, to weep, to fall asleep like a tired child.

'Maevy says you mustn't go back without having something to eat. She says I have to persuade you.'

'There's Thomas . . .' she conceded. 'He's having his supper somewhere and turning up at the theatre at ten. I could scarcely go without him.'

'That settles it, then. Nothing could be simpler. We'll come back to the theatre in time for Thomas.'

'Are *you* going, Dan?' She was trapped.

'Yes. Don't worry. I'll take care of you.' He must have thought he was being appealed to.

He did, assiduously, never leaving her side. There was a respectful sobriety in the restaurant. People talked in hushed tones about the death of the Queen, about her long reign, sixty-four years, Dan told her. No one, he said, could remember any time when she *wasn't* there.

'It's the end of an era,' Mr Donaldson said across the table to her, and that seemed to be the general feeling. No one knew exactly what difference it would make to them, except that they knew it would never be the same again. The Queen mourned for Albert for most of her life, Lizzie thought, and felt a corresponding sadness.

And yet, strangely enough, there seemed to be a slight rift in the dark shadow which hung over her, a chink of light. Nigel had died in the age of Queen Victoria; she, with Jonty, was going into a new one. And with this sense of the ending of something, there was a faint feeling of hope in her heart.

She tried to explain this to Maevy on their way home. 'Do you feel it, Maevy? Things are going to be different for everyone. Ellie and Jonty are going to know tremendous changes.'

'And many more opportunities. At one time when I was nursing I wondered if I ever could become a doctor. Ellie will receive a better education than I ever had. Doors will open for her.'

'And Charlie. Once the War's over and he's back again I'm sure there will be great advances in medicine. There always are. The only good thing about wars, he once said. And maybe you'll get a motor car, an Argyle or an Albion. Oh, you have such a lot to look forward to!' She could not stop them. The tears ran down her face. 'Oh, Aunt Maevy,' she said against her shoulder, 'I'm not jealous, least of all of you, but my life's so blank without Nigel. Each day succeeding each difficult day. He's in my thoughts day and night. It's so cruel . . .'

'Hush, hush,' her aunt stroked her hair. 'A lovely girl like you spoiling her face. There, now.' She wiped her cheeks. They were hot tears, scalding tears. 'You're surrounded by love and you have a son to rear, and who knows? It may well be an era of change for you, things you never expected. You'll be able to go to France to see the Barthes – you always liked Emily, didn't you? – and to America to visit Patrick and Maria. You'll meet widows like yourself who'll be making the best of their lives and carving out new ones. You're a brave lass. You've proved it many a time, and a braw one too. Hush, there, hush, my lovely . . .'

She was able to present a calm face when they went into the drawing-room and found grandmother and Lord Crawford patiently waiting. She did not have to smile or look vivacious. The Queen was dead.

7

My Dear Husband,

I write with a full heart. The War is at last over! It's hard to believe, all that waiting time soon to be behind us, to see you again, to be in your arms, to see your face when you look at Ellie, now grown so tall.

'I've never known such deep personal joy, nor such universal joy. It leaves the joy of the relief of Ladysmith far behind, and the wild jubilation of Mafeking Night when the whole country went mad.

I think we all thought then that the War would be over in a matter of months, but we hadn't reckoned on the brilliance of De Wet, nor his guerilla fighting. At times I even wondered if all Kitchener's blockhouses would deter him. And I grieved for those Boer women and children suffering such misery where they were herded like animals – some say, tortured. That is a wrong which should be quickly righted. Sometimes I felt like starting my own protest group here in Scotland!

I'm beginning to see this tendency in myself, to want to take up the cudgels on behalf of the poor and oppressed, the downtrodden, like our trace boys so poorly clad and fed in the bitter winter, as are some of the carters' bairns. That's why I'm in favour of the SCA, that's the Scottish Carters' Association, and advise our men to join it, as not every employer does. Ernest teases me and says I'll kill all our profits if I encourage them to ask for increases in wages, but many are incapable of doing it for themselves. No business ever failed by being fair to their employees. I sound like my mother!

All the same, being a working woman has made the time pass more quickly for me, and looking back, this year seems to have been full of event. There was the King's coronation in August – I always meant to say to you, Charlie, that it was postponed because of his being operated on for appendicitis, and how I'd thought of that time when I was in the Royal with the same trouble. Poor Mr Wilcox, the surgeon! Having a Sister for a patient and a doctor whom he knew breathing down his neck all the time! It must have made him distinctly nervous. By the way, now that the King has had the operation, I hear the aristocracy are clamouring to have the same!

I wonder what happened to Mr Wilcox's daughter, Letitia? The one you were sweet on. (You hate to be teased about her, don't you?) Well, you can't be perfect! I only saw her once and that was with you at the Kelvingrove Exhibition. Now I can confess I was fiercely jealous. It did one good thing. It made me realize that I was in love with you, but it took that illness to make me confess it. Mother always talked about my "stubborn bit".

Now that the War's over, I can tell you that the real reason for my going to work at McGraths was to set my mother's mind at rest. I used to sit in the quiet afternoons when I had exhausted all my household chores and think about you, and I'd be seized by the most fearful apprehension. I couldn't live without Charlie, I'd think. Other people, I know, had done so when they lost their loved one – I had only to look at Lizzie – but I told myself that our love was different. *I* was different. Such arrogance. But you know, dear heart, that you have always been the only man in my life. I would sit in the Braidholme garden and say, this would be meaningless, Ellie would be meaningless, if I lost Charlie . . .

How right it was to go and work in McGraths. I was so busy and interested during the day that there was no time to worry about you, and in the evening when I got home there were the precious hours with Ellie before she went to bed, hearkening to her reading, answering her questions – she has a bright enquiring mind – and perhaps visiting the Hall when she was safely tucked in bed.

Mother still looks magnificent, but she's lost her bloom a little, tires more easily; Lord Crawford is decidedly frail, but then he's older than Mother. The loss of his son was a bitter blow.

And I'm thirty-nine. Is it too old to have another baby, my dearest doctor? Do you think we might be lucky at last? I long for a son, especially when I see that grand little fellow Lizzie has, with his brilliant blue eyes and his baby smile.

He has been the saving grace of Lizzie. She's young enough to put grief behind her now, or appear to, and it's good to hear her laughing again. Ernest Murray-Hyslop is a frequent visitor to the Hall. Mother says Lizzie needs young company but she enjoys him, too. He's urbane, like his father, and doesn't take life too seriously, like me.

Your last letter telling me about all the operations you're doing made me wonder if you'll ever settle down again in general practice. Belle Geddes has filled your place admirably, but women don't like her, although she specializes in their complaints. I suppose if I were to be strictly honest I'd say I don't like her either. I try to be logical about it. She's pretty, with dark hair and silver-grey eyes, well, more beautiful than pretty, more voluptuous than beautiful, and her appeal to men is obvious enough. If her bell goes in the surgery and she appears at the door, you see the men looking at each other with that male look. A woman who makes other women feel dowdy is never very popular – with women! It's mean to talk that way about someone who has held the fort for you. I'm sorry.

It's quiet in the house tonight, a soft and happy silence. Susan has gone to bed, Ellie is fast asleep. No wonder, because she and I have danced round the dining-room table this evening to a home-made tune based on *The Keel Row*, "Daddy's coming home from the *Boer* War, the *Boer* War . . ." Susan came in to clear and stood clapping her hands in time to our song, her long face lit up in the way it does. I think, in a way, she must be the only one who's sorry that the War is over. The hate she's expended on the Boers, the love on Roberts and Kitchener! I wouldn't have *dared* mention the admiration I had for de Wet. I should have got black looks from her for a month of Sundays. It's the best drama she's been involved in for a long time, and to Susan involvement is everything. I've a feeling that the paradise she looks forward to is going to be far too tame for her.

Nearer home there's been Glasgow's hour of glory as well, the electrification of the tramway system. You won't know the old place. The last horse was taken off the trams in April, and a great new generating station has been built at Pinkston. The system's easy to follow, a different colour for every route, and once you know these you're all right. The drivers and conductors wear smart green uniforms. Oh, that drink-sodden city of ours is coming on! Poor Catherine . . .

But in spite of approving of the new trams, I have a sentimental side for horses, completely illogical when you think of the work they entail for the men. In the early days more value was put on them than their drivers, and those men had many a drookin' waiting on their open carts at stations and the like. There's an old carter's saying that if only they could put a roof over Glasgow the carter would be all right.

Already in haulage work there are quite a few motor vans,

and Patrick's prediction of motor transport is fast coming true. That's why I encourage the men to join the SCA and look out for their own interests. If their leaders are sensible they'll extend it when the time comes, and I think they are. They've now got a Sick Fund, and the problem of overtime and Sunday labour is being tackled. But we still do well, and Ernest, who is a young man of vision, says that as long as we keep up with the times that's all right.

Do you know what one of my earliest memories is? It's being taken to the Sunday School picnic here in Sholton when I was a wee lass, and our father winning the first prize for the best-kept horse. And guess who presented the prize? None other than the Honourable Alastair, then the laird's son, now mother's husband. Life's queer-like, isn't it, but wonderful.

I've stopped and read over this letter so far and find it's nearly all about carters! But you used to talk about medicine all the time in the old days. Remember how you went on about Lister? Now I'm boring you about *my* job.

But what's much more important, and hardly believable, my darling, is that our long waiting time will soon be over. Maybe you'll arrive at Braidholme any day now. Oh, I hope I'm not at York Street! But I know if I sat at home and waited for you I'd go mad with impatience. Come quickly, dearest, and safely. Every minute is going to seem like a year. Your loving wife, Maevy.

Charlie was in a forward hospital in Pretoria when the Peace Treaty was signed. He did a totally unnatural thing for him. He went out that night with a few fellow officers and got drunk on root beer. After that it was back to normal, albeit with a sore head, but he did not regret it. You couldn't let the War end without some kind of celebration. There was no cessation in the work although hostilities had ceased, and it only fully came home to him when he got Maevy's letter. How her character and sweetness came over, he thought. Immediately he was desperate to get home to her.

But, as he read, he saw the difference in her. She was fulfilling herself at McGraths. Her involvement came over strongly, but then she had always been like that. She had to have a commitment in her life. He remembered the Carters' Strike in 1889 when Arthur Cranston had been injured. She had seen the procession starting when she had looked out of the Ward window and had been compelled to join it. That was his Maevy, concerned always with the welfare of those around her, never pleasure-loving for its own sake.

She was like her mother in her need for wider interests. She needed 'something of her own' as well as looking after a home and family. Well, he was the least chauvinistic of men, he told himself. They had always understood each other. He had always respected her as an individual as well as a housewife and a lover. If she was as good at working in McGraths as she was in those two capacities, she would be very good indeed.

Besides, she had been used to responsibility as a Sister in a large hospital, and had at one time wanted to become Matron. But then she had fallen in love with him. And what Maevy did she did thoroughly. His pulse raced at the thought of making love to her again. 'This,' she had said to him one night in bed, 'will always be the most important thing in my life.'

But she was still 'Today's Woman'. That had been a joke between them when they had both worked in the Royal Infirmary. And no home, even one as much loved as Braidholme, would ever be big enough to hold her. You approve, don't you? he asked himself.

And if his dearest Maevy was Today's Woman, what would that make Ellie? Tomorrow's Woman? Oh, the whole world was opening up for them! He went to sleep and dreamed of Maevy wearing a straw boater and carrying a banner with the words 'Votes for Women' on it.

He awakened with a vague feeling of disappointment, and laughed at himself as he was shaving. You don't want to play the returning soldier role, do you, he asked himself, to be cosseted and cuddled by an adoring wife? Their marriage was different.

In the morning he was detailed with other medical officers to be ready to embark on a hospital ship which would be leaving for home the next week.

8

He saw them from far off as he walked the length of the platform at Central Station. All their meetings and partings so far had been at the Broomielaw; this time the boat had docked at Tilbury, and it had been a few days before he had been cleared.

He could never have mistaken them: that indefinable McGrath something, the tallness, the straight back; Ellie, now ten, was surely tall for her age, and she had the abundant McGrath hair, although fair like her mother's. Today it had been released from its usual plaits and put into ringlets – rag curls, he remembered Maevy calling them.

'D'ye see them, sir?' The elderly porter pushing the barrow with all his belongings raised an enquiring face from his load.

'Yes, they're at the barrier.'

'Hoo long hae ye been owr there?' The pert curiosity of the Glaswegian.

'Two years.'

'D'ye tell me that, noo? Seen a lot o' fightin', then?'

'Only the results. I'm a doctor.'

'Oh, aye. Well, there's got to be some fur that.' He sounded disappointed, then brightened, 'A lot o' fatalities, were there? Cuttin' aff legs an' sich like?'

Nigel's young, calm face, still, deprived of life . . . 'No, mostly typhoid,' he said shortly, and hurried his steps.

They had both seen him. They were waving. Ellie was jumping up and down, and as he came through the barrier Maevy came forward and into his arms so naturally, a coming home. He steered her out of the way of the crowd.

The softness of a woman, his woman, he'd forgotten the sweetness. 'Oh, my wife,' he whispered against her face, tears pricking his eyelids.

She released herself, her eyes luminous. She looked beautiful, trim, perhaps thinner – she had always wanted a really slender figure although it had never been his wish. There would be no mysteries, he had said. 'Charlie, oh, Charlie . . . home at last. Ellie?' The girl was hanging back shyly. 'Oh, there you are. Come and say hello to your Daddy.' And to Charlie, lovingly, 'Do you see a difference in her?'

'A difference?' He swept Ellie into his arms, lifting her. 'She's a young lady now . . .' He hugged her against him, his own daughter, their daughter, the seal of their love, such a multitude of feelings . . . 'It's good to see you, lass.' His voice broke. 'Well, we'd better get to the front for a cab, Maevy. Oh, I'm sorry . . .' The porter was standing, taking it all in. 'Will you follow us?'

'There's no need for a cab,' she said. 'Mother sent us in with Thomas. Do you remember him, the Hall coachman?' Her eyes were searching his face as she spoke, as if she were relearning it.

'Yes, he's an old friend.'

The porter was obviously impressed by the turnout, especially the crest on the carriage doors, but unabashed by Thomas. 'Jump doon an' gie us a haun, mister.' The task completed, Charlie felt it deserved a large tip.

'Half-a-crown extra for the crest,' he said, smiling at Maevy, when they were being driven away.

There was no strangeness in bed. 'You'll want an early nicht, doctor,' Susan said, her eyes shining with undisguised glee. 'I've laid oot that special nightdress you bought, Maevy.' In times of excitement she forgot titles. But they had delayed to give Ellie time to get used to him, and to show him her lesson books, and the exercises

69

she could play on the piano and the new kitten Susan had in the kitchen. Maevy never saw them grow into cats, and suspected Susan of giving them away to one of the farms nearby for mousing.

It was natural, the coming together. Theirs had never been a shallow relationship, and they lay in each other's arms to begin with, deeply at peace.

'The times I've imagined this,' she said. He could feel the satin of the nightdress, and smiled, thinking of gaunt Susan in her single bed nearby. Was vicarious pleasure enough for her, poor soul? He had once questioned this, and Maevy had said, 'She's one of us. It's not vicarious. That and the promise of eternal salvation fulfils her.'

'I too, my dearest,' he said. 'The thought of you kept me alive through it all.'

'Was it terrible for you?'

'No. Only being away from you. The work was absorbing. I did more surgery in two years than I'd have done in twenty in an Infirmary.'

'I feared you might get enteric fever yourself.'

'Doctors are immune . . . no, that's a fallacy. A good friend of mine, married with three children, died. I was lucky.'

She moved against him and he felt her breasts, the swell of them, the soft swell. 'Nigel . . .' she said. 'Do you want to talk about it?' He could not answer. 'I *was* you, in that terrible situation, with you in your grief . . .'

'They couldn't get anyone else. They tried, but it had to be done if there was any chance for him. You have to do in war what you wouldn't do in peace, but if ever anything was proved right it was that you should never treat your own kin. It's the . . . involvement. I thought of your operation, and how at the time I longed to push old Wilcox out of the way and get on with it myself. Now I see it wouldn't have done. I've suffered enough over Nigel . . . but had it been you . . .'

70

'But you're sensible, logical. You've put it all behind you now?'

'I've done my best. I had several nights of not sleeping and then I began to see I was no good as a surgeon if I was obsessed by might-have-beens about Nigel. Your letters, your wonderful letters, sustained me. But I'll confess to you now I dread my first meeting with Lizzie. I couldn't blame her if she thought of me as a . . . murderer.'

'Oh, Charlie.' She got up on one elbow to look at him. 'Never feel that, because *she* doesn't. There was bitterness, but it was never directed towards you, it was the War, God, fate. I encouraged her to work through it all, the pain of loss, the terrible grief, especially when she was carrying their child. But she loves you, loves you very much. She knew you tried to save Nigel's life. There's never been any criticism.'

'Has she got over his death?'

'In one way she has because she's young and resilient, and she has her baby son. I think it's slowly becoming a dream to her, love's young dream. She's too beautiful not to have other men falling in love with her, and she's not a cold girl. She has strong passions.'

'I know another one.'

'Another . . .?' Her hair was falling over her face and he tugged gently at a lock.

'Another girl of strong passions.' She was in his arms, her hair spreading over him. 'All the stronger for having been kept for such a long time.'

'That's true enough.' Her voice was muffled. 'Some nights in this bed, our bed, I went mad with longing . . .'

'Ah, that's what I like to hear.' He held her closely. 'You were always truthful, my darling.'

'Not backward at coming forward?' She laughed against him. 'That's like Dan Johnson. Never an ordinary phrase where a cliché would do.'

'Never mind Dan Johnson.' He rolled over on top of her. 'This is a night, my darling,' his voice had roughened, 'when there will be no finesse. Maybe tomorrow,' he kissed her, 'or the next night,' he kissed her again, 'or the night after.'

'No finesse,' she said, her body arching towards him. Oh, she was ready. You always knew where you were with Maevy. Honest, in and out of bed. There was no need to talk any more. Their bodies said it all.

'I'm like a camel,' he said, weakly, laughing, too soon after, 'a camel who's just met his first oasis.'

'The trouble is,' her voice was thick, 'it's a very big desert and there are more oases. After he's had a wee rest he'll have to set off again for the next one.'

'Poor camel,' he said, laughing against her mouth. He would have gone through ten wars for this.

'Do you feel fit to go, Alastair?' They were in the drawing-room of the Hall, the three of them in their best: Alastair in white tie and tails, Lizzie wearing a mauve chiffon dress which bared her shoulders and whose skirt was caught up with bunches of violets over a lace petticoat. Hadn't she worn it for her engagement night, the night of my retiral ball? Maeve thought. If so, it took courage to wear it again, but then Lizzie had never been short of that.

'Perfectly fit, my dear.' He smiled. 'And since you've always told me I look my best in this regalia, nothing would prevent me from going to Charlie's party.'

'And they say women are vain!' Maeve laughed and raised her eyebrows at Lizzie. '*You're* bonny, as always.' She would not mention the dress. 'How do *I* look?'

'You're wearing the gold you wore for your retiral. I wasn't going to let you outdo me.' She was quite calm. 'And you know you quite stole my thunder that night with even the dining-table decked out to match you.'

'Yes, it was a nice colour scheme. What a trouble I had

getting orchids the same colour! They're not an everyday flower.' She had thought, looking in the mirror, that she did not look so blooming as on that night, but after all, it had been three years ago, and the War had aged everyone. Even Lizzie, who was young in years, would never have that same look of vulnerability and sweetness. The death of Nigel had robbed her of her first youth. She got up and rang the bell. 'We might as well get started. It will be grand to be back in Braidholme again. A happy house.' A house of memories, she thought, but she could not voice that to Alastair. They were all of Kieran.

Charlie felt, possibly for the first time in his life, a trifle shy as they stood in the hall to welcome their guests as they came in. But it was soon full of people and laughter, and he went from one to the other greeting them.

Maevy's mother looked splendid, as she always did, just a little more splendid than the others in her gown of gold with its orchids in the corsage. But, yes, the bloom was beginning to go, although she could still put out everyone's eye in the room . . . except Maevy's.

'My Queen of Beauty,' he had said to her earlier in their bedroom. Her fair hair was piled on top of her head, her dress was low-cut – more so than before, he thought – she held her head high, she was beautiful, fulfilled. There was a new sophistication about her which had not been there when he went to South Africa.

'Aren't you proud of Maevy tonight?' Maeve whispered to him as he found her a seat in the drawing-room.

'Very,' he whispered back, 'but she has to work hard to outshine you.'

'Do you hear this wicked man, Alastair, paying me compliments and him only a week back with his wife?'

'Well-deserved, my dear.' He sat down beside her, stiffly. His face was grey. 'You'll have to work some of your wonders on this old leg of mine, Charlie.'

'No better, is it?' He thought the man had aged considerably since he had seen him last. The death of his son had been a bitter blow. Did *he* bear him any grudge?

'Your business will be blooming, sir,' he said. 'The demand for steel goes up and up, doesn't it?'

'Yes, indeed. We're opening a further plant on a site we've bought nearer Glasgow. Fortunately I've got a good man in the place I was keeping . . . for my son: Sir Edward Hamilton. He's well-known in City circles. Young to be a captain of industry. I can leave things in his capable hands . . . Ah, here's Lizzie.'

'Good evening, Uncle Charlie.' She kissed him. 'I've never seen Braidholme so full!' She laughed. 'Susan's upstairs supervising the ladies' cloaks. She's in her element.'

'She'll be that. The excitement of it all is going to her head. She's being allowed to bring Ellie down for an hour, then she has a team of village women in the kitchen to order about, and of course, see you all off the premises and lock up afterwards. It's Susan's day, really.' He was speaking too much from embarrassment. 'She doesn't bear you any grudge,' Maevy had assured him. 'Give her your love.' Her suddenly remembered words made him smile in the old way at Lizzie, the girl who had always come to him in trouble. 'My, you're a bobby-dazzler tonight! I can't get over all the beautiful women floating around here: Maevy, and then your grandmother, and now you! It's too much for a simple man like me.'

'You were never simple, Uncle Charlie.' Her eyes reassured him. Two days after he had come home he had gone to see her and told her in detail about the days leading up to Nigel's death. 'I know you did your best to save him,' she had said, 'I grieve for you too, don't ever forget that.' 'And as for beautiful women, wait till you see Honor.'

'Are *they* coming? Is Terence coming?' Maeve sat up,

her eyes bright. Her first-born had always been her favourite, although she denied it.

Lizzie had her hand to her mouth. 'Oh, Maevy will kill me! I've let the cat out of the bag! Yes, they're bringing Robert. He still wants to come and work in McGraths when he finishes at Trinity, so Maevy thought they could kill two birds with one stone.' She half-turned, 'Oh, here they are!'

Charlie watched Terence McGrath advance into the room with Honor, his wife. How Irish he looked, he thought, as if he had taken on the patina of the country he had adopted. He had a jaunty air but was as handsome as ever – that McGrath presence, he thought – his red curls thinner now, his face more florid, his evening wear a bit dandified. And Honor was a typical Irish beauty, a cloud of dark hair, a wild rose complexion, a slightly fey air. Behind them was Terence's son, Robert, whom Charlie had last seen at his and Maevy's wedding eleven years ago, just a small boy.

Did Robert know that Terence was Lizzie's real father? He thought briefly of that long-ago love affair between Terence and Bessie Haddow, and her early death. He watched Terence, his eyes searching the room, then his eyes lighting up and him crossing the room, arms outstretched. 'Lizzie!' he heard him say as he embraced her, 'you look like your old self again! Different from the last time!' Charlie remembered Maevy telling him in a letter that her brother had come post-haste from Ireland to see Lizzie when the news of Nigel's death reached them.

Now he had turned to Maeve and he heard the loud, happy voice. 'Here she is, the apple of me eye, and sitting there quite jecoe!'

'I'm speechless, Terence!' She was on her feet. 'What a grand surprise, but see what it's done to me,' she was dabbing at her eyes, 'I'm crying my eyes out.' Honor had joined them and the two women embraced. 'I wouldn't

miss a chance of seeing you as well as the returning hero!'
Honor's fine eyes were bright.

'And aren't you the fine flatterer! And as lovely as
ever.' Maeve's eyes were no less bright. 'Now tell me, are
you still writing all those books, and why haven't you
brought those beautiful girls with you?' She caught sight
of Robert, hanging back shyly. 'Who is this handsome
young man? Don't tell me! Not Robert?'

'Yes, it's your grandson,' Terence put an arm round his
son, 'come to pay his respects to his grandmother and to
see if it will suit him.'

'Suit him, indeed!'

'Father's joking, Grandmother.' Robert bowed.

'Now, that's too formal. Come and give me a kiss.'

Charlie watched the boy giving Maeve a peck on the
cheek, bending to kiss Lizzie, then shaking hands politely
with Lord Crawford. He was dark-haired and serious, like
Catherine, his mother. But what a happy choice Terence
had made in Honor to be his sons' stepmother.

Later, when Robert was speaking to him and Maevy,
he said to him, 'You'll have to have a talk with Ernest
when he arrives. He'll tell you all about McGraths. Or,
for that matter, your Aunt Maevy. She's in the business,
too.'

'Are you, Aunt Maevy?' He looked surprised.

'For the time being. I'm keeping your place warm.' 'If
we have another child,' she had said to Charlie, 'I'll leave
at the drop of a hat.'

'You see, it's going to be a home from home,' Charlie
said, 'the more McGraths the merrier.'

'You'll be frightening the life out of him.' Maevy smiled
at the boy. 'Now come along with me, Robert, and I'll
introduce you to the others. I think we've some young
girls here for you.'

Charlie seated Honor and Terence, excused himself
and went into the hall in case there were any late arrivals.

Ellie was there, dressed to kill in her best party dress. She was helping Ernest off with his coat, laughing with him.

'Susan said I was to do this, Daddy,' she said.

'Well, what Susan says goes. Good-evening, Ernest.'

'Good evening, Charlie.' Ernest shook hands, dapper as ever. 'I've got a much better idea, Ellie. Will you be my partner and lead me into the drawing-room? I'm shy.' He hung his head.

Ellie giggled delightedly. 'Can I, Daddy?'

'Yes, on you go.'

'Oh, thank you, kind sir.' Ernest bowed and went off with Ellie clinging to his arm.

'Hello, Charlie. Sorry we're late.' He turned. His partner, Jim Geddes, was holding out his hand. 'We had a big surgery.' His daughter was beside him.

He shook hands with both of them. 'This is a great pleasure,' he said to Belle. 'I haven't seen you since I got home.'

'No, that's true.' She had a singer's voice, deep-throated. She spoke slowly. 'I expect you're far too busy.' She seemed to linger on the words, giving them a deeper meaning. Her eyes held his.

'I'm looking forward to getting back to the practice,' he said lamely.

'Belle has a favour to ask you, Charlie,' her father said.

'I'm at your disposal.' He smiled at her.

'Are you?' Why did he keep on noticing her eyes, the expression in them, silver-grey with thick dark lashes. There was no colour about her, he thought – thick white skin, thick black hair dressed in a chignon. Maevy appeared beside him.

'Good evening, Dr Geddes, and,' she smiled, 'Belle, or do you prefer the title?'

'Not on social occasions.'

'I'll remember that. Leave your cloak on that chair. You've arrived just in time for supper. Would you take

77

Belle in, Charlie, and perhaps you could escort me, Jim? I want to start the ball rolling. People always hang back when you mention food.'

His slight discomfort with his partner disappeared when they were seated. After the grace which John Craigie made into a small sermon, he chatted to people across the table from him and those on either side. The atmosphere was happy, informal. Maevy had said to him earlier, 'There are to be no speeches. I think it might be hurtful to welcome you back officially because of Nigel. You understand?' He had agreed wholeheartedly.

But it did not prevent him from feeling deeply thankful to have a place like Sholton to return to, where he felt at home, and where he was surrounded with the people he loved. He looked round the table happily from time to time. Maevy, of course, shone like a star, had never been more beautiful, and her mother was still a handsome woman. His love spread to all of them, to Isobel and John, to Terence and Honor and Lord Crawford and Ernest – how citified he looked as he talked to Robert, although he seemed to change when he turned to Lizzie, become, was it his imagination, tender? In any case, they had a lot to say to each other.

And Maevy had invited Arthur Cranston because she said no McGrath party was ever complete without him. His father and Maevy's father had both worked down the pit together, and had toiled for the miners' welfare in the little spare time left to them. 'And now, poor soul, his wife has died,' she had told him. 'She never understood Arthur's burning desire to fight for the rights of the workers. You've got to be tough to be married to a man like Arthur.'

He had commiserated with Arthur about his wife's death but the latter had brushed it aside. 'I manage. The children are growing up. And I'm a dedicated man, doctor. Maevy knows all about that. By God, that lass has a head on her shoulders. And she's compassionate. You should be proud of her.'

'You're the picture of a contented man, Charlie.' He heard Belle's deep voice.

'I *am* one.' He turned to smile at her.

'Can I ask you my favour, then?' Her silver-grey eyes seemed to slide along the lids. Was it the colour which made them odd?

'Fire away.'

'Well, I'm concentrating on gynaecological work and Sholton is as good a place as any. Plenty of confinements. Maybe they've nothing else to do in the dark nights.' The disconcerting emphasis on certain words . . .

'Maybe not. What was . . .?'

'Father's beginning to get tired. He's ten years older than you, and I wondered if you'd like to have me in his place. Mother and I thought that if he began to ease out of the practice gradually for the next year or two . . . I know the ropes now. Would you take me on?'

'Well . . . I'd have to discuss it with Jim.'

Her eyes swept over his face, slowly. 'Father will fall in with my plans. He always has.'

He did not want her. She had a disturbing presence, and he had not forgotten what Maevy thought of her. But against that he ran the risk of offending Jim Geddes who had worked long and faithfully with him. And she knew the practice. She would be good at her job. But that was not the same as people liking her. Then, there was his own secret dream, not even voiced to Maevy, for Ellie to study medicine, unless they had a son, even now. Belle could help Ellie, tell her how *she* went about it. Women doctors were still scarce on the ground.

'You'd certainly be a great advantage to the practice,' he said.

'So you'll take me?'

'I'll let you know.' The silver-grey eyes were suddenly cold.

They had a post mortem sitting up companionably in bed. 'I think it went well,' Maevy said, sipping her hot milk.

'Yes, everybody seemed happy,' he smiled at her, 'including Susan.'

'And Ellie. She was entranced with all the lovely gowns. And Ernest.'

'Yes, he's got an easy way with everyone, young and old. I saw him spending a lot of time with Lizzie. Do you think he's smitten?'

'I don't know. He has a kind heart underneath the clowning. Maybe he realizes she'll miss Nigel more in company. He's always cheerful and talkative, but you never really get to know what he's thinking.'

'I liked young Robert. He reminded me of Patrick, your brother.'

'In a way, or it's his mother's seriousness. I hope not her temperament. I don't think so, somehow. It's strange he should be like Patrick, and yet his own son, Gaylord, from what Kate says in her letters, gives them a bit of worry.'

'In what way?'

'Inability to make up his mind about a career. Keeps doubtful company. Her Kieran tries to steer him in the right path. There have been one or two peccadilloes already.'

'Oh, it's natural in a lad of nineteen.'

'Maybe so. You don't want them to be angels. I don't know if you remember, Charlie, but Maria's Uncle Gaylord, her mother's twin brother, died in mysterious circumstances in Tidewater, Virginia. He'd never married. I never got the whole story, but apparently Caroline, Maria's mother, had a nervous breakdown when it happened. Maria was only seventeen at the time, and had the

worry of nursing her mother. She and her father went
through a bad time. Caroline was in a home eventually.'

'A mental home?'

'I would think so.'

'So there's a skeleton in the family cupboard?'

'Isn't there in all families? Anyhow, I don't think we
need worry about Robert when he joins the firm. Mother's
pleased. "That will be two McGraths now," she said.'

'You're staying on?'

She put down the glass and turned to him. 'Do you
want me to give it up?'

'I want you to do whatever you want, my darling.' He
drew her to him. 'I know how you missed the challenge
of nursing. And I've not forgotten what you said when I
came home. That you'd give it up if we had another
child.'

'It doesn't look like it.' She did not raise her head.

'Are you really torn apart by it? Look at me, Maevy.'
She withdrew herself from his arms. 'You know what I
think, medically speaking, that your operation might have
upset things. Against that you had Ellie, but maybe we
should regard that as good fortune. Don't think I'm not
as keen to have a son as you, but sometimes you have to
accept . . . Now, we could start going round gynaecolo-
gists, if you like, or bow to what John Craigie would call
the will of God. Tell me truthfully, does it still obsess
you?'

She had turned to face him. Her face was pale, with
circles of fatigue under her eyes because of the long day,
but their expression was as honest as ever.

'I'm forty now. I agree with you that the operation did
something to me, rather than God's will. If I stop to
analyse it, I realize a child to look after at my age might
be difficult. But it was a son I wanted, a son who would
become a doctor like his father, a son who might take

your place if you didn't come back from the War. But you did, and there I thank God.'

'What's wrong with Ellie studying medicine, if she wanted to?'

Her eyes widened. 'Do you know, that hadn't occurred to me, the great feminist, "Today's Woman".' She laughed. 'If she wanted to, that would be fine, a step beyond my nursing, and logical. That's a hope. But besides that, I know if I were simply a housewife I wouldn't be completely satisfied. McGraths is a challenge to me. And it's *ours*, Charlie. My mother and father built it up from nothing, and I'd like to do my bit in keeping it going, in his memory, in their memory.'

'I appreciate that.' He put his arm round her again. 'Ellie's at school all day and Susan's here to keep the bools running. And I'd be proud of you.' He hugged her. 'Today's Woman.'

'I don't deserve a husband like you,' she said.

'Nor I a wife, so we're quits. By the way, Belle Geddes asked me tonight if I'd take her on as a partner in place of her father.' He felt awkward mentioning her. He didn't know why.

'Did she?' Maevy's voice was level.

'Yes, she and her father have discussed it. He's had an incipient ulcer for a long time. I think that's what made him crabbit occasionally, and he wouldn't mind slowly easing out of the practice.'

'Would you like her?'

'I'm not sure. There are many advantages. It saves me looking for someone else, she's local, she knows the practice and she seems clever enough.'

'Oh, she's clever enough.' He could feel the dislike.

'If I turn her down I risk offending Jim and Aggie Geddes, slighting their one and only. They've always been proud of her.'

'You want to go on in general practice?'

'Meantime. I've got to find my feet again. But if a tempting offer came from the Royal to do two or three days' surgery every week, I wouldn't turn it down. There are great opportunities now that we have X-rays. I'm easy. Being at home with you and Ellie is more than enough for me.'

'And you don't mind me being away for part of the day? I'd always be there for Ellie coming out of school.'

'No, I don't mind. Why should I? It's time I became a Today's Man.' He laughed.

'You're a good man, whatever else. Well, I don't mind if you take Belle on. After all, it might not be for long anyhow.'

'What makes you say that?'

'Women get married, don't they?'

'So they do!' He laughed again. 'That makes me feel much better about it. It's funny, I never thought of Belle Geddes getting married . . .'

'She's not averse to men.'

'Oh, I know that. But married . . .' They lay down, and sleep overwhelmed them with their arms round each other.

9

Lizzie bent down to cuddle Jonty once more before she left. He was seated on the floor surrounded by his toys. At three years old he was a solemn little boy, scarce of hair as yet, and what there was of it was a soft brown like Nigel's, which had always been abundant. She no longer felt the acute grief when she recognized traits in Jonty which came from the Crawford family, the thin frame which steadfastly refused to fatten, the narrow, well-shaped head, although his eyes were the brilliant blue of those of her grandmother and herself. 'Be a good boy, won't you, while Mummy's in Glasgow?'

The child paid no attention to her, and again the single-minded concentration was Nigel's. She remembered his habit of not answering if he was absorbed in his own thoughts, but the memory scarcely disturbed her now, only brought a soft sadness.

'Don't make such a fuss, Lizzie,' her grandmother said. 'He's perfectly happy. You're only making it into a grand drama.'

Lizzie kissed him and got up. 'You're sure he won't be a trouble to you?'

'Now, why should he be?' Maeve smiled at her. 'Didn't I bring up five children, six till John drowned, and no help whatsoever? He's far more independent than if you'd had a nurse dancing attendance on him.'

Contrary to the custom in the Crawford family, it had been decided not to have one. At the time she had been too grief-stricken to enter into the discussion. Maeve had been outspoken. 'You'll find the child your salvation with Nigel gone. If you hand him over to a nurse your arms will be empty as well as your heart.' Lizzie suspected her Aunt Maevy of having had a hand in the decision, too, although she had said only that, for her, bringing up Ellie had been the most enjoyable time in her life, and that she would not have missed it for anything.

But despite Jonty's lack of excitement at her leaving him, when she turned round in the carriage as it was rolling down the drive, she saw the little figure energetically waving at the window. Grandma had put him up to it, of course.

It was a glorious morning, mellow, golden, with a hint of crispness in the air, sufficient excuse to have worn her dyed ermine cape and toque. She had seen that the softness of the fur was becoming when she had stood at the mirror, and Maeve had confirmed it. 'A pretty woman wearing furs is ten times prettier. Now, you enjoy yourself today,' she said, 'and don't hurry back.'

She was going to have lunch with Ernest because he had something to ask her. 'I can't think what it can be,' she had said at breakfast that morning. 'And what's Lord Balfour up to today?' Grandmother had turned her attention to father-in-law who was reading his paper. She could be as close as a clam when she liked. Maevy had suggested she come to the office at York Street first and see round. 'And meet Robert,' she had added. 'He's installed now and seems to be liking it.' It was going to be an exciting day.

Glasgow was seething with people as usual, she thought, as she walked under the Central Station Bridge after she had got off the train. What a wonderful cavern of shops it was here, permanently lit because of the lack of daylight, and all the more mysterious because of that. She must bring Jonty soon to travel through it in a tram. There must be a feeling of wonder for a child to be at the window of one of those clanking monsters and to look out on what seemed like some kind of fairyland.

There was the shop where she had bought this very umbrella she was carrying, and here was that wonderful sweet-shop – 'All Home-made Confections', it proclaimed on its windows. Had she time? She darted in and asked the girl behind the counter for quarter of a pound of treacle toffees. They were messy, but that was the joy of them, one's mouth filling up with the brown sweet liquid as one sucked. And there were pink and white sugar almonds, Grandma's favourite. 'A box of these, please,' she said, pointing. She hurried out again, well pleased with her purchases, and made her way towards York Street.

She had not visited the new premises, and they were a surprise to her in their magnificence. All that shining mahogany and engraved glass, and telephones ringing. Telephones! Her father-in-law had them in his offices, but Crawford's Steelworks were known world-wide. And she noticed as she rang the bell that there were quite a few girls sitting at desks amongst the men. One of them got up and came towards her. She was wearing a neat white blouse with a black bow tie, and a black skirt. 'Yes, Miss?' she said.

'It's not "Miss",' she said, smiling. 'It's Mrs Crawford. I've come to see Mr Ernest.'

'Oh, it's the Honourable Mrs Nigel Garston Crawford?' the girl said, colouring. 'I'm sorry. Will you come away in, please. Mr Ernest is expecting you.' She opened the door set in its mahogany panelled wall. 'Follow me, if you please,' and she led her down a wide corridor between the desks. Someone was coming towards her, a young man, sober-suited. He stood back politely. 'Robert!' she said. 'Fancy meeting you!'

'Good morning, Lizzie.' He was in black with a high white collar, and was carrying a rolled umbrella in one hand, a pot hat in the other. They've made him into a

City businessman already, she thought, poor soul. She herself couldn't bear to be incarcerated in an office.

'Oh, you look grand, Robert,' she said, 'when did you start?'

'Er . . .' he looked quickly on either side of him. The heads at the desks were discreetly lowered, she could hear the pens busily scratching. 'Last Monday. I'm staying at a hotel in Bath Street meantime, till I find suitable lodgings.'

'Do you think you'll like it?'

'Oh, yes, Glasgow's a fine place. Nearly as good as Dublin. I'm just finding my bearings. Er . . . I have an appointment to see a client, I'll say good-bye.'

'You must come and see us soon. Come home with Aunt Maevy in the train.'

'Yes, I will, thank you. Good-bye.' Lizzie turned, and saw the girl beside her was shining-eyed in admiration.

'The girls are all mad about Mr Robert,' she said. 'This way, if you please.'

Maevy was there also when she was shown into Ernest's room. 'I'm beginning to think I'm the only member of the family who doesn't work here,' Lizzie said, laughing.

Maevy kissed her. 'We'll give you a job too if you like. And you're going out to lunch with Ernest, he tells me.'

'Haven't you guessed?' Ernest smiled at them both impartially as he fetched Lizzie a chair. 'I'm going to propose that we elope to a coral island with waving palms in the South Seas where Lizzie will wear a straw skirt and beads and dance for me every day.'

'It isn't safe to go out with Mr Ernest Murray-Hyslop,' Maevy said. 'He has a terrible reputation with the girls.'

'I'm sure you're right. I'd be much better off with Robert. I've just seen him looking very important. How is he getting on?'

'Really well,' Maevy said. 'Isn't he, Ernest?'

'He'll be running the place in no time. Takes life very seriously. So different from his father, Maevy says.'

'My real father,' Lizzie said. 'You knew that?'

'Yes, Kate told me ages ago.' She always marvelled at his easy way of talking about his stepmother. Was it an American custom? 'I don't think you could have had a better one.'

'Oh, Terence as a young lad, Ernest!' Maevy shook her head smilingly. 'How he led Patrick into mischief! But they're the best of friends, both happy now after all their trials and tribulations. Well, I'd better stop gossiping like an Arbroath fish-wife and get on with my work.'

'Why don't you come with us?' Lizzie asked.

'No, thank you. I shouldn't like to be *de trop* when secrets are flying about.' She put an arm round Lizzie and hugged her. 'Besides, I just have a sandwich because I leave early in the afternoon to be there for Ellie when she gets home.'

'Well, if you're sure,' Ernest said. 'I'll see you afterwards about that contract.'

'The only one I didn't meet this morning was Dan Johnson,' Lizzie said as they were walking along Gordon Street towards the Grosvenor Restaurant.

'Oh, he'll be busy somewhere. He's a grand worker.'

'Does he take quite well to Robert coming?'

'I think so, but time will tell. Here we are. I've booked a table for us.'

When they were seated opposite each other at one of the tables at the top of the marble staircase, Lizzie leaned towards him as she took off her gloves. 'You're being deliberately mystifying, Ernest. What is it you want to ask me? I've a feeling that Grandma knows, and Maevy, indeed the whole world except me.'

'Would you marry me, even without the coral island and the waving palms?' His brown eyes were merry.

'Ernest!' She laughed at him. 'Don't put me off! Come on, tell me your secret.'

'Well, since you won't take me seriously I'll tell you . . . but first you must order.' The waiter had appeared at their table, and was proffering a large menu to each of them with a white-gloved hand. Ernest looked up from his. 'The oysters are good here.'

'Oh, may I have some? It's so *special* to have oysters.'

'You may. How many can you manage?'

'The same as you.'

'That makes you a very greedy girl.' He laughed. 'A dozen each, please,' he said to the waiter. He bowed and went away.

'I'm all ears,' she said, smiling at him.

'Don't smile at me like that. You'll break my heart. You know I'm going back to America soon?' He became serious. 'That was always the arrangement with Patrick. And now that we have Maevy and Robert and Dan, not to mention a good accountant and head clerk . . .'

'Yes, I knew.' The news had saddened her when she had first heard it. No Ernest to joke with. 'You were so good to me after . . . I'll miss you. You make me laugh.'

'You do the same for me. You polish the sun and the stars for me, make them shine brighter. There, isn't that romantic? Remember what you were like when you came to Wanapeake with Maevy and you rushed into everything? And how you flung your arms round me when you were going back home? Oh, you were a forward little girl for your age!'

'Was I? I was full of life . . . then. I thought you were so sophisticated. At Yale, no less!'

'And poor Kieran eating out his heart for you.'

'Oh, he was too young for me, I thought. Actually he was only seven months younger but it seemed a lot at the time. And then I forgot both of you when I met Nigel.' She felt the laughter draining out of her.

'Don't be sad.' He put his hand on hers and when she looked at him his eyes were tender. She had become like a sister to him, she thought.

'If you don't tell me your secret,' she said, 'I will burst.'

'Well, if you burst you won't be able to eat your oysters so I guess I'll have to tell you, or ask you. Would you and Jonty come with me on a visit to America when I go back?'

She was speechless for a second or two before she found her voice. 'Go to America with you?' She shook her head. 'No, I couldn't think of it.'

'You liked it last time you were there.'

'But that was different . . . I was different . . . it was another life. No, I couldn't . . .'

'Look, Lizzie.' He put down his fork. 'It's over three years since Nigel died. I know you'll never forget him, and I'm the last person to urge you to do that, but you're only twenty-six. The war's over, Jonty is no longer a baby, you've never been away from the Hall for more than a day since then . . . don't you think you owe it to yourself?'

'That's the last thing to talk about, "owing". It's I who owe. I've been cosseted by grandmother and Lord Crawford, Jonty and I given a home, every wish of mine gratified. Nigel gave his life . . . oh, don't talk about owing!'

'I'm sorry. It was a tactless remark. I know Nigel gave his life willingly, just as Lord and Lady Crawford have willingly taken care of you and Jonty. But I've sounded out your grandmother about you going back with me and she thinks it's a grand idea and that her husband would say the same.'

'He's not very well. I read to him and we look at old photographs together . . . I think he depends on me.'

'I know you're devoted to him, but have you thought that maybe they'd like a little time to be on their own?'

90

'Oh, I don't get in their way! And the Hall could take a dozen families without you noticing it.'

'Lizzie, did you ever think of getting a house of your own?'

She looked at him. 'Strangely enough, I have. I sometimes wonder if Jonty is a disturbance to them . . . no, that's not the whole truth. It's their home, and I'm the interloper, however welcome they make me feel. And the idea of my own place appeals to me. I've thought of it, and wondered if it would hurt them if I suggested it.'

'I shouldn't have asked. Forget it. Things sort themselves out. You can blame, or thank, your Aunt Kate for this idea of mine. She started it, by saying in one of her letters that she wished you'd come to visit them and use me as an escort on the voyage. Then Maevy got hold of it and said I should ask you. So, here I am, asking you.' He smiled at her. 'What do you think?'

She looked at him, biting her lip, her eyes moist. 'I've always been adventurous at heart. Maevy says she's a homebird and now that she has Charlie back nothing would drag her away from him. But I'm eager to see new places, different people. Of course I've been to America before, but that only whetted my appetite. We could have another bicycle trip to Wanapeake Point and you could wear your cycling costume.' She smiled.

'I thought I was no end of a swell. Happy days! We could have a car run. Patrick and my father both own Oldsmobiles.'

'My goodness! Does everyone have cars there? I'd love to see Patrick's new house, too.' The idea was beginning to appeal to her. 'Aunt Maria has described it to me in her letters, and Sarah, and Gaylord . . . let me see, what ages will they be?'

'Sarah's twenty-one now. Gaylord two years younger.'

'And of course there's the baby, the successor to poor little Mary who died. Virginia, isn't it?'

'Yes, but they call her Ginny. She'll be seven now, no longer a baby, and I'm sure she'd fall in love with Jonty.'

'He'd love to see his cousins, I know. And think of the experience for him. Crossing the Atlantic at his age!'

'Well, for his sake, if not for your own, won't you say yes?'

'All right, yes!' She laughed. 'You've persuaded me, Ernest, but it wasn't difficult. Actually, I'm a very cosmopolitan young woman, I'll have you know. Quite used to eating oysters.' She squeezed lemon juice over one of them, lifted the shell between her finger and thumb and let the succulent morsel slip down her throat. Delicious.

She would not tell him that Sir Edward Hamilton had insisted on ordering them when she had lunched with him in his expensive club in Blythswood Square. Of course her grandmother and father-in-law had been there too. 'Business lunches are so much more enjoyable with the addition of such charming female company, Alastair,' Sir Edward had said, raising his glass. The ostensible reason for the luncheon was so that she and grandmother could meet formally the new Managing Director of the Crawford Iron and Steel Works.

She did not think her grandmother and her father-in-law were matchmakers, especially since in a way Sir Edward was taking the place Nigel might have held in the firm, but looking at the man, his strong chin, his square, bulky shoulders in his well-cut suit, the regulated waves of his hair, she knew he could never take Nigel's place in her heart. He was too square, even his hands were square, there was a lack of fluidity in him, a hardness, and yet his eyes had not been hard when they looked at her.

'There's something very wicked and indulgent about eating oysters, I always think.' Ernest's laughing brown eyes were on her as he held one up to his mouth. 'Certainly you're no country miss, but why cosmopolitan?'

'Well, I've visited Ireland twice since Nigel . . .' there

were still times when she couldn't say it, '. . . to see my father and Honor, and that's home to me, and don't forget I went to a finishing school near Paris for a year at Emily's recommendation. Do you ever see your sister?'

'I try to go every year, if possible. She and Charles steer a rather shaky matrimonial course together. It worries Kate.'

'A brilliant little humming-bird, grandmother sometimes calls her. She's never forgotten that Emily thought her very much *du monde*.' She laughed.

'So are you. Your finishing school may have polished you up a bit but I think it's inherent.'

She touched her fur toque. 'That's one of the nicest things I've had said to me for a long time.'

'Just wait till the Americans see you. You'll bowl them over.'

'No, I shan't.' Her eyes were sparkling. 'Oh, I'm beginning to get excited already! And I'll see Great-Uncle Terence, grandmother's brother, and dear little Great-Aunt Caroline with her ringlets, in their lovely house across the Hudson. Oh, Ernest, I can hardly wait.'

'Well, could you be ready to go in a couple of weeks? The Fall's a lovely time there.'

'Easily, oh, easily! Those oysters are absolutely delicious, Ernest. Much better than . . . any I've ever tasted.'

When she was rolling up the drive behind Thomas who had been waiting with the carriage to meet the Glasgow train, she saw a large and opulent motor car standing on the wide sweep of gravel in front of the house. There was a grey-uniformed chauffeur sitting in the driving seat, looking straight ahead.

'What a lovely motor car.' She bent forward to Thomas. 'I wonder whose it is?'

'Nasty smelly things!' He drew in behind the car and parked his whip. 'King Edward's to blame, if ye ask me.

He started it a'. Ye even hae to hae number plates! Ma Betsy and Brownie hae nae need o' them, thank the Lord.' He leaned forward and patted the two broad rumps. 'A don't know whit the world's comin' tae, Mrs Nigel, and that's a fact.' Lizzie watched him climbing stiffly down from his perch to open the carriage door. At least you'd be under cover, she thought.

'I still prefer the carriage, Thomas,' she said, smiling at him. 'Thank you.' She accepted his proffered hand.

Once inside she went running up the stairs and burst into the nursery, destroying a scene of peace and quiet, Cathy and Jonty seated at the table in front of the fire. Their faces were rosy from the flames, and they were both laughing at some private joke. 'Is he all right?' she said.

'As right as rain.' Cathy surveyed her calmly. 'Eating his tea like a wee man. Aren't you, pet? Her ladyship says can you go downstairs to the drawing-room, Miss Lizzie. There's a visitor.'

'Is there? Did you miss Mummy, Jonty?' She went down on her knees and hugged the child against her. How had she managed to forget him for most of the day? 'What did you do?' He was wriggling.

'I'm having my tea. Cathy's telling me about . . .'

'Yes, my darling, but what did you do all day?'

He freed himself and turned to her. 'We went for a walk by the river and Cathy made me a net with my handkie and a stick and I caught a big *fush*!' His blue eyes shone.

'Is that what you're eating?' She could not correct him with Cathy standing there, smiling.

'She's silly, isn't she, Cathy?' The gap in his baby teeth showed as he tittered. 'We threw it back because it would have died without water. It swam away to its friends. It was a great tare! That's what Cathy said.'

'Did she now?' Lizzie laughed at the maid. 'We'd better not let Lord Crawford hear him say that!'

'No, he was aye gey particular with Master Nigel, but yince they go away to they schools they're licked into shape, the English shape. Now, the lad's fine, Miss Lizzie. You go and see what her ladyship wants while he's finishing his tea.'

'All right. But I want to bath him, remember.'

'Aye, aye,' she nodded, 'you'll get bathing him.' She was indulgent, as if to a child. They'd known each other for a long time.

When she went into the drawing-room she was surprised to see Sir Edward Hamilton there. He was on his feet and evidently taking his leave, but he turned towards her. How crag-like he looked after Ernest, and that tightly-waved hair so closely covering his scalp . . . he was so *contained*, she thought, finding the word.

'Here she is at last,' Maeve said. 'Do sit down again, Sir Edward.'

'I'm afraid it isn't possible.' He came forward and greeted Lizzie formally. 'How are you, Mrs Garston Crawford?'

'Well, I thank you.' She could think of nothing to say.

'Sir Edward very kindly brought me some important papers to sign to save me going into the office.' Lord Crawford filled in the gap.

'That was good of you,' she said, 'coming all that way.' Perhaps he looked slightly less crag-like in that light suit, worn obviously because of the dust on the roads. And younger. And his complexion was tanned, making his smile whiter.

'It's no distance in the Daimler. It's still a new toy to me.' He seemed to relax from his stiff stance.

'Yes, I saw it as I came in. It must be a great thrill to ride in it.'

'And to drive it. Most exhilarating. Well . . .' the light went out of his face, and he turned towards his host and hostess. 'If you'll excuse me, Lord and Lady Crawford, I must get back to the office before closing time.' He bowed. 'I'll say good-bye.'

'If you must,' Maeve said. 'Show Sir Edward out, Lizzie.'

'There's no need, thank you.' He bowed again at the door and was gone.

'Well,' Maeve said when she had waited a second or two, 'that was a quick exit. You must have chased him away, Lizzie.'

'I hardly said a word!'

'Do you like him, Alastair?' She appealed to her husband.

'We didn't hire him for his social behaviour, my dear. He came to Crawfords with wonderful recommendations. I must say it was extremely thoughtful of him bringing those papers. He could have sent a minion.' His amber eyes were amused.

'He's in love with his new motor car,' Lizzie said. 'It's quite obvious. Dont't you think there's something . . . rock-like about him?'

'Well, if he can build up Crawfords into an even more rock-like edifice I'll be pleased. We're losing a lot of trade now that pig-iron's being exported. Steel is ousting cast-iron in any case, and we need someone who understands the new processes. We've been too conservative, and I'm too old to make sweeping changes. If only . . .' She knew what he was thinking. Hadn't she wept often in bed, thinking the same thing? If only . . .

Her grandmother had crossed to him, put an arm round his thin shoulders. 'We'll always miss him, my darling, but we mustn't go on grieving about might-have-beens. Lizzie especially must put sadness away. She's young.'

'Nothing will ever make me forget Nigel,' she said. 'And if I did, there's Jonty to remind me.' She saw them for the first time as old people, and her heart was wrung

96

with pity and love. She would not talk about the trip to America just now. It would be too hurtful.

Dalton House, Draffan. 25th September, 1904.
Dear Mrs Garston Crawford,
It was a great pleasure meeting you recently if even for such a brief time.

As you showed interest in my new motor car, I wonder if you would care to take a ride in it with me sometime? Most weekends would be suitable, but I would place myself at your entire disposal.

Yours sincerely, Edward Hamilton.

The Hall, Sholton, Lanarkshire. 30th September, 1904.
Dear Sir Edward,
'I thank you for your kind invitation to take a ride in your new motor car, but I am afraid it is impossible for the time being. I leave for America in a few days.

'Yours sincerely, Elizabeth Garston Crawford.

10

The voyage to New York, which was much quicker than
the one she had made with Maevy fourteen years ago –
was it all that time? – was even more luxurious. It was a
smoother crossing on the *Saxonia* than it had been on that
homeward voyage with Maevy, but the meals were of the
same gargantuan kind and, as Ernest said, you had to
walk at least five miles round the decks every day to work
up an appetite for the next one.

He was a delightful companion, proved to be an expert
at most of the deck games, and was soon in demand to
captain teams, to make announcements and to organize
games for the children, a general factotum. In fact, as she
told him, he was the most popular man on board, and all
she could do was share in his reflected glory and accept
the attentions of the ship's officers, which turned out to
be more pleasurable than she had imagined.

'You're a born organizer,' she said to him when they
were having dinner. He had just been asked to judge the
best fancy dress at the ball tomorrow night, the last
function before they docked at New York.

'No, I'm not,' he said, 'I just like people.'

'And people like you. And children. You have Jonty
eating out of your hand.' Nigel never knew his son, she
thought. He had been more reserved than Ernest, a kind
of detachment which made him appear haughty. She
remembered grandmother telling her of his grandmother,
'A shy-like creature. Went walking in the Sholtie Woods
on her own, listening to the birds . . .'

'I like to see people happy,' Ernest was saying. 'Are
you happy, Lizzie? Sometimes you look . . . reflective.'

'Do you mean now?' His brown eyes were on her, that smile which went up on one side.

'Yes, this very minute. The present. Not the past.'

'Yes. Very happy. And there's the pleasure of what's ahead, meeting all my American relations again, and seeing if they look the same, and their houses, and Patrick's and Maria's new house, and America, and, oh, everything!'

'You're going to have a difficult time deciding who to stay with.'

'Perhaps they'll share me.'

'I guess that's best. Are you going to finish that sugar monument you've been toying with for a long time?'

'I guess not,' she mimicked him, laughing. 'I've got some new gowns especially for the relations. I want to be able to get into them.'

'Well, shall we go up on deck and walk? It's supposed to be good for the waistline. There's dancing, but you'll get plenty of that tomorrow.'

'All right. I'll just go downstairs and get a shawl and see that Jonty is all right. Though he's slept like a log since we set sail. The sea air must have done something for him.'

'I wish I could say the same.' For a second his face was serious, and then he was on his feet, smiling, making some joking remark to the captain.

The child was fast asleep and she bent to kiss him. I feel strange tonight, she thought, a feeling of something impending, something I know and don't know, something which draws me and yet makes me turn away, a feeling that this is more than a voyage from Glasgow to New York, but one of discovery, of leaving those last three years behind me and starting again. You wouldn't mind, Nigel . . .? She did not know if the words formed on her lips or not. Should she tell Ernest? He had been so good and kind. No, I'm twenty-six, too old for confidences . . .

He was waiting for her. He had a white scarf round his neck but no coat.

'Won't you be cold?' she asked him.

'Not a bit of it. I have my love to keep me warm.' He executed a dancing step. His patent shoes gleamed. 'Here, take my arm. You might get blown away.'

'People will think things. Already one lady asked me if you were my fiancé.'

'What cheek! You should have told her I was your uncle.'

'She'd never have believed me. What age are you, really?'

'As old as Methuselah. Thirty-five.'

'My goodness! You should have been married ages ago.'

'I didn't want to, at first. I was having too good a time in New York to want to settle down.'

'You were a lady-killer, that was it. What about now?'

'Now?' He turned his head. 'Look, isn't it too trite for words! A full moon. I bet John Brown supplied it with the ship, attached by a string.'

There were quite a few people strolling on the deck, and after a few rounds Ernest said, 'I'm getting tired saying "Good evening". Here's a good place.' He steered her beneath the davits of one of the lifeboats. 'We can look at the sea from here. It's much too beautiful a night to go to bed.'

'But I must quite soon . . . Jonty.'

'The stewardess will keep an eye on him. She always does.'

'Why am I fussing? Yes, it's beautiful. I've never seen a moon as big as that at home.' The silver path on the water seemed to her magical.

'Everything gets bigger the nearer to New York you come. Are you apprehensive at all?' He turned to her, and she saw the straight lock of hair had fallen over one eye. She pushed it back, patted it.

'There!' she said. 'Apprehensive? No, but I have mixed feelings. I can't help thinking of that young girl who set off so confidently all those years ago. Isn't it good we don't know what's going to happen to us?'

'Yes.' His voice lowered. 'But never regret the past, the good or the bad bits. I try not to.'

'There weren't many bad bits . . . before Nigel. I mean when I was young. I think the worst was when I found out that Uncle John and Aunt Isobel weren't my real parents and I had to confront them with it.'

'That was bad enough.'

'Now I see it was just as bad for them. It was then, or afterwards, that I realized everyone didn't *see* as I did. D'you know what I mean? That was a revelation. I believe that with two people the most important thing is that they should have the same way of *looking* . . . oh, it's so difficult to explain, but I remember the feeling of desolation when I realized Isobel and John didn't believe they had done anything wrong in keeping the truth from me. Now I accept it. Like-mindedness. It's nearly as important as love, perhaps it *is* love. Nigel and I were like-minded . . . I think. Maybe, looking back, we didn't know very much about each other. We were so busy loving.' Suddenly she found herself weeping, a soft kind of weeping which didn't hurt. 'It was so beautiful, Ernest. I miss the loving so much . . .'

He took her in his arms and rocked her against him. 'Oh, you shouldn't ask *me* to comfort you . . . try and say to yourself, "Isn't it good that I had those wonderful years with him?" Enjoy the melancholy of it, now that the pain's gone, if it is gone. And think that perhaps his dying kept it perfect . . .'

'What do you mean?' Her face was against his shoulder.

'We all get, well, sullied in the market-place, except

perhaps the saints. Nigel wasn't given time to tarnish your memory of him. Think of it as a shining sovereign you can take out and hold from time to time . . .'

'You're very wise, Ernest.' She came out of his arms to look at him.

'No, I'm not, just that I've had longer at it than Nigel.'

She put her hands on his shoulders and kissed him. 'You're my dearest cousin and I can never thank you enough for having this idea . . .' His arms went strongly round her. They were close joined.

Familiar sensations were in her mouth against his mouth, in her limbs a trembling, in her breasts a pain; yes, that was well-remembered, a prelude to a greater pain, a unique pain which thrilled . . . her head swam. Was it she who had started all this, or Ernest? Yes, it was she who had kissed him, had lingered because the sensation of their mouths together was delicious, she had even opened hers . . . 'Jonty,' she said, 'I was forgetting . . .'

'So was I.' His face looked very white. 'I'll see you down.'

They did not speak going along the corridor until they reached the cabin. 'Give me your key, Lizzie.' He opened the door. 'Sleep tight,' he said. It was the old smile, and she pushed back her memory of what had happened, if it had happened. Perhaps she had been moon-struck.

'Don't let the bugs bite,' she said, laughing at him. 'It's an old Scottish saying.'

He shook his head at her, still smiling.

11

Long ago she remembered making the same train journey
with Aunt Maevy and Uncle James, with the Hudson
lapping, it seemed, at the very rails, and the little stations
seeming to rise out of the river at each stop.

Then his carriage had met them, but this time a smart
motor waited at Wanapeake Station, and seated at the
wheel was a young, thin man who on seeing them gaily
waved his panama hat. Lizzie, waving, immediately recognized the dark-haired girl beside him.

'It's Sarah, isn't it?' she said to Ernest as she stood
beside him, holding Jonty's hand. I would have known
her anywhere, she thought, the quiet darkness of her. She
had last seen her talking to Nigel at Grandma's ball, a
serious girl of sixteen, and she had been jealous, willing
him to look at *her* . . .

'Yes.' Ernest was waving and shouting, 'Hello!' And
then shaking hands vigorously with the young man who
had climbed out of the car and half-ran towards them,
'Gaylord, old son! Do you drive the Oldsmobile now?'

'Of course I do! I learned on the Curved Dash, but this
is opulent! Your father has one. "In my merry Oldsmobile
. . ." Do you know the song? Welcome, cousin Lizzie!'
He had turned to her. 'And your little boy. Isn't he a
dream?' He was as she remembered him with his parents
when they had lived in Glasgow, then a small thin child,
but now at nineteen with a laughing charm and a nervous
vitality in all his movements.

'You may kiss your cousin, Gaylord.' Ernest laughed.

'Oh, may I? Well, since we're cousins!' She felt his thin
body against hers for a moment, his soft mouth on her

cheek, and then Sarah was there with her sweet, serious smile.

'Welcome to America, Lizzie.' Another soft kiss on her cheek. 'And your dear little son.' She bent to kiss him too. 'Oh, Ernest!' Ernest had put his arms round her and hugged her as she straightened. She was faintly pink. 'It's a wonder we arrived in one piece the way my brother drives! We're so glad to see you both. Come along. I think Jonty looks tired.'

Lizzie lifted him in her arms. 'He's shy, that's all. Say hello to your cousins, my pet.' The child hid against her shoulder.

'Leave him to grow accustomed to things,' Ernest said. 'Shall we get into the car, Gaylord? The rest of the luggage is following. You take one case, I'll take the other.'

'Aye, aye, sir!' Gaylord clowned, touching his forelock. 'I'm a hopeless organizer,' he smiled at Lizzie. 'Come along. Mother and father are dying to see you. The arrangement is, Ernest, we drop you off at Wolf House where you are to have a tearful reunion with your parents, return of the prodigal son and all that, and then you've all to come on to our place for another tearful reunion with cousin Lizzie and little Jonty.' Sarah had her arm round Lizzie and Jonty as she guided her to the motor car.

'You come into the back with me, Lizzie. Shall I take him?'

'No, thank you, Sarah. Best to leave him just now.'

'Father and mother thought you should stay with us,' the girl said as they settled against the padded back of the motor. Lizzie remembered Sir Edward Hamilton's Daimler in the drive of the Hall. Had he been disappointed when she had refused a ride in it?

'Father particularly wanted it that way,' Sarah went on. Her dark eyes on Lizzie were understanding. Aunt Maria had always been direct. She would have told them long ago that she was a second wife, and that Patrick had been married to Bessie Haddow . . . my mother, she thought now, who died when I was too young to remember her.

'That's lovely, Sarah,' she said, settling down with Jonty on her lap. 'I'm longing to see Uncle Patrick and Aunt Maria.'

'I know someone who's longing to see you!' Sarah smiled at her. 'Kieran. He's talked about nothing else. He'll be coming with Aunt Kate and Uncle James.'

'Kieran! Does he still live at home? Oh, that's grand! He and I wrote letters to each other for ages after my last visit here with Aunt Maevy. You were living in Scotland then.'

'Yes, I look back to Scotland often, but there was a lot of sadness then. My little sister, remember?'

'Mary? Oh, yes, that was so sad for you all.' Gaylord had picked up part of what she was saying.

'No sadness, please, for our lovely cousin. We're going to give her the time of her life. You'll see how we enjoy ourselves in America, Lizzie. You shan't want to go back to dreary old Scotland. I guess *you're* glad to be back, Ernest. Life is dark and earnest back there, isn't it, Ernest?' He laughed out loud as he drove with a flourish along the country road leading uphill from the station. There were the tall trees again, so many of them, as if just sufficient room had been cleared for each house from the original forest.

'Talk less, Gaylord,' Sarah said, 'and concentrate on your driving, please. We want our guests to arrive in one piece.'

'Yes, solemn Sarah.' He hummed loudly, then said, 'Do you know the "Merry Widow Waltz", Ernest? Marvellous.'

'Yes, I do,' Ernest laughed, 'and I'd like to correct you. I did *not* find Scotland dreary. I felt at home there.'

She remembered Wolf House so well when they dropped off Ernest at its gates: brick built, with the gleaming white window frames and shutters and the French-style roof built up square like a cottage loaf. There was the solid front door, also painted white, with the rounded arch above it and the wide porch where they had so often sat to admire the foliage of the trees.

'Won't you come in?' Ernest said to Lizzie, jumping out. 'They'd all like a quick look at you.'

'Well . . .'

'Not allowed, not allowed,' Gaylord sang out.

'There are strict instructions from Mother,' Sarah said. 'You're all coming to our house later for dinner. I have to bring Lizzie and Jonty straight there so that she can have a rest and freshen up.'

'All right.' Ernest saluted. 'See you later, Lizzie.' His eyes were laughing as they met hers, holding them for a moment. We're more than friends now, she thought. I wonder . . . life was suddenly interesting and complex and unpredictable, as if she had emerged from a long winter, a long winter of the spirit. She held the sleeping Jonty close to her as Gaylord drove smartly away from Wolf House with a loud blowing of the klaxon.

Sarah gave her a brief description of their house, Claremont, as they bowled along to Gaylord's singing, through quiet roads where only a gleam of roof through the trees showed the presence of other houses. 'In Wanapeake they're mostly clapboard. Wolf House is unique, and ours, too. It's built of stone which Italian masons had quarried for some Government project, and the remainder was bought by a private builder.'

'Didn't Aunt Kate have an Italian housekeeper called Mrs Vanaressi?' She was pleased she remembered.

'Yes, she's still with them. A lot of Italian immigrants came to Wanapeake towards the end of the last century to quarry stone, and they stayed on. I think when Mother and Father saw Claremont they felt it was theirs. Father said the stone reminded him of the little cottage in Sholton where he was brought up, and they decided to name it after Claremont Terrace where their Glasgow house was.'

'I guess Wanapeake is a whole lot different, though,' Gaylord said, who was listening. 'Not as quiet as Sholton. Just wait till I take you to some of my howffs on the Wanapeake river. You're going to get the surprise of your life.'

'Lizzie wouldn't like the places you frequent,' Sarah said sharply. 'You know Kieran's always warning you about the company you keep.'

'Oh, Kieran's an old stick-in-the-mud! As bad as the parents. Everybody's entitled to a bit of enjoyment, don't you agree, Lizzie?' He slowed down, made a wide turn through stone pillars and drew up, the wheels crackling on the gravel. 'Here we are!' He blew the horn loudly and Jonty wakened and sat up, rubbing his eyes.

It could not by any stretch of the imagination be called a little cottage, and its only resemblance to Colliers Row in Sholton was indeed the stone it was built from. It was more like Claremont Terrace: a gracious house, solid, imposing, and with some of the cragginess of Scotland in its rough-hewn bulk, softened by trailing creeper now tinged gold and red by the 'Fall', as Ernest had taught her to say.

Aunt Maria and Uncle Patrick were at the top of the wide flight of steps to greet her, Uncle Patrick of the solemn manner, almost as craggy as his house now, and Maria, totally at home in her own land, dark-haired, strong-chinned, welcoming, smiling, her voice ringing with its renewed American inflections.

'Lizzie, my dear! Welcome! And your lovely little boy! How we've counted the days. Isn't she lovely, Patrick? So like your mother, but not so tall.'

She went into their arms, the tears running down her

face. 'Oh, it's grand to see you both again! I can scarcely believe it.'

'Come along inside,' Maria said in her rich voice, 'you must be tired. And here's Ginny to help with Jonty.' A pretty little girl had appeared from behind her mother and knelt down to put her arms round him.

'I'm your cousin, Jonty. We have a lovely little room off your Mama's especially for you, and lots and lots of my toys, and a new toy called a teddy bear, just for you. Come and I'll show you.' She straightened and held out her hand. He took it confidently and went up the steps, although obviously finding them a big stretch for his small legs. Lizzie watching him thought how like Nigel he was, shy, but always willing to meet a challenge.

'Now, there's a conquest for you,' Maria said. Looking at her glowing face, Lizzie remembered the other child who had died, and how once long ago, she, herself a child, had sat on the floor in their house in Claremont Terrace and held her on her lap. Her head had lolled, her eyes had been vacant under the pretty birthday ribbons.

She walked with Kieran in the lovely garden of Claremont after dinner. The quarried stone had been used outside as well: in the pillared folly at the foot of it, in the stone urns, arches and jardinières full of salvias and dahlias, in the paved paths. Beyond the trees was a view of the Hudson, as wide as the sea at Rothesay, she thought.

'Do you remember the bicycle trip last time I was here, Kieran? And Great-Uncle Terence and Great-Aunt Caroline following in a carriage?'

'With the champagne.'

'Yes, with the champagne.' She laughed. 'The first time for both of us. This time I'd like to sail on that grand river.'

'Oh, we have all kinds of plans for you, especially Gaylord. He loves excitement. Too much, sometimes.'

'Loves a tare?' She saw his look of puzzlement. 'That's a Scottish saying. But isn't he at Yale? You and George, and Ernest, went there.'

'No . . . well, he wouldn't study. It isn't that he isn't clever. He's just . . . easily diverted. His father is going to try and get him appreticed to an architect in Wanapeake, the one who designed this house, as a matter of fact. He has quite a good reputation.'

'Does Gaylord have any . . . leanings towards architecture?' She was beginning to gather he was somewhat of a problem, and she thought of his dead uncle who had drowned himself, although no one had ever said that. And she thought also how strange it was that we were marked by our ancestors. People had told her she had her mother's ready smile and her grandmother's carriage, and yet there was Uncle Patrick, as solid and reliable a person as you could have found, who had had that tragic little daughter and now a son who seemed to give them all cause for worry.

'You look pensive,' Kieran was saying. She saw his sweet mouth, his gentle eyes. 'You've had such a bad time, losing your husband when he was so young. I often felt guilty I wasn't fighting too, and yet the War seemed remote here . . . I wish we'd kept up our correspondence and then I could have at least tried to comfort you.'

'Oh, I had plenty of that.' She felt very close to him. Everyone said he was like grandmother's first husband who had brought her from far-off Ireland to settle in Sholton – a true gentleman, even his successor, her father-in-law, had said. 'But you'll understand because we're practically the same age, how nothing is a comfort when you lose the person you love.'

'I can understand that.' His eyes were full.

'I only began to climb out of the slough of despond after Jonty was born, and then, apart from loving relatives – especially Aunt Maevy – Ernest was the one who made me feel young again. I was creeping about in darkness, oh, I can't tell you the grief . . .'

'Ernest has great gaiety of spirit. We missed him when he went to Scotland. I remember how you admired him when you were last here.' He smiled at her. 'And how you sent your love to him in all your letters, even from your finishing school in Versailles. I was quite jealous.'

'Were you?' She looked between the gap in the trees to the gleam of the Hudson. 'I thought you would have been married by this time, Kieran.'

'Did you?' She turned and saw his wry mouth. 'The girl I loved didn't love me.' He was a tease, of course, always had been. She remembered him making fun of Ernest in his cycling costume, the sage green breeches, the befrogged tunic with silver buttons, the yellow Yale badge on his pork-pie cap.

'Oh, that's sad.' She spoke lightly. His look was making her uncomfortable. He had been only a boy when they last met, and in any case it was Ernest who had taken her fancy. Both had been forgotten when she had fallen overwhelmingly in love with Nigel on their first meeting. 'But there must be hordes of girls in New York. You work there, don't you?'

'Yes, in father's export business. He's practically retired now. I live with my parents here in Wanapeake to escape the hordes!' He laughed. 'Besides, I'm not fond of cities.'

'There you're different from me. I loved Paris, and I long to see New York.'

'I'll be happy to show it to you . . .'

'Now, now, what's all this?' Gaylord was suddenly standing in front of them, tall and spectacularly thin in his black dinner jacket. He had a great elegance. 'I noticed you two leaving the drawing-room so I thought I'd spy on you.'

'So you've been creeping about the bushes?' Kieran said, laughing. 'I might have known, you crazy clown.'

'Don't bluster, cousin dear. I thought we should plan some events for Lizzie's delectation.' He turned to her, his eyes sparkling. 'There's a wonderful inn on the Wanapeake, Lizzie. All the best people go. And there are gondolas one can glide about in, and an orchestra playing on the verandah, and paper lanterns and lots and lots of bubbly . . . let's make up a party. Are you on, Kieran?'

'If it's the Venetian Inn you're talking about, yes, by all means. Not the other one.'

'Listen to this puritanical little man talking! Showing off in front of you, Lizzie. Trying to make a good impression. Don't pretend the Paradise is any worse than the places you go to in New York which the family don't know about. Ernest will come, of course, and we can ask Sarah and Jack – that's her friend, Lizzie. He's besotted by her, but our solemn Sarah is not allowing herself to be bowled over . . . and there's George and Abigail . . .'

'You know they wouldn't go,' Kieran said. 'It's not their style.'

'No, prayer meetings are more their thing.'

'I don't think I could leave Jonty,' Lizzie said. She was excited at the thought of the outing. She wanted excitement, to feel that she was living again. She could let her hair down in Wanapeake, far from home, just as Kieran did in New York, according to Gaylord.

'But this place is bristling with servants!' Gaylord waved his thin hand back at the house. 'And there's Mama who's good with children. She'd love to be in charge.'

'Well, if your parents agree.' She caught Kieran's eye. Was he disapproving? But not Ernest. He loved fun, just as she did, and it was so long since she had had any, only that brief glimpse on the ship when they had stood close together and kissed. It had only been fun, hadn't it, a romantic moment helped by the full moon sailing on the water and the faint sound of the orchestra? Yes, she would love to go. The old excitement which she had once felt at the idea of an outing stirred in her.

Her aunts and uncles were sitting companionably round the fire, except for Ernest and Sarah who were playing cards at a side-table. Sarah looked up when they came in, laughter in her face.

What fine-looking women Aunt Kate and Aunt Maria were for their age, Lizzie thought. They must each be about fifty. Aunt Kate, particularly, was still beautiful. It was the everlasting quality of her beauty, the serenity of her expression, her fine eyes. It came from grandmother's family, the Muldoons of Woodlea. Terence, her own father, had it, a kind of nobility, and Aunt Maria too, in a way, because *her* father was grandmother's dearly loved brother. She had still to cross the Hudson and visit them at Springhill.

James Murray-Hyslop was sixty-nine now. It was difficult to believe, but then Aunt Kate was his second wife, and George and Ernest his children from his first marriage, as were Emily in Paris and Victoria who lived in Wanapeake. He was showing his age now, but he had the wryness which Kieran had inherited, a Scottish pawkiness. 'Here comes Lizzie surrounded by her admirers,' he said, looking up. 'Now we have two beautiful young ladies in our midst!'

'Oh, I can't hold a candle to Sarah,' Lizzie laughed, 'I'm just a country bumpkin. Gaylord's telling me all about the wonderful inns you have here, on the Wanapeake River.'

'As long as you steer clear of the Paradise Inn,' Maria said. 'That, I believe, is a blot on our landscape, fast people from New York driving down, drink, even drugs . . .'

'I'm sure Gaylord's thinking of the Venetian Inn.' Kate smiled. 'A charming place. They have boats . . .'

'Gondolas, Aunt Kate,' Gaylord corrected her, wagging his finger. 'I went to a birthday party there last week. It was one of the Van Dam girls.'

'That's George's wife's family.' Ernest raised a smiling face to Lizzie. 'How confusing it all must be for you. You haven't met him yet. Are he and Abigail all right, Kate?'

'Blooming, and their children. They're looking forward to seeing you and Lizzie as soon as you can visit them. There's a new baby there, just a year old – Zachariah, Zach for short.'

'They're trying to catch up with Victoria and Jason,' Ernest laughed. 'How many little Vogels are there now?'

'Five.' Kate's eyes danced. 'Perhaps they've stopped with Benjamin. I'll take you to see all the little ones some afternoon, Lizzie. They're my pride and joy.'

'I'd like that, then I'll be able to tell grandmother all about them.'

'How is she?' Her face became tender.

'Happy. She's concerned about Lord Crawford's health, but you know Grandma. She has a great gift for enjoyment. I don't think it will ever leave her.'

'James,' Kate said, turning to him, 'we must go and see her. She's getting on. We mustn't leave it too late.'

'Are you talking about me, or your mother, dear heart?' Lizzie saw the look which passed between them.

'You! You're just a young thing yet! You'd be dancing the Highland Fling as soon as your feet touched Scotland.'

A spasm of sadness went through Lizzie as she watched them. A long and happy marriage – something that had been denied her. The prospect of the enjoyment ahead of her palled. She was lonely. She was meant to be loved, to live with a man. Nigel . . . the essence of him came back to her, his amber eyes, his tender hands, the slightly *farouche* air he had had at times, her husband, her lover . . .

113

12

But she was too much Maeve's grand-daughter to be unhappy for long, especially amongst relatives who were so intent on making every minute of her stay enjoyable and memorable.

Aunt Maria took her shopping and visiting, they had several trips across the Hudson to visit her great-uncle Terence and great-aunt Caroline, now both frail. He was older than grand-mother, Lizzie realized, which made him seventy-six, and his wife Caroline, Maria's mother, was a pathetic little creature with grey curls hanging limply on either side of her withered cheeks but still with her penchant for bright colours and little bows.

Springhill was as lovely as ever, its wide lawns running down to the Hudson, and still immaculately kept although the stables were empty of horses now. Her Aunt Maria told her of her horse called Starlight. 'That was when your Aunt Isobel came to visit, long ago,' she said. 'How happy we were together! She had her twenty-first birthday here.'

'Isn't Springhill too big for you to manage now?' Lizzie asked her great-aunt when they were having tea in the shaded drawing-room. The sun hurt her eyes now.

'Far too big, my dear, but there are so many memories in it: your Aunt Isobel and my darling Maria sweeping down the stair-case in their ball gowns . . . sometimes I think I can still hear their laughter. Even the sadnesses count. At one time I thought Maria and Patrick might come here to live, but it's the wrong side of the river for Patrick getting to New York by train. There were no trains when we first came here.' She sighed. 'Times change. But we're too old to move now, isn't that so, sweetheart?' She addressed her husband who was balancing a cup on his fat stomach.

'I need room.' His face was purple-red, a bad colour, Lizzie thought. 'I'm a big man, my dear Lizzie, as you can see.' He was still jolly. 'Both my sister and I were never used to hen-houses, although the Hall is bigger than this by a long way, I imagine.'

'Yes, I suppose so. The grounds are certainly larger.'

'Well, there you are, then. If we have the money to keep up these places, why not? It's a good inheritance for the younger generation, and goodness knows, there are plenty of them.'

'What do you think of Gaylord, Lizzie?' Caroline asked. 'Isn't he a beautiful boy? So like my dear twin brother who . . . passed on. We were so close, so close. I never really got over his death. Why did he do that . . .?' She put her handkerchief to her eyes.

'Now, now, Mother.' Maria got up, motioning her father to stay where he was, and put her arm round her mother's shoulders. 'There's no point in living in the past. Just look at this lovely little boy sitting so well-behaved on the carpet beside you, and remember that he is fatherless and Lizzie without her dear husband.'

'Oh, yes, of course, I'm selfish. I know that. Dear Lizzie. But someone as beautiful as you will have many men anxious to marry you.'

'I know of two across the Hudson already.' Maria caught Lizzie's eye over her mother's head. She misses nothing, she thought. 'And goodness knows how many back in Scotland.'

'What flattery, Aunt Maria,' Lizzie said, laughing.

'Is my dear Gaylord in love with you, then?' Caroline asked.

'Don't make the girl blush, dear one,' Terence said, stirring his tea loudly, and taking a bite from an iced cake in his saucer. His appetite seemed to have grown with age.

'I don't mind.' Lizzie smiled across at him. 'No, not a bit, Great-Aunt. I'm far too old for him. He's keener on enjoying himself with lots of ladies rather than one.'

'Well, that's at least healthy,' Terence said gruffly. Lizzie wondered why her Aunt Maria looked away, her face grim.

Then there were visits with Aunt Kate to see her 'pride and joys', and to give Jonty other children to play with, but truth to tell Lizzie enjoyed Aunt Kate more than she enjoyed Victoria's and Abigail's broods and their incessant talk of domestic details.

Seated in the back of the Oldsmobile, driven by the chauffeur since Kieran and James were in New York at their export business, Kate would talk about Scotland when she had been the eldest of a large family and had first gone to be nursemaid to the Murray-Hyslop children.

'When I brought them to visit mother at Colliers Row she would have a lovely Irish lace teacloth on the scrubbed wooden table, and bake such dainty scones and cakes. Oh, she was always a lady, even in that little kitchen! I can see her now with her black silk apron and her shining red hair. And now she's a real one!'

'I should hate to leave her and Lord Crawford,' Lizzie confided. 'He's old now and I can relieve her a little. I can listen to him when he talks about Nigel.'

'That must hurt.'

'It does, but it's a soft hurt now, a passing sadness. At first we used to weep together and that helped us both . . .'

Ernest came often to Claremont to discuss business with Patrick after they had spent the day in New York. The American branch of McGraths was going from strength to strength. The rapid spread of railways all over America had helped rather than hindered the firm. They

116

already had a reputation for quick deliveries to any part of the continent. Uncle Patrick's drive had full scope. At fifty-one he was still full of energy.

He said at dinner to Ernest one evening in the dining-room with its pillars and polished floor, 'You see, I was right, Ernest. Motor transport here is far advanced compared to Glasgow. I have a fleet of vans which meet every train in a radius of one hundred miles, or where there are no trains we guarantee to deliver goods to any part of the United States of America.'

'You have the advantage of a comprehensive railway system. They've been moving fast while I've been away.' Lizzie liked it when they talked business. She could admire Ernest's lean, intelligent face, the merry eyes, even when he was concentrating, the straight lock of hair which he had to push back from time to time.

'Yes, I foresaw that, but trains aren't suited for everything, you know. My latest idea is to have a fleet of pantechnicons for house removals. I could do with you to organize that side. It would have been a grand opening for Gaylord, but,' he shook his head, '. . . hopeless.' It was a good thing Gaylord was not there, Lizzie thought.

'His talent lies in other directions, don't forget,' Aunt Maria said. Was that what she really thought? Lizzie wondered, watching her as she dished out food in her usual competent fashion. 'Judith,' this to the maid, 'pass those round, if you please. And tell Cook we need more squashes. He goes on sketching parties with young men, you know,' she spoke to Lizzie. 'I've some of his work upstairs. I must show it to you.'

'I'd like to see it.'

'He's certainly artistic,' Ernest said. 'I remember he was always drawing when he was a small boy. He may well make a success of this new venture in architecture.'

'He'll make a success of it if he gets up in the morning,' Patrick said. 'He's still lying in bed when I set off for New

117

York, and no wonder, with all that partying that goes on at night. If it weren't that he'd be no use to the firm back home, I'd send him there to see what the Scottish air and capacity for hard work would do for him.'

'Now, now, Patrick.' Aunt Maria's glance was admonishing. 'Don't let Lizzie go back with the wrong impression of Gaylord.'

'He's a charming young man,' she said, 'I'm sure he'll do very well.'

She walked with Ernest to his Oldsmobile when he had taken his leave. It was a moonless night, the trees rustled in the wind, and occasionally she could hear the ghostly hoot of a river steamer. 'There's a Fall feeling,' she said. They had seen so little of each other since they had landed. She stood close to him, shivering slightly.

'Are you cold, wee Lizzie?' His voice was tender. 'Sit in the motor car with me.' He opened the back door and handed her in, coming in beside her. 'You've been whipped away from me by all those relatives, and you'll soon be going back home.' He put his arm round her. 'See, I'm saying "home". I wish I was going back with you. I'm sorry I made that agreement with Uncle Patrick and the firm. Especially now.'

'Why especially now?' It was even darker in the Oldsmobile. There was a smell of leather and cigars, a man's smell.

'Because I've fallen in love with you and I can't bear to see you go.' He put his cheek against hers. 'Did you mean to kiss me on the ship, was it friendship, or . . . love?' She could not see his face, but felt the leanness of his jaw. She could imagine the merry eyes, the straight lock of hair falling over them.

'It was friendship at first, and then . . .'

'And then?' he said gently. Were his eyes still merry?

'All the old feelings which I thought were dead came

back. I felt young again, alive for the first time since Nigel died. You . . . stirred something in me.'

'Oh, I hoped you'd say that!' She felt his mouth on her cheek. 'You're constantly in my mind, your face in its sadness, and then when it lights up, your excitement. I saw, that time we had lunch together in Glasgow, the Lizzie you were meant to be, full of life and gaiety . . . Lizzie, I have to say it before you go.' He turned her to face him. 'Would you consider marrying me?'

'Marrying you!' She was astonished. 'I never thought . . . But you're going to be *here*.'

'Is that your only reason? Other women have crossed the ocean to be with someone they loved.'

'No.' She was shy, and put her face against his shoulder. 'It's the first thing that came into my head!' She laughed. 'I was *dumfoonered* at your proposal! But I couldn't, you see, leave grandmother and my father-in-law in their old age. They've been so good to Jonty and me. They depend on me, and there's the Hall. If either of them . . . went, the other would need me more than ever to run it. Already I see to the greenhouses – well, supervise them – order provisions, engage the staff sometimes . . .'

'But if it weren't there, and, forgive me, if grandmother and your father-in-law weren't there . . . oh, I understand how grateful you feel to them but that's not *us* . . . Do you, could you, love me enough to marry me and come to live here?'

The feeling was there again, the stirring of her senses, so welcome after the barrenness. Why was it one man could do this to her and not another? She thought of Sir Edward, and Kieran here . . . how to explain the delicious trembling sensations unless it were love. 'I could, Ernest,' she said, 'I think I do.'

He kissed her. She had not been kissed like that since Nigel left her to go and fight. His ardour had been youthful; Ernest at thirty-five was experienced in kissing,

119

his words of endearment were his own and new to her, his thin body different to her. There was no doubt about it. She loved him.

'Yes, you do,' he said. He was panting. He laughed. She was sure his eyes were merry. 'But what are we going to do about it, you on one side of the world and I on the other?'

'We can write.'

'Write! What a cold fish thing to say. Lizzie, I want you. You know you want me.' He caressed her face, his voice soft.

'Ah, but I'm a Scots lassie,' she said. 'I'm older than when I married Nigel, and more mature. I've been through the whins. You would call it being cautious. I would like to test this love, see if it held up to a separation. I know one can do without a man's love, if one has to. We can get to know each other better through our letters, confide our thoughts to each other. You will be over on business from time to time. There would be that to look forward to.'

'That wouldn't satisfy a girl like you. I know you. You're passionate, starved . . .'

'No, it wouldn't satisfy me,' she laughed, teasing him, 'but it wid dae fur a bit though mebbe no' fur long.' She kissed him lightly. She was a different and wiser girl than the one who had married Nigel.

'But you can't love me to talk like that.'

'I must, because I know I'd be tortured by the thought of all those fine ladies you meet up in New York while I'm being helpmeet at the Hall with only a little lad to keep me company.'

'Twaddle! A beauty like you! What about Sir Edward Hamilton?'

'Don't tell me you're jealous of him! He's not at all like you. Stiff and awkward. The only resemblance is that he has a dearer motor car than yours!'

'What is it?' he said, making her laugh and think, Men . . .

'A Daimler.'

'I give you that.' He hugged her, laughing too. 'Oh, Lizzie, you and I are meant for each other. Say you'll marry me.'

Their kisses were bitter-sweet now. Why, she thought, when I'm so much in need of love, should I choose someone who will be thousands of miles away from me? She drew away from him. 'I'll have to go now, Ernest. Aunt and Uncle have enough worries with Gaylord.'

'Say it, my darling.'

She shook her head. 'It may be your home, Ernest. It isn't mine.'

13

Their party at the Venetian Inn was fixed for the night
before Lizzie's departure. The time had gone so quickly,
and she had begun to feel at home in Wanapeake,
thinking less and less of Sholton. Jonty, too, spent many
afternoons with his little cousins. There were few children
in Sholton he could play with. There was still the barrier
of class in the village, and the mothers of the children
there would have been more embarrassed than flattered
if she had invited any of them to come for tea. Here in
America it was different. The children of the staff in both
Victoria's and Abigail's houses often joined in their
games.

Kieran had a few days off work and took her sightsee-
ing. Uncle James seemed less of a taskmaster than Uncle
Patrick. Since Ernest had asked her to marry him she had
only seen him briefly at Claremont when he called with
Patrick on their way home, both looking a trifle weary
after the bustle of the city.

But in their few exchanges she knew she loved him.
What she did not know was whether she could bring
herself to leave her grandparents on their own. She would
confide in Aunt Maevy, she decided. She would help her.
She might suggest a solution, or sometimes a solution
came of its own accord if one kept one's mind quiet. That
was Uncle Charlie's teaching.

Kieran did not take her to New York. He left that to
his mother and aunt. He took her on what he called his
favourite expedition, into the hinterland behind Wanapeake, tracing the course of its river as far as they could
by motor car and foot. She told him laughingly that he

had a bit of David Livingstone in him, and he agreed, in so far that he was at home with nature. Cities had no appeal.

'Now, Ernest,' he told her, 'is a different type. Urbane is the word I'd use to describe him. And he enjoys the challenge of cities. He doesn't mind being incarcerated all day. He and Uncle Patrick suit each other in their driving ambition.'

'Yes, that's true,' she said, but perhaps her eyes or her expression betrayed her. She felt his thoughtful glance on her.

They found little-known tracks up river where they could watch the brilliant little humming birds and sometimes a solitary blue heron. He told her about Audubon, the painter and naturalist, and promised to send her some of his prints. There was a tropical feeling, she told him; the sun, even in early October, was hot on her shoulders, so different from the image of Sholton in her mind – its grey stone, its small hedged fields with their circumspect cows, nothing lush, and dominated often by the coal bings rearing to blot out the sky.

But, then, the Sholtie burn was pleasant, and in the Hall with its vast wooded grounds one was shut away in a private world . . .

On another blue and gold afternoon he taught her how to fish, and showed her how, nearer the mouth of the Wanapeake where it was tidal, one could find crab and sometimes shrimp.

They glimpsed the quiet lagoon which was a mirror for the Venetian Inn. 'It's even lovelier at night,' he said, 'with the lanterns lit. But, then, there are people.' She did not say that the thought of the gaiety excited her. They sat on the rocks with their picnic and they were companionable, avoiding intimacies or conversations about the family, or Ernest. She knew she had given herself away by her expression.

'There is an island,' he told her, 'a mysterious place called Sachem Island where the river divides. I wish we had time to go there. There are the most wonderful tall hemlocks,' and seeing her questioning look, 'evergreen firs. It's like being in a cathedral, silent, hardly any birds. And, then, there's the Blue Pool, surrounded by cliffs. That's where the other inn is, Paradise Inn.'

'Is that the one the family don't approve of?'

'Yes. They're against the New York set. They think they bring their own bad habits with them. Gaylord loves it.'

'You worry about him, don't you?'

'Yes, I do.' She was struck again by his sweet expression as he turned to her. 'Goodness knows why, but he's always confided in me. Uncle Patrick is strict with him, and Aunt Maria, although she loves him truly, puts her husband first. But he's so vulnerable! That's one of the reasons why I live at home. I'm there for him if he needs me.'

'He's lucky to have you.'

'Do I sound like a prig? I know I'm not cavalier like . . . others.' She thought he would have liked to say 'Ernest'. 'But sometimes too much sophistication can spoil things. I've a feeling that the people who go to the Paradise Inn see it simply as a rendezvous, a place for excitement. Even the village boys get to know about them. They're paid fifty cents for diving into the Blue Pool.'

'Things are changing, Kieran,' she said, feeling infinitely older than he. 'It's the same at home. Even douce old Glasgow has its new rendezvous – howffs, they call them.'

'You're right.' His gentle eyes were on her. 'Of course I accept change. It's inevitable. But it doesn't mean to say that I like it.' He smiled at her. 'The favourite picture in my room is a copy of a pen drawing done in 1760. Idyllic.

124

The trees are spindly like a foal's legs, and delicate little deers are cropping the grass between them. Through the trees you can see the river where it widens at Sachem Island, undisturbed except for a few white sails. Everything fresh, new, unsullied, as it was when the Indians left here.'

She was touched. 'You make me see it. And I remember Grandmother telling me about your mother's first letters home, and how she could imagine an Indian coming out from the trees brandishing a tomahawk.' They laughed together.

'You can still get that feeling,' he said.

They were quite a party at the Venetian Inn on Lizzie's last night: Ernest, Kieran, Sarah, with Jack Henken, an amiable young man obviously very much in love with her; George and Abigail: George still serious, Abigail, blonde, pink and plump-armed in her ruched pink gown; Victoria and Jason Vogel: Victoria a pale copy of her sister Emily in Paris, with none of her sophistication, not at all '*du monde*', Jason, tightly buttoned into his black suit, already in his middle forties a prominent citizen of Wanapeake; and Gaylord, full of animation, in a light suit with a cummerbund and light buckskin shoes, making Jason look twice as sombre.

It was a beautiful evening, and the laughter and music took all Lizzie's latent sadness away. She was going to live for the present. She would always have tender memories of Nigel, but he, lying in that far-off field in South Africa, would want her to be happy. She laughed and danced, she was taught the new America polka by Gaylord, and waltzed to the tune of 'I Love You Truly' with Ernest.

After supper they boarded one of the gondolas and drifted over the lagoon with the music from the orchestra coming to them faintly on the still air. Fireflies darted.

The lagoon had many moons in its depths, reflections of the paper lanterns.

Ernest was beside her, his arm along her shoulders. They could not speak privately, but love flowed strongly between them. Once she turned to look long into his eyes, and when she turned back she caught Kieran's gaze on her. She was aware that he smiled awkwardly, apologetically. Perhaps it would have been better if she had allowed Ernest to do what he had wished, announce their engagement tonight.

But she was not ready. It was no more than an instinctive feeling. Although she had known him in Glasgow for a long time, her falling in love had been sudden. She had not been ready. Ernest was the first man she had really seen as a man when she had got over her grief. She had to think. It was not only herself who was involved, there was Jonty, grandmother and her father-in-law, all her relatives back home. Here, in America, she knew there would be no opposition. Aunt Kate would welcome her with her usual warmth into their family.

Gaylord was on his feet, brandishing a glass. He had arranged for champagne to be brought on the gondola. 'This is to wish God speed to cousin Lizzie! Will you drink, ladies and gentlemen, to the Scottish beauty, the breaker of Wanapeake hearts!' He swung his arm and collapsed backwards, his legs sticking up in the air. There was a burst of laughter, but Lizzie saw Victoria and Abigail looking away as if ashamed.

Kieran and Ernest were on their feet, helping him up from the bottom of the boat. He righted himself, his face flushed, but still holding his glass. 'Trust Gee-gee!' he shouted, waving it again. 'Haven't spilled a drop! Oh, no!' His face expressed exaggerated concern. 'It's empty! I've lost it! Waiter, more bubbly, *s'il vous plaît!*'

'You've had enough,' Kieran shouted, laughing.

'Now, now, dear coz, no holding hands, please. I've

126

told you before. Just look at Ernest. He doesn't interfere, but then he's otherwise engaged. Trust little Gee-gee, he doesn't miss a thing. I know who fills Ernest's mind these days. All together now, "I love you . . . truly . . ."' He swung his arms, swaying as he swung, '"Truly . . . dear . . ."'

Ernest was unperturbed. 'You're a fool, Gaylord,' he said. 'Sit down or you'll fall into the water this time. But I give you fair warning, if you do, I'm not fishing you out.'

'I don't need you. I've got Kieran, kind Kieran. *He* keeps an eye on me, too much of an eye. Wouldn't let me take you to the Paradise Inn instead of here, afraid I'll find you the wrong playmates . . .'

The evening was going sour. Abigail and Victoria were tight-lipped. Jason seemed to be trying to look as if he were not a member of the party. His round face was puffed with disapproval.

When they landed from the gondola Ernest took things in charge. 'The party's over, Gaylord. Lizzie has to set off tomorrow morning. We'd better get home.'

'Just another drink for Auld Lang Syne?' His mouth was turned down pettishly. He looked dejected.

Ernest shook his head, smiling, and placed a hand on his shoulder. 'We've had a lovely time and you've been a grand host. We'll all get back now. I'll drive you, Lizzie, Sarah and Jack; Kieran will take our Oldsmobile and see the others home. Agreed?' He turned to their group.

Jack Henken seemed untouched by Gaylord's behaviour. 'That suits me, Ernest, since I haven't any transport.' The others were silent.

Gaylord sulked in the back of the motor car, his head bowed. Sarah and Jack carried on a polite conversation with Lizzie. When Jack was dropped off at his house Sarah kissed him on the cheek without much show of emotion. Was she shy, or did she really love him? Lizzie

127

wondered. She was such a self-contained girl it was difficult to tell.

Ernest saw the three of them to the door of Claremont, Gaylord still sulking like a small boy, his hair ruffled, his hands in his pockets. He pushed past them in a blundering fashion and Sarah looked apologetically at Lizzie. 'That's Gaylord, I'm afraid. Either the swings or the round-abouts. He'll be bright and breezy tomorrow, you'll see.' And then, hesitatingly, 'You'll want to say good-bye to Ernest. I'll see you tomorrow at breakfast, Lizzie.' She kissed them both, and left them.

'That was considerate,' Ernest said.

'Poor Sarah. She shouldn't feel ashamed for her brother.'

'People like Gaylord always make people feel ashamed and then when he's charming they feel guilty for feeling ashamed . . . Ah,' he said, drawing her towards him, 'don't let's talk about Gaylord. He's his own worst enemy. This is good-bye, my dearest. I shall be off to New York long before you.'

'Yes.' She leaned towards him. 'Well, it's best this way.' She did not think so.

'We'll write, and you'll keep telling me you love me?' He caressed her face, looking into her eyes.

'Yes, and you'll write and keep telling *me*? And I'll think about it and if I can't stand not seeing you . . .' She closed her eyes at the pain of it.

'I've had a word with Uncle Patrick. It's likely that I'll be in Scotland before long. He wants to institute the pantechnicon trade there as well.'

'Christmas?' Her heart lightened.

'I don't know. But as soon as I can. My love,' he kissed her mouth, looked at her a long time before he kissed her again, 'let's make our parting light. Otherwise,' he smiled at her, 'my love will burst its banks and I'll forget myself.' She wanted to forget herself.

'Yes, let's keep it light.' She drew away from him. 'I'm the happiest girl in the world. It's not good-bye. I'll go now, quickly.' She got out of the motor and went swiftly up the steps, not looking back. Sarah had left the door unlocked, and she went into the hall. She leaned against the other side of the door, trembling, before she could make herself go upstairs to her room.

She had been unable to sleep because her body had been awakened. And then when her blood calmed she tossed and turned, racked with doubt. Jonty would like it here with all his little cousins. She had looked in to see him in the adjoining room and he had stirred in his sleep and said, 'Come on, Zach,' and then laughed.

Should she, before she left, write a note to Ernest and say she had changed her mind and she would come back and be married here? Was that a betrayal of Nigel? But hadn't she already decided that she needed a testing time so that she could be sure it wasn't only her body that wanted him?

She was tired and not sleepy. It had been an exciting evening in strange surroundings with strange voices, the orchestra with its black musicians, the dancing couples. One girl had worn a gauzy scarf which floated out as her partner spun her to the music. She had seen him bend and kiss one of her bare shoulders.

What would they say back home if they knew about such goings-on? Lord Alastair insisted on formality, Nigel had been the same, 'distant', the villagers had thought him, in spite of his perfect manners. He had not had the easiness of Ernest, Kieran or Gaylord, although *he* had gone too far this evening. There was a lack of control inherent in him, something strange . . .

She heard a small incessant tapping on her door, and was not alarmed. Was Sarah, like her, unable to sleep, or did she want to apologize for Gaylord's behaviour? She sat up. 'Come in,' she said softly. The door opened. There was sufficient light through the open curtains to let her see it was not Sarah, but someone in a red dressing-gown, lean, tall, with ruffled hair . . .

'Gaylord!' she whispered, afraid. She pulled the bed-clothes over her shoulders. 'What are you doing here?'

He came swiftly towards her and sat down on her bed. 'We must whisper.' His face showed white in the diffused light from the moon. 'You won't scream, will you, cousin Lizzie? I couldn't sleep for remorse. I lay in bed wishing I hadn't disgusted you.'

She made herself speak calmly. 'But you didn't disgust me.' She sat up and felt for her wrap. It must have slipped off the bed. Now her bare shoulders were exposed. Aunt Maevy had advised light nightwear because of the warmer climate. 'It's all right, Gaylord. Now, please go.'

'I was *so* miserable.' His voice broke. 'I can't tell you the misery I felt. It came over me like a black cloud. Can you forgive me?'

'Of course I can.' She had started to shiver. 'Now, please go. Aunt Maria might . . .'

'They're at the other end of the house.' She knew that to be true.

'Jonty . . .' she said feebly.

'Children sleep like kittens. They've nothing to worry them. I looked in on dear little Ginny next door and she was *so* asleep.' She began to feel less fearful. He was disarming, there was no harm in him, and yet she had to get him to leave her room.

'We'll talk in the morning, Gaylord. I'm tired.'

'Kiss me, then,' he put his head on one side, 'and say you've forgiven me for spoiling your last evening.'

'But I told you you didn't.' She was impatient with him. 'Oh, well . . .' she leaned forward, and then so suddenly that she was unprepared, he had pinioned her on the

130

pillow with his arms and was kissing her roughly, his mouth open. She smelled the liquor on his breath.

'If you scream I'll tell them that you invited me in.' He raised his head but kept her pinioned. 'I'm capable of it. You don't know me, Lizzie, how mixed-up inside I am, how confused. When I saw you and Ernest together it was like a sword going through me. I wanted to feel like him.'

She struggled fiercely in his grip. 'Get away from me, Gaylord! I don't care. I *will* scream.'

'No, you won't. You're sensible. But passionate. It's in your eyes and in your body. Show me, show me, I want to know . . .' Once more his mouth had fastened on hers, and then she felt the weight of his whole body on top of her. One of his hands came free and was tearing at the shoulder-strap of her nightdress, he was pushing his legs between hers although the covers were still partly over her. 'I want to feel the way you do, you and your dead husband, now you and Ernest.' He took his mouth away to speak. 'Show me, show me! You've been married! You know! You aren't like the callow girls around here who must ask their parents if I may kiss their cheek . . .'

She was suffocating. Before she became weak, she must do something. With a tremendous effort she managed to push his body away from her and, swinging her arm, she struck him across the face. There flashed through her mind that picture which had kept her sleepless for so long after Beenie Drummond had told her about it, the great flailing red arms descending . . . She must have been crazy with anger when she struck grandmother, and for a moment she shared the same madness. To think that Gaylord should assault her in this way! It was intolerable, dirtying everything, her marriage to Nigel, her new-found love of Ernest.

He was sitting on the side of her bed, his hand to his face. He looked dejected, his head bowed. She got out of bed, found her wrap on the floor and put it on over her

131

bare breasts. She had to try twice before she could summon her voice. 'I'll never forgive you for this.' Her voice rasped in her throat, hurting it. 'Not only for myself but for your parents. Oh, don't worry. I shan't breathe a word of it, I'd be too ashamed. I can only believe you've taken leave of your senses.'

'They left me a long time ago,' he said, not raising his head, 'when I realized . . .'

'Don't tell me anything, don't explain, just get out of my room!' There was something there she did not want to contemplate.

'You weren't in any danger,' he said, getting up and facing her. His voice had a flatness, a finality. She saw a black scratch from her nails on his cheek against the terrible whiteness of his face. 'You didn't have to fight.' He turned and went slowly to the door, stopped, his back to her. 'Nothing would have happened. That's the saddest part . . .' A surge of pity went through her, quickly changing to anger. He had ruined everything. Nothing in her life would be the same again.

She wept when he had shut the door quietly behind him, and then she got up and locked it. Her hand was trembling so badly that she could scarcely get the key to turn. I'm not going to think of it, she told herself, the implications. I want to feel anger, not pity. She clenched her fists, whipping up anger. That would save her from thinking . . .

She looked in at Jonty and found him still fast asleep. 'Children sleep like kittens,' Gaylord had said. She went to the pitcher, poured some water into the basin and sponged her face. It was burning. She got back into bed. When her anger finally cooled, the sick kind of pity was there again.

132

14

It was difficult settling down in the Hall. Now its vast rooms, its palatial air, the formal grounds and the grey-green quality of the atmosphere after the brilliance and colour at Wanapeake made it seem even more vivid in her memory. And she missed Ernest. She was the type of woman who needed a man beside her. She had the capacity and need for a loving relationship just as grand-mother had, first of all with Kieran McGrath and then Lord Crawford.

She found him frailer than when she had left, and somewhat querulous, but Maeve dealt with him in her warm-hearted fashion, teasing him, cosseting him a little, laughing him out of his complaints – most of all, loving him. He was overwhelmed with pleasure at seeing his grandson again. 'Here's my little successor,' he said, holding out his arms to Jonty, 'it won't be long now.'

'Now, Alastair,' his wife said, 'we'll have no more of your gloomy talk or Lizzie will be regretting that she ever came back again. She'll tell us all her news, and I'll relive my time there again. Is that beautiful river still as wide and handsome, Lizzie, and what did you think of the health of my dear brother at Springhill and my crown and jewel, my beautiful Kate? And what about Patrick? How many millions has he made now?'

She nodded when she told her of Kieran, and said that yes, she had always known he was the living image of her own dear Kieran and you won't mind me saying that, Alastair, because you had a great opinion of him as well. 'Young Kieran used to write letters to you, Lizzie, didn't he? Has he given that up?'

'Yes, a long time ago. When I fell in love with Nigel. He's busy now keeping an eye on Gaylord.'

'The namesake of Caroline's twin brother? Patrick has a bee in his bonnet about cousins marrying. He thought that poor little Mary was the result of his close relationship with Maria. And he didn't approve of Kieran being fond of you either, Kate once told me. Afraid that it would lead to something. I think he made it plain to Kieran.'

'He never said.'

'He wouldn't. And as far as Gaylord's uncle is concerned, well, we had a suicide in our own family, Terence's Catherine. There's no such thing as a happy family, but the sadness can make the joy seem greater.' And then with a mischievous smile, 'You haven't mentioned Ernest. He, at least, isn't a blood relation.' Lizzie had the advantage that, like grandmother, she never blushed.

'Oh, he settled down quickly with Uncle Patrick, or had to.' She laughed. 'But I think they're two of a kind.'

'Maevy tells me we have another one in young Robert in the office. Goes from strength to strength. But that's all you have to say about Ernest?'

'For the time being, Grandma.' She would not worry them with her doubts and anxieties. They had enough worries. 'Gaylord's the one they worry about, at least, Kieran.'

'Ah, yes. Is there anything in heredity, I wonder? I don't mean looks, something deeper.' She gave a shake of her head as if to say that was enough of that.

'Sir Edward Hamilton has been visiting me,' Alastair said. 'Most kind of him. And he seems to have taken a tight rein on Crawfords and its general management. He's certainly increasing business for us.'

'As long as he doesn't oust you completely,' her grandmother said sharply.

'That's a foolish remark, my dear.' Lord Crawford's

mouth had a downward turn. Again Lizzie noticed the change in him. 'It was the best thing I did, bringing him into the business, taking the load off me, especially now that I haven't Nigel.' He's never got over it, she thought. I have. She admitted it now. She did not want to live in the past any more.

It was difficult finding a suitable time to see her Aunt Maevy because she went off to McGrath's office in York Street every morning and was becoming later and later in returning. Susan was very much in charge when Lizzie called at Braidholme.

'There's a big meeting on today of the Scottish Carters' Association, with that Hugh Lyon, and she's staying late to see the committee. She's a great one for the workers, Maevy.' She was in her favourite stance, arms akimbo. 'She encourages them to join to get their rights, and sees that they have a Sick Fund an' aw that. And she was that keen on them keeping up their Annual Horse Parade this summer . . .' Susan was evidently now an authority on all matters pertaining to the Scottish Carters' Association, Lizzie thought, concealing a smile. If ever anyone lived through others, it was Susan. The McGraths and their doings had been meat and drink to her for as long as she could remember. Did nothing ever happen in her own life?

'Ellie isn't back from school yet?' she asked.

'No, but ony meenit noo. Since she went to Hutcheson's Grammer in the toon she's aye later. Their star pupil, I'm hearing.' Since she had hardly any friends except another old maid in the village, Tibby Simpson, it was difficult to imagine how the news would reach her. 'She comes and goes hersel in the train; right independent, she is.'

'I thought I'd take her back with me to the Hall for tea. Is Uncle Charlie in?'

'Aye, the surgery will be feenished noo. Away ben and

135

see him. I'll have to get on wi' the dinner and no' stand crackin' here.' She dismissed Lizzie.

The waiting-room was deserted, but Charlie's door was shut. She knocked and went in when he called out, but stopped inside, hiding her surprise. 'Dr Belle! I'm sorry. Am I butting in?'

'Of course you aren't!' Charlie's face was free from guile. 'My, what a grand young woman you're looking since your American trip!' He got up to greet her, kissing her fondly. 'Isn't she, Belle?'

'She certainly seems to have filled out a little.' The girl's silver-grey eyes slid coldly along their lids. 'Some people have all the fun while you and I slave away in Sholton, Charlie.' Her eyes were not cold when she looked at him.

'Ah, but you have the pleasure of being one of the first doctors to qualify in Glasgow, while I've nothing to show for *my* expensive education.' Grandmother had said she could be quite nebby at times.

'There's more to life than doctoring.' The cold eyes again, the cool voice. She had no time for women. 'Well, I'll get away on my calls, Charlie. Father won't be out today at all. I told him to stay in bed. And I'll see to that change in Mrs McCafferty's medicine. Good-day, Lizzie.' Her hair was luxuriantly black against the white jacket she wore for the surgery – another of Charlie's 'fads' as some in the village called it. 'It's like gawn to Broon the bakers noo,' someone was supposed to have said. Charlie himself had repeated the story, laughing, unperturbed. Lister was still his saint.

'You and Aunt Maevy are so busy I can't get a chance to talk to you,' she said. 'I came to see if I could take Ellie home for tea. I know she's very grown up these days, but Jonty misses his American cousins.'

'And do you?' His bright black eyes were on her.

'Do you mean Kieran, or Gaylord, or . . . Ernest?'

136

'Now, take your pick,' he said, laughing, but he would not press her, like grandmother. 'How's Lord Crawford?'

'I see a difference in him since I've been away.'

'Aye, he's failing, too rapidly for my liking. His heart's bad and he hasn't got over Nigel. I can say that to you now. At one stage I thought you wouldn't either.'

'But I'm young.'

'Yes, that's the secret. And before we really appreciate it, we've lost it. Well, I'd better get on with my calls. I tell you what, come to Braidholme on Sunday afternoon and see us. Bring Maevy's mother if she'll come. I wouldn't advise it for Lord Crawford. He needs great care. I'm glad you're back to give them both that, Lizzie. They depend on you.'

Maeve declined the invitation. She would rest in the afternoon beside Alastair, she said. He liked her close by. Lizzie knew that they still liked to treat dinner as a formality and took pleasure in dressing for it, although the process took longer and longer. Sir Edward Hamilton was coming.

'Do you like him, Grandma?' she asked her.

'I'm not right sure. He's competent enough, but there's a hard streak in him, ruthless. And I might as well warn you, Lizzie, I think he's got a double reason for coming.'

She shook her head. 'He's wasting his time.'

'I thought that. You don't have to say anything. You were a different girl when you came home. You have my capacity for love and a willingness to give it when the time's right. Oh, lass, to be young again . . .' Her face with its beautiful crown of red hair was wistful, the blue eyes luminous.

Braidholme restored Lizzie's temporary disenchantment with Scotland. Yes, I belong here, she thought, it's in my bones and my heart from that dark passionate girl, Bessie Haddow, who was born and brought up in Sholton, even more than from my father with his Irish parents.

137

Grandmother still yearned for her old home from time to time. 'I'm due a visit to Woodlea and Terence and Honor,' she had said, 'but as long as Alastair's poorly . . .'

Aunt Maevy was and always would be her anchor . . .

> Trusty, dusky, vivid, true,
> With eyes of gold and bramble dew,
> Steel-true and blade-straight,
> The great artificer made my mate.

Charlie had once quoted Stevenson's poem to her. 'Change it to a fair-haired lass and that's my Maevy,' he had said, his eyes shining with love.

Ellie was a fine girl now of twelve years, fair like her mother, with all her earlier brashness gone, but still with the light-heartedness which came from a happy family background. If Maevy still regretted that she had only one child, she could have no complaints about the one she had.

When Charlie got a call to visit a patient, she jumped up too. 'Can I come too, Daddy, and bring Jonty? It would be a treat for him.'

'Don't use Jonty as an excuse,' he said, laughing. 'You want to drive the pony, don't you?'

'Yes.' She dimpled. 'Caught out!'

'Come on, then!' He put his arm round her. 'For Jonty's sake!' He looked at Maevy and Lizzie. 'Do you think she'll want to drive that motor car when I get it?'

'Of course I will,' the girl said. '*Can* I take Jonty, Lizzie? I'll take good care of him.'

'Just try and stop him. Look at his face.' The child was jumping up and down, clapping his hands with delight.

'He's a grand wee lad,' Maevy said when they'd gone. They were seated in the summer-house at the foot of the garden. It was a mellow day, and they had the windows and doors open to the air. The garden was vivid with autumn colours, less intense than Wanapeake, but with their own beauty.

'He enjoys Uncle Charlie's company. He misses having a father.'

Maevy had her mother's directness. 'Are you going to tell me? I know by your face you're happier than you've been for a long time.'

'Could I ever keep anything from you?' She leaned forward to pat her aunt's knee. 'Ernest has asked me to marry him.'

'Do you love him?'

'Yes, it suddenly came. America clinched it, or maybe being on the *Saxonia* together.'

'Ah, there's nothing like being on a ship, but it's how you feel on dry land that counts.'

'I didn't change. But it's not as easy as that. He's based in America now, that was the agreement with the firm, and I can't leave grandmother and father-in-law. You know that. They've been so good to me.'

'Oh, I know that fine. It isn't just duty, it's love.'

'What do you think I should do, Aunt Maevy? I don't want my life to go past, yearning . . .'

'Now, don't feel too sorry for yourself. You've been luckier than most. You had a perfect love with Nigel, you have a son to prove it. I know you lost him, but you're still young. A lot can happen in a year, maybe less. Did Ernest say anything about coming back to pay a visit?'

'Yes, he mentioned Christmas. He's managing the removal side for Uncle Patrick and they have the idea that they could start the same thing here. Of course I know you have to build up the motor transport side first . . .' She stopped because Maevy was looking at her with a droll expression.

'Is this you teaching your grandmother to suck eggs just because you've been in the land of the brave? Don't belittle the Scottish McGraths, if you please. I happen to work there.'

'Oh, I'm sorry.' She put her hand to her mouth.

'I'm teasing. Do you know, there are four thousand motors on the road now, and we have a copy of Patrick in the office in young Robert?'

'Yes, Uncle Charlie was telling me.'

'No, we aren't as backward as they think, but that's enough sprowsing. Take my advice, Lizzie, and leave it until Ernest comes to Glasgow. He'll come at Christmas, I'll bet my boots.'

'You're right, as always.' If he did not, it would mean he was not as keen as *she* was. 'Oh, it's so good to talk to you. If I ever go to America permanently, I'd have to stow you away in my trunk.'

'You know I'd never leave Charlie.'

She said, without thinking, 'What's your opinion of Dr Belle, Aunt Maevy?'

'Why do you ask?'

'I met her the other day and it only confirmed what I thought when Jonty was born. I don't like her.'

'She's a good doctor and more than useful to Charlie now that her father's given up. She can take over when he's operating at the Royal, and you know what that means to him.' Did cutting off Nigel's leg give him a taste for it? The terrible things that came into your head . . .

'Yes, I suppose so. Funny how you take or don't take to people. Like Sir Edward Hamilton. He's coming for dinner tonight.'

'He's coming to see you, more likely.'

'So Grandma seems to think. I can't take to him, either.'

'He sounds a thrustful man. Charlie hopes he isn't pushing too far with Lord Crawford when he's not in such a good state of health.'

'He won't hear of anything against him. I think in a way he's putting Nigel's mantle on him.'

Maevy looked at her. 'You've matured, Lizzie. Whoever you choose in the long run will be lucky.'

'Get away with you!' But although she had been frank she had not told her about Gaylord. That was still too sore a place in her heart.

Sir Edward Hamilton was there when she went down to dinner a few hours later, wearing a new white silk gown bought in New York, with side panniers and a broad white collar, which she acknowledged to herself in the mirror set off her shoulders and her dark red hair. She wore the string of pearls Nigel had given her before he went off to fight, and die. Pearls for tears, but he would want her to be happy.

Sir Edward was immaculate, his crag-like face losing its sternness when he greeted her. 'Did you enjoy your sojourn in America?' he asked formally, kissing her hand.

'More than I can say,' she said. 'I saw your Daimler in the drive when I came in. My relations favour the Oldsmobile.'

'Yes, I have heard of it, but I think there are only two motor cars one can take into consideration, the Daimler, and the Rolls Royce when it's available.' No quarter given, she thought.

'I like the Oldsmobile,' she said perversely.

For the rest of the evening she only engaged in general conversation with him. Maeve was gracious, as usual, but she noticed how her father-in-law seemed to listen intently to Sir Edward's views, and how they lingered long over their port. Her grandmother made no comment. She had never been one to meet a situation before it was necessary.

When he was going away he took her hand in the hall. 'My invitation is still open to you to take a ride in my motor car, Mrs Garston Crawford. We might drive down to my yacht at Wemyss Bay before the fine weather goes.'

'Have you got a yacht?' She must have sounded impressed instead of curious.

'Yes. I think Sir Thomas started the craze.' He had a pleasant smile, she had to admit. 'Now many business people in Glasgow have taken it up, the Campbells, for instance . . . you know Campbell-Bannerman is one of them, he changed his name by deed poll when he married into the Bannermans, a Manchester family.'

'He must have thought it sounded better for a Prime Minister,' she said. You're a snob, Sir Edward, she thought.

'Shall we fix a date?' he was saying, 'I need to know a little in advance. With Lord Crawford unable to come to Glasgow now, he's charged me with . . .'

'That's just the point,' Lizzie said, interrupting him, 'I don't care to leave either my father-in-law or my grandmother for the time being. Especially since I've been away. Perhaps you'll excuse me.'

'As you wish.' His face was grim as he was shown out by Redfern.

15

November brought with it a thick yellow fog in Glasgow which hung even over Sholton, and with the short dark days Alastair Crawford seemed to decline. There was nothing spectacular in his illness. Each day he seemed frailer, and by the end of the month he was not managing to go down to dinner. But he insisted on Maeve dining downstairs with Lizzie.

'You know he's always liked formality,' Maeve said to Lizzie as they sat at the large mahogany table immaculately laid as always by Redfern with its glass and silver, and waited upon by Cathy. 'And he still takes a delight in seeing me dress. I've always dressed to please men,' she said with a wry smile. 'Never underrate the small pleasures of life.'

'What does Charlie think about him?'

'You know Charlie. He doesn't beat about the bush. His heart's very poor and the slightest exertion might be fatal. He's warned me. But I'm going to live each day as it comes and give him what pleasure I can. When my Kieran was so ill at Braidholme we used to have such pleasant evenings up in that airy bedroom overlooking the garden. We had a good fire roaring in the grate and our trays on our knees and we were as happy as Larry. But he recovered.' She smiled again. 'Still, I'm doing the same thing with Alastair. I never did believe a sick room should be a place of gloom.'

'It isn't that, Grandma. And those lovely flowers! You make it a bower.'

'Aye, those officious nurses want to banish them out of the room. Even Maevy, if I'd let her. I'm taking Jonty to see him tomorrow. He asked for him. He dearly loves to have the wee lad sitting on his bed and prattling away about his doings. Then after Charlie's visit in the afternoon Sir Edward's coming to see him. He's always wearied after his visits, but Alastair sets great store by his ability and advice. He says he's a fine man.'

'I'm sure he is.'

'But you aren't interested?'

'No. Ernest is coming over at Christmas, Grandma. I had a letter from him this morning.'

'So that's what has put a glow in your face.'

'That,' she smiled, 'and being here with you and grandfather. It's strange, together I think of you as that, on his own as father-in-law.'

'As long as you think of him with love.'

'I do that. He's always been so kind to me. America's a fine place, but this is home. You've both given me a home here, and I've been very happy.' Her voice broke. 'I love you very much.'

'Tell Alastair that the next time you go up to see him. You're the apple of his eye. You married his son.'

'Nigel's death's an everlasting sorrow to him, I know.' She got up and went to stand at the drawing-room window to hide her tears. Grandma did not care for 'sloppy displays', as she called them. The garden was formless. Only a vast blackness stretched to the horizon where it lightened and formed a pearl-like background to the bare trees.

She thought of Sachem Island which Kieran had described to her, 'like a cathedral', and of Gaylord and the whiteness of his face and the black streak her nails had made, and to banish that thought she turned in her mind to Ernest, his charm, his urbanity, the best type of Edwardian, maybe. 'We'll keep it light,' he had said. Yes, you needed lightness in this sad world.

The following evening, when Sir Edward had been and

gone without being announced in the drawing-room, she was summoned to Lord Crawford's room by Jessie. 'He's propped up on his pillows, Miss Lizzie . . .' She had noticed that when there was trouble in the family, the staff reverted to former titles. Susan in moments of stress called Aunt Maevy by her Christian name, and Jessie was an old friend. She it was who had put a cloak round her shoulders that night the tree crashed on the conservatory.

Her father-in-law held out a weak hand to her. How frail he looked, his face sunken round the mouth, the narrow skull, the sparse hair. Nigel would have looked like this eventually . . . 'Come and sit beside me, Lizzie. Your grandmother is in her bath, and I can tell you . . . she takes an unconscionable time over it.'

'It's very relaxing. How are you today?'

'Charlie says I'm no better, no worse; he always calls a spade a spade. But he says he's going to lend me his phonograph . . . a new type of medicine. Can he mean that music soothes the savage breast? Mine isn't very savage.' He stopped speaking to regain his breath.

'He's a great believer in music for himself, I do know that. He plays almost every night.'

'He's an . . . exceptional man. I'm afraid . . . I can't sit up properly so you'll have to forgive me.'

'Forgive you for what?' She bent to kiss his cheek. 'You do what Uncle Charlie tells you. He'll soon have you better.'

He smiled faintly, shaking his head at her. He preferred Charlie's frankness. 'Lizzie, I must come to the point because talking tires me and I've had . . . rather a lot today. Sir Edward has asked me if I would have any objections to him paying suit to you.'

'Oh!' The sound was involuntary. 'He shouldn't have done that.'

'Why not? Are you not in my care?' He was autocratic in spite of his frailty.

'Yes, and I love you truly, Father-in-law.' She remembered Maeve's advice. 'Maybe I should have told you before how much I love you and grandmother, how much I appreciate your goodness to me, and Jonty.'

'You are my son's widow, he loved you, as we do.' His eyes seemed to plead. 'Aren't you at all interested in Sir Edward? He's sensible. He wouldn't rush you. He only wondered if I could lend a little weight to his proposal, and I have to say to you, Lizzie, that since my dear son is . . .' his voice broke, 'no longer with us, I can't . . . think . . . of anyone more suitable than Sir Edward.'

'Except that I don't love him.' She could have wept. 'I'm happy here as long as you'll have me, but when the time comes, Ernest and I love each other . . .'

'Ernest . . .?' He looked bewildered.

'Ernest Murray-Hyslop. We've known each other for a long time, as you know. I realized when I was in America that my feelings . . . had grown stronger.'

'But he's family.' His voice was cold. 'You should look further afield.'

'But only by marriage. He isn't Aunt Kate's son, remember.' Had he the same prejudices as Uncle Patrick?

'You're bent on this . . . alliance?'

'Yes. I'm twenty-six. If I'd had my wish I could have thought of nothing better than spending the rest of my life with Nigel, but it wasn't to be.' Had he not been so ill she would have said, 'You were proud enough of him when he went away to fight the Boers. "It'll make a man of him," all your generation said, as their sons marched away. Well, it made a dead man of him, and thousands of others . . .' 'Don't distress yourself,' she said, taking his hand, 'nothing will happen to upset you . . .'

'While I'm here?' Those amber eyes, sunken in his face, were still shrewd.

'I didn't say anything like that. Please . . .'

'I'm thinking of my grandson's future, my heir. Sir

146

Edward could have taken care of his affairs until he was old enough to go into the business.' Or go and fight in another war? Where did those thoughts come from?

'Surely he can do that whether or not I marry him?'

He lay back on the pillows, and she waited, sorrowing for him. 'I'm tired,' he said at last, 'too much talking . . .'

Maeve came into the room in a corn-coloured gauzy peignoir. 'You're trailing clouds of delicious perfume, Grandma,' Lizzie said, glad she had come. Her father-in-law's face was grey with fatigue.

'Am I?' She went swiftly to the bed. 'Are you all right, Alastair?' She sat down beside him, taking his hand. 'I told you not to talk too much.'

'It's my fault . . .' Lizzie begun.

'It's nobody's fault. He has to learn his own strength.'

'I wanted . . . things . . . tidied up, dear heart.' His eyes went up to her, and then closed with weariness.

'Don't be in such a hurry.' She bent and kissed him, then stroked his hair gently. 'There's no hurry, no hurry at all, my dear one . . .' Lizzie went out of the room quietly.

Lord Crawford died on Christmas Eve. He had failed so rapidly in the next few days that even Charlie was caught out. Someone was cleverer than he. He had had to admit this before.

Maeve, brushing her hair at the dressing-table mirror, more for her husband's enjoyment than her own, saw life run out of him, his face stiffen on the pillow, heard the small outlet of breath. She sat still for a moment, gathering all her resources together, then got up and closed his eyes. She bent and kissed the cold lips, then sat at his bedside gazing at his face in death. This was her time alone with him, before the tumult and the shouting.

He looked serene, his brow smooth, the lines gone from his cheeks, and he was the Alastair she had known a long time ago, the young man who had bent over her when she had been thrown by Walpole, his mother's horse. His amber eyes had been on her, her loosened hair. 'Oh, beautiful . . . you need love, you need . . .' he'd said. Why was youth so fleeting? She wept quietly for the loss of it. Alastair was safe, as Kieran was safe, wherever they were. Only she remained . . .

16

Funerals and weddings are the great gatherer of families, where some breaches are healed and others made, where the pleasure of renewing old acquaintances becomes uppermost and the sad reason for the coming together, in the case of a funeral, is almost forgotten.

And Lord Crawford was not really family. He was the husband of Maeve McGrath that was, who had come with her husband, Kieran, across the sea to this little village on the banks of the Sholtie and created by their loving union a large part of this company of men and women linked by blood and marriage ties.

Terence came with Honor and young Terence and Honor's three girls, Moira, Dymphna and Clare – now twenty, eighteen and seventeen respectively – because Terence felt it right that they should honour Lord Crawford's passing, but also to pay homage to his mother's loss. He looked well, happy and settled, as Irish as the Irish now, a younger edition of his Uncle Terence in far-off Wallace Point on the Hudson, who with his wife, Caroline, had been too frail to make the trip.

But from Wanapeake came Kate escorted by Kieran and Ernest; also Maria and Patrick, who had left Sarah in charge of their household and Virginia, the youngest, but had brought Gaylord so that he could make the acquaintance of all his cousins, Scottish and French. Maeve's warning letter that her dear husband was sinking had made them decide to accompany Ernest.

And in response to her telegram Charles and Emily Barthe came from Paris with Giselle, now a young lady of twenty. The twins, Olivier and Marc, were in Germany on business and unable to attend, but to the eyes of young Terence McGrath from Ireland, his Parisian cousin was like some exotic creature with her dark eyes and her elegance, her *je ne sais quoi*. He was forced to use the rather hackneyed phrase.

He listened to her stories of Paris and the art world there, and said that certainly he intended spending some time in that most glamorous of cities to further his artistic career. His Aunt Emily, 'that brilliant little humming-bird' whom his grandmother had described to him often, said that he must feel welcome always at their home in Monceau Park, and that she could introduce him to all the important people in the field of literature and art. He thought of Apollinaire and the *Futuristes*.

'Isn't that so, Charles?' she said to her husband, and he nodded with a weary but acquiescent air. He was a changed man from the one Maevy and Maeve had seen when they visited the Barthes so long ago, when Maeve in her inimitable fashion had helped Emily out of a tight spot – wasn't it over a duel or something – and had qualified for the ultimate accolade from Emily as 'very much *du monde*'.

Young Robert spoke a great deal with his Uncle Patrick, forgetting all too soon, perhaps, the reason for the gathering, questioning him closely about how things were done in America and impressing his uncle by his astuteness.

Kate was the support of her mother. Perhaps that was why James, her husband, had stayed at home and not only because of his troublesome bronchitis. Dressed like her mother in elegant black, and still showing that beauty which defeats time because she set no great store by it, she sat by Maeve, the widowed Lady Crawford, both smiling and full of loving kindness to all who spoke to them, because Maeve had said she wanted no weeping amongst her family. Alastair had had a good life. He had been seventy-two when he died, and she had been there when he went, his eyes on her.

Ellie was brought by Maevy and Charlie because they had never believed in sparing her from the darker side of life, and also she was nearest the age of Jonty, now Lord Crawford but still a small boy of four who ran amongst the grown-ups' legs and giggled when Ellie chided him.

Gaylord enjoyed himself hugely once he had got over the hurdle of meeting Lizzie. Her eyes were cool, not cold, when they were forced to greet each other formally. She was not going to split on him. His fear of that was over. She had obviously accepted his excuse of being drunk when he had written a letter of apology, although she had never answered it. She had the old lady's character, you could see that by her raised chin.

This was an even better party than those at the Venetian or even the Paradise Inn, except that Kieran had warned him that if he drank too much and disgraced himself at a funeral, he would never forgive him. But Kieran did not know that he had other means of combating the darker moods. That bad back had been a blessing. The only one who might have any inkling was that black-eyed husband of Aunt Maevy, outwardly genial and questioning him on the way of life in America, but fixing him occasionally with those eyes which were as keen as the scalpel he was supposed to wield with such skill.

But he could always excuse himself and charm those three delightful girls from Ireland, Moira, Dymphna and Clare, especially the young one who seemed to be a bundle of fun and even in the wilds of the west of Ireland had heard of the Bunny Hug and the Turkey Trot. *She* would make a fine companion on his arm if he could ever take her to the Paradise Inn. He could just see her whirling her parasol above that jaunty little red head. That was what life was all about, fun. Don't think . . .

The two of them got into a corner with her step-brother, Terence, and that elegant miss from Paris, Giselle Barthe, and several times they had to stifle their laughter when he said something which amused them. It opened up a completely new world to him. From what Giselle hinted, there were places in Paris which made the Paradise Inn look provincial, although as a well-brought-up young lady she had never frequented them.

Oh, there were some great times ahead, and if he fell into one of those dark holes (that was how he thought of his moods), he knew how to make his eyes sparkle again. Once he caught his cousin Ernest's eye as he looked around, and he thought, there's another astute one. It's a pity he ever came back from Scotland.

But mostly Ernest's eyes were on Lizzie. They would seek her out, and sometimes he was able to manoeuvre himself near her so that they could speak together, although not very privately. But always his eyes were asking the same question that he had asked in his many letters to her. 'Will you marry me?'

John Craigie, obese now and pasty-faced, gave a carefully-prepared oration to Alastair which went on far too long and reminded Maeve of those interminable sermons in the Kirk when the children were small. Isobel, as always, with her thin, still pretty face and her wasp waist, looked as if she had a frail hold on life, although it was surprising how she always managed to turn up on those important occasions dealing with life and death, where her husband officiated.

Maeve, watching them all, was sad and happy at the same time. She had lost a very dear partner. She was now, like Terence and Caroline, and even James Murray-Hyslop, an onlooker rather than a participator. There was a feeling of loneliness, and even sadder, of completion. She looked at her family around her and knew for the first time the detachment which is the penalty of age.

'I've had a happy life,' she said to Kate, and failed to keep the sadness out of her voice.

'Now, Mother,' Kate turned to her, smiling, 'you always told us not to look back. I won't have you speaking like that. You'll start visiting us all soon now that you're freer, and just think of the welcome you'll get in all our houses. It's a new life you you.'

'Is it?' she said, for the first time in her life not so sure. 'Maybe you're right. Well, maybe I'll start with Ireland.'

'Ah, Terence was always your favourite, your own boyo,' Kate said, making her mother bridle.

'Wasn't I forever telling you I didn't have any favourites in my family?'

'Yes, Mother, you were forever telling me.' She mimicked gently her mother's Irish brogue. 'Well, first amongst your favourites, then. Who's that distinctive-looking man talking to Lizzie?'

'That's Sir Edward Hamilton. He would like to acquire Lizzie along with Crawford's Iron and Steel Works.'

Kate shook her head. 'I don't know about the Iron and Steel Works, but Lizzie's like you. She knows what she wants.' The man's face was like a crag, she thought. He looked dangerous.

In the evening Maeve and Lizzie dined alone with Ernest as their only guest. He, Kieran and Kate were staying at the Hall, but Maevy and Kate between them were having another family gathering at Braidholme, which they'd thought would be too tiring for their mother.

Lizzie had had a brief walk in the grounds with Kieran before darkness fell. He was quieter than she remembered, but he was a sensitive man, she reminded herself, and it became the occasion. 'I hope, once this sadness is all over, Lizzie,' he said, 'you and Ernest will be very happy.'

'Has he told you?' she asked.

'He's not a great talker about his own affairs.' His

sweet expression touched her as it always did. 'But we all know. His . . . sophistication leaves him when he talks about you. He's just like anyone else in love . . .' He looked away.

'And are *you* happy, Kieran?' she said.

'I've a lot to be thankful for.' He didn't answer her question directly. 'And I'm kept busy being nursemaid to Gaylord.'

'I can well imagine.' She felt her features stiffen, and went on quickly, 'I'm deeply interested in America and my relations. Couldn't you take on the job of keeping me informed about them? You used to write me such lovely letters . . .' She remembered it was she who had stopped writing because of Nigel.

'I would like to do that, Lizzie.' On impulse she turned to him and kissed his cheek. She thought she had embarrassed him by the way he drew away from her.

Maeve did not demur at the arrangement for their quiet dinner. The day had exhausted her, and so long as she would see all her dear ones again, she was content to remain at the Hall.

She wanted, for instance, to have a word with Patrick and Maria and ask them what Gaylord intended to do with his life. The sense of detachment she had felt at the funeral had not blinded her to the fact that Patricks's only son looked as if he could well be a problem. His behaviour had lacked decorum, which meant he lacked judgement. Maybe a driving father like Patrick was partly the cause – although she loved her family she had no illusions about them – or perhaps the weakness stemmed from that unfortunate uncle of Maria's with the same name as his great-nephew.

And she looked forward to a visit, perhaps tomorrow, from Honor and Terence, who on the other hand seemed to have few problems. She was fond of that dark-eyed Irish girl who wrote books as well as making her beloved son happy. Besides, had she not restored Woodlea to its former beauty and assured her that there was always a welcome on the mat?

Lizzie, that evening, was tremulously happy at dinner with only Ernest there. He was kind and solicitous to Maeve, and made the sad day less sad by his presence. But her grandmother excused herself after coffee had been served in the drawing-room. 'I admit to feeling weary now. I just want to lie in bed . . .' her voice broke, '. . . and think of Alastair.'

'I'll go up with you, Grandma,' Lizzie said.

'There's no need. You and Ernest want some time together. When must you go back?' She addressed him.

'Our sailing is booked the day after tomorrow. Your son is a slavedriver, Lady Crawford.' He smiled at her. 'We've some big deals pending. We're going to McGraths tomorrow to have a meeting with Maevy, Dan Johnson and young Robert. Uncle Patrick intends to put forward some new notions.'

'My goodness!' She became interested in spite of her sorrow. 'When I think of our wee office in Sholton and Isobel and Maevy doing the books, it scarcely seems credible.'

'You and your husband founded an empire. We're all proud of you.'

'A business is like a family,' she said. 'You don't realize it at the time, and there it is, growing under your very nose, spreading outwards. That's why I think women ought to be in business. They're used to the process. It's natural to them to hold the reins, if the men would admit it.'

'I do for one,' he said. 'I know what you were like, and you've a worthy successor in Maevy. There's none to touch her for administration.'

'Aye, she learned that at the Royal Infirmary. And she's got a deep interest in the workers as well. Always

155

sees their point of view.' She got up. 'But I'll say good-night now, Ernest.' She held out her hand and he kissed it. His eyes met Lizzie's, for once without laughter in them.

'I'm coming up with you, Grandma, and don't say no. I've to see to Jonty as well, make sure he's asleep.'

'The little lord,' Maeve said. 'It beats everything. All right, my lovely. I won't say no since you're determined.'

Lizzie put her arm round her as they went up the wide stairs together. 'A memorable day, Grandma.' No sloppiness.

'Aye, to be sure.' Her face was serene.

She would not need any help with her undressing, she told Lizzie. She wanted to take her time. Her beautiful face was waxen pale, making the red hair redder. The blue eyes were sunken. 'Call me if you want me, Grandma,' she said as she kissed her. She knew she would not.

Ernest took her in his arms when she went downstairs again. 'Come, my lovely. That's what grandmother calls you. But you're *my* lovely as well.' He led her to the big sofa in front of the fire, and when they sat down he drew her to him. 'A sad day for her, but the dignity of her, and the courage. I want to . . . and yet I feel the effect of the day too strongly yet. Do you?'

'Yes,' she nodded. 'In a way it would be . . . sacrilege.'

'But be sure I love you.'

'And I love you.'

'"Ae fond kiss"? I read that in Kate's book back home . . .'

'Ae fond kiss'll do.' She turned to him and raised her face.

'You're like a flower.' He smiled down at her, stroking her face gently. 'Tell me the name of a Scottish flower. I've forgotten them all.'

'The bluebell?'

'My Scottish bluebell. That's it.' He bent and kissed her mouth. 'Can we talk for a moment or two, close, like this? Does Lord Alastair's death make a difference to us? Won't you want to marry me?'

In answer she put her arms round his neck and kissed him in small kisses, making him groan.

'Ah, Lizzie, don't. I'll forget myself.'

'I only did that to let you see I haven't changed. I'll never change. It's you I want. You. But, yes, it makes a difference. You see how sad she is in spite of her brave face. There are so many things to settle, where I can help her, and legal affairs. Shall I, for instance, be expected to live here with my little lad who is now the owner? What happens to the business which I presume he has inherited along with the title? And what about Grandma? Will she want to stay on here, or find a place of her own or go back to Ireland? All those decisions. You can't rush them. We'll have to see how the bools run, as she'd say.'

'I'll add that to my Scottish list.'

'There will be the reading of the will and a meeting with the solicitors and discussions with the rest of the family. You can see how complex it all is. And you have your own business affairs to attend to. You and I are very small fry amongst all that.'

'Not to each other. Yes, of course I see that grandmother comes first. There's no alternative for the moment. I go back with Kate, Kieran and Gaylord. But I might put the situation before the board at the McGrath meeting. It concerns them too since I'm a partner, and I believe they're all interested in our welfare. You haven't that suppport on the Crawford side.'

'No. My father-in-law had no relatives living. His sister died some time ago. There's only Sir Edward Hamilton who's become his righthand man latterly.'

'Yes. I met him.' His face was set. 'It's wait for the time being, then?'

157

'It's got to be, Ernest, but not for long. I feel it in my bones. So,' she leaned towards him, 'don't let's talk any more.'

In his arms she had a foretaste of the passion she knew they would share when they were together. Grandma would have understood. She was a woman of passion herself.

The days following the departure of the family to their various homes were dreich. There was no other word for it.

Terence, her father, had had a long talk with her on their own before he caught the Irish boat. 'I want you to promise, Lizzie, to take care of mother for a bit. She's very dear to me. Oh, don't look sad, I'm not suggesting for ever. Sure and a blind man on a blind donkey could see that you and Ernest are in love. Just for the next month or so. She's not looking so well. When you think of it, she had a hard young life, and it takes its toll.'

'Don't worry,' she said, and shyly, 'Father.'

He hugged her. 'Bessie would have liked to hear you say that. It wasn't to be . . .' His eyes were moist when he released her. 'Maybe you could gently introduce the idea of mother coming to stay with us at Woodlea for a time, for good, if she'd like it. After all, it was her home first. But don't you worry. I want you to have your happiness, too. You deserve it after losing Nigel.'

'Don't *you* worry.' She laughed. 'I made a promise to myself when my father-in-law died. Ernest knows that. He's understanding and prepared to wait, though not very patiently. Besides, as you know, there are a lot of business affairs to be settled here.'

'Aye,' he nodded, 'and maybe there will be a few surprises. And, should anything out of the ordinary happen – wills can be the very devil – Honor wants me to say that she would treat you as her own daughter if you came to Woodlea, and you can't say fairer than that because those three are the apple of her eye.'

'And yours,' she said, smiling at him.

'I've four daughters,' he said, 'and the first-born is the dearest.' That pleased her.

The reading of the will in the great dining-room of the Hall had more than a few surprises. Terence had been right: Lord Crawford had left his whole estate to his grandson, Nigel Jonathan, Sholton Hall to his wife and subsequently to his daughter-in-law. The latter would act as guardian to his grandson, and on her death the house would revert to him.

Lizzie and Maeve were to go on living at the Hall as long as it suited them. 'It is their home,' he had dictated to his solicitor, 'but in any matters of business I should like them to be guided by Sir Edward Hamilton who has their welfare at heart.' Crawford Iron and Steel Works would be held in trust and managed by him until such times as Nigel Jonathan had attained his majority.

His fortune, after bequests to servants, was to be divided equally between Lizzie, Jonty and Maeve. They would all be rich, Mr MacNair pointed out, saying that they would be apprised of the exact figure shortly.

Here he looked up, slightly bemused. 'And there's a concluding paragraph addressed directly to you, my lady. Do you wish me to read it?'

'Please,' she said calmly.

He cleared this throat: ' "Because my wife has given me unending joy, I should like her when she is in residence at the Hall to drink my health each night at dinner. I die with the image of her beauty imprinted on my heart." '

That was the first time Lizzie had seen her grandmother weeping since her husband's death. She had to rise and go out of the room to compose herself

* * *

Maevy's opinion of the will was unequivocal. She said to Charlie in bed, after her mother had called to see her and acquainted her of its contents: 'Sir Edward has got at Lord Crawford when he was too frail to argue.'

'My lovely,' Charlie said mildly, 'that's unlike you. Am I sharing my bed with a hard-hearted business woman now?'

'We'll attend to that side of it later,' she said crisply. 'What will it be like, I ask you, if Ernest and Lizzie marry and live at the Hall, as she must do with Jonty, and that man is breathing down her neck all the time?'

'Perhaps Sir Edward is hoping that that won't happen and that it will be *he* who'll be there – that is, if you're determined to make him the villain of the piece.'

'No.' She shook her head. 'We aren't dealing with children here, nor is he. Lizzie was a child when she married Nigel, as he was, two children madly in love; now she and Ernest are mature people. *They'll* marry, all right. But I'm telling you, dear doctor,' she tapped him on the nose, 'it would have been better if Sir Edward hadn't come on the scene.'

He stopped joking. 'I'm inclined to agree with you. I caught sight of his face at the funeral. The Rock of Gibraltar. Funerals, or weddings, for that matter, are grand places for observing human nature in all its vagaries. People don't realize how much their faces give away to the onlooker. You and Kate, and your mother, all so beautiful and upright; Terence sprightly and doting on that beauty, Honor, with her brood like cygnets round a swan; John Craigie, cynical in spite of being in daily touch with his Maker; Isobel like a wraith but a singularly strong wraith; Ernest, a true sophisticate; Kieran, a sad sweetness in him for a man – I wonder why – and did you see how that young Gaylord's eyes glittered? That was strange . . .'

But Maevy, in spite of the fact that she was a trained

nurse and might have picked up his allusion, was not listening intently. She was busy making plans to write to Patrick in a few weeks and say that, because of this new idea of his about pantechnicons, she would like to come to America fairly soon and see them in action. And there was also another matter which she would like to discuss with him. Too delicate to commit to paper . . . 'What was that you said,' she said, snuggling into his side, 'about sharing your bed with a hard-hearted business woman?'

17

The winter of 1905 was bitter, and it seemed in the short dark days that the most important thing was survival. Maeve's health declined; there was nothing radically wrong with her, Charlie said, just a lowering of her spirits brought on by the influenza which was rife in Sholton. He believed that people, as well as the birds and beasts, all lost some of their vitality in the winter. It was a natural thing.

'Don't apologize to me for finding you in bed,' he said to her when he was visiting her one morning. 'If I had my way half of us would curl up like dormice and sleep the winter away.'

'It's not like me, Charlie,' she said. 'I've always been full of energy.'

'Grief is exhausting, as well as influenza. When you lost Mr McGrath you were younger and more resilient.'

'And there's that lass running the place, waiting on me, looking after Jonty, pining all the time for Ernest . . .'

'Lizzie's all right,' he assured her. 'She and Ernest will sort out things for themselves. They're neither of them so young that they don't know their own minds, and they're both too sensible to "pine" as you put it. That's for the lovesick lads and lassies . . . although I must admit I pined for Maevy when she wouldn't have me and I wasn't in my first youth.'

'Ah, but she was worth waiting for.'

'You know that, Mother. She's my reason for living, and that, from someone who loves life, is an admission.'

He told Maevy about her mother when they were having supper together that night. Ellie was upstairs doing her homework which she had taken seriously ever since she had gone to Hutcheson's Grammar School in Glasgow.

'When the weather gets better she should go off to Ireland and stay with Terence and Honor,' she said. 'It's still home to her, even more so as she grows older.'

'You're right. And there's the matter of Lizzie and Ernest. The girl has a warm heart. She wouldn't dream of pushing her own affairs when her grandmother isn't well, but she and Ernest ought to be married. They need each other.'

'Need each other . . . we know all about that.' Her glance was loving. 'Would you mind . . . if I went to America, Charlie? I mean on a buisness trip.'

He looked at her in surprise, but with a wry smile. 'You mean without me, your own dear husband?'

'Yes, without you. Put that in your pipe and smoke it! You and I will escort mother to Ireland later on when she and the weather improves. That would be a fine jaunt, if you can arrange it at the Royal and the practice. But I've a few things I've been turning over in my mind, about pantechnicons and such like, and I've a notion to discuss them on the spot.'

'It's the "such like" I'm interested in, dear heart.'

'That may be so, but I'm superstitious. I'd rather tell you when it's a *fait accompli*, as Emily Barthe would say. Besides, I'd like to report on Uncle Terence and Aunt Caroline, for mother's sake. They're both far from well. I don't know which is the worse.'

'Well, you have such a variety of reasons for going that I can't stop you, nor would I. When would you make this trip?'

'At the beginning of April. Just as soon as this cold spell is over.' She smiled at him across the table, beautiful in his eyes with her still fair hair piled on top of her head, her warm blue gown with its touch of lace at the neck and wrists. 'I'll feel like a real business woman travelling on my own for the first time. I wonder what I should wear?'

'As long as it isn't that gown which sets off your eyes to perfection and would drive sane men daft. No, a shirt and tie and a sober black skirt, otherwise I'll be consumed with jealousy the whole time you're away.'

'You're constant, Charlie McNab. It was the best thing I ever did in my life, marrying you.' She stretched her hand across the table to him.

'I couldn't bear to lose you,' he said.

Jim Geddes was coming less and less to the surgery now, his daughter, Belle, more and more. Her working hours seemed to have increased since Maevy left for America, but perhaps that was Charlie's imagination. He had to admit she was a great help to him. She had a straight-forward manner with the patients, although not overly sympathetic, but her astuteness appealed to him. She could root out the malingerers quicker than he could.

But he was uncomfortably aware of her at times, not as a colleague, but as a woman. She had a voluptuous figure which was shown to perfection in her shirt-waist. She seemed to stand too near him at times; once he had seen the sweat on her upper lip where there was a slight, dark, seductive shadow. Why had he thought of *that* word? he wondered.

He was playing the piano one night after supper, Ellie in bed after their romp together. 'You're not as strict as mother,' she had told him, laughing, as he banished her. 'She still thinks she's a Sister at the Royal.'

'Don't talk about your mother behind her back,' he had said, but he had laughed too.

He heard someone talking to Susan and recognized Belle Geddes' voice. He glanced at the wag-at-the-wa'. Nine o'clock. Scarcely what you'd call a reasonable time to visit in a place like Sholton. There was a knock at the door and he said, still playing, 'Come in.'

'I've just come to borrow a book, Charlie,' she said behind him. 'Don't mind me. I'll browse about. I like to hear you play. You're a man of many talents.' Her tone was mocking.

'Some think so,' he said. Ravel was a new composer to him. There was something attractive in the impressionistic technique of his music. Ah, well, he thought, almost forgetting Belle, it never did to stagnate. That was the secret of keeping young. Keep trying something new. This little contrapuntal run, now, that was effective . . . Her silence made him turn on his piano stool to look at her. She was sitting on the sofa, her eyes on him. Her blouse was unbuttoned. He could see the swell of her breasts.

He got up. 'I thought it was a book you came to borrow.' He kept his voice cool.

'That was just for Susan's benefit. Come and sit beside me.'

'If you fasten up your blouse.' It was a pity that, while being sensible, one should sound priggish.

She laughed, throwing back her head. 'Don't tell me you've never seen a woman's body before, apart from your wife's.'

He stood for a second, then crossed the room and sat down beside her, took her by the shoulders and gave her a good shaking. He had never done that in his life to Ellie, and here he was . . . he marvelled at himself. 'You're a rascal, Belle,' he said. 'You know that. You're far too young for games like this.' Had he meant old?

'And you're daft, Charlie McNab. I'm twenty-eight. I'm not innocent. How could a qualified doctor be innocent? I bet you weren't. I thought with your beloved away you could do with some comfort . . . all in the line of duty, doctor?' Her silver-grey eyes slanted up at him, her tongue ran along her lips. He felt himself shiver inwardly, a warning shiver.

He got up. 'We're early bedders in this house, Belle, and I was just thinking of going up myself. Maybe you'll lock the outside door on your way out.'

She looked at him, slowly fastening the buttons of her blouse. Her full red lips were pursed. 'I can't make up my mind about you, Charlie, a man like you . . . shouldn't be satisfied with someone so . . . upright . . . as Maevy McGrath.'

'You'll not rile me,' he said. 'Away you go now and get to your bed.'

'And I haven't to come back?'

'If you come as a friend and a colleague, you're welcome. But only that.' He went to the door and held it open, and she walked through it slowly. His feeling of rectitude was disseminated somewhat by an entirely masculine desire to pinch her round bottom as she passed him.

Maeve had an unexpected caller one afternoon as she lay resting in bed. Charlie had convinced her that there was no shame in it, and although she had recovered from the influenza attack, there was something very pleasant in being in bed in this fine bedroom with its view across the Hall park, and the roaring fire in the grate.

Jonty had been to visit her and had tumbled about on the eiderdown and generally enjoyed himself in a hide-and-seek game with great-grandma, until Lizzie had borne him away, kicking his legs and shrieking his displeasure. Aye, she'd thought, you had to be young to thole bairns for long . . .

'Susan MacInnes to see you, my lady.' Cathy was at the door with Susan in a fur tippet and her ancient black velvet hat squashed on her head and fiercely pinned, her black coat which came out every winter and still bore its smell of moth balls. She had her handbag stuffed underneath her arm in a determined kind of way, and Maeve had the impression that but for that she would have taken up a position in the middle of the floor with her arms akimbo, her usual stance when she had something to impart.

'Oh, this is nice of you to visit me, Susan,' she said. 'Come away and sit in this comfortable seat beside me. I'm sorry I'm not up to receive you.'

'You're better in bed, Mrs McGrath . . . Oh, dearie, dear.' She clapped a black-gloved hand on her chest, 'I mean, my lady. And here's Cathy telling me to mind my ps and qs. And how are you keeping?' She sat down stiffly and slightly forward in the chair, clutching the tortoise-shell clasp of her handbag with both hands.

'I'm an old fraud. Dr Charlie has declared me recovered, but I've still to have a wee rest in the afternoon.'

'And so you should after all you've been through.' Susan looked fierce. 'He was a kind gentleman, Lord Crawford, liked and respected in the village, which is mair than you could say about his awld faither. Generous, too. Aye, it's a sad loss for you.'

'A sad loss, Susan.' She put her hand on one of the woman's. 'You've been through so much with me, stood by me and the McGraths. We don't get round to saying that often enough.'

'You're ma life, the lot o' ye. Ah haevny ony o' ma ain.' She raised her chin. 'And that's why a'm here.'

'I hope there's nothing wrong, Susan.' She was alarmed. 'Lizzie tells me you're managing fine to run the house in Maevy's absence. Is Ellie all right?'

'Aye, she's a grand lass now that she's at the Grammar School. It's quietened her down a bit. It's a pity Maevy and the doctor couldny have had mair o' the same kind when you think o' aw they puir shilpit things runnin' wild and half-clad aboot Colliers Row, dragged up by the heels . . .'

'I lived there, don't forget, and brought them all up.' Maeve smiled at her.

'Ah, but you're different. The McGraths are different.' There's no argument about that, her voice said.

'Well,' she was mystified, 'I know Charlie's all right because he's been in here most days to see me. So what is it, Susan?'

'It's Doactor Belle, Mrs . . . my lady. She's hangin' aboot the doactor, takin' the chance while Maevy's in America. Oh, a never trusted that yin! She's a sly creature. A've heard tales a wouldny repeat . . .' Maeve cut her short.

'What do you mean, "hanging about", Susan?'

'She comes to Braidholme at times that are no' respectable to a decent community, nine o'clock, and yince twenty past. A grant ye she doesny stay long, but it'll gie the doactor a bad name wi' his wife awaw . . .'

'But it will be to discuss the practice! They don't get much time during the day.'

'If it's to discuss the practice she wouldn't come oot o' his room like a cat that's licked cream . . .'

Meave said grimly, 'You're not a troublemaker, Susan, never have been, so I respect that. But don't you think in your zeal to look after Braidholme and Ellie and Charlie for Maevy you're letting your imagination run away with you? Young folk have different ideas from us. I'm constantly having to tell myself that. They think nothing of nine o'clock, or even twenty past.' She restrained a smile. 'There's more to keep them up now. They even go into Glasgow at nights on those new motor buses they're running. And did you know, you can get one all the way to London? No, Susan, times are changing, and Dr Belle is a modern young lady, especially with her training. If you have struggled through studying medicine surrounded

168

by men who look at you as if you had two heads, you'll think nothing of paying a call on your employer at nine o'clock.' She felt strangely exhausted by her speech, but she saw Susan's rigid features relax.

'Maybe you're right, my lady. I never thought of it that way. But a'm that anxious to keep everything nice for Maevy. You know what a think of her and the doactor. They're the salt o' the earth, just as you are. Not a day goes past but I thank God that I've been called to serve you.' There were two burning spots in her cheeks.

'You did right to come and tell me, Susan. It relieved your mind and you with all that responsibility on your shoulders.' The woman pulled her shoulders back. 'But take my word for it, Charlie thinks far too much of Maevy ever to look sideways at another woman. Only the other day he was saying that to me. Now you get up and ring that bell. I want you to drink a cup of tea with me before you go back to Braidholme.'

'Oh, Missus, a wouldny dea that!' She drew her brows together.

'Yes, you would. You've walked here and you've to walk back and I'm very grateful to you. Come on, now, the bell's at the fireplace. And you'll take off your tippet and sit with me while we talk like old friends about the days when we were both young.'

'Aye, that's a long time ago now. Well, if you think a should.' She got up and pressed the bell, leaning forward with her forefinger extended to do so, gingerly – it'll not bite, Maeve thought, watching her with a smile – took off her fur tippet and laid it carefully over the back of a chair, then came and sat beside Maeve. 'A long time ago,' she sighed, smoothing her black cotton gloves, 'and those lovely bairns o' yours . . .'

'Just as a matter of interest, Susan,' Maeve said, 'how old are you now, if it's not too delicate a question?'

'Sixty-one come May. I can hardly believe it. Maybe no

sae skeigh as a was, but good for a long time yet, God willing.'

'You can still give me ten years. Aye, we've plenty of life in us yet. Now, tell me, how's that old crony of yours in the village, Tibby Simpson . . .?'

But when Susan left, although she had been disturbed by her news, she found that she was not as upset as she might have been. She had no real liking for Belle Geddes – she was not a woman's woman, nor had she any wish to be, she was sure – but she knew Charlie. He would never encourage her. He had waited too long for Maevy. If ever there was a perfect marriage it was theirs, marred only by the fact that they had wanted more children. But even that desire on Maevy's part had gone, it seemed. She never talked about it, and the business had given her the extra interest she had always craved. Like me, she thought smugly.

I'll not interfere, she decided, not say anything. It's not my business even if Belle has been trying to lead Charlie on. She would not put it past her. Wasn't she supposed to be running about with a man at Crannoch who sold those new-fangled motor cars?

This is the first indication of getting old, she thought, a wish to be uninvolved, as if I'd been tethered by a myriad silk threads, and one by one they're being broken, until at last there's a very tenuous hold on reality. That was why, if death came, the wrench would not be so much for myself as for those left. It would simply be the last thread broken. No, she thought, I trust Charlie. I'll give him the benefit of that trust.

18

On a balmy April evening Lizzie and Maeve were invited to Braidholme for dinner, to hear about Maevy's visit to America.

If Maeve had any worries about a rift in the relationship between Charlie and Maevy, her visit dissipated them. Maevy was radiant and assured, a beautiful woman who looked happy and fulfilled. Charlie was obviously over-joyed to have her home, proud as a peacock of her, and showing his joy by teasing them all.

'I'm like that old cockerel we had, do you remember, Ellie?' he said, because she had been allowed to stay up for dinner. 'With my harem, although I can't call such beautiful ladies as I'm surrounded by barnyard fowls.'

'Do you mean, Jock, Daddy?' Ellie asked.

'Yes, you used to stand in front of him when he was crowing and say, "Do it again, Jock!"'

She, too, looked beautiful in her party dress of green taffeta with its wide bertha collar of Honiton lace and her golden hair, a paler gold than Maevy's, dressed in long ringlets and held back by combs.

And yet, apart from the hair, Maeve thought it was Lizzie the girl most resembled with her quicksilver volatil-ity, more, indeed, herself, come to think of it. Maevy was of a calmer disposition, more deliberate – well, look at the time she had taken to decide to marry Charlie McNab with all her doubts about sacrificing her career. A man's love came first, but if you were clever enough, and not too impatient, you could have both.

'You look quite restored to your own young self,

Mother,' Charlie said, looking up from carving the roast beef.

'My, what a tactful husband you have, Maevy! Yes, thanks to your doctoring and Lizzie's nursing I'm back to normal. Alastair is a sore loss and has left an empty place in my heart and at the Hall, but we have Jonty to cheer us up. A rollicking wee lad, isn't he, Lizzie?'

'Yes, he keeps us busy, that's true enough.' The girl's vitality seemed dimmed, Maeve thought, but then she was in love. She had seen the letters arriving from America. Lizzie was not secretive about them, sometimes she read out suitable parts to her. Sometimes she came across her rereading them at the fire; once, when she looked up, her eyes had been swimming with tears. 'How was Ernest when you saw him, Maevy?' This was family. She was not going to hide her love.

'Well, and very busy. I had to wait till after seven at night before I could clap eyes on him at Wanapeake, but then I made a few trips to the New York office to disucss the pantechnicon scheme with them. Do you know, Mother, they've got them running all over New Jersey and New York State, and Patrick has plans to extend them further.'

'Would they take on here in the same way? It's a small place in comparison, and our roads and railways aren't so far-flung.'

'Oh, yes, in time they would. People are on the move between Scotland and England nowadays, and even all round Glasgow. It's much more convenient to have a flitting from door to door than trust to the railways. Then we would train men to handle furniture properly and how to take care of valuables. We'd have to go into the question of where we could buy vans of the size we required, here or in America, but that's a matter for Robert and Dan. The scheme will take a few years to get going . . . but don't let me go on about business and me just back home. That's not what we're here for.'

'No, it's not,' Charlie said, passing plates of roast beef, 'otherwise I'll begin to describe my latest operation at the Royal.' There was no malice in his voice. 'Now, if you've all got your plates, let me fill up your glasses. I want us to drink a toast to our returning heroine, my dear wife, safe and sound from across the seas. To Maevy!' He raised his glass to her, his black eyes bright with love. No worry there, Maeve thought.

'To Maevy!' everybody said, even Ellie who had been given a thimbleful, her eyes sparkling with the high life she was leading and her first sip of claret.

'Well, if ever a husband was glad to see his wife back, it's Charlie,' Maeve said, raising her glass, 'worked off his feet, flu rampant . . .'

'Didn't Dr Belle help you, Charlie?' Maevy said, her voice free of guile.

'Yes, indeed. She's a grand doctor. No time for the soft approach, but she gets the results. I couldn't have done without her.'

'She's a beauty in her own way,' Lizzie said innocently. 'I saw her in the village the other day, bare-headed, if you please, driving her pony and trap. A few eyes were turning to look at her, especially the men's.'

'Is that so?' Charlie said. 'I only see her as a doctor, and someone who gets through the surgeries faster than her father did. That's all that matters.'

Maeve was satisfied. 'Tell me about Terence and Caroline, Maevy. How did you find them?'

'Not grand, and a bit pathetic into the bargain in that big house across the Hudson. Uncle Terence is jovial, but I think he has to spend a lot of time ministering to Aunt Caroline. I don't like to say this, Mother, but she's become a complaining old woman, only happy when he's dancing attendance on her.'

173

'She's frail of spirit, my lovely. Always remember that. And she had a serious illness when her twin brother died. Sometimes in old age those old sores reappear stronger than ever, regrets, memories . . .'

'I remember her on the day of the bicycle picnic,' Lizzie said, her face alight. 'Oh, Ellie, you should have seen our get-up, especially Ernest's in his Yale outfit, but very debonair. Great-aunt and uncle followed us in their carriage with lovely food and champagne! Have you a bicycle?'

'Yes, a Raleigh. I'm thinking of riding to Hutchy on it soon.'

'You'll do no such thing,' Maevy said. 'The traffic's geting terrible in town now with all that motor transport . . .'

'Well, you'll make it worse with your pantechnicons!'

They all laughed. Maevy said, 'It's Patrick's idea! I'd just be carrying it out.'

'Now the pot's calling the kettle black,' her mother smiled at her. 'Give us some more of your news.'

'I had a talk with Kieran one night. We both wondered if perhaps Patrick expects too much of Gaylord. He isn't ambitious like him. Gaylord has a lot of talent, you know.' She looked round the table. 'He does lovely water-colours, and now that he's training to be an architect, his drawings are quite professional. But then he goes out at night with what Patrick calls undesirable people, and short of banning him, they can do nothing about it. He's desperate to leave home. Kieran and I think this should be allowed, at least on his twenty-first birthday. That's just a year away. It would prevent Maria and Patrick worrying so much. What the eye doesn't see, the heart doesn't grieve over.'

Maeve, listening, thought she might write to Patrick, a diplomatic letter, and then thought again that she would not. No one, least of all your own family, ever took your advice, certainly not at the time, and if they did much later, they pretended it had been their own idea.

I shan't go to America first, she thought, much as I would like to see Terence and Caroline. I'll have a holiday with Terence and Honor in Ireland first, where life is easy-osy, and that will set me up for crossing the ocean. But then there was Kate, who drew her with her warmth, and that fine husband of hers, James Murray-Hyslop, a deal older than her and getting frailer, too. And that fine son of theirs who reminded her so strongly of her own dear Kieran with his sweet mouth. He'd make a fine husband for someone. Well, she thought, we'll just have to see how the bools run.

They were drinking their coffee when Charlie said calmly, 'I didn't realize you had such a sense of the dramatic, Maevy. Why don't you tell Lizzie now?'

'Tell her what?' she said, looking at him with limpid eyes.

'Come on, now, good news never improved with keeping. Look at the lass. Her eyes are shining. She's been as good as gold, hardly mentioning Ernest, although she's dying to know more about him.'

'I didn't want to forestall Ernest's letter. Haven't you heard from him recently, Lizzie?'

'Yes, but nothing . . .'

'Well, in case it gets delayed, I *will* forestall it. Before I went to America I had an idea about Ernest, and I discussed it at a board meeting here. Young Robert's dying to go to America, and Ernest is dying to come back here to you. I've sounded out both parties, as they say.' She laughed. 'Patrick had to be approached, of course, and he agreed, indeed he saw some virtue in it from the firm's standpoint, as Ernest can pass on the knowledge about removal transport he's gained in America. We all thought fair exchange was no robbery, so . . . his letter

175

will be in the post, or more likely, he'll be stepping off the boat any day now.'

Ellie jumped up, ran to Lizzie who'd put her hands to her eyes, and threw her arms round her. 'Oh, she's crying! Don't cry, Lizzie, it's good news. Here's a handkie!' She looked up at her mother, her young face distressed. 'What shall we do?'

'It's with happiness, pet.' Maevy smiled at her.

Lizzie raised a streaming face. She mopped at her eyes with Ellie's handkerchief. 'Thanks, Ellie. Yes, it's happiness, I can't believe it. Oh, thanks, Aunt Maevy. My goodness!' She looked at Maeve. 'We'd better get home right away. He might be at the door, he might be . . .'

'I should drink your coffee first,' Charlie said, smiling, 'it'll sustain you. And I think after you drink yours, Ellie, you should get off to bed. You were a grand wee nurse, there.'

'She takes it from her mother. Come and kiss your grandmother, Ellie.' Maeve watched the girl coming towards her, her fair face alight with happiness for her cousin, and she thought, this one will add lustre to the McGraths. She hoped she would be there to see it.

19

Ernest and Lizzie were married quietly in May with what Ernest referred to as unseemly haste, the church decorated with sheaves of white lilac from the Hall gardens. Lizzie herself arranged a great basket of bluebells culled from the Sholtie Woods in memory of her mother, Bessie Haddow. Her father had told her once that Bessie had been 'partial to bluebells'. Perhaps they had wandered there together, perhaps . . . She felt very close to her mother in the days before her wedding.

She complained to Ernest smilingly, 'I've never been a white bride. It was a rushed war marriage with Nigel, and now that I'm a widow, it wouldn't look right.' Indeed, although John Craigie performed the ceremony with his usual aplomb, she felt there was a slight edge of disapproval in his voice. Maybe he would have preferred her to remain in widow's weeds instead of seeking once more the pleasures of the flesh.

Because there was no doubt she sought them avidly. The first night of their honeymoon was spent alone at the Hall. Jonty was staying with Maevy – it was no penance to him as he enjoyed being spoiled by Ellie – and Terence had set off for Ireland with his mother that very afternoon. Lizzie had walked up the aisle on his arm. How many people in the village knew he was her father, she wondered. She did not know, nor did she care.

Maeve had said she did not want to be in their way, and Lizzie had agreed to her going to Woodlea on the one condition that it was for a holiday only, and that she would still regard the Hall as her home and live there with her and Ernest.

So now they were in bed together in her own bedroom overlooking the park, and Ernest's arms were safely round her and she was the happiest woman alive. She had to tell him.

'I'm made for love, Ernest,' she said. 'I've longed for you since the day and hour you went back. This is how I want to be, with you for the rest of my life.'

'You have no idea . . .' his voice was unusually hesitant, '. . . what it does for a man to have an honest wife.' He kissed her bare shoulder lingeringly, Ernest would not stampede her – she marvelled at herself for thinking such thoughts – he was too sophisticated for that.

'What's the point of lying in matters of love? Tell me truthfully, is it in your mind just now that I was married to Nigel, that you're not the first?'

'Not unless it hurts you to know you're not the first with me,' he kissed the other shoulder, and then lower still, making her quiver deliciously, 'although *I* haven't been married.'

That was difficult. But there could not be one-sided honesty. 'It does, for a second or two, and then I think, well, obviously there has never been anyone you loved enough to marry, so I must be generous.'

He laughed, his mouth against her breast. 'That's the right word to use, my darling, generosity. Oh, ours will be a fine love, generous, wide, accommodating, trustful, no taking umbrage; truthfulness.'

'And you won't mind living in the Hall instead of a home of our own?'

'No, because it is where you want to be for your son's sake, and your grandmother's, and I shall tell myself that Nigel doesn't mind me in his place so long as I take care of you and love you as he did.'

But it was more than Nigel had done, or perhaps different. The expression of love in a young man of twenty and a mature man of thirty-six is different. There are attributes in both cases, innocence against knowledge, but Lizzie was no longer a trembling young girl and what Ernest gave her would have been impossible for Nigel.

She was a woman of passion and of taste. She appreciated and was ready for Ernest's kind of loving which was as debonair as himself, except when towards dawn they wept in each other's arms because of the intensity of their love. And then laughed at each other as they put on their night-clothes again and prepared themselves for sleep. 'And we said we would keep it light,' Ernest said, helping her to smooth the silk nightgown over her limbs.

'How do you know what's light if you haven't known the opposite?' she asked him, in his arms again, at peace, exhausted. 'We were no longer two people. After tonight wherever we are we'll belong to each other.'

'Yes, there had to be tonight to know that. Now, compose yourself for sleep. Say your prayers if you want to. I don't want a haggard-eyed bride in the morning when we set off for Paris.'

It was Lizzie's idea. She had memories of her schooling at Versailles, and the Barthes' family home and the excitement of being in such a beautiful setting after the starkness of the manse, of sitting in the Café de Paris with Nigel and believing she was in heaven.

She wanted to see Paris now through different eyes – a mature woman's, she hoped – loved by a mature man who could enjoy with her the sophisticated delights, perhaps even visit some of King Edward's haunts, the racecourses, the music-halls, and, for culture, study some of the churches with a little help from Mr Ruskin. And as well, she had some very beautiful gowns trimmed with lace and equipped with clips for the hem because of their excessive length, which Grandma had helped her to choose.

The Barthe family welcomed them on their first night, in the salon with its huge gilt mirror above the Louis

Quatorze table by Boule, which Emily thought so *démodée*. Lizzie remembered the little Boudin painting of the Normandy seaside because it in turn reminded her of the Barthes' Normandy farmhouse where she had been so happy. And she remembered also the ormolu clock and the Sèvres vases, which Emily had affected to scorn, but which she saw were still in their place on the mantelpiece.

But most of all she remembered the people: Giselle whom she had last met at her father-in-law's funeral, and her parents, Emily and Charles, who, although they did not realize it, made a perfect foil for each other, one so brittle, the other so phlegmatic. And it was charming to see how the twins, Marc and Olivier, had become exquisite young Parisians of twenty-three. They were both employed at the Sèvres factory in the south-west of the city. Ernest had a perfect rapport with them.

'You must come often to Paris, the two of you,' Marc said. 'You are made for it. We can show you the lesser known sights. And we have a *pied-à-terre* on Rue St Denis if you wish to borrow it.'

'We've already invited them to stay here, *mes enfants*,' Emily said, touching her swinging earrings, 'but they've refused.'

Ernest thanked them. 'We are at a hotel in the Rue St Hyacinthe on Lady Crawford's recommendation.'

'Ah, yes, I remember that,' Emily said. 'You're an independent lot, you McGraths, although I forget, *Leezie*, you were of the Scottish aristocracy before you became a mere Murray-Hyslop.' Lizzie hid a smile. She would give Aunt Maevy, grandmother and Ellie an impression of Emily when she got home. 'Grandmother insisted on staying there with your aunt, although we wished to entertain them at Monceau Park, *n'est-ce-pas*, my love?'

'*C'est vrai, chérie*.' Charles Barthe had the air of a man who for a long time had found it easier to concur than disagree.

Giselle was charming, still not affianced much to her mother's chagrin and the victim of some pointed barbs, and she too volunteered to be at their disposal while they were in the city.

'You have all been so very kind,' Ernest said, correct and equally charming in his fine-fitting dinner jacket, his smoothly-polished hair with the stray lock firmly pomaded in place – my elegant love, Lizzie thought. 'I'd like to take you all to dinner tomorrow night at a place of your choice, and then Lizzie and I, I fear, are going to Normandy for a few days. She has very pleasant memories of the lush countryside there, and I'm at the stage, I confess, where I'm prepared to gratify my wife's slightest whim, although I don't know how long that will last.' This remark was received with laughter from the children and a *moue* from Emily – over the years she had become an expert at French *moues* – and a distracted look from Monsieur Barthe. Was there still a love-nest on the Left Bank? Lizzie wondered. Grandma had told her all about the duel.

'Then you must borrow our farmhouse,' Emily said, brightening. 'There's a resident housekeeper and her husband there. They would make you very comfortable, and horses, and a motor car . . . is there a motor car there, Charles?'

'The Delaunay-Belleville.' He examined his nails.

'We shouldn't dream of disturbing your arrangements,' Ernest said. 'We shall be moving on each day along the Seine, staying at simple inns, savouring the countryside.' His look in Lizzie's direction said, 'and each other'.

'Then that's settled,' Charles Barthe said suddenly, as if coming to life. 'Take the Delaunay-Belleville. Return it when you have completed your stay. It's lying there not being used. We prefer the carriage in Paris because of the traffic. I insist.'

Lizzie admired the gracious way Ernest accepted, hiding his pleasure. He dearly loved to drive.

They discussed her half-brother, Terence. Apparently he and Giselle had been corresponding. 'He's finishing his art course in Dublin this summer,' she said, 'and he would like to come and stay in Paris for a year at least. I'm encouraging him, and the twins would love his company.'

'Yes, we would,' Marc said, smiling wickedly. 'We'd show him the sights.' Sights not found in Baedeker, Lizzie thought.

'Gaylord, Uncle Patrick's son,' she said, 'is also fascinated by Paris . . .' She heard her voice lose its confidence. Once or twice, in bed with Ernest, she had thought to tell him of that terrible episode in her room at Claremont, but she had hesitated. Perhaps later. Their loving was too perfect yet to spoil. 'I know he's tried to persuade his father to let him come here. He's studying architecture so it would benefit him, but Uncle Patrick seems adamant.'

'There are quite a few distractions here, of course.' Charles Barthe looked wistful.

'I thought him a charming young man,' Emily said, 'when we met him at Lord Crawford's funeral – quite different in temperament from his father.'

'And his sister, Sarah,' Ernest agreed. 'She's sensible to a degree.'

'For a person of spirit like Gaylord,' Olivier said, 'this little place buried in America must be *triste*.'

'Gaylord's like a racehorse, difficult to handle,' Ernest tried to explain. 'I've watched him for a long time, although he has more rapport with my stepbrother, Kieran. It would be a good thing if he *were* allowed to come to Paris. Uncle Patrick would find he'd settle down after he'd sown a few wild oats.'

'"A few wild oats",' Charles Barthe repeated. 'You English have such interesting expressions.'

'Except that we're Scottish,' Lizzie said. This seemed to amuse Marc and Olivier who burst out laughing. She remembered that when she had been a schoolgirl she had thought them a comical pair.

She was in a golden haze of happiness, she told Ernest. Normandy would always be her favourite place, her refuge. They collected the Delaunay-Belleville at the Barthes' farmhouse (more of a *gentil-hommière*), situated on the green waters of the Epte near Gisors, and made their way slowly through the rolling countryside of the Vexin. Fleury-sur-Andelle was wooded in comparison, but after that they were in the land of vast horizons, as Ernest called it, where the only trees were the vast copses of beech, oak, and elm which screened the farms.

There was something in the calmness of Normandy which soothed her volatile spirit. She was in love and loved. She felt beautiful. Ernest told her a hundred times a day. She was so happy that she wept sometimes, but in private. She wanted, like Ernest, to keep it light.

Maeve, in far-off Woodlea, was relaxing in *her* refuge: the green deepness of south-west Ireland where even the loughs looked green at times, and, she swore, the sheep also, a deep, peaceful greenness. She was revisiting old haunts, old friends, and being spoiled by Honor and her three young daughters, especially Clare, the youngest. She had always liked lively children. Clare was after her own heart, spirited, mischievous at times, in her eyes, adorable. Honor would have to watch her.

It was a home to relax in because it had been her home, full of memories of her parents, Terence, her brother, and her own dear Kieran. She liked young Terence, who came home at the weekend, quiet, thin, artistic, who was content to sit with his grandmother and listen to her stories of Woodlea. He had the same love of the place as his father, and he also had a strong rapport with his stepmother who teased him and yet loved him so obviously.

'Honor's like an Irish sprite,' she said to him once. 'Here one minute and gone the next. And that faraway look in her eyes sometimes, as if she was with the fairies . . .'

'It's her writing,' he said. 'Ideas come into her head. I know it with painting. You're in a different world. You listen with one ear to people talking, but inside your head you're thinking things out. It's like being two people.' She listened while he tried to explain the artistic temperament to her, and thought, my life's been too busy for all this, but knew that was not the real explanation. They were different people.

'Are you going to Paris, do you think?' she asked him.

'Oh, yes!' His face lit up. 'How could I not! Father and Honor are encouraging me to go. Honor says I need different horizons, that I must absorb, absorb . . . it's her favourite word. But I'm like father. I'll come back to Ireland eventually. It's home to me now, not Glasgow. That's practically disappeared from my mind now.'

'You may fall in love with a French girl and stay there.'

'Well, we'll see.' He was too bland. 'Now, Grandma, before I go back I'm going to ask you to sit for me. Would you mind?'

'Oh, I'd like that. I've never been painted. Alastair did talk of it . . .'

'I don't say this one will be worth anything, but honestly, Grandma, I don't know a more beautiful woman than you and that's a fact.'

'Didn't I always say you were my favourite grandson?' She smiled with happines. This lad had *jaloused* what she missed with Alastair's death, a man's admiration. 'Now you must tell me exactly what you would like me to wear.'

184

'Gold,' he said, 'I see you in gold . . .' She saw he was in that different world he had spoken about.

But her greatest joy was to be with his father, now the complete Irish country gentleman, happy with his second wife, his horses, at times going to Dublin to research for her, and, as well, taking an intelligent interest in world affairs. He was twice the man he had been when he was married to Catherine Murdoch.

'I see things more clearly in Ireland than I ever did in Scotland, Mother,' he told her, 'the wrangles about Home Rule, but important as that is, the question of Germany. They're becoming the enemy of Britain. People are having a fine time under Liberal rule. They don't notice the menace. Germany is trying to gather the whole of Europe against us, including France and Russia.'

'And what will be the outcome, son?' she said, fearful in this pleasant house where she felt so much at home.

'War,' he said. His usual happy face was stern. She felt cold.

20

When Lizzie got back from France, amongst her correspondence she found a letter from Kieran which she read first with pleasure and then with growing concern.

I write first, (she read) to wish you and Ernest every happiness in your life together. He's a lucky man. Tell him so from me, but I know he knows it already. Ernest doesn't give much away, but I realize now his time here was only a waiting time.

Your marriage has gladdened us all. Mother talks about you often and her face shines with happiness. I sit and listen and imagine you when you were here so long ago with your red plaits and your bright enquiring face. I thought of you often in your sadness when Nigel died, and now you have what you deserve, a man who loves you.

Life goes on here the same as usual, more or less. Great-Uncle Terence and Great-Aunt Caroline a little frailer each time we see them, father giving up the reins of the business bit by bit, the younger members of the family, Victoria's five and George's three, flooding into Wolf House at frequent intervals and filling it with their chatter, to Mother's delight.

Apart from work my principal task at the moment seems to be that of keeping an eye on Gaylord. I had plans to cut adrift from the family, get an apartment in New York and make a separate life for myself, but he seems to need me.

He has conceived a great desire to go to Paris, and I can sympathize with this, but Uncle Patrick won't have it. Aunt Maria, who is a strong character as you know, nevertheless allows her husband to be arbiter. Nothing will change that. It is their kind of marriage.

There have been family rows. Gaylord has stormed out of the house a few times and I know he's keeping bad company. He has arrived here the worse for drink and I've had to smuggle him up to my room. George will have nothing to do with him because of the children, nor Victoria, Sarah is shocked by the behaviour of her brother and guards Ginny from him. Poor

Gaylord! Added to that he has had back trouble for some time due to a fall from his horse a long time ago. He suffers a lot of pain . . .

Why am I burdening you with this recital of woes when your cup of happiness must be so full? I expect for the same reason that Gaylord comes to me. There must always be someone in one's life to whom one can turn, or at least confide, someone not in one's immediate family. Remember those letters you wrote to me during your schooldays and your moans about certain schoolteachers?

But nothing stays the same and that's the sadness. People grow up and have grown-up problems, and yet sometimes inside they feel as unable to cope with them as with their childish ones. Don't feel you have to say or do anything about what I've told you about Gaylord. Indeed, when I started this letter it was to be one of friendship only, from your dear cousin who wishes you and Ernest continuing happiness . . .

She showed it to Ernest and he looked at it thoughtfully after he had read it. 'One reads between the lines,' he said.

'About Gaylord?'

'About Kieran. As for Gaylord, that's not a problem even Kieran can solve.' He took her in his arms. 'Believe me, my dearest,' he said, 'I know how lucky I am.'

Once more she could not bring herself to tell him how Gaylord had assaulted her. It was in the past, and why should she spoil their happines? Ernest might feel some kind of gesture was required of him, although in her heart of hearts she knew that would be too conventional a reaction for Ernest. The real reason for keeping it from him was that she wanted to think about it, to try to understand it. The disgust she had felt had long since receded. Slowly, or perhaps not so slowly – perhaps some of Ernest's sophistication was beginning to rub off on her – she was beginning to realize that Gaylord's unhappiness was due to something more than temperament. When she had thought some more she might discuss it with Ernest. Not now. It was sufficient to be loved.

187

21

'I've found out about that motor car,' Belle Geddes said to Charlie.

'The one my friend told me about.' They were making out their visiting lists together on a bright sunny morning a year after Ernest and Lizzie's marriage.

'Have you?' Charlie, busily writing, did not look up. 'Are you going to see Lizzie this morning?'

'No, I don't think she needs me. Mother and daughter are doing well. Father also.' She laughed at him. 'I'd never have thought such a suave character as Ernest Murray-Hyslop could be in such a state.'

'It's natural if you're in love with your wife. I was the same.'

'Were you? And you a doctor!' Her black eyebrows went up over the narrow silver eyes. A peculiar-looking girl, Charlie thought, with her own kind of attraction. Not for him.

'Did you hear what I was telling you?' Belle said. 'About the motor car? It's a Rover.' He paid attention.

'Is it? As easy to steer as a bicycle, then? If you want to know, it's only two bicycles put together with a motor . . .'

'But think of the advantages in the practice! No horse to look after, a good hood over your head to keep off the rain, up to fifteen miles an hour . . .'

'Ellie has a Rover safety now.' He admitted to being interested. He and Maevy had discussed it often. She was all for it. Ernest had a powerful Napier and he had taught Lizzie to drive it in the grounds of the Hall until Charlie pointed out that it was not too wise for a pregnant woman.

'Well, there you are. Surely you can have *two* with a motor added, if that's all it is. If Hamish Black delivered it today we could drive it out this afternoon and maybe do the calls at the same time.'

'We?'

'Yes. Don't look so surprised. Hamish has let me have a go in quiet roads. He knows all about them. He's an agricultural engineer in Crannoch, and he's so sure about their future that he's gone into the business of selling them.'

'I've heard of Mr Black,' Charlie said dryly. 'Is this a put-up job?'

'Why are you so suspicious?' She shrugged. 'You know we've talked before about a motor car for the practice. That's what finished my poor father, riding out in all kinds of weather even before he had a trap. Here am I giving you a chance to try one out and you infer that I'm trying to make you buy a pig in a poke!'

He smiled at her, giving in. 'I'm quite taken by the idea. All right. If you can get Mr Black to bring it to the surgery after lunch and demonstrate it, we'll try it out.' He had a mental image of Maevy and Ellie if he drove home in it tonight, their bright, loving faces. He could take them runs on the summer evenings to places they'd never been, far up into the country . . . 'I would buy it for the practice, of course.'

'Of course.' She smiled, a tongue-in-cheek smile.

'I admit it would be a grand help in winter. I'm getting to the stage where my bones are beginning to creak, far less your poor father's.'

'That's hard to believe. You're in your prime.' The way her eyes rested on him made him remember that time when Maevy had been in America and Belle had unbuttoned her blouse in his own sitting-room. Shameless bitch, he thought without rancour. She did not stir him. Never would. There was only Maevy.

Mr Hamish Black made it sound as if it was as easy as eating a mealie dumpling, and indeed it was. After he got over the strangeness of holding a wheel instead of reins, and driving round the village on his own, he found he and Belle were chugging away steadily but in comparative comfort. He enjoyed the surprise on the faces of patients or patients' relatives when they opened their doors and saw the strange-looking object he had come in. The general opinion was favourable. It would be a collective feather in Sholton's cap if they were the first village to have a motor-propelled doctor. One old man summed it all up. 'Aye, doactor, I'm right glad ye hae wheels under ye at last!'

The calls finished, Charlie drove with aplomb in the direction of the surgery. He recognized in himself a certain cockiness.

'So you like it?' Belle said.

'Yes, I like it. There might be a few minor alterations . . .'

'Hamish would see to that. He would do anything for me.'

'I can well imagine.' He had seen the hot eyes of the agricultural engineer turned motor dealer on his female assistant. 'Would you like to try it?' He smiled. 'Since you say you've been taught by the redoubtable Mr Black.'

To his surprise she accepted. 'I would indeed. You could stop here and we'll change over, if you like. It's nice and quiet.'

He put on the brake and got out of the car, helped her to descend. Would Maevy want to have a go? Maybe in time she would be driving to Glasgow . . . 'I'm calling your bluff. I wanted to see if you were telling the truth about being able to drive.'

'I never lie.' She walked round the bonnet, got into the driving seat and pulled on the leather gloves he had left on the seat.

He was surprised at her adroitness, and then corrected himself. Maevy would not approve of that way of thinking, why should he be surprised? Belle was the best doctor he had ever worked with, cool, efficient, and with an open mind to advances in treatment. She showed an intelligent interest in his work at the Royal, was always willing to stand in for him . . .

She seemed to get far more out of the car than he had. The run was smoother, it responded with more ease to her handling of it. She was light-fingered . . . she made a smooth right-hand turn from the main village road.

'Why the Sholtie Brae?' he asked her. 'This isn't the way back.'

'I wanted to try it on a hill.' Her voice seemed to stream from her mouth with the wind. 'And we'll see the Sholtie in spate after all those heavy rains.'

'All right.' He was enjoying himself. He would certainly buy one. He and Maevy would go for runs, even down to the Clyde coast. They might get a bigger model so that there would be plenty of room for Ellie. Oh, they would have fine times! And Maevy would get some air. She was too long in that office of McGraths. That was Maevy, in for a penny, in for a pound.

The thing which did not suffer was their love. She had asssured him of that frequently when they were in bed. 'All day, my darling, you are there with me. As I am with you. And there's the joy of meeting at the end of the day . . . it makes it sweeter . . .' The wheels were rattling under him. The car was picking up speed. 'What are you doing, Belle?' he asked.

'Nothing.' She was wrenching at the brake. 'I'm doing nothing! It was going too fast, and I braked, but you can see . . .' her voice rose in agitation, '. . . it isn't working!' She wrenched again, her back extended. He saw her knuckles stretching taut the leather gloves.

'Pull harder!' He put his hand over hers and put all his

191

strength into helping her, he had the sickening sensation of the ground slipping away under them.

'Something's broken! Charlie! Something's . . .'

'My God!' He hardly heard her as he looked round. The speed they were doing must be above the fifteen miles Mr Black had promised. Keep cool, think . . . The trees of the Sholtie estate rearing above their high stone wall were a flashing green blur. 'Here, let me!' He knocked off her hand from the brake handle, bent and wrenched with all his might, a great solid-looking steel brake with its clutch handle. He had the sensation of it coming away in his hand.

'It's no good!' Her voice was high, she was losing her nerve, a thing he had never seen her do. 'Can't you manage it? What shall we do? Could we jump?' She was shrieking now, 'Oh, no, it's far too fast . . .!'

He looked wildly round. Impossible to get the heavy doors open at this speed. If he had only been in the driving seat, to get purchase . . . perhaps if they managed to turn it into the tow-path when they came to it . . . but that was too long to wait . . . not at this speed . . . 'Here's a grassy bit!' He suddenly decided. 'Turn the motor into it!' He seized the wheel with one hand and helped her to steer it round. 'That's it! It's slowing, I think . . . Christ! Mind that *tree*!' The thud as they crashed into the stout oak had a dreadful dull heaviness, like thunder. It could be heard all over Sholton . . .

Dr Jim Geddes' poor injured heart missed several beats when his daughter stumbled into their sitting-room, dishevelled, streaked with dirt, her hair hanging loose, her voice scarcely audible. He had to tell the frightened servant to bring a glass of water before he could induce her to sit down, far less speak.

'What is it, Belle?' His hand was trembling as he held the glass for her.

'Charlie . . .' She was shuddering, her face ashen. The water ran from her mouth. 'We were in a motor . . . trying it out . . . over-turned on . . . Sholtie Brae . . . I crawled from under . . . Charlie . . .' She covered her face with her hands, making queer, broken noises. He thought she was going to be sick, then saw the tears coming from between her fingers. He had not seen her weep since she was a child. 'Go, for the love of God. Father . . . I can't stand . . . it!' He felt faint, useless. If only Aggie were here. She had been so capable . . .

His training asserted itself and he became Dr Geddes, not the father of this distraught woman who bore no resemblance to his self-assured Belle. He said to the frightened servant who was still standing twisting her apron. 'Get your mistress upstairs to bed. Cover her well and pack plenty of hot water bottles round her. Stay with her.'

He went into the hall, shouting in a voice he had not used for a long time, 'Jack!' The groom appeared from the kitchen, his jaws working.

'Just haen' a sup, doactor . . .'

'Put the pony in the trap! Hurry! There's been an accident.'

He was surprised at the adrenalin which was coursing through his veins as they clattered down the Sholtie Brae. What would he find at the foot? It did not bear thinking about. Anyhow, he reassured himself, tried to stop the trembling of his mouth, he was in full command of his senses. He had to be, to be able to help Charlie, his friend over the past twelve years – his doctor as well, when he had to send for him because of this heart of his. The salt of the earth, Charlie McNab, and that lovely wife and child. More than respected in the village, loved . . .

He knew when he saw the posture of the body lying in the grass that Charlie had left them. The pain in his heart was like the angina, only worse. Oh, there would be a weeping and a wailing in Sholton, he thought, as he bent beside the mangled figure, straightened the broken neck, closed the staring black eyes. But that would be nothing compared with the agony of Maevy McNab. The adrenalin drained out of him, leaving him an old man unable to face what lay before him.

'Help me with him into the trap,' he said to the lad whose eyes were falling out of his head.

'Oh, doactor . . . A canna . . .'

'Do what I say. Gently, now.'

There was no room to lay the body flat. They had to put it propped up in the seat opposite him as Jack got into the front and lashed the poor horse up the Brae again, the tears pouring down his face. Jim Geddes, sitting beside him, thought Charlie looked surprised as well as dead. He had not been ready. Life had been too good . . .

BOOK TWO

And Rumours of War . . .
1910–1914

1

Ellie and Maevy were at breakfast at Braidholme on a sunny September morning. Charlie's death, rather than the simple passing of four years, had made a different girl of Ellie. Her spirited temperament, although still evident, had been dampened, and the necessity to comfort Maevy in her great grief had made her at eighteen more mature than most girls of that age.

And, to Maevy's joy, she had begun her studies this autumn at the Queen Margaret College for Women in Glasgow. Perhaps subconsciously she wanted to fill her father's place.

'And do you think you'll like it, Ellie?' Maevy asked. Charlie's death had made an indelible impression on her. Her fair hair had dulled, although as yet it had not gone grey. Only the life had gone out of it, as it had gone out of her expression. No one would ever bring back the Maevy who had been buried with her husband.

At times, she could still look like someone who had been blighted. Maeve, hurrying over from the Hall on that terrible day, had found a daughter who lay prostrate, tearless, silent, in her room upstairs, with a distraught Ellie sitting beside her. 'I'm ashamed, Mother,' she had said in a lifeless voice. 'All my training, to collapse like this . . . Ellie . . . see to Ellie . . .'

'Oh, I like it,' the girl was saying. 'The lectures are grand. But it's a good thing I'm travelling home every night, because the girls from Edinburgh – they're going to be medical missionaries – were telling me they can hardly get a landlady to take them in. They say they'll only take single gentlemen!'

'The cheek of it!' Maevy said. 'Don't they read?'

'Oh, the male students are just as bad, and the doctors. Some of the professors, even. Patronising. The Royal's better than some places, though, the Western for instance. They've set aside a third of their beds for female students, and the Maternity Hospital will only allow female students at their West End branch.'

'Aye, trust the Royal. Your father always thought the world of it, and of Lister.' She could talk about Charlie now.

'I don't know what we would do without Hubbards – that's the bakers nearby. You can buy a glass of milk there and a cookie to see you through the day. Now you know why I'm eating so much when I get back to Braidholme.'

'Well, you aren't putting on any weight. Your waist is like a bluebell stalk . . .' That had been one of Terence's expressions. 'When I was your age I used to think I was too plump. Charlie knew the daughter of a surgeon in the Royal, Mr Wilcox, and I was a bit jealous of her. Letitia . . .' She smiled. 'I saw her at the Kelvingrove Exhibition with him – the 1888 one – and her slim figure worried me more than the fact that he'd escorted her there.'

'He never saw past you, Mother.'

'No, you're right, though I shouldn't boast. It was because I could see past *him* at the time, thinking of my great and wonderful career, that he'd asked her out. If I'd known . . . what was going to happen, I wouldn't have . . . wasted precious time.' She shook her head impatiently. 'You'll have to put up with me, lass. Sundays are days for backward thoughts, regrets.' Her smile was shaky. 'Maybe it's because you and I are such busy ladies that it's the only time we get a chance to talk. What are you doing today after church?'

'I'm invited to the Hall for lunch because Lizzie has Sir

198

Edward Hamilton coming, and she thinks I'll liven things up. I don't think she likes him very much.'

'He wanted to marry her.'

'Did he? Oh, she's far better with Ernest! Sir Edward's far too ponderous, like one of Rabbie Burns' "toon cooncillors".'

Maevy's smile was easier now. 'He may be ponderous but he's clever. He's running the Crawford business and takes care that Ernest doesn't know anything about it. I know Ernest worries Sir Edward might take control and there would be no place for Jonty when he's ready.'

'That's a long time yet. He only had his tenth birthday last Wednesday. It's a pity we couldn't go.'

'He'd have Annabel and Kit there. He dotes on his little brother already. He told me last time I saw him that he was going to teach him to play cricket and the wee soul's only two!'

'I think Lizzie wouldn't have sent him away to school if it hadn't been for the sake of Nigel's memory and Lord Alastair's. "It's the Crawford tradition," she said to me. "Who am I to break it?"'

'Ernest is understanding. There's a lot to be said for people not marrying in their first youth. They've wiser heads on them.'

'That's what I think *I'll* do, take my time. With medicine you don't want to rush into it, and there are some women doctors who haven't married at all . . .'

Like Belle Geddes, Maevy thought, as she listened to Ellie planning her life. She could not yet bring herself to mention the woman's name aloud.

She was still in the practice, along with a new young doctor, Colin Thomson. She had come to see Maevy, white-faced, a fortnight after Charlie's funeral. Her own father had died the previous week. At first Maevy had thought of telling Susan to say she did not want to see her . . .

199

'I know my grief can't be compared with yours, Mrs McNab,' she had said, sitting across from her in her black dress, her jet earrings and her luxuriant black hair. No hat. That was her style. 'It would be an insult. I've taken a fortnight to risk coming here and being turned away. I shouldn't have blamed you if you had. Father died because of Charlie and me. The shock was too great for him.'

'I was sorry about your father. Sorry I couldn't come to the funeral . . .' Belle Geddes waved her interruption away.

'Charlie died,' she said clearly, 'not because of me, although I certainly urged him to buy a motor. But he would have got one anyway. He moved with the times. There was a fault in the brake. Hamish Black confirmed this, the Procurator Fiscal accepted it. I'm here to ask you if you'll let me come back to the practice, at least until you get someone permanently. That locum they sent is no use.'

How direct she is, Maevy had thought, even in her state at that time of half-life, swimming through shadows with people emerging and disappearing, meaningless, like this black-dressed white-faced woman sitting facing her, whom she had to force herself to listen to, which was an even greater effort than stemming the bitterness, the ugly words which rose to her lips. 'I don't know,' she said, dully, 'I can't . . .'

'. . . stand the sight of me? Well, I don't blame you. Let that lie. There are people in Sholton needing doctoring and I'm hearing the complaints.'

She had nodded, said, 'Do what you like, we'll talk about it later,' and then the agitation which gripped her at times had forced her to her feet. 'I can't take any more . . . let me go . . .'

Belle Geddes was on her feet also. 'I can give you a sedative to make you sleep, Mrs McNab . . .'

A flicker of flame had shot up in her cold heart and she had felt her mouth twist. 'I don't want to sleep . . . I'll never sleep again . . .' She had stumbled out of the room.

The shame had kept her from doing something to herself, like that poor uncle of Maria's, or Catherine. Anything to make her forget. That had been four years ago . . .

'I've been invited to John and Isobel's,' she said to Ellie. 'They got in first, although Lizzie asked me, too. So we'll be going different ways.'

'Well, it will save you and Ernest talking shop. Are you still worried about the strike?'

'I think it will come. A ballot's been taken and the men are overwhelmingly in favour of it.'

'Well, you're in the clear. Ernest says you're always on the workers' side.'

'Who wouldn't be? It's high time they had a 56-hour week. I've seen the conditions they worked under since McGraths began, and my mother and father were more lenient than many carting firms. She always said a business would never prosper if you didn't give your workers a fair deal. We were the first to pay Sunday working overtime. Yes, I'm on the side of the workers, all right.' She felt a flicker of excitement, welcome enough. 'They're men, not beasts. And I'm on the side of the women, too. I can't tell you the joy it gives me to see you doing what I always had a secret desire to do, study medicine. Your father would be proud of you.'

'I know.' Ellie reached her hand across the table to her mother. 'It's partly why I'm doing it . . .'

Susan came in, making a noise about it. 'Ur ye two gawn to sit there and blether aw the day?' The older she got the less attention she paid to formality. 'A've ma kitchen to tidy up and get ready for the dinner.' She refused to call it luncheon.

201

'We'll both be out, Susan,' Maevy said, smiling at her. 'I told you. Just have a quiet wee bite on your own.'

She sniffed as she cleared the plates on to her tray. 'A don't fancy much at dinner-time noo. A biled egg will dae me. A'll maybe take a dauner doon to the village and see Tibby Simpson.'

'You just do as you like or put your feet up. I'm going to the manse. The kind of lunch they give you there will make me turn away even a boiled egg at night.'

'Aye, that wumman they have in the kitchen is gey heavy-handed. If she threw yin o' her scones at ye, you'd be felled like an ox.' She lifted the tray with a pleased expression at her sally and went away.

'What would we do without Susan?' Ellie said, laughing at her mother.

'Some day we might have to. She's getting on.'

She wished several times during the course of the manse lunch that she was at the Hall. Ernest and Lizzie's happiness permeated the big house. Her mother added grace and wryness to any table. There was Jonty, a ten-year-old copy of his father, handsome like the Crawfords, and the prattling of the little ones, not restrained to the nursery as Nigel had been. Oh, she was blessed, and deservedly so.

'You don't look so well today, Isobel,' she said, pushing the stodgy potatoes about on her plate and trying to swallow the bullet-like peas.

'No,' Isobel smiled faintly but bravely, 'it's one of my bad days. Isn't it, John?'

He looked up from his plate, his jaws working. 'When are your good ones, may I ask?' He smiled at Maevy as if inviting her to share his *bon mot*. 'Isboel likes her bed, Maevy. She's never happier than when she's tucked up in it.'

'Aye, during the day,' Isobel said sharply. What did she mean, Maevy wondered. Were her constant illnesses a

202

defence? Charlie had often said that there was nothing organically wrong with Isobel . . . well, at least, she had her husband.

'I tell you what, Isobel,' she said, 'when you finish eating you go up and have a rest till tea-time. Sunday's a busy day for you two with kirk services. I don't know how you do it.'

'See, John,' Isobel said. 'And often we have people back for lunch as well, if John takes the notion. I tell you, it's all go at the manse.'

'I'm sure it is.' She sat patiently listening, thinking how often people, even this sister and brother-in-law of hers, forgot that she worked every day at McGraths and ran a house as well. And then, more importantly, should she ask John about . . .? He was a minister, after all. She was tired of this gnawing doubt. Surely he would be able to give her some comfort.

It was difficult to start once she and her brother-in-law were ensconced in his study and he was fiddling around getting his pipe and tobacco, and then filling the room with an evil-smelling smoke which turned her stomach, which had already been partly turned by 'that wumman's' solid fare.

Then there was the endless ruminating as he lifted and laid, puffed and sucked. How self-pitying and querulous he had become of late. And he was like a loosely-tied sack in that chair. The man did not take enough exercise as well as over-eating . . . she must be charitable.

'I've given my life to this village, Maevy, but there's no gratitude. The constant demands drain you. And Isobel doesn't help much with this constant retiring to her room. She's even done it when I've had some of the elders for a bite. No support. You expect a wife to be a helpmeet . . .'

'John,' she said, 'I came to have a talk with you. It's about something that's been festering inside me since . . . Charlie died.' He looked up. She had caught his attention.

'Long ago, when I was ill in the Royal, I confided in you about burning that letter written to Catherine, Terence's wife, and keeping it from the Procurator Fiscal. I know you never told anyone. I'm grateful for that. Anyhow, I did tell him eventually, at Charlie's instigation.'

'I recognized it as a confidence, but you may remember I too advised you to divulge your secret to the proper quarters.'

She did not remember that he had. 'Well, everything turned out all right, and Charlie and I got married. We had a wonderful life together, sixteen years of it. Too short . . .' The words escaped her. 'I ought to be grateful for that but I can't. I have a daughter who couldn't be more devoted, friends and relations round me, a good home and work that fills my life . . . but I'm full of bitterness.'

'Bitterness?' he said, packing the tobacco into his pipe with the flat of his matchbox. 'I don't understand.'

'Bitterness because he was taken away from me, bitterness against God. Bitterness against Belle Geddes whom I blame. I have suspicious thoughts, that she might have told lies about the brakes being faulty, that she and Hamish Black in Crannoch might be in collusion . . . Can you help me to get rid of this bitterness, to get back my faith? Can you give me . . . something?' It had cost a lot to say these things. She was trembling.

He looked at her. There was no compassion there. 'You surprise me, Maevy, that you should have thoughts like that. Now, if you were in my shoes . . . Look what I have to put up with – an ailing wife, a parish which shows no gratitude for my constant ministry,' he looked around the room as if seeking new grievances, 'very little money. Look how you and Isobel's mother live. You want for nothing. She goes off to Ireland and America whenever the spirit moves her, she lives in luxury at the Hall although she started off in Colliers Row; you had sixteen

204

years of married life with never a care, a good innings some might say . . . As for your suspicions, Mr Black at Crannoch is a respected individual, and here in the village they speak highly of Dr Belle for her devotion to her work.' He sucked vigorously at his pipe as if to gain sustenance. 'No, it's I who should be bitter. But do you see me showing any signs of it?' He did not wait for an answer. 'Shall I tell you why? Because I pray. We converse at night, God and myself, I on my bended knees. Isobel says I go on too long, but if people would only do as I do . . .'

She said she would not wait for tea. The only thing to prevent me throwing myself in the Sholtie, she told herself, walking fiercely through the village, is to join them for tea at the Hall. Lizzie had said she would be welcome.

To go into the drawing-room at the Hall after the manse was like entering paradise. There were great bowls of flowers everywhere, some of them hothouse blooms; a cheerful log fire burned in the marble grate against the early chill of the autumn evening; on the floor the children, Annabel and Kit, played with a bright scatter of toys. Jonty was sitting at a small table with a game of patience. Cards on Sunday! John would have a fit.

The faces lifted to her were welcoming. Lizzie, beautiful, her copper-red hair bright against her green dress, came forward. 'Oh, good! We held up tea in the hope you'd come. We had bets on it!' No one more than Lizzie knew the stultifying atmosphere at the manse. 'Now, where are you going to sit, Aunt Maevy?'

She's complete, Maevy thought, completely happy, as she accepted a chair beside her mother who patted her hand. 'Well, Mother. I don't know who's looking better, you or Lizzie.'

'I *feel* fine, but Lizzie's *looking* better. You must be proud of her, Ernest.' Her mother smiled across at him.

'I am.' Ernest was mending a child's toy. 'There you are, son.' He bent down to Kit, patting his fair head. He looked elegant himself, Maevy thought, in his light suit cut in the latest fashion with its high buttoned jacket, the smart bow tie. He and Lizzie must spend a fortune on clothes. Was it John's monologue which had made that thought rise in her mind for the first time? Who would have thought that he envied the other members of the family their affluence? 'And you know Sir Edward, Aunt.' She had been aware of him sitting silently, waiting to be included in the conversation. Now he rose from his chair and came towards Maevy to greet her.

'I was invited for luncheon,' he said, 'but I'm afraid I've overstayed my welcome, although I assure you it was your niece who persuaded me to remain for tea.' He seemed more relaxed than when she had last seen him, a craggily handsome man. But, then, he must have got over Lizzie by this time.

'You and I can walk home together, Mother.' Ellie looked up smiling from the rug beside the children. 'Aren't they lovely, those two wee ones? Look how Annabel takes care of wee Kit.'

'A precious pair.' She looked at the brother and sister: Annabel with her wispy brown hair round the thin face, the lively brown eyes, Ernest's child for sure; Kit fair, more a McGrath, with his regular features and well-set eyes.

The talk became general as the sumptuous tea was brought in, Redfern hovering over Cathy as she dispensed scones rich with butter, fresh strawberry jam in silver dishes, pancakes, sandwiches of all kinds, fruit cake, cream sponges.

As she watched, at the same time keeping up a running conversation with her mother, she saw how often Sir

Edward's eyes slid to Lizzie and rested on her. Like an animal, she thought, but what kind? He was not swift in his movements. Everything about him was deliberate. He was the kind of man who would become heavier as he aged, a big handsome . . . lion. Was he still stalking Lizzie? She chided herself for her vivid imagination, and yet, when he spoke to Ernest, surely his dislike of him was evident in his excessive politeness?

The talk turned to the case of a carter. When the King died there had been funeral services all over the country which had necessitated a great deal of work in carting timber and the like. The man in question had worked a total of seventeen hours one day, carting timber for crush barriers, and he had claimed three shillings overtime which his employer had refused to pay.

Sir Edward was lofty. 'In my opinion the sheriff was right in disallowing this claim. There is no fixed or standard day in a carter's day's darg, so there is no justice in his claim. He probably only worked seven hours the next day.' Maevy bit back her annoyance at his tone, but she let Ernest speak. He was cool. No one would ever rile Ernest.

'I'm afraid you're in the minority, Sir Edward. This is a test case to further the agitation on the part of the carters for a fixed working week. Who can blame them? No advance in their working conditions has occurred since the last time they struck, in 1889. We at McGraths,' he looked at Maevy and her mother, 'have always advocated a sympathetic approach, but often we've been a lone voice amongst the other haulage firms.'

'And consequently we're heading for another strike,' Maevy said.

Maeve put her hand on her arm, her face worried. 'Do you think so, Maevy? I'm not up with the latest developments.'

Lizzie seemed to be trying to lighten the discussion.

'Well, if you insist on being a globe-trotter, Grandma – '
She had Kit on her knee now, making a beautiful picture,
Maevy thought, the red head against the fair one.

'You know it's because you treat me so badly at the
Hall.' Maeve smiled, but she wasn't to be put off. 'Has
something been happening while I was away, Maevy?'
She turned again.

'Yes, there was a meeting of the men. It was so crowded
that they had to shift it to Glasgow Green. I was there at
the last strike. I ran out of the Royal at the dinner hour
with another nurse to watch it. That was when Arthur
Cranston broke his knee and Charlie . . . operated . . .'
She saw herself in the quiet ward, looking up and seeing
Charlie there, his loving black eyes on her. Grief, as fresh
as on the day she had heard of his death, swept over her.
There was silence in the room. Annabel's piping voice
broke it. '*My* wee dolly's got a broken knee . . .' Everyone laughed as if in relief and she made a tremendous
effort, speaking directly to her mother. 'Do you ever hear
of Arthur?'

'Oh, yes,' her eyes were full of understanding, 'there
was something in the Crannoch paper the other day. You
see, I do keep up with some things. He's one of Mr
Lyon's right-hand men now. And his father's still hale
and hearty at over eighty. He and Kieran – ' she looked
at Sir Edward, 'my first husband – were good friends,
worked on truck together. But it would take me too long
to tell you young ones about truck and what it was . . .'
She was talking to give Maevy time to recover herself.
She was grateful, taking up where she had left off.

'At that time, August 1889, they requested a ten-hour
day, with six hours on Saturday, making a fifty-six hour
week. And further payment for Sunday duty. They're still
waiting, twenty-one years further on. We're one of the
few who pay extra for Sunday work.'

'It's blackmail, of course,' Sir Edward said, disregarding this. 'We're strict at Crawfords. It always pays. Give them an inch and they take an ell. If you're not careful,' he was looking at Ernest, not her, 'you'll have the workers running the whole show instead of the other way round . . .' Jonty was a quiet lad, like his father, and young enough not to push himself forward in grownup company, but Maevy saw his eyes on the man for a second, piercingly blue, then veiled as he looked down again at his cards.

'Now, Sir Edward,' Lizzie was on her feet, trim and smiling in her green gown, 'I'm going to ask you to sample Cook's sultana cake. She prides herself on it. And while you're eating it my grandmother's dying to tell us more about her visit to America. Ellie and Maevy haven't heard it all.'

He accepted the reprimand graciously. 'Nothing would give me more pleasure,' he said. Maevy saw his eyes lift momentarily to Lizzie as his hand stretched out towards the plate.

At the back of her mind, as she listened to her mother, she turned over her visit to the manse. Perhaps her suspicions about the motor car were unfounded. It was an outrageous thing on her part to believe that Belle Geddes and Hamish Black had collaborated in any way. And surely it was a sign of her grief to wish to find someone or something to blame for Charlie's death. Perhaps John had been right to treat her suspicions with the contempt they deserved.

In that pleasant drawing-room with Ernest sitting beside Lizzie on one of the large sofas, both relaxed and yet so obviously in love, she felt that awful loneliness creep over her heart like cold water, numbing it. Will it be like this until I die? she wondered.

2

'I couldn't have done without McGraths in the last four years.' Maevy and Ernest were in her office on a dull November morning waiting for Dan Johnson to appear. 'Mother was right. "Something outside yourself". She always said that.'

'She's a wonderfully wise woman,' Ernest said. 'She has a complete acceptance of life. Look how she took her brother's death. All she said when she came back was, "I was glad I was there at the end. Terence and I began together."'

'But it's affected her. "That's when you feel your age," she told me, "when one by one your dear ones leave you."'

'She's a rock in the family. So different from Great-Aunt Caroline. *She* won't last long without *her* dear one. He was her oak. She was like one of those climbing shrubs that cling to the host.'

'A pale pink rose with butterflies fluttering round it.'

He laughed. 'The Grant side seems to be weaker than the McGraths or the Murray-Hyslops. Gaylord, for instance. Aunt Maria and Uncle Patrick visited the Grant family home a long time ago at Chesapeake Bay. Kate says it was to lay a ghost. That was the origin of Virginia, I guess, little Ginny, although she's not so little now, thirteen, I think, their pride and joy. Aunt Maria would be forty-five when she was born.' He laughed. 'What's got into us this morning and us with work to do?'

'Nostalgia.' She smiled at him. 'It's potent. All right. You were going to tell me what you think about pantechnicons. That side of the business has been hanging fire for a long time now.'

'We haven't forgotten them. Dan's done more research than I have. By the way, he said we were to go on without him while he's finding out about the strike. But, apropos pantechnicons, the decision is we both think it's too soon to start a service here.'

'But surely there are heavy commercial vehicles on the road, Ernest?'

'Oh, yes, from as far back as 1898. Thornycroft pioneered them. They're steam-powered, either coal or oil. France has been forging ahead with single cylinder internal combustion engines, but those are for light vehicles – a firm called De Dion-Bouton. No use for us.'

'America is ahead of us as usual.'

'They've more to conquer. The sky's the limit. Think of all that vast territory. Scotland would go into one of their states. They're using electric traction for goods vehicles, Studebakers, mostly. We've discussed it thoroughly, Dan and I. We think we should leave the idea of door-to-door removals in abeyance meantime. The railways are coping with the main part of the journey in the case of long hauls, and we can concentrate on the short hauls to and from the stations, making two or three trips. Are you disappointed?'

'No, I abide by your findings, though I still want to see that fleet of pantechnicons with our name across them, "McGraths, Door-to-Door Removals". But we have enough on our hands at the moment, especially with this strike pending. It's a period of transition for the carters.' She shook her head. 'Oh, I wonder how Dan's getting on! I can't do any work until he comes in. I'm on edge.'

'Think of something else.' Ernest was always cool. What was he like in bed? Maevy wondered, and then wondered at such an irrelevant idea passing through her mind. Was it because she missed Charlie physically, sometimes desperately? There was no one she could say this to. Her mother was too old to be bothered by such things, and Ellie was too young. Ernest would understand . . .

'It's a great joy to me to see you and Lizzie so happy, Ernest. The difference between your place and the manse . . .' She smiled.

'Poor John, poor Isobel. Maybe they have their own joy . . . in the Lord.' His smile was mischievous. 'Yes, we're happy, Maevy.' He only called her 'aunt' in company. 'I never believed there could be such happiness when I was a carefree bachelor. I thought I had it all. But she's everything I ever wanted in life, it's a case of "my cup is full and runneth over". I'm sure John would be glad to hear me quoting the scriptures. Sometimes it comes over me, when we're all together, Lizzie and the children – and, make no mistake, you and Ellie and grandmother . . .' He laughed. 'The only fly in the ointment is the occasional visits of Sir Edward. It's become a habit with him, and Lizzie feels it's only right because he holds the reins at Crawford. He's still in love with her, you know.'

'Oh, he's got over that, surely?' She did not think so.

'I'm not at all sure. Sometimes I catch him looking at her. And he doesn't like me. I feel it in my bones. Maybe I'm being fanciful, but I'll tell you one thing, he's steadily appropriating that business. Lord Crawford didn't tie it up properly as far as Jonty and Lizzie, and for that matter, his wife, are concerned. He lost heart when his son died. Sir Edward won't let me have a look in, and you know Lizzie, she isn't business-minded. Sometimes I think Jonty will be left with no inheritance when it comes to the time.'

'Well, we'll take him into McGraths.'

'Perhaps. And besides, there's the Hall . . .' His face was pensive, not sad. Ernest, she thought, had always been a realist. Although his happiest years were undoubtedly being spent in Sholton and Sholton Hall, it would not break his heart if he had to leave it. He was resilient, truly sophisticated.

'Braidholme means everything to me,' she said, 'it's Charlie, and before that, mother. It's in my blood. I hope Ellie will live in it after me . . . I find it difficult to look forward.' She turned away.

'You still suffer,' he said, 'I know. I've watched you. Once you accept that you'll never get over Charlie's death you'll feel better. Keep him alive, don't bury him. In any case, someone like Charlie couldn't be buried. He had too great a spirit. Bask in the love he inspired . . .'

'Ernest,' she raised her eyes to him, 'you're going to make me weep, hardened business woman that I am. Trot out some figures to me while I recover, anything . . .' She sat, her eyes brimming, not wiping the tears away. It was a soundless, healing kind of weeping; love, she thought, I must learn to live in his love . . . Ernest was talking.

'You don't have to listen to this. "The Heavy Motor Car Order came into force in 1905, and that permits a load of five tons, so that's a step forward. What we want for McGraths is a purpose-built goods vehicle rather than an adapation of a horse vehicle . . ."' He was holding a sheaf of papers.

Live in his love . . . *'I'm not going to jump on you like a fox on a poor wee hen. I'm going to take you in my arms, like this, see, it's nice and friendly . . .'*

'. . . Carter Paterson have gone ahead with buses on those lines, from Leylands, but the breakdown record is pretty high. Steam presents problems to the drivers although they're easier than petrol, but then if the driver doesn't pay proper attention to getting steam up or runs out of water suddenly and has to fill up at a duck pond . . .'

Don't turn away from the memories . . . *'When I imagine life without you, the void is . . . frightening. I don't know what I'd do . . .' 'You'd live. For Ellie, for*

213

your family, for yourself. Busy people are the ones who feel loss most keenly. If your life is . . . shapeless, there would be no void. . .'

'. . . and then we'd have baggies blocking the inlet pipes!' She heard the smile in Ernest's voice. 'It would mean us employing skilled mechanics and building repair shops. It's a whole new concept. Dan and I think if we give it a year or so more, all those difficulties will be ironed out. Meantime we've plenty of work to keep us going and there's this strike. I wish he would come in and put us out of our misery.'

She came back to the present. 'Have you heard the verses on the carters written some time ago? I had a copy of it somewhere. Let me see if I can remember it . . .

> 'Noo, cairter chaps are pushed gey sair,
> Their pay, ye ken, is ocht but fair,
> Their hours are lang the hale week roun',
> Nae men wark langer in the toon . . .'

Dan burst into the room, his usual sober face alight. 'It's off! The strike's off!' He collapsed into a chair. 'My goodness, what a to-do! The Railway Companies have capitulated, sixty hours a week, and conceded the right to overtime!'

'They've seen sense,' Ernest said. 'Have you got a copy of the agreement?'

'Aye, here it is.' He was unfolding a piece of paper as he spoke. 'We'll need more carters at this rate. They'll be wearing bowler hats next! Still, I suppose it *is* grand news if the work keeps coming in.'

'Read it out, Dan,' she said, 'we're too overwhelmed.'

'Right ye are.' He coughed, flattened the sheet, began. '"It is hereby intimated that the following conditions of service, as affecting the Companies' carters in Glasgow, will come into operation on Thursday, December 1, 1910, viz:

'"Hours of Duty: 60 hours per week shall constitute the standard hours of work, inclusive of stable duty on weekdays, but exclusive of meal hours.

'"Overtime: Overtime at ordinary rate shall be paid in respect of hours worked on weekdays in excess of the standard weekly hours, viz., 60 hours.

'"Sunday Duty at Stables: In cases where carters are not relieved of Sunday stable duty, such duty shall be paid for at the rate of 5s per day, not exceeding 10 hours, exclusive of meal times."'

Maevy and Ernest exchanged triumphant glances. 'We've no quarrel with that,' she said.

'No, indeed. It will have far-reaching effects, even amongst the Welsh miners in Tonypandy.'

She nodded. 'Now the Railway contractors will have to sit up. If the carters are kept waiting to load and unload at the docks they'll no longer have to wait in their own time. That should make the loads move faster.'

'We're not out of the wood yet,' Dan said. He was always inclined to be gloomy.

'Oh, there will be difficulties, but leave it to Mr Lyon. He's got the bit between his teeth now. And don't forget,' she smiled, 'he has Arthur Cranston to back him up.'

'Aye, it takes a Crannoch lad to tell them what's what. Do you think we could have a drink of tea, Maevy, before we get back to work? My mouth's parched.'

'You can have something stronger if you like.' She felt suddenly happy. It had been a good morning. For the first time since Charlie had died she felt purposeful. There was a lot in life for her yet.

3

That Saturday in late March when Kieran went downstairs for lunch he found Gaylord there, dressed in a casual jacket and moleskin trousers. Sometimes Kieran thought *his* mother and father would have made better parents for his cousin than Aunt Maria and Uncle Patrick. But had not his mother once laughingly said to him that the 'little angels' who went to other children's parties could not possibly be hers?

'Here's your cousin to see you,' Kate said, looking up smilingly at him. 'I think he has plans.'

'I thought you and I could go rabbiting, Kieran,' Gaylord said. 'I've got my shot-gun in the motor.'

'On a day like this?' The lamps were still on although it was midday. There had been an uneasy hiatus between winter and spring all week. The snow had gone – it always went earlier in the Hudson Valley – but it was gloomy, depressing and dank.

'Hasn't he become a city type, Aunt?' Gaylord said. 'Do you keep him wrapped up in cotton wool? I tell you, sir,' he looked at James, including him, 'you should see me when I go out inspecting sites, rough clothes, wading boots . . . you can't be a city gent in Wanapeake.'

'I think Gaylord has something there.' James gave his wry smile. 'Sometimes I regret the years I gave to the city, and now when I have more time, the fireside draws me more than the great outdoors.' Kieran noticed his breathlessness. It was getting worse.

'Come the spring you'll be out and about, Father. You know how you like croquet. It's damp and muggy today. No one except Gaylord would think of it.'

'That's because I'm a wanderer on the face of the earth.' Gaylord spoke gaily. How bright his eyes were at times, Kieran thought. 'Ma and Pa are visiting Great-Aunt Caroline and I didn't want to go there – such a sad house with her in bed most of the time – and Sarah is going out with Robert McGrath. Did you know he's never away from our house? She's given poor Jack Henken his marching orders. No, thanks, if I'd stayed at home I should have been left acting as nursemaid to Ginny.'

'Nursemaid, at fourteen!' Kieran laughed at him.

'Well, dancing attendance on her. She's a little madam. Anyhow, are you coming? If not, I'm going myself.'

'Yes, you must, Kieran,' Kate said. 'And you'll both have a stirrup cup before you go, or the equivalent, a beagle cup, except that you haven't brought a dog, have you, Gaylord?'

'I don't like dogs. They fawn. I prefer cats. And no, thank you, aunt, to the stirrup cup. I'm a reformed character now. But if you care to ask Mrs Vanaressi to put us up a flask of coffee and some sandwiches, that would be most welcome.'

'Won't you stay for lunch?'

'No, thank you. There isn't time.'

'It appears I've no choice,' Kieran gave in, smiling. 'Well, you chat to my parents while I go up and change.'

He was glad Gaylord had called. Weekends in Wanapeake in winter could be dull, but he usually came home. His mother looked forward to seeing him. She was tied to the house more and more because of his father's persistent bronchitis, and her only diversion was visiting Abigail and Victoria to see her grandchildren. She had given up most of her voluntary work and they rarely entertained. The distressing shortness of breath which his father suffered from made speaking a penance. He had talked often about returning to Scotland when he retired completely. Kieran doubted if they would ever make the trip.

217

'Where are we going?' he asked Gaylord when they were in the Oldsmobile.

'I thought Abigail's people's place. I've *carte blanche* to wander about their woods, and there's the river running through it. We might see some otter as well.'

'You seem very cheerful this morning. Have you been left a fortune?'

'Left a fortune? By God, what wouldn't I do with that? I'm paid a pittance by that measly small-town architect, and father doesn't augment it by one jot or tittle. "Live on what you earn, my boy. That way you'll appreciate the value of money."' His mood had changed as he spoke. The gaiety Kieran had noticed had gone. When he stole a glance at his cousin he saw that odd glitter in his eyes again. And he was wrenching the wheel as he drove.

'Don't take it out on the poor old Oldsmobile,' he said. 'Where would you like to be?'

'Need you ask? Paris, of course. Gay Paree. *He* stopped me going there. I could have got the fare together but I couldn't live on nothing, could I? He's bloody hard on me.' His voice broke. 'You don't know how lucky you are, Kieran.'

'I don't know about that. You'll soon be finishing your apprenticeship and then you'll be rolling in money, building fine houses along the Hudson for the rich New Yorkers . . .' It was as if Gaylord had not heard him.

'I dream of Paris. I know the ambience would be right for me. I long to stroll along the boulevards, go to the music-halls, the museums, sit in the cafés, it is my kind of place, Paris.' His anger seemed to be mounting. 'And to think that Irishman, Terence, is there! I envy him his father. Uncle Terence had the decency to let *him* go. *He* didn't stand in his way.'

'But it was part of Terence's training as a painter.'

'And wouldn't it have been part of *my* training! I'd like to see the Trianon, Notre-Dame, the Hôtel Dieu, the

218

Opéra, all those places. Even grandmother has been to the opening of the Tour Eiffel. She heard the firing of the cannon, went up the stairs, she even showed me her *Permis D'Ascension*! Aunt Maevy was there, too, and all the Barthes. Everybody's been everywhere except me!'

'Calm down.' They had reached the Van Dam driveway. 'I don't want you to bang into those gates. They'd never forgive you.'

'Jump down and see old Siegel in the gatehouse, there's a good chap.' And when they were driving through the wrought-iron gates with the Van Dam crest on them, he went on as if there had been no interruption, 'Oh, God, I'm miserable!'

'I believe this is part of the old road from Wanapeake,' Kieran said to distract him. 'Can you imagine the traffic in coaches there must have been? Now it's the Van Dams' own special drive.' And as this elicited no answer, 'Where are you going to leave the motor?'

'At the ferry-house. The man there gives me permission to borrow a boat and row up the river for a short distance. The track isn't wide enough for the motor. We'll get out when we're in the woods.'

When they had unloaded Mrs Vanaressi's picnic basket and the guns into the boat, Kieran took the oars. Sitting facing Gaylord, he was aware once again of his eyes. They were strange, with an elusive glitter which made him feel uneasy. After his outburst, he had fallen into a silence, his arms wrapped round his body.

It's either one thing or another with him, Kieran thought as he looked around him. What a difference there was between this cold, surly river with its overhanging bare branches compared with that lovely day he had spent with Lizzie not far from here. Darkness and light. They had seen brilliant humming-birds and the occasional flash of a blue heron. The sun had shone. The water had sparkled.

And there was that other sunny afternoon when he had taught her to fish. He had put his arm round her so that he could place her hands in the correct position on the rod. Her closeness, her perfume, were so strongly imagined that he closed his eyes. Gaylord's voice was mocking.

'Your face has gone all soft, Kieran. I know who you're thinking about: Lizzie. You're mad about her, aren't you?' He was suddenly fiercely angry, and ashamed.

'Shut your mouth!' he shouted. 'Just shut your mouth! Don't talk about her!'

'You're jealous, aren't you?' He was laughing. 'Jealous of Ernest. Well, of course, she was always in love with him. I know. The thing about people like me is our acute perception. The onlooker sees most of the game. She's a passionate woman, Lizzie. Ernest is a lucky man, a *very lucky man* . . .' He sang out the words, his eyes glittering. 'I know.'

'You're mad,' Kieran said, taking hold of himself. And the oars. They had slipped out of his grasp. He must not let this fool anger him, or let him see how much he was affected by talk of Lizzie. 'You really will have to watch it, Gaylord.' He made himself smile. 'What age are you? Twenty-five? You're no longer a child, or even a young man. People will grow tired of your erratic behaviour. Not all of them are as long-suffering as I am.'

His answering smile was disarming. 'Sorry, old man. I didn't mean to offend you. Don't know what got into me. I get this desire to hurt – and it's always those whom I love the best. I want them to feel as I do. I grow tired of myself . . . Here we are. Pull in here.' They had reached a small jetty and Kieran shipped his oars. 'This is where old Siegel wants us to tie up the boat. He's scared we'll get caught up in the weeds further on.' He was the lovable Gaylord again, and Kieran accepted it because he always did.

Perhaps he had to examine himself. Why was it *he* who

took care of Gaylord, felt a responsibility towards him? In a strange way, did he need him, too?

They ate their sandwiches and drank the welcome hot coffee companionably enough. Gaylord had said they needed sustenance before they started so that they would aim straight. He was quite a good shot, and kept the cook at Claremont supplied with rabbit and hare. Fishing did not appeal to him, he had often said. It was too slow.

'Have you given up the demon drink?' Kieran said to him.

Gaylord shrugged. 'I can take it or leave it.' He spoke casually. 'If I go out with friends, I might be persuaded, but that's seldom.'

'Don't you patronize the Venetian any more?'

'Not much.' He looked around. 'Those trees glower at you, don't they?'

'Hemlock.'

'"My heart aches, and a drowsy numbness pains
My sense, as though of hemlock I had drunk . . ."
Keats. Did you know it? That's what *I'd* like to drink.' His voice became impatient. 'Shall we push on? It's oppressive here, like a jungle.' He held out his hand. 'Pull me up. My back stiffens when I sit.'

'Are you still having trouble with it?'

'Not anything I can't remedy. You pack up while I wander behind the bushes.' He smiled boyishly. 'It seems to have another effect on me as well.'

'Right.' Why didn't he have something done about that back of his? He did go to the doctor occasionally, but he should see a specialist in New York. He would mention it to his mother, Kieran decided.

Gaylord was a good tracker. He led the way through the woods, avoiding the swamps, leading Kieran safely over the trembling wooden bridges on to the small islands where the river widened. He was in high spirits, jumping with joy when he shot his first rabbit, whacking Kieran on the back when he followed suit. On Thrush Island they stalked a hare which got away, but back in the woods again he bagged a young one. It was not killed outright, and its eerie squealing turned Kieran's stomach. 'We've had enough now,' he said, 'let's get back. We've a long way to go.'

'They say they have souls.' Gaylord, ignoring him, was expertly tying its feet together. The head with the huge staring eyes was now swinging over his shoulder. Now it was revulsion Kieran felt. They did not need game as the Indians had needed it, to live. Food was freely available. Both came from wealthy homes with well-stocked larders. He listened to himself. Was he becoming a squeamish old bachelor?

'It's getting dark, Gaylord,' he said. 'We've bagged enough. We should be making tracks for home.'

'How appropriate that word is . . . tracks. A left-over from our ancestors. Yes, it's eerie, isn't it? The light's gone.'

'Like a cathedral.' Hadn't he said that to Lizzie?

'They say there's a headless horseman who gallops through these woods. Can you hear the sound of hooves?'

It wasn't the sound of hooves in his ears, it was the sound of silence, a prehistoric, atavistic silence. Nothing changes, he thought. Under our veneer of sophistication our passions are the same – love and hate, greed and lust. He did not formulate the words, it was an inchoate germ of an idea only, that he was somehow stripped, just as Gaylord was stripped, of pretence: Gaylord a man who liked men, he saw that fully and for the first time; he a man who lusted after a woman who was married to his step-brother. 'It's . . .' he began, then stopped, his heart pounding in his ears as he stared at his cousin.

Gaylord had turned the barrel of the shotgun towards his face. The muzzle was in his mouth. He felt his heart jump painfully, sickeningly, against his ribs. He could not speak. Was the trigger-guard on? 'What's the idea, Gaylord?' It did not sound like his voice. 'Trying to frighten me?'

He pulled the muzzle a fraction from his mouth. 'Not trying to . . . frighten you. Just . . . trying . . . for the sensation. Wondering what it would be like if I pulled the trigger.' His eyes were odd, glittering.

'You're mad. Give it to me.' Gaylord shook his head, his mouth closed over the barrel again. The mouth had widened slightly in a smile. Keep him talking, that was the main thing. 'You've no idea how . . .' Ease forward, balls of the feet, silently . . . 'silly you look.' Yes, now he could see the trigger guard *was* on . . . 'Like someone playing a flute . . .' Ease forward a little more, a slight see-sawing motion, scarcely noticeable . . . 'Phil the Fluter's Ball.' The name of the song came to him from childhood. Should he distract him, or should he just grab the gun? 'That would be one of grandmother's songs . . .' It was a matter of timing and which was safer . . . 'from Ireland . . .' It would be impossible for it to go off if he could just get Gaylord's fingers away from the trigger-guard. They were round it. 'Woodlea, South west, the Green Isle. I wonder if she'll go back . . .' Was he sure the trigger-guard was on? Yes, he remembered examining the two guns lying beside the log they had sat on to eat their sandwiches. James had instilled the habit in him at an early age. Was Gaylord on to him? Those strange eyes . . . he looked damned ridiculous like that, like a child at the breast . . .

The lunge was involuntary, not a matter of thought. He fell towards Gaylord, knocking the shot-gun away from his mouth and at the same time grabbing the stock. They were now both holding it. He saw Gaylord's white knuckles again, uncomfortably near the trigger. Treat it as a joke. He felt the sweat running down his face. 'Let's go, you ass!'

'No.' Gaylord's face was pouting, like a child's. 'You stopped my game. I was only teasing at first. You go into those . . . *fugues* when you aren't with me and I know who you're with. It's written on your face. No, I shan't let go.' He was bubbling with laughter. 'It's *my* shot-gun. Remember we used to say that long ago, when we were playing? "It's *my* hobby-horse." "It's *my* ball . . ." Stop twisting it! You know I'm strong.' He could see the white-knuckled fingers, saw the index finger creep out.

'Let it go.' The sweat was running into his eyes now, stinging them. 'I have the strength of ten.' His face was ugly, almost unrecognizable. 'I'm out and about with my theodolite every day while you're sitting in a stuffy office with slack muscles. *And*,' he was smiling now, 'I've found something better than drink to give me courage. What do you think of that, oh, moon-struck cousin!'

Why hadn't he thought of it before? Laudanum. That back of his . . . 'Let go, Gaylord,' he kept his voice calm, 'and we can talk. It's much better to . . .'

'*You* let go. Because you're older you aren't stronger . . .'

There was a sudden blinding noise. He thought he heard birds crashing in the trees, but there were no birds . . .

4

Lizzie had decided on a spring ball. Christmas and the New Year were always busy with functions in Glasgow, the annual staff dance of McGraths, which had been instituted by Maevy, and the more formal dinner and dance at the Grosvenor Hotel of the Crawford Iron and Steel Works.

It would also serve as a launching for the Exhibition to be held at Kelvingrove Park, as she and Ernest had been involved in it. Ernest, whose interest was in its historical aspect, had given a generous donation towards its fund for a chair of Scottish History and Literature at the University, she had raised money by organizing a Fancy Dress dance with a Grecian theme. She had always enjoyed theatricals. Ernest said she should have been on the stage.

She had to admit they had different tastes. Ernest liked the plays put on at the Theatre Royal which she regarded as being sometimes stuffy. She preferred the King's Theatre, where as well as seeing musical comedies one had the pleasure of dressing up and being seen. But they had a mutual love of pantomimes, and this Christmas they had taken Annabel, Kit and Jonty, the latter home after his first term at prep school, but still young enough to enjoy the frolics of 'Puss In Boots'.

The Hall always looked at its best in spring with the grounds a sea of yellow daffodils on the lawns and under the trees. She had taken their colour as her theme. Daffodils and fresh spring greenery were banked up in the ballroom, the tables in the dining-room and conservatory were set with yellow linen, she herself wore a pale

225

yellow chiffon gown with her cornelian drop earrings. She felt she had lived up to her reputation as 'that smart young matron of the Hall, Sholton.' 'Did you know her son by her first marriage is Lord Crawford?' she had heard one woman whisper to another at a Glasgow committee meeting. She herself had no 'side', whereas she found that the west end of the city bristled with it. She was not without insight.

'You look ravishing,' Ernest told her before they went downstairs together. 'Who would believe that you had had three children?'

'And that I'll never see thirty again?' That was better than saying 'thirty-three'. One of her 'adorable little foibles', as Ernest called them, was not being able to admit to her age. She knew why. She had always had a keen appreciation and regret at the swift passage of time. Happiness did that to you more than sadness, and Nigel's death had provided a yardstick for sadness which she would never forget.

'I'm more honest than you,' he said, smiling at her. 'I've had my forty-second birthday. I'm becoming an old man.'

'You don't look it.' Most Glasgow men of his age had developed a portly presence, a corpulence testifying to rich dinners and wine, but which they hoped gave them the dignity they sought. Ernest was as slim as a reed, agile, and when that wayward lock of his fell over one eye he could look engagingly young. And he danced beautifully. No one could whirl his partner faster than he did to the 'Merry Widow Waltz', and his tango, a new dance which had just made its appearance, was a dream of delight. 'Are you as happy as I am, Ernest?' she said. She stood close to him, raised her arms and put her hands behind his neck.

'Happier, if anything.' He smiled down on her. 'Sometimes I feel life has been too good to me. I haven't had to

226

meet any great sorrows or tribulations. I run on easy lines.'

'Perhaps because you have a light touch with it. You aren't intense, like . . . Uncle Patrick, for instance. Perhaps it's your father in you. He's always been wry.' She kissed him lightly on the mouth. 'Nor are you jolly like Uncle Terence. You're just . . .' she kissed him lightly again, butterfly kisses he called them, 'right.'

'So madam has no complaints?' He was insouciant. It was the wrong time for passion when they were both ready for their public appearance.

'None.'

'And your eyes never stray?'

'Never.' She thought she saw a shadow in his. 'Why do you say that?'

'No reason, my darling. Absolutely no reason. Shall we go down?' He touched carefully, lovingly, her superbly dressed hair.

He stood idly, occasionally passing a word to some of their guests, and watched Lizzie dancing with Alec Crichton, their banker. He noticed how Crichton looked down on her laughing face, the aware but circumspect look which sensible men reserve for pretty married women. Alec would not put a foot wrong. Besides, Catriona, his own wife, was a pretty woman too, not to be compared with Lizzie, of course, but with her own Highland charm.

Where had this seed of suspicion sprung from, and how to explain this strange feeling? Was it because of his passing years? He had always lived a day at a time, but did men begin to doubt themselves once they had passed forty? He had never been introspective nor doubting before.

'Your wife is a beautiful woman.' He recalled a conversation in the smoke room of the Glasgow Chamber of Commerce. 'I overheard someone say so at the Liberal

Club the other day. We were discussing the plainness of politicians' wives in general. I don't know what the new one's wife is like.' And Hamilton had said to him at a business dinner last night, 'I hear your wife's in with a set over at Park Terrace, a city set, rather . . . well, you know . . . they don't live as they do in Sholton.'

Of course Lizzie was admired and of course she was becoming well-known in Glasgow because of the amount of charity work she did. It was her forte. Sholton was too small to contain her. No one could organize, plan, manage the details as Lizzie could, and all done with a flair which was her own. She had not her aunt's or her grandmother's business capacity, or if she had she preferred to use it in other directions, but when she was interested in some project she was a tireless worker, and who could resist her charm?

She was constantly in demand, and his own devotion to his work at McGraths gave him little time to accompany her. Sometimes she had escorts, but she had always been honest about them. 'Mr Logan sat on the platform with me last night, Ernest. Very handsome. A power on the Stock Exchange, they say, but I'd rather have my darling.' She was no less loving, nor passionate, than she had been six years ago when they were married, no less a devoted mother to their three children.

No, he had no worries about Alec Crichton, nor Mr Logan. It was Hamilton he did not trust. He saw through his occasional asides to Lizzie, just as he saw through the business machinations of the man, but in the matter of Crawfords he was powerless to do anything about it. He had consulted his lawyer. 'I have no access to the firm's documents,' Mr Baird had said. 'You know that as well as I do, but I've studied their balance sheets as I'm sure you have. You know how many shares Sir Edward holds. I think it's on the cards that when your stepson reaches his majority Sir Edward will, to all intents and purposes,

228

have bought him out.' The boy's grandfather had not been astute enough for that one.

But he remained on their guest list, and although neither he nor Lizzie liked him, they had to put up with it. At least he hoped Lizzie did not like him. An open rift would be dangerous from Jonty's point of view. But in a few years Jonty would be asking questions if the reputation of his great English public school was of any account. The danger then was that it might be too late.

He scanned the ballroom and saw Sir Edward dancing with Catriona Crichton. Even her fey charm was having little effect on him. He was impervious to all women, except Lizzie. He had always wanted her, still did. He knew that with certainty, standing there in the ballroom with its masses of yellow in every corner, the multicolour of the swirling dancers, the skirl of the bagpipes, for they were dancing a reel.

There was young Ellie in her first year at Queen Margaret College for Women, dressed in white with her fair curls piled on top of her head. Who would not get better if they had her for a doctor? Charlie McNab would have been proud of her. What a tragedy that was, he thought. Others could have been spared easier than he, the finest man he had ever known.

And there was Maevy, dancing with Dan Johnson in a stiff-looking suit that looked unused to the occasion. Dan was happier at McGraths than in a ballroom, already cast in the role of a devoted shadow to the McGraths, but no doubt with his own feelings. He had always been an admirer of Maevy, maybe more.

She looked well, stately in her green satin with her Madonna-like face. Was it his imagination, or had she at last come to terms with Charlie's death? There seemed a new lightness about her. The McGrath women were wonderful, jewels, with the possible exception of Isobel who was not here tonight. John and she felt they could

229

not venture out much in the evenings now. The March winds could be treacherous. Would she become like Great-Aunt Caroline, a mere wraith, if John went first?

And look at the Dowager lady herself! He smiled. He had begun to call her that, three-in-one: first the young Maeve Muldoon, then the married Maeve McGrath, and now the Lady Crawford, seventy-seven and sitting like a queen there with her bevy of admirers around her paying their respects. When he saw her coterie drift off, and before they were replaced by others, he crossed the ballroom floor and sat down beside her.

'Aren't you dancing, Ernest?' she said. 'I rely on you to demonstrate to me the latest steps.' She was still beautiful. It was amazing, that richly red hair still without a shred of grey in it. True or false (he would never know, nor would anyone else), her matchless skin, her dignity set off by her grey taffeta gown and her diamonds, the family diamonds which would come to Lizzie when she died.

'I came to ask if you'd take a turn with me, your Highness,' he said smiling at her.

'Wouldn't I just like that, but the daft thing is I get a wee bit giddy sometimes, and it would never do if I disgraced you and fell flat on my face!'

'I admit I could never live that down! Well, we'll sit jecoe here and criticize everybody else. There's that woman whom Lizzie worked with on the Poor Children Appeal. Hadn't Ramsay MacDonald something to do with that?'

'Maybe so. No dress sense whatever. Will you look how that dress is bumfled round her hips! Her dressmaker should have advised her better. Lizzie, of course, makes them all look like cabbages. They won't like her any the more for that.'

'But the men will.' He did not know why he said that.

'She's like me.' She looked at him, calmly. 'She likes

230

admiration. Even when Alastair was gey ill I craved it. Men are important in our lives, Lizzie's and mine. Maevy's different. There was only ever one in hers and that's why she's finding it so dreich without him.'

'At least she's got McGraths.'

'Yes, she's a fighter. And something else will come along for her once Ellie goes off on her own. She's always been on the side of the oppressed. Now it's women she's talking about. Did you know she's joined that Women's Union in Bath Street? Ever since she heard Mrs Pankhurst speaking she's been fired.'

'No, I didn't know that.' If she put as much quiet energy into the NSPU as she did into McGraths, there would be fireworks.

'I've never been a joiner, but then I've never felt oppressed, but she thinks it's high time women got their fair share of things. She likes women, could always deal with them; Lizzie and I, well . . .'

'. . . you like men.' His eyes were on Lizzie swaying round in a waltz with the young son of Lord Duntocher who was on the board of McGraths. After that it would be Hamilton himself feasting his lascivious eyes on her. 'Well, if you're sure I can't tempt you, my lady,' he said, 'I'll go and see if I can tempt my wife. Someone else might get in before me.'

He saw the smile in her eyes. 'I've always known, Ernest, that men begin to doubt themselves when they get into middle age. You're the last one I would have thought it of.'

'Oh, I'm not immune.' He stood up, then bent and kissed her cheek. 'But I have an inestimable advantage over the others. I'm married to her.'

'May I have this dance?' he said later in their bedroom. The ball was over, the last Argyll, Daimler and Napier and even the odd carriage had rolled down the drive, the augmented Crannoch Ensemble had packed their instruments and gone home in their wagon. He came up behind Lizzie as she sat in her *peignoir* taking the pins out of her hair. It fell about her shoulders, darkly red. Her face was white against it with tiredness.

She laughed at him in the mirror. 'It's three o'clock, in the name of goodness! We ought to be asleep.'

'You owe me that last dance. I couldn't get near you for your suitors.'

'I was doing my duty with all those important people you asked, my duty as a wife.' She spoke lightly, but she saw the shadow in his eyes. 'All right, then.' She got up and came into his arms. 'You sing,' she said, 'I like to hear you sing softly in my ear.'

He spun her round the room, humming softly, and she felt him relaxing. He was tired too, but his nervous energy would not run down. He worked too hard, and it had been a long and tiring winter with further trouble with the men. Not all haulage contractors, she knew, were as amenable as McGraths. The original fifty-six hours per week had not materialized, and Lyon had had to step in and force an agreement of 62½ hours. It was Maevy who had told her – Ernest did not bring his worries home with him – and she had also read in the papers last month of the strike at Paisley under John Elliott. She knew more than Ernest gave her credit for.

Maybe she had been a little flirtatious with all these men, but she had to admit it, their admiration was heady. She needed to be assured. But why did she need to be assured when she was so loved by this man holding her?

Grandmother was the same. Now, Aunt Maevy had nothing like that in her. Constant, true, as faithful to Charlie's memory as she had been to him when he was alive.

'I think I'm a wee bit flighty,' she said, pouting. 'Or maybe you're getting too busy to tell me . . .'

'Tell you what?' He said against her cheek.

'Tell me that you love me.'

He stopped dancing to face her. 'But I'm always telling you!'

'No, you're not.' She could only say things like this because she was so tired. 'You're afraid of your own emotions, you treat them as a joke, and you've taught me to do the same. "A light touch", you're always saying . . .'

'But you know I hate heavy-handedness. And groaning and sighing . . .'

'You don't like to let yourself go, that's what it is. Maybe it's the way you were brought up. Your father's a wry man, a dry man. Or the kind of education you got in America. I'm a child of . . . passion.' She made herself say it. 'Bessie Haddow gave herself to my father, knowing he was a married man. Maybe that's . . .' He interrupted her. His voice was rough.

'You think I'm afraid . . . to let myself go?'

She looked up at him, half-afraid, half-laughing. 'Oh, I'm not *challenging* you, Ernest!' Her laughter faded at the passion in his eyes. 'Maybe we're both tired . . .' He took her in his arms, spun her towards the bed and collapsed on to it, still holding her. He turned on top of her and kissed her time and time again, like a thirsty man drinking at a burn. 'Too tired?' he said at last. They were both breathing heavily.

'Not that tired.' Their dancing and his kisses had sent the blood coursing through her limbs. They had never made love at three o'clock in the morning except in their honeymoon days in Paris. Maybe it was time . . . 'Help me off with my robe . . .'

It was a new experience in the quiet house, with only the quiet ticking of the clock. This time there were no light touches. She discovered once again the real Ernest beneath the sophistication, someone who needed reassurance just as she did. It was like mining, she thought, remembering the gentle man, Kieran McGrath, her grandfather. They were mining for love, getting to the depths of each other, in the only way, by loving.

It was a new kind of loving after six years of marriage, deeper, painful even, revealing: there were certainly the heavy groans and sighs that he had so despised. And she had to bite her lips to prevent a moan or two escaping. Although it was a big house there were servants and three children, the eldest rapidly approaching manhood.

'There, there,' she said when he lay panting beside her. 'There, there, my darling.' A dim memory came to her of being in Argyle Street on Saturday afternoon and finding a lost child. She remembered the tear-stained face, the tragic eyes, the running nose. 'Hae ye loast yer Mammy?' she had asked him tenderly. Were all men little boys?

5

He was his insouciant self the following morning at breakfast. Annabel and Kit were playing on the floor with their toys, but Jonty sat at the table with Lizzie and Ernest looking fresh and young and reminding her of Nigel with his narrow head and that patrician air. It was no longer a painful nor a reproachful memory.

He would be glad to see me happy, she told herself, and wondered if that were true. He had been her first love. Perhaps it was best not to wonder, just be glad she had now a mature love with Ernest and a token of that first love in this fine young lad facing her.

'Did you enjoy the ball, Mother?' he said politely, looking up from his plate of home-cured ham, sausages, black pudding, two eggs, fried bread and tomatoes – her eyes travelled over the array. They were sure in the kitchen 'that the young maister was hauf-starved at that school o' his'.

'It was lovely. You should have stayed down longer.' She had taken him in with her to see the start of the dancing, but he had soon slipped away.

'It doesn't appeal to me.' How like the Crawfords he was at times! 'Besides, we get lessons at school and we have to dance with each other. Once I had to partner Rolston Minor and be the lady!' He looked disgusted. 'He stood on my feet and I felt like giving him a good kick on the shins!'

'Most unladylike behaviour.' Ernest looked up from the *Glasgow Herald*. His smile was far from disapproving.

'Just wait till you're a few years older and you'll feel quite differently,' Lizzie said, and because she was still full of love, 'Your father and I had a wee dance to ourselves last night in our room.'

'Did you?' He looked surprised. 'Didn't you have enough downstairs?'

'Not of the right kind,' Ernest said from behind his paper. And then lowering it but not looking at Lizzie, 'Are you going to manage to get a cricket team together at Sholton?'

'Not a chance, sir.' Jonty shook his head. 'I sounded them out at the Sunday School but they think it's a heathenish game. They prefer "fitba'".' He laughed.

'We'll never see the green playing fields here. They prefer asphalt and a couple of jackets for goalposts. They never took to it in America either. Too slow.'

'I should like to go to America sometime,' the boy said shyly. 'I've read all Fenimore Cooper's Leatherstocking Tales, Hawkeye, Deerslayer . . .' his eyes shone.

'You can still sense the Indians there. I look forward to showing it to you soon . . . Yes, Redfern?' The butler had come in with a tray. There was an orange envelope on it.

'A telegram for you, sir.' Over the years Redfern had grown taciturn. Lizzie wondered if he resented Ernest being in Nigel's place. The Scots were funny folk, she thought, although she was one of them.

'Thank you.' Ernest took it. 'I wish they'd wait till I get to the office. Thank you.' His face showed no concern. She watched him while he tore open the envelope. Telegrams always alarmed her ever since that terrible day when she had had news of Nigel's death. They were bad omens.

'What is it?' she thought of Great-Aunt Caroline with her frail hold on life, something dreadful happening to that happy family at Woodlea . . . 'Is it bad news?'

'Very bad. It's from Uncle Patrick. You'll have to bear

236

up, my darling.' He shook his head, his face grim. 'Dreadful news.'

'Read it.' She could hardly speak. She looked at Jonty. He was too old to be told to leave. She caught his eye and tried to smile reassuringly. Her face felt stiff.

Ernest's voice was low, shocked. '"Tragic shooting accident. Kieran badly injured."' He stopped reading, as if to compose himself. '"Gaylord . . ."' his voice dropped to a whisper, '". . . dead."' He raised his head to meet her eyes.

'Oh, my God, Ernest . . .' She put her hand to her face. Kit whimpered, frightened at her tone, and she took her hands away. 'Come to Mammy.' She bent down and took him on her knee. Annabel was pulling at her skirts, distressed at her distress.

'Are you hurt, Mamma?'

'No, no. Hush, there's a good girl. Oh, Ernest, what does it mean? I can't take it in. Oh, hush, Annabel,' the child was wailing with fright. 'Look at Kit. He's not crying.'

'Come to Jonty.' The boy got up and took Annabel on his knee.

'If only we had a telephone!' Ernest said. 'Not knowing the details. Uncle Patrick said he was writing . . .' He was still holding the telegram, his face pale with shock.

'They say it's coming soon,' Jonty said, as if to make conversation, and then, 'We're taught at school never to point guns . . .' He looked from one to the other, lost. And his nice breakfast, Lizzie thought, wondering at herself.

Ernest was speaking, drowning Jonty's hesitant voice. 'We'll have to plan, Lizzie, what to do.'

'Do you want me to leave, Father?' The boy looked miserable.

'No, no. It's your family too, Jonty. Perhaps you can help us.'

'Are you going to tell great-grandmother?'

'That was in my mind, too.' Lizzie nodded. The first shock was leaving her. 'What do you think, Ernest? Shall we tell her, or wait till we get Uncle Patrick's letter? It might not be as bad . . .' But he had said 'dead'. What could be worse than 'dead'? And 'badly injured'? 'Oh, poor Aunt Maria! She's had such worries with her family. And your mother, Ernest. Kieran badly injured. I wonder *how* badly?'

'Kate will stand up to it, but she'll be fearful of the effect it will have on my father. This is when you wish the sea didn't separate us . . .' He got up and walked about the room. She had seen tears in his eyes.

If she could have wept with him it might have helped, but she was dry-eyed, and besides, she had never been an easy weeper. Like grandmother again. Gaylord, she thought . . . gone, that charming, unpredictable young man. It was unbelievable. And almost as unbelievable was the fact that Kieran, that sweet, gentle friend of hers, had been badly injured.

And with the thought of that gentleness the tears flooded her eyes. Kit was resting against her breast, enjoying the closeness, and she rocked him against her. 'Oh, dear, oh, dear,' she sobbed, 'I've suddenly thought of Kieran. He looked after Gaylord, worried about him. I think he almost gave up his own life for him . . .'

'Don't distress yourself, my darling,' Ernest said.

'When Gaylord was miserable he always sought out Kieran. They would be out walking, that would be it,' she raised her face, streaming with tears, 'or hunting, as they call it there, and there would be this dreadful accident with the gun. Maybe they stumbled . . .'

'Don't conjecture.' Ernest came round the table to her and put his arms round her and Kit. 'It will only hurt you the more.'

'Will you come and play with me in the garden, Jonty?'

Annabel said, her little face raised up to him. She had such a shrill, piping voice. Grandmother had commented on it. They must send her to Crannoch for elocution lessons . . . she was shocked at how she could even think of such trivialities at a time like this.

'All right, Mouse.' This was his favourite name for her. 'Let's go and get your ball. Would you like me to take Kit, Mother?'

'Would you?' She looked at him gratefully. 'Take him into the kitchen. The girls will make a fuss of him there.' Maybe she had been wrong not to engage a nurse. 'Oh, you're a good lad.' She put her hand on his arm. 'It isn't fair and you on your holidays . . .' He smiled at her boyishly, lost for words.

'I'm not doing anything else. Come on, Annabel. Don't dawdle, if you please.' He was the young lord for a moment. He lifted Kit from Lizzie's knee and hoisted him on his shoulder to excited squeals. 'Ride a cock-horse, to Banbury Cross!'

Ernest sat down beside Lizzie and took her hands. 'I think we should tell grandmother. It wouldn't be fair to keep it from her until Uncle Patrick's letter comes. Do you agree?'

'Yes, oh, yes.' She put her handkerchief to her eyes. She had stopped weeping. 'She'd only guess anyhow. You can never keep anything from her. We shan't show her the telegram, all the same. That would be too much.'

'No. We'll just say there has been an accident.' His lock of hair had fallen out of place again. She gently stroked it back from his eyes, thinking, and we were so happy . . .

'Do you think we should go up to her room now?'

'Do you feel up to it?'

'Yes. It's got to be done.' She liked action. She felt better on her feet. 'We'll support each other.'

Maeve was sitting up in bed with her breakfast tray which Lizzie had insisted on some time ago. She had protested against such an indulgence, but not too much. She would never have admitted it, but it had become a strain dressing to go downstairs for breakfast, and it was unthinkable that she should appear other than properly attired. Robes were a sign of sloppiness.

She looked up at her grandchildren coming into the room, heard their bright, false, 'Good-morning, Grandma!', and knew by their faces something was wrong. She fought off the knowledge for a second or two. You had to prepare yourself, gather your courage. She had done that ever since she could remember, eloping from Woodlea with Kieran, facing up to the Colliers Row women in Lady Crawford's riding habit . . . it took a little longer with each passing year.

'Well, this is nice. A visit from the two of you. What ploys have you on for today?' She made herself smile.

'We've bad news.' Lizzie came to her and put an arm round her shoulders. Trust Lizzie. She was as direct as she would have been herself.

'Tell me, then.' She gripped the handles of the breakfast tray. There, that was a little support. She raised her chin. Lizzie was looking at Ernest. He had a thin, pale skin. It looked like paper this morning.

'A telegram came from Uncle Patrick,' Ernest said. 'I'm sorry to bring you this news. There's been a shooting accident . . . Gaylord and Kieran.'

'Could I see the telegram, please?' She knew her voice was icy, but that was because her blood was running cold in this warm, comfortable room with the leaping fire in the grate.

'Do you think you should? It might distress you . . .'

'It will distress me more if I don't know as much as you do.' He took it from his pocket reluctantly. 'Thank you.' She could still read without glasses at her age and was proud of the fact. It was strange, therefore, that the words did not make sense for a moment. 'Tragic news. Shooting accident. Gaylord dead. Kieran badly injured.' She looked at them until they seemed to be engraved on her brain.

How had that son of hers managed to write such harsh words? 'Dead.' Not passed away. So final. And 'badly injured'. Did that mean close to death? Had someone written them for him? His lawyer, or James, or maybe Kate? Maria would be prostrate. What was the reason for Patrick and Maria having so much trouble with their children? Sarah was a dullish girl, far too serious, that poor little soul, Mary, had died, and now Gaylord. It was too much.

And what about Kate? How was she standing up to it? She had been luckier, certainly, with fine stepsons and stepdaughters, but now her own son 'badly injured', that gentle lad with the same name and nature as her own Kieran.

'Oh, Grandma!' Lizzie had not been able to bear the silence. 'It's terrible for you! You'll be thinking of Aunt Kate and Uncle Patrick, your own children, how unbearable it must be for them. If only we were there to help them!'

'It's hard to . . . take in,' she managed to say. 'You have to wait till . . . it settles. What's to be done, Ernest?' She had a sudden pain between her eyes which made her frown.

'I think we should wait till we get Uncle Patrick's letter. It will explain things. Though how he'll be able to bring himself to write . . . maybe someone will do it for him. In any case . . . even if we left now we shouldn't be there in time for Gaylord's funeral.'

'Unless there's an inquest.' She thought of Catherine, Terence's first wife, and the agony they had all gone through, especially Terence and Maevy. Was it the lot of all families to have such sadness? But there were the happy times. You had to hold on to that.

241

'Yes, I'd thought of that, too. I still think we should wait till the letter comes but be making our plans about who should go. Maevy and me, perhaps. Lizzie's tied with the children.'

'You both can't go and leave McGraths in the lurch. I know the trouble you're having with the men just now. *I'll* go. I have to be with my children.' She knew it was the right thing as she said it. It was nothing crossing the Atlantic now, as she had found out since Alastair died, not like when Kate had gone as nurse with the Murray-Hyslops. And think of all those pioneering women in the old Queen's time, who put up with such hardships climbing mountains and penetrating into darkest Africa, like Mary Livingstone.

'Should you?' Lizzie looked doubtful. 'You must think of yourself.'

'That's the last thing I want to do,' – she spoke sharply – 'at my age. I'm thinking of my dear son and his wife, and Kate, my Kate. Besides, it's as easy as winkie, now, just a hop, skip, and a jump. And if you can't come, Ernest, I'll take Ellie. She's on holiday just now and she would look after me fine with her medical training.'

Ernest nodded. 'We'll leave it at that. I'll talk it over with Maevy when I get to the office and make enquiries about sailings. And I'll send a telegram to Patrick from the GPO in Glasgow. I'll think what to say when I'm driving up.'

'You'll say the right thing, Ernest,' she said.

He kissed them both. 'Look after each other.' Yes, he was a fine lad. They would never know if Nigel would have turned out as well.

'You have a good husband there,' she said when the door closed behind him. 'Reliable and loving.'

'Yes, he's that all right.' Lizzie put her arms round her. 'Last night, Grandma, after the ball, we were so happy. Maybe too happy.'

'There's nothing to stop you going on being happy. This hasn't happened to you.'

'I know. And yet the tears keep coming, for them, and maybe for myself a bit. How you can't count on anything, even when you're happy. I knew Gaylord was . . . different. He . . .' She stopped herself on the point of telling Maeve about him coming into her room. She had not told Ernest. Why should she tell anyone now that he was dead? She was a married woman with three children, not a silly young girl. She had not reached this age without knowing that some men were different. The real tragedy was that he had been forced to conceal it. 'The sadness of it,' she said, her head bowed so that she should not meet her grandmother's eyes. She was sharp.

Maeve looked at the bent head, heard the sobs. Lizzie had always been tender-hearted. *Her* tears would come later. Meantime, she was still the centre, the lynch-pin of the family. When they saw her arriving, an old woman, but determined to be with them, they would know they hadn't to give in.

The lad had been a misfit, that was the tragedy. Was that why this lass was weeping so bitterly? She stroked the head of red hair, abundant and richer than her own nowadays. 'Cry it out, my lovely. Cry for him . . . and for all those who don't . . . conform.' The word came to her. It was strange, but at this age she seemed to be able to take blows better than when she was young. And understand more.

'If you'd had a nurse for Annabel and Kit you could have come to America,' she said. Scolding was better than weeping. 'I know you wanted to have them to yourself, but a husband comes first, always remember that.'

Lizzie raised her head. Her face was tear-stained but indignant. 'And who was it who advised me not to have a nurse for Jonty, I'd like to know?'

243

'It was for comfort . . . because of losing Nigel.' She was sheepish.

'You can always surprise me, Grandma, even at a time like this.' Lizzie was wiping her eyes. 'But I'll do what you say, I'll get them a nurse before they're *wasted*, isn't that what you're getting at?'

'Ah, a wee bit of wasting never did a bairn any harm, especially those two. They're a pair of beauties. Here, give me a kiss and away to them.'

She was glad she had waited till Lizzie went away before she put her head in her hands. It never did to have a crying match.

6

Maevy was appalled when Ernest showed her the telegram, but unlike Lizzie she did not weep. There was too much to be thought of. 'How did mother take it?' she asked.

'As you would expect. She's determined to go to America.'

'There's no reason why not. She managed fine before. People always give her special attention. She's that kind of woman.'

'I'll go with her, of course.'

'I can understand how you feel, Ernest. Your poor mother. She must be shocked beyond speaking about. I wonder how badly Kieran is injured? But Aunt Maria and Uncle Patrick have nothing to hope for. Maybe they've known for a long time about Gaylord.' She looked at him with clear eyes. 'Have you?'

'Yes. But you?'

'I'm still a nurse. Charlie and I talked about it, but you couldn't speak to Patrick.' She sighed. 'It's a terrible business. And just look at all those.' She pushed across the desk to him a sheaf of documents. 'It's going to be difficult for you to get away.'

'Is there still trouble?'

'It couldn't have happened at a worse time. With this strike at Paisley under John Elliott we have to take over a big part of the Paisley employers' work. You're fixed up with meetings with the Glasgow contractors and the railway companies for the next week or two, and they want you to speak at Edinburgh and Leith as well.'

'It's wages rather than hours now.'

She nodded. 'You know my feelings are with the men, but on the other hand McGraths has to remain solvent. I've never been any good at public speaking and Dan's hopeless. Lyon has fixed a meeting with the contractors next week. Edinburgh and Leith have fared better than Paisley, as it happens. Oh, there are an awful lot of decisions to be made!'

'I'll go through this lot this morning. In the meantime, would you get someone in the office to enquire about sailings and we'll make two bookings for the end of next week? That will give Patrick's letter time to reach us. Do you want to take time off to go to your mother, Maevy?'

Her eyes were steady. 'No. Lizzie's there. They've always been close. I'll work hard and get through quicker and call in on the way home. She wouldn't want me to leave McGraths in the lurch.'

'That's what she said, too.' He smiled.

'Well, she started the business. We wouldn't have been here without her.'

Kate was sitting with Kieran when the maid came in and whispered in her ear that her mother and niece had arrived. She looked at his calm sleeping face, and got up quietly. She had brought him home from hospital as soon as they had given permission and had declared him out of danger.

It was a flesh wound to the hip. There had been severe loss of blood before he and Gaylord had been found, but most of the shot had buried itself in the tree behind them during the struggle which must have taken place. She had not pushed him, but bit by bit she was piecing the story together.

She went into her mother's arms, but took her lead from Maeve – there were to be no tears – then greeted Ellie. 'I'm so very glad to see you too, Ellie,' she said, kissing her. 'I'm sorry your first visit couldn't have been on a happier occasion.'

'I'm just a deputy, Aunt.' The girl's black clothes accentuated her fairness and her slenderness. She was like and yet not like Maevy, maybe livelier, more volatile. There was a lot of Charlie in her. And she was certainly intelligent. You could see it in the steady eyes. 'Uncle Ernest was so upset when he couldn't get away. He was all for cancelling the meetings he had to speak at but Grandma wouldn't let him.'

Maeve, seated in a comfortable chair, was taking off her black gloves and folding them on her knee. There were lines of fatigue on her face but her back was straight. 'I knew you would appreciate his situation, Kate. It might have affected hundreds of men's livelihood if he'd cancelled. Maevy's not any good on a platform and Dan's running about doing the donkey work. But he'll be coming to see you just as soon as he can.'

'He's written to me. I know Ernest. He's always been good at decisions and sticking to them. How did you stand up to the voyage, Mother?' The maid had come in with a loaded tray, and this was safer talk.

'There was no "standing up" required. It would have been a right picnic if it hadn't been for the sad circumstances. How is Kieran?'

'Mending daily, thank God. I have him upstairs now. I'm used to nursing and it's easier for James. He can't get about much because of his emphysema. He's resting at the moment. You'll see him later.'

'We can wait. And how about Maria and Patrick?'

'They'll be here any minute. I told them when you'd be here. Patrick's sorry about not meeting you at the station, but he felt it would be too upsetting for Maria. She . . . fears meeting people.'

'What a sad house Claremont must be.'

'Sarah's good, always does what's required of her, and

she's a second mother to Ginny. And Terence's Robert has been a great help. His father would be proud of him. He's taken on Patrick's share of the business while he's been with Maria, and is often there in the evenings to give the household some semblance of normality, maybe, because, oh, Mother, it's like a tomb there! I remember you telling me about Terence's house at Great Western Terrace after Catherine's death and the black flatness of it.'

'And look at him now. Far happier with Honor than he's ever been. Maybe this will be the last of Patrick's troubles.'

'Let's hope so. Now, take a cup of tea and refresh yourself. Thanks, Ellie.' The girl had risen, eager to help. 'Pull that wee table over beside your grandmother. That's right.' There was a knock at the door. Patrick and Maria came in. Kate went quickly to them and embraced them, then led them over to Maeve, her arm round Maria.

'Don't get up, Mother,' Patrick said. He and Maria knelt beside her and she put her arms round them. Kate looked at Ellie. The girl's face was expressive, her eyes moist. The second family tragedy in her young life, but the first had been worse, the death of a dearly-beloved father.

'You poor souls,' Maeve said. 'I had to come. Now, get up off your knees. There, Ellie will help you, Maria, and Kate's got a nice cup of tea ready. Tea's the thing. We'll talk about what's happened because it's the best way, and see if there's anything to be done to ease the hurt.'

'That will never be eased, Mother.' Maria was sitting beside her on the chair Ellie had placed for her. What a poor soul indeed, Kate thought, all her robust beauty gone, the square chin seeming squarer because of her badly-dressed lank hair, her eyes sunken with grief and lack of sleep. And Patrick. His face was like a stone.

'Pass them some of that nice plum cake, Kate,' her

mother said. 'Little things, even a nice taste helps, to bring back feeling.'

'It's finished my mother,' Maria said. Her voice broke but she did not weep. Perhaps she had no tears left. 'We've brought her over from Springhill to be with us. Finished her.'

'No, my dear, it was losing your father that did that.' Maeve turned to Patrick. 'Kate tells me Robert McGrath is a great help to you in the business.'

'Aye, he is that.' He nodded. She noticed his hair had gone quite white since she had last seen him. Terrible, she thought. He had such grand black hair. And Terence in Ireland is grizzled, too. There was nothing which made you feel older than to have grey-haired sons.

'Perhaps you don't have the labour problems here that Ernest's having. He and Maevy are up to all hours. Sometimes I think Maevy's heart is more with the workers than with McGraths, but fortunately Ernest's even-handed. We couldn't do without him.'

'My lad's gone,' he said, his face expressionless. The finality of his words caused a silence in the room until Kate spoke.

'Yes, he's gone, Patrick. That's a terrible thing to face. A sweet lad, but with his own sorrows. Maybe he's happier where he is.'

'I can't help thinking he took his own life,' Maria said. 'The doctor says . . .'

'Leave it, Maria.' Maeve touched her arm. 'Wait till the inquest. You've lost him whatever happens. That's what you have to accept.'

'We should have talked to him more, tried to understand . . .'

'There isn't a parent alive who doesn't have the same feelings, even when their children are alive. 'If only . . .' How often I've said that. You've had a wearier time than most, you and Patrick, starting with Mary, but maybe

249

that only happens to the strong ones, those who can thole pain. Look how you supported your mother when your Uncle Gaylord died, Maria. My brother told me about that, and how he and Caroline couldn't have managed without you. And look how you crossed the ocean to be with Patrick when it wasn't so easy. You're both strong, and now you can support each other. And you have two lovely girls in Sarah and Virginia – Ginny, isn't it? I haven't got used to that new-fangled name. I can tell you, *my* girls, Kate, Maevy and Isobel, have given me as much pleasure as my sons, if not more. You have to look forward. You get back to the business, Patrick. You're laying too heavy a burden on young Robert's shoulders. We'll take care of Maria.' She looked at her. 'Have you a nurse for your mother?'

'No, I hadn't thought . . .'

'Well, Kate will arrange that. You must learn to delegate. That's a word I learned in McGraths, and also how to do it. Martyrs are no favourites of mine. And Kate and I will be on hand every day to help you through this sad time, get you back to living again. That's what families are for. And here's Ellie, just bursting to help too, full of life and halfway to being a doctor.'

'Not quite, Grandma,' Ellie protested.

Maria looked at her. 'I've scarcely greeted you, Ellie. Forgive me.'

'Oh, don't apologize.' Ellie went over to her and put her arms round her. 'I want to help. That's why I'm here. Uncle Ernest charged me with that.'

'You can sit with Kieran,' Kate said. 'He could do with a younger face than mine. And you can give him all the Scottish news. He and Lizzie used to write to each other.'

Kate insisted on her mother resting after Maria and Patrick had gone. It would be time enough to meet James at dinner, and maybe have a word with Kieran.

'You're saying that I've talked enough, is that it?'

'That's it.' Kate put her arms round her. 'You could always talk the hind leg off a donkey.' I'm going to lose her too, she thought. That will dwarf all the rest. Death was becoming part of life.

She sat down with Ellie when she was showing her her bedroom. 'Big houses,' she said, 'seem to fill up with sadness as well as happiness. It's a strange thing. If they could talk . . .'

'I know what you mean, Aunt Kate.' Ellie was unpacking her dresses and hanging them up in the wardrobe. 'Braidholme's like someone in the family, mother often says. It's got special memories because grandmother lived there with grandfather McGrath. And the Hall, well, it's even older, and look at its history, right back to Covenanting times. And now it's got three generations under one roof, as well as the heir. Lord Crawford. It doesn't sound like our Jonty, does it? It must have been difficult for Ernest at first to be there, and him not a Crawford. Do you think he ever felt . . . resented?'

'He never said. He's a realist. Never introspective. But, yes, I think Alastair might have resented him a little seeing him in the place of his own dead son, but I wouldn't blame him for that. And maybe the servants minded him a wee bit.' She still had her Scottish way of speaking after all those years, Ellie thought, although her accent was Yankee. 'They can be, well, conservative, and I've discovered how much they know about what goes on. My first hint that Gaylord was taking drugs came from my housekeeper, Mrs Vanaressi.'

'Taking drugs?'

'I'm telling you because you're a medical student. I would have told your father. He had a bad back and the doctor originally prescribed laudanum. Gaylord kept complaining and the doctor kept giving it. I don't know whether the trouble was chronic or whether he became

251

addicted. He was charming, Gaylord, and clever, and Dr Studebaker's getting old.'

'But how did your housekeeper know?'

'She's lived in Wanapeake all her life. Her husband worked at the quarries near a place called Paradise Inn, and one of her daughters was employed there. A fast New York set frequented it, I'm told, and Gaylord sometimes patronized it, unknown to Patrick and Maria, of course. This girl picked up snatches of conversation as she waited on the tables. People under the influence of either drugs or drink can be indiscreet. James and I told Kieran about it, but I think he already knew. It takes Kieran a long time to believe ill of anyone. He's loyal. But he said he would warn Dr Studebaker.'

'That's terrible. So his parents wouldn't have any idea?'

'No, and unfortunately we only got to know just before the accident. I'm praying it doesn't come out at the inquest. It will be bad enough if they find he committed suicide.'

'Like his uncle. Do you think it runs in the family?'

'Who knows. You might as well say young Robert and Terence McGrath are tainted since *their* mother committed suicide, although there's no sign of that kind of temperament in either of them. Terence is well on to becoming a fashionable painter in Paris, and a frequent visitor at Emily's house, I believe.' Kate smiled. 'To see Giselle, perhaps? Well, at least there's no blood tie there. You're bound to find out all about those things in medicine, Ellie. I'm looking forward to having talks with you. How times have changed since my young days, when the only thing I could do to earn a living was to go as a nurse to the Murray-Hyslops. Still,' her face was luminous, 'that's how I met James.'

Ellie spent most afternoons sitting with Kieran while Kate and Maeve were with Maria. He was getting up for a little each day, and she usually visited him then. She took a clinical interest in his injury and they had discussed it together.

'I'm lucky to be alive,' he told her. 'If it had hit the liver or my spine I should have been dead or paralysed, which is almost worse. As it is I'll always walk with a limp, or a stoop, or both. The hole's as big as my fist.' She would have liked to ask to see it – not that *she* would have been shocked, but she thought *he* might have been.

He was fourteen years older than her, but there was a quality of youth and even innocence about him which at times made her feel his senior. Her medical studies had quickly disabused her of any romantic notions she might have had, and she had lost a beloved father at a vulnerable time in her life. She had become, living alone with her mother, more a friend and confidante than a daughter. At nineteen she was mature beyond her years. But her saving grace was her sense of fun which she had inherited from Charlie.

'You and I will soon be able to have a waltz together,' she told him laughingly one sunny afternoon.

He shook his head. 'Even when I was fit I was never a dancer.'

'Do you mean to tell me that an eligible young man like you didn't get asked to balls in New York? I thought the ladies would have roped you in to try all that new stuff, ragtime and such like.'

'Eligible young man?' He smiled at her. 'I'm thirty-three!'

'Well, you don't look it. I know doctors of your age in the Royal Infirmary and they're very dignified . . . as if they'd never been young. And are you telling me you've never been in love?'

He laughed shamefacedly. 'No . . . well, no one here. I never gave anyone a thought because . . .' he looked away from her.

'Your heart was with another?'

'Why do you say that?' He spoke sharply, for him.

'I don't know. It suddenly came to me. I'm . . . intuitive. I get flashes of illumination. My professor says I'll make a good diagnostician, that I have a flair . . .' She decided to say it. 'It's always been Lizzie for you, hasn't it?'

'I'm not being diagnosed, young Dr McNab,' he said. She saw how his pale, indoor skin had flushed with colour. It's sad for him, she thought, if I'm right. Lizzie and Ernest were an ideal couple: he rich, handsome, obviously in love with his wife, she with her radiant beauty and that 'air' which Ellie hoped she might acquire in time. To her they were the embodiment of married love.

Sometimes she found her Uncle James in Kieran's room, and the three of them would have what she thought of as 'a grand tare' together, in spite of the sorrow which surrounded them. Kieran's father had a wryness which appealed to her. She could well see where his attraction lay for Aunt Kate, apart from the fact that he was still a handsome man with his height and fine head. It was a pity that Kieran could not acquire some of that wryness. Perhaps, she thought, it was his vulnerability, his tender nature, which had kept him in love with Lizzie for so long, a hopeless love since Lizzie adored Ernest and she was adored by him.

Her uncle provided what she missed at home, a father figure. He joked with her, sometimes fighting for breath, and he asked questions which Charlie might have asked. 'What are they thinking of back home? Don't they read? German millionaires being created one after the other because of their booming factories, and here we have Carnegie working for peace. What a paradox!' He had to stop for a second to get his breath back. 'We were warned by Jean Jaures a few years ago, and they did what they do to all prophets, assassinated him.'

'Maybe they should let women run the country,' Kieran said.

'My mother goes occasionally to Suffragette meetings,' Ellie told them proudly. 'She's a member of the Scottish Branch of the Women's Social and Political Union.'

'Good for your mother,' James said. 'I'm beginning to think it's the women who have the vision, not men. We've certainly made a sorry mess of things up to now.'

'Do you think there will be a war?' Kieran asked.

'I don't see how it can be avoided.' He stopped, said quietly, 'Ernest wasn't called up the last time, but it would be different now . . .' Oh, no, she thought, Lizzie couldn't stand it. First Nigel and then Ernest . . .

'It's evil,' she said, 'war. When I have more time I'll join something, anything . . .'

Once, when she and her uncle were going downstairs together he said to her, 'You're a good influence on that son of mine. At thirty-three his head's still in the clouds. Sometimes it's unwise, I don't say wrong, to believe the best of everyone. Hope for the best, but be clear-eyed.' She knew he was thinking of Gaylord.

She remembered his words when she found Kieran downcast the following day. 'I know what's in your mind.' She bent forward and kissed him before she sat down. 'It's Gaylord, isn't it, and what happened?'

He nodded. 'You're a wise girl,' and added, with his gentle smile, 'for your age. Yes, you're right. Some days I waken up with it like a load on my back, wondering whether I could have acted differently if . . .'

'If only. Grandma says they're the most used words in the English language. It's because you're not well yet, Kieran. It takes a long time to recover from an injury as bad as yours. Why don't you tell me about it? You know I won't talk.'

'I couldn't burden you, a young girl . . .'

'I'm older than my years, and I'm the soul of discretion.' She smiled. 'And I've taken the Hippocratic Oath.'

He said, not looking at her, 'It was when I saw him with the gun in his mouth . . .' and stopped.

'Go on.'

'It's difficult . . .'

'Not if you don't concentrate too hard. Tell me. You'll feel better.'

'He was . . . fooling . . . at first . . .' And then the words came tumbling out as if he were describing a scene in front of him. 'I got such a shock when I looked, and saw the gun . . . I knew, you see, that he was taking laudanum. My mother knew, too. I was trying to decide what was best, who to tell. Dr Studebaker was past it, due to retire. I couldn't hurt Uncle Patrick any more. He always treated Gaylord as a problem, you know, instead of a son, and so he became a problem. He's still doing the same thing, or was, up until Gaylord's death.'

'What do you mean?'

'Robert wants to marry Sarah, but Uncle Patrick has forbidden it. He has this belief that cousins shouldn't marry because of that poor child they had who died. Now, because of Gaylord, he'll feel more strongly than ever. Sarah's afraid of him. She'll try to please him. A long time ago she was obviously fond of Ernest but that was nipped in the bud. Ernest, of course, was always in love with Lizzie, although it took him longer to realize it than some . . .' He stopped abruptly. She saw the look of strain on his face.

'You should let me help you back into bed, Kieran. This isn't one of your good days.'

'No, that was a digression. I was telling you about Gaylord with the muzzle of the gun in his mouth. I watched him like a cat watches a mouse. I was being so careful, anticipating his every move – although he'd said he was only fooling – and then suddenly, I'll never be able to explain this to myself, I lunged at him, entirely without forethought as if my heart had taken control of my head. As if I'd lost control . . .' He was white-faced.

'Don't reproach yourself.' She saw his distress. 'It was the adrenalin in your body, a purely physical thing. How else would soldiers fight in battle? Generals rely on adrenalin although they may never have heard of it.'

'Nor had I, to be perfectly truthful.' He was looking at her doubtfully. 'Perhaps under another name. Still, I begin to see what you mean. But this is the terrible thing which plagues me. When I lunged at him he was still alive, and I *precipitated* his death. I must have knocked the gun, and he pulled the trigger. The full impact of the shot missed me and went into a tree.' He spoke almost in a whisper. 'I think he shot himself, deliberately, when he saw me lying on the ground.'

She was horrified. 'You only *think* that, Kieran. *He* could have got the major impact.'

'The ground where we lay was soaked with blood. His head was half-blown away.'

She closed her eyes momentarily. 'Who told you that?'

'Father. Very reluctantly. I got it out of him bit by bit. I had to know. Siegel, the boatman, who found us, told him.'

She was silent. Now she could see the two bodies, the dark wood, the blood on the grass, spattered on the bark of the trees . . .

'I shouldn't be telling you this. I forget how young you are . . .' She brushed that aside.

'If I'm not used to it I should be, will have to be. I'll see plenty of it.'

'Your father would be proud of you, Ellie.' He has a sweet mouth, she thought. There's something about him . . .

'You've got it the wrong way round. It's I who am

257

proud of *him*.' She was afraid she was going to weep. 'Gaylord's uncle drowned himself, didn't he?'

'Yes.'

'Do you think they both had a secret worry?' She had been afraid to say this to him. She and Maevy had once discussed it, fearfully to begin with, and then frankly: 'Charlie would have liked me to be frank and honest with you about everything, Ellie. I know you're just nineteen, but you're his daughter.'

'Yes,' Kieran said, 'that was the problem.' He looked straight at her. 'You can understand the drink and drugs, can't you, the escape they gave from . . . knowledge. His father missed a great opportunity. He forbade him to go to Paris. The social climate is more lenient there, more bohemian. He would have met artists and writers, people who understood him. He felt, and I agreed with him, that it was his spiritual home. His uncle, after all, found what happiness *he* could sailing a bug-eye on Tidewater Virginia.' And seeing her incomprehension, 'A small boat.'

On the day of the inquest she spent most of the time with her grandmother. James had insisted on going to support Maria and Patrick. Kieran had been a little feverish and the doctor had advised rest and quiet. 'He's worried,' Kate said to them when she came down from his bedroom.

'He's sensitive.' Maeve looked up. The lines of strain showed on her face. I should take her home soon, Ellie thought. She's tired of bearing other people's burdens.

At tea-time James came slowly into the room and sat down on his favourite chair. His chest was heaving.

'Not a word from you for five minutes,' Kate said. She got up, poured a cup of tea and took it to him. She stroked his hair lovingly. 'Drink this, my darling.' She said over her shoulder, 'Mother's a great believer in cups of tea, aren't you, Mother?' Tried and tested love, Ellie thought. 'Take your time, now. We can wait.'

He took a sip of tea. 'Didn't you . . . think of offering me . . . anything stronger?' His smile was mischievous.

'Tea first and a sandwich, then you can have your whisky before dinner. You know what the doctor says . . .'

'Moderation in all things. Yes, I know. Very dull.' He took another sip of tea. His voice was stronger as he looked at the three women. 'Death by misadventure.'

'Ah,' Maeve said, 'that's what I hoped for! Nothing to be gained . . .'

'And Patrick and Maria?' Kate asked.

'They went home relatively happy, or should I say, less sad, however you like to look at it.'

'Oh, yes, they can both live with that,' Maeve said. 'Now off you go, Kate, and tell your son. We'll attend to your husband.'

7

A few days after the funeral Ellie went to Claremont. She had had a short note from Sarah inviting her for tea. 'We must get to know each other better before you go back to Scotland. There hasn't been much opportunity during this sad time . . .'

Maeve was pleased. 'You can't sit with Kieran all the time and neglect your other cousins,' she said, 'and the sooner we return to normality the better. You and they have your lives before you. On you go, and give the lass my love.'

Sarah was waiting for her in the drawing-room at Claremont – such a grand room, Ellie thought, a symbol of Patrick's success, almost as big as the one at the Hall, and with French windows giving on to the large wooded garden, showing spring touches of yellow in the bushes. Sarah followed her to the window after they had greeted each other.

'It's beginning to come alive again,' the girl said.

'It looks even now a beautiful garden. It will be a solace to your parents.'

'If anything can be. Yes, it's very beautiful. We'll soon have the creamy blossom of the dogwood everywhere, and the rockery becomes a mass of colour.'

'Where's the rockery?' Ellie peered.

'That mass up there, to the right. It's much larger than a Scottish rockery. I think it was made with the hewn stone left over when the house was built. There's even a young larch or two in it, and stone steps leading to the wood. It'll soon be smothered with berberis and japonica and chokeberry, as well as the smaller flowers, windflowers and primulas and heathers – I don't know their Latin names.'

'You know more than I do.' Ellie smiled round at her. 'Does your father like gardening?'

'Not much, but he enjoys walking in it to admire it. We have a very competent gardener. It's a joy to mother. I'm hoping she'll get back to it soon.'

'My mother gets great joy out of ours. Is Ginny at school? I thought I might not see her.'

'Day school. She travels each morning with father to a girls' academy in New York and comes back with him in the evening, or if he's going to be too late, by train. He wanted her to have a good education, but mother is so attached to her she couldn't bear to have her at boarding school. She's her pride and joy.'

'I can see that.' There was a melancholic note to Sarah's voice. Ellie glanced at her. What age was she? Twenty-eight and not married? Grandmother had said she resembled her maternal grandmother, Caroline, lying upstairs with a nurse to look after her, hopelessly confused, 'fortunately', in grandmother's words. Caroline was never the kind to stand up to hardship, and it was better she did not know of the latest calamity. 'When my brother died she was like a house blown down by the wind,' she had said. But Sarah was only like her maternal grandmother in her small, dainty build. Her dark eyes and hair were Uncle Patrick's. And she was quietly dressed, no bows or frills . . .

'It will be a good thing when you get back to your normal life,' Ellie said, putting an arm round the girl's shoulders. 'Everybody says what a tower of strength you've been to your mother and father.'

'They've no one else. Oh, thanks, Bridey.' A maid had come in with a tea-tray, placed it on a table between two opulent sofas, curtseyed and gone out again. 'She's a girl from a family Uncle Terence knew in Ireland,' she said. 'Come and sit down by the fire, Ellie. I intended to show you the garden and our lake, but it's too raw a day.'

'Is your mother joining us?'

'No, she's asked to be excused. She has strict instructions from the doctor to rest every afternoon. She's worn out with grief, and strangely enough, she's sleeping a lot. In a way it's a good thing Grandma is so very demanding, although she doesn't know what mother has been through. I doubt if she even realizes Gaylord has . . . gone.' Her voice trembled.

'How is Robert?' Ellie said, to change the subject. 'I've seen him a few times but we haven't had much conversation. I suppose he *does* recognize me! I was a gawky little school-girl when he left Scotland.'

'*You'd* never be gawky.' She handed Ellie a cup of tea.

'Oh, rubbish!' She was pleased. 'I understand he's a great help to your father.'

'Oh, he's that!' She did not smile. 'Father couldn't have managed without him, but, being father, he wants to keep him in his place.'

'In his place?' She looked at Sarah over her cup, surprised. The small face was a muddy white, the eyes sunken. She should be resting, too. She was pleased to see that she was developing quite a professional observation. 'But he's your cousin!'

'Yes, he's my cousin. That's the difficulty.' She looked into the fire.

'Doesn't Uncle Patrick like him?' she ventured. She remembered the quiet seriousness of Robert, very little charm.

'As a partner in McGraths, yes, a man after his own heart, hard-working, devoted to the good of the firm, able to take responsibility, a true McGrath with none of his father's . . . unreliability. But not as a suitor.' Her voice quickened, she turned to Ellie a pitiful face. 'I had to confide in someone. Ginny's too young, and Abigail and Victoria are wrapped up in their children. Abigail's mother, Mrs van Dam, rules Abigail, as well as Wanapeake, and Victoria . . . well, she's not at all like her sister in Paris. All that glitter went to her.'

'A brilliant little humming-bird . . . that's what grandmother and my mother called her.'

'And Victoria's a wren, a contented little wren on her nest, with Jason feeding her and the children. Oh, I'm letting myself go, please forgive me.'

'I think that's what you need to do, Sarah.' Ellie put down her cup and touched her cousin's hand. 'I'll treat anything you say to me with the strictest confidence.' She felt as if she were sitting behind her father's desk in his consulting room, even that he was helping her to say the right thing. She said, gently, 'Has Robert proposed to you?'

'Yes, a long time ago. I'll tell you the truth, Ellie. I don't have an overpowering love for him. I haven't a passionate nature like grandmother, and perhaps Lizzie, I discovered that with Jack Henken. The only time I fell head over heels in love was with Ernest and he didn't even notice me.'

'Oh, I'm sure he did . . . but I think it was always Lizzie for him.'

'Yes, they're right together, I see that. I'm not . . . exciting enough. When Robert came to work here and Ernest went to Scotland, I knew that was the end. You'd think I could look further afield than cousins, but father has never liked entertaining much, and I've never had the good fortune to go out into the world as you're doing. Even Ginny has been sent to school in New York . . . so, I know it must seem very dull, I began to spend more and more time with Robert.'

'Do you love him?'

'I love him, yes, but I'm not *in* love with him. He says

263

that doesn't matter, that it would come with married life. Perhaps he's right. What do you think, Ellie? You're an outsider to our family here. You'll see things clearer. Your mother and father were always in love, weren't they? My mother says they never saw past each other.'

'Yes, I think that's true, but I don't think their kind of love happens very often. Most marriages are what Grandma calls the make-do-and-mend kind. And she says they can be very happy, too. I think in her case her true love was my grandfather McGrath. Lord Crawford was a good second-best.'

'I can't marry Robert till I see Mother better and, this is a terrible thing to say, until Grandmother is safely dead and off our hands . . . but even that's not the important part.'

'Is it your father?'

'Yes,' she said bitterly. 'Well, of course everyone knows my father and how dogmatic he is. He won't countenance cousins marrying. You probably know why. If I married Robert he'd probably disown me. He might even put him out of the business.'

'Oh, he'd never do that!'

'You don't know him.'

'Maybe . . . Gaylord's death will have softened him.'

'Or convinced him. A confirmation of his beliefs, don't you see? The trouble lies with me, too. I'm not adventurous. If I had done as Grandma did, run away with Robert, I should have been tortured with guilt. Ginny, I know already although she's only fourteen, would be entirely different. She would put herself first. She's not afraid of father because she was in a way a gift, a special gift after their worries with my sister who died, and she's perfect in their eyes. She can twist him round her little finger.'

'Anyone can change their nature if they want to.' What would her father have advised? Her borrowed omnipotence left her and she was a vulnerable nineteen again.

'Don't you think you should wait for a little, Sarah? It's too soon after Gaylord to do anything definite. You leaving the house, for instance, would be the last straw, and if, as you say, your father might put Robert out of the business, what would you live on? And, think of your mother.' She saw with startling clarity the wisdom of her decision to study medicine. It had not been a conscious move on her part: it had evolved, naturally. But how wise it had been. She was her own woman, not a chattel. And mother was so right to fight for the rights of women. This state of affairs, a girl of twenty-eight being afraid of her father, should not be tolerated. 'Perhaps you could confide in her, Sarah,' she said.

The girl shook her head. 'No, she follows father in everything.'

'Well,' she was at a loss, 'why not give it a month or so and then see what the situation is like? But don't spoil your own happiness. You'll be here after your mother and father aren't. It's your life.'

But she felt she had failed Sarah. She did not answer, looking into the fire, and then giving a deep, quivering sigh. Her face was white and strained when she turned to Ellie. 'That's enough of me.' Her mouth trembled in a smile. 'Tomorrow I've to take you to Abigail's house, then Victoria's. They want to get to know their Scottish cousin.'

Sarah had painted a pretty accurate picture of the two younger households. Abigail was plump, jolly and with a commanding presence already, probably inherited from the great Mrs Van Dam. George was happily henpecked and obviously proud of his buxom wife and brood of children, Polly, Sam and Zach who, with a large collection of pets, seemed to spill all over the house, the garden and their parents. They were the picture of married bliss, contented, even smug, with little understanding or wish to understand how other people lived.

265

Victoria and Jason seemed to have the same attitude, but while perhaps eclipsed by the exuberance of the Van Dam children since theirs were so quiet, they could measure five against their three, which consequently required a larger establishment with a larger staff of servants. Jason Vogel was from a richer family than the Van Dams, if not so long in heredity or so illustrious. While enjoying the company of Abigail and Victoria, Ellie soon realized there would be no help for Sarah from those two satisfied young matrons.

Ellie spoke to Kieran about Sarah the day before she and her grandmother left for Scotland. 'If she's not careful she's going to ruin her life,' she said, when they were walking slowly along the flagged paths of the grounds. He could now manage short walks, albeit painfully, with the assistance of two sticks.

'*You* would never behave as Sarah is doing,' he said. She took it as a criticism.

'I don't know how I'd behave,' she said, 'but at least I'd always have my work to fall back on, I hope.'

'You really believe in a career for women?' Was he teasing her? 'Look at my mother. She's contented enough.'

'You forget she did work till she married your father, and that there weren't the same opportunities for her. Besides, she's one in a thousand, a truly happy woman. For those of us like grandmother and my mother, and myself – maybe the discontented ones – we need . . . something else.'

'And what about Lizzie? Where does she fit in?'

'Now, that's difficult.' She slowed her steps even more to accommodate his. 'I can't place Lizzie. She's got character, charm, beauty and brains. Maybe she's too well-endowed. Sometimes I think she could have been an actress, but that's regarded as even worse than being a doctor. I reserve judgement about Lizzie. Time will tell.'

'What a wise head on such young shoulders!'

She thought he was laughing at her. 'Do you feel me young?' she asked him. 'I'm not aware of it.'

'Not when you're talking. You're like Socrates himself. But when I look at you, so *very* young, so untouched . . .' He stopped in the path, leaning on his sticks, smiling at her.

'Don't laugh at me, please.'

'I'm not. I'm loving you, my sweet, wise, young cousin. Kiss your old cousin, Ellie. If I took my hands away I'd fall on my face. He loves you very much.'

She came close to him and put her mouth against his. She did not know whether to make a kissing sound or not. It was the first time she had felt the mouth of a man.

8

Lizzie was sitting in the drawing-room alone over the tea things. It was past five o'clock, but she had not got the energy to move. Ernest would soon be home, and she had her news for him. He was never exuberant, but surely he would show quiet satisfaction. After all, it was his exuberance and passion, and her own, she reminded herself, which had resulted in her paying a visit to the doctor's surgery today.

She had asked to see young Colin Thomson. Maybe it was a slight to Belle Geddes, but she never felt comfortable in her presence. Aunt Maevy evidently felt the same, and no wonder. That terrible accident on the Sholtie Brae must have bitten deep into her soul. She never met Dr Belle at Braidholme. She had always thought her aunt had shown considerable courage in agreeing to her continuing in the practice.

He was a nice lad, Colin Thomson, tall, chestnut-haired, broad-shouldered, a hint of a farmer in him, which was not surprising as his father had a fine farm beyond Crannoch. Colin had been the brainy one of the family – his mother was a schoolteacher – and had been sent to the Glasgow High School and after that to the University. He was quite unlike Charlie, sunny and open where Charlie had been quietly smiling and complex, but then Aunt Maevy would never have had anyone who resembled Charlie in the practice. It would have hurt too much.

Young Dr Thomson had welcomed her with boyish pleasure. 'Well, Mrs Murray-Hyslop, this is a nice surprise. I wish all my patients looked as blooming as you do.' His look had been admiring, and so it should, as she had taken the trouble to dress herself in a tightly-buttoned jacket and skirt of green barathea – maybe the last time she would be able to wear it. The discreet neckline of the high-boned *écru* lace blouse counteracted in its modesty the figure-fitting of the suit. After all, it was a visit to the doctor's, not an afternoon tea party. But she could not resist tilting her neat boater of green straw well over her left eye. There was no fun in wearing them straight.

'Oh, I'm feeling fine, Dr Thomson. It's just . . .' she told him as delicately as she could what it was 'just'. She remembered him not so long ago winning the running prizes at the Kirk Sunday School picnics, and she felt she had to spare him too much detail.

He surprised her by his polish and complete lack of embarrassment. 'There is very little doubt, Mrs Murray-Hyslop, as I suppose you know yourself. You're pregnant. Seven weeks, I should say. I'll give you an exact date to look forward to. Would you like me to examine you? I could call in Dr Geddes.'

'No, no thanks.' Belle Geddes would take a poor view of that. 'You're only confirming what I thought.'

'You'll be very pleased, then, I'm sure, and so will Ernest, I mean, Mr Murray-Hyslop.' He was charming. 'Three fine children and a fourth on the way, a nice quiverful . . .' he grinned, showing his youth, and his fine white teeth, 'Sorry! Maybe it *won't* be a quiverful!'

'I hope it is. Four's quite enough these days. I'm a very busy woman. Luckily I've a good nurse for the two younger ones, and Jonty's at prep school and will go on to Eton, like his father.'

'Ah, yes, I knew the Honourable Nigel. I remember him visiting our farm with his father when I was a boy. So distinguished. Such a tragedy. Luckily I was too young. . .' Maybe he saw her slight frown. 'So you won't have to give up so much, then, having a nurse.' And as he helped her on with her fur wrap, for the spring was chilly and it had to get an airing even in Sholton, 'How is Lady Crawford keeping?'

'She's in fine fettle, thank you. You know she took Ellie with her to America recently. We had some bad news in the family.'

'Yes, Mrs McNab told me. A sad business. Ellie would look after your grandmother, though, if I know her. She comes in here from time to time, to tell me how to run things!'

'Aye, she's like her mother, throughgawn. Did you know my aunt's now involved with Votes for Women?'

'The Suffragettes?' He smiled charmingly. 'As a mere man, I'd lend them my support if they needed it.'

'I read about a Men's League in the *Citizen*. "Their poodles of the male sex", it called them,' she laughed, enjoying her conversation with this young man, 'though I don't think anyone would ever call *you* a poodle.'

'More like an Airedale.' He laughed with her. 'Yes, it's high time men realized women aren't inferior objects.'

Lizzie felt faintly envious of Aunt Maevy with all her ploys, and here she was at thirty-three having another baby. Still, her face softened, there was no pleasure without pain, and that night after the ball had been more than pleasure. Sitting opposite this young, fresh-faced farmer-cum-doctor, she knew he had noticed her expression by his masculine look, quickly disguised as he looked down at his papers then up again. 'Well, I don't think I have to give you any advice, Mrs Murray-Hyslop, but I'd like you to keep in touch with me during the next six months or so. Lead a healthy life with plenty of exercise. I don't believe in women putting their feet up. It's a perfectly natural process.' Men, she had thought, smiling at him as she pulled on her gloves. I wonder if they'd say the same if *they* were in the throes of it . . .

There was a knock at the door and she said, 'Come in.'

Cathy would want to clear the dishes and she must get upstairs and tidy herself for Ernest coming home, as well as look in on the children at their nursery tea. The new nurse expected it. That one sometimes put the fear of God in her, and how she missed those rough and tumble games she had had with Annabel and Kit before this wonder came!

'Sir Edward Hamilton, Madam,' Cathy said. The burly figure came from behind her, hat and cane in hand.

'Forgive the intrusion, Lizzie. I was on my way home . . .'

'Take Sir Edward's things, Cathy.' She hid her surprise. 'Can I offer you a cup of tea?'

'No, thanks. I mustn't wait.'

'Sit down for a minute.' She wondered why he had come.

'I really wanted to have a little business talk with your husband. I didn't realize it was only five o'clock.'

'Ernest doesn't get in much before seven, I'm afraid. He's a hard worker.'

'Not like some people, is that the way of it?' He smiled at her. There was never much mirth in his smile, she thought. It was as if the muscles round his mouth obeyed him, but not his eyes.

'Oh, I wasn't inferring anything,' she said hastily, 'but Crawfords is so much bigger in every way than McGraths. You probably have only to be there in an . . . advisory capacity.'

'Well, a little more than that. Lord Crawford left me in control, you may remember. I have a few papers for his grandson to sign. I thought your husband could deal with the matter. It's hardly your territory.'

'It is if it concerns my son.'

'Don't worry. May I say, Lizzie, that anything to do with you and therefore your son always receives my most careful attention.' She felt uneasy. And why did his eyes rest on her face and forget to leave it . . .? Well, of course she knew. She was not a simpleton.

'Ernest keeps a close watch on Jonty's affairs,' she said. She did not know how this conversation had sprung up. Maybe it was because she was faintly disturbed at the confirmation of her pregnancy and unduly sensitive. She needed Ernest, his lightness. He would laugh with her, remove her doubts, make the prospect seem altogether delightful. *And* see through this man in two shakes of a lamb's tail.

'I'm sure he does.' His voice was icy. 'Of course you must remember that Lord Crawford did not recognize him in his will. Perhaps he resented him taking the place of his son.'

'I would prefer if you did not bring my first husband into the conversation.' Her disturbed frame of mind over her pregnancy surfaced and combined with the unease she felt. Why had this man arrived at this particular time? What had he to tell Ernest that was important, to Jonty, if not to her? He had always been a thorn in her flesh.

'Please forgive me. If I'd known it would upset you . . .' He did not look contrite. 'When I see you with Mr Murray-Hyslop, I think of Lord Crawford and how he had hoped that perhaps *I* would be your. . . helpmeet. I was his mainstay before he died. I knew his wishes . . .' Had be been drinking? She imagined she caught a faint smell of brandy in the room. She held up her hand.

'You seem determined to be offensive,' she said. 'I'd be pleased if you'd leave.'

'I'm sorry, oh, I'm sorry, Lizzie!' His face became a dark red. 'My tongue runs away with me. And this is a special day.' There seemed to be some kind of exhilaration behind his words. He got up and sat down beside her on the sofa. She had been right. She caught a faint whiff of spirits. 'I wouldn't offend you for the world.' He took her hands. 'You know how I feel about you. Why do you think I've never married? Sometimes I can't bear that great barn of a place up the river on my own. Haunted by thoughts of you. Work has had to be my salvation, ambition has comforted me. Today has been the culmination of my hopes, but it hasn't brought me happiness, it hasn't brought me . . .'

She got up. She was trembling. 'It'll be difficult to forget . . . your attitude. I've never given you any reason . . .' He was on his feet beside her, far too close to her . . .

'Lizzie, it was because of you . . .' He stopped short. In the doorway, looking at them, was Ernest.

'Oh, it's you, Edward,' he said. 'They didn't tell me.' He came forward and shook hands, then looked from one to the other. 'Am I interrupting something? A quarrel?' He smiled. 'Exciting news?' He turned to Lizzie. 'Are you trying to winkle some money out of Edward for one of your charities?' He kissed her lightly on the cheek.

'No.' She shook her head, tried to convey a warning with her look. 'I think Sir Edward has something to say to you. I'll go upstairs.'

'Are you all right, my darling?' His eyes were keen.

'Yes, perfectly all right. I'll say good afternoon, Sir Edward.' She did not hold out her hand, and hoped she swept out of the room with suitable aplomb. Her hands were trembling.

She went up the wide staircase burning with anger. What was behind the man's strange behaviour? Resentment, or drink? And had he found a way to pay her back through Jonty? Oh, her father-in-law had made a great mistake trusting him with Crawfords, a firm established by his grandfather, with each son of the family taking charge as he became old enough. He's killed it, she thought, he's taken Jonty's inheritance away from him because of me. She had to stand outside the nursery for a few moments to collect herself.

'The children thought you were never coming, Madam,' the new nurse said severely. 'I've had quite a job keeping them happy.'

'Well, you'll just have to give me a good spanking, won't you?' She looked coolly at this paragon of virtue whom grandmother had helped her to engage. She would have to get to work on her and make her more human.

'Go on, Jane,' Annabel said, looking up from nursery tea, her mouth ringed with strawberry jam. 'Spank Mammy!'

'*Mummy*,' the estimable Jane said. 'Mammy isn't quite . . .' She got up with a wet cloth and wiped Annabel's face briskly. 'It's "spank *Mummy*".'

'Well, that's what I said, isn't it? Go on . . .'

'Mammy, Mammy, Mammy!' Kit looked up from his tea, oblivious to the niceties as practised in the best nurseries. She swept him into her arms.

She waited anxiously for Ernest to come up, lying on her day bed in a lacy *peignoir*. She thought it gave the appropriate sorrowing impression.

'You look like Sarah Bernhardt,' he said when he came into the room. 'Are you trying to seduce me?'

'Do I have to try?' She forgot her pose and sat up. 'Tell me what happened downstairs.'

'It's as I feared.' He sat down on the edge of the bed. 'Crawfords has been made a public company. Jonty won't suffer financially, nor will you or grandmother for that matter, but the continuity's broken. Another link with the past broken. I suppose Jonty could insist on a seat on the board when he's old enough, but that's the extent of it.'

'I feared it too. It's the end, then, of Crawfords as we knew it. Grandma's told me often about Nigel's grandparents at the Sunday School picnics, and the pomp and the ceremony. The whole village looked up to them. Oh, she'll be sad. It's over, the old days. She'll be sad for Jonty's sake.'

'Maybe not so sad. She's practical. Everything comes to an end, and if it doesn't before this war rushing towards us, it will after that – family firms, old methods, inheritances, even houses like this. Oh, they'll go on, but different folks will live in them, jumped-up industrialists like Sir Edward . . . Look at that Baroque monstrosity he's living in just now . . .' But she was not thinking of Sir Edward. Ernest had said 'war'.

'You don't think there's another war coming? Oh, they couldn't be so cruel.'

'We don't count, but if it comforts you, I won't talk about it. You've suffered enough with wars, God knows, but I'm sorry for Jonty.'

'He's too young for wars, it's you!'

'And I'm too old. Your cheeks are burning, my sweetheart. Is it Sir Edward who's upset you?'

'I'm going to cut him out of our life!' She was thoroughly upset. This was going to be such a lovely evening . . . 'I should have done it long ago.'

'He's in love with you, poor chap. I've always known it. What a good thing you didn't marry him. It would have been like living with Crannoch Crag!'

'Oh, Ernest!' She put her hand to her face. He could always make her laugh.

'You haven't encouraged him, have you? I thought you were standing devilishly close to each other when I came in.'

'How can you say such a thing to me?' she said, 'and me still head over heels in love with you and going to have your child!'

'What did you say?' He took her by the shoulders.

'You heard me. You can't dance in the bedroom at three o'clock in the morning and expect nothing to come of it.'

'Oh, Lizzie, my Lizzie.' His arms went round her, and he held her close. 'Do you mind?'

'A wee bit, to be honest. But on the whole, I don't. I saw young Colin Thomson today. I'll have *him* the next time, not Belle Geddes. Do *you* mind, about another baby, I mean?'

He shook his head. 'I'm delighted. There's room in my heart for as many reproductions of you as you can manage. But bearing in mind that you're a beautiful woman and you don't want to spend your life in maternity gowns, I think we'll stop at this one.'

'Well, no more dancing,' she said.

He said he would go and have his bath, then he was going to sit down and write to Jonty and his lawyer before dinner.

'Should I go and tell Grandma?' she asked.

'Yes, about the baby, but not about Crawfords. I thought she looked tired when she got back from America, in spite of her brave face.'

'Well, lie down beside me for two minutes and tell me nice things about myself, and the baby . . .'

'You are a seductress.' He smiled at her but stretched out alongside her. 'Let me see . . .' His voice was soft. 'There was once a happy couple called Lizzie and Ernest who lived in a lovely house by the river. The husband wasn't completely happy because it had never been *his* house, and so if it ever came that they had to move out he wouldn't mind because he would build another one for them and for their beautiful children, including the newest one called . . .'

'I never knew you felt like that about the Hall, Ernest,' she said.

'Oh, you were more important, always will be to me, but yes, I minded a little. A man wants to provide for his own. To go on with my story . . . Living further up the river was a dragon in his big turreted castle and he was so envious of the happiness of this lovely couple that he did everything to destroy them, and their house. He carried horrible tales, but nothing he said to Ernest made any difference because his love was as strong as steel . . . not Crawford's steel.'

'So he took his trusty sword and hacked the dragon to pieces?'

'No,' he said, 'you're wrong. He used his own love to make him understand the dragon's love, which although it was thwarted love was true enough to the dragon. But he took care to guard his beautiful children and his beautiful wife, and hoped that some day the dragon would meet a lady dragon who would mend his sore heart . . .'

'Oh, Ernest,' she said, 'you make me ashamed . . . but I'm still going to cross him off my visiting list.'

9

The summer was over, Maevy thought, and now there were only the short dark days of winter ahead. It had been a year of strikes, dockers, miners and railwaymen, and also grumblings of an even deeper kind of unrest in Europe.

Charlie would have been able to explain to her why money from British investors was pouring abroad to undeveloped countries like India and China and wages at home were reduced, but it was not difficult to see why the workers felt they had to come out on strike.

He could have interpreted her unease for her both at home and abroad, calmed her fears with his balanced outlook, relaxed her with his music. She rarely went to orchestral concerts these days, the pleasure had been in sharing. She would never again know anyone with such a breadth of vision. She would always miss him.

Once, long ago, two years after Charlie's death, when she had been obliged to go to London for the firm, she had accepted an invitation to go to a concert at Covent Garden. The business associate, a middle-aged man, had been circumspect and attentive. He had told her politely how lucky they were to be at such an affair in the presence of the King, no less, and with such wonderful singers as Madame Tetrazzini and Madame Melba. The tickets had come to him by a strange chance.

But, suddenly, in the middle of 'I Pescatori di Perle', when the wonderful voice of John McCormack was filling the auditorium, she had been seized with such a fit of weeping that she had to excuse herself and hurry out.

She had never forgotten the man's understanding as he

joined her in the foyer. 'There is no need to apologize, Mrs McNab. I know only too well how grief can catch you unawares. My wife died last year.' He had taken her to supper afterwards, and they had listened to each other.

There had been compensations this summer, blessings in plenty. Ellie had been on holiday from Queen Margaret's, and her bright presence had filled the house. She was an ideal daughter, communicative and yet independent, reminding her often of Charlie in her definite opinions and yet her lack of aggressiveness. She had a rare degree of tolerance in one so young.

Together they had gone 'doon the watter' to Rothesay, where the Women's Freedom League had summer headquarters, and, greatly daring, had both accepted bundles of *The Vote* and sold them along the front. Ellie had been in her element; Maevy had been at first shy, then, scolding herself for being 'a big wean', as they would have said in Sholton, had added her cries to Ellie's. 'Buy *Vote*! Votes for Women! No taxation without Representation!' As she had confided to Ellie in the tearoom when they were resting from their labours, it was as good as a shot in the arm.

Together they had made little expeditions: sad ones, to the manse where Isobel and John had to be comforted. Belle Geddes had diagnosed cancer in John – it was Ellie who told her this, not her brother-in-law, who remained in ignorance of his condition, and still thought he 'just wasn't quite so sprightly these days'. 'Not to be wondered at, Maevy, in someone who has devoted his whole life to the parish with very little thanks.'

Isobel, deprived of his constant chivvying since his appetite had gone – 'If you'd eat a decent meal as I do . . .' – seemed lost, a pathetic figure who went out less and less. 'I try to tempt him with nice dishes, Maevy, even go into the kitchen and make them myself, but he turns them away. If only Charlie had been here he would

279

soon have made him better.' And he would have made me better, too, she thought, while she comforted her faded sister.

'He's running down a little, Isobel. We all are. What age is John now? Fifty-eight? He's bound to feel weary at times.'

'Maybe he should think of retiring. He seems to forget I've been at the constant beck and call of the parish, too, for all those years. We both need a rest.'

'He should mention it at the elders' meeting. Drop a hint or two. You could retire into a nice wee cottage in Sholton and enjoy yourselves.' They'd never do that, she thought. They hadn't the capacity, nor the length of time . . .

The happy visits were to the Hall. Maeve, thinner since her visit to America and not so full of vitality, always welcomed them. She had taken to staying more in her room overlooking the garden, but as always it had taken on her personality – bright flowers, a glowing fire, mementoes here and there of her visits to Paris, Ireland and America, photographs in silver frames of the family. She had a spirit lamp and a silver kettle for making tea, some delicate china cups, and she kept a box of fancy biscuits in a drawer. She could make it seem like a picnic.

Jonty was there sometimes, and he and Ellie were firm friends despite the difference in their ages, making expeditions on their bicycles into the countryside, and seeming to have a lot in common. Ernest said he had taken the loss of his inheritance very sensibly, and had even said he was glad. Now his future was not mapped out for him. He might travel for a year before he went to Oxford, as his father had done. The young had different ideas now, Maevy thought. The Edwardian age of leisure had gone. This was one of experiment, and the world was growing smaller.

Lizzie was keeping well and looking more beautiful

than ever in her sixth month of pregnancy, her face fuller, her hair a richer copper, her eyes bright. She loved and was loved. It was evident in her every gesture towards Ernest, and his to her, a truly happy marriage. She would never envy Lizzie.

Besides, she had her own interests. Today she was going to stay on in Glasgow after work and have tea in the Women's Freedom League tearoom in Sauchiehall Street, browse amongst their books and then go to a meeting to be addressed by none other than the great Flora Drummond, 'The General'.

She had joked about it with Colin Thomson when she had met him in the village this morning, out on his rounds. 'Women are allowed in free, but men have to pay 2/6d. There, that ought to put you in your place for once.'

'But I'm in favour of the Movement,' he had said. 'I believe Mr Graham Moffat has started a Men's League. I remember seeing his play at Crannoch, *Bunty Pulls the Strings*.'

'His wife's an actress. There are a lot of actresses interested, and artists . . .'

'Well, they couldn't look smarter than you do this morning,' he had said. She had stepped to the train on light feet.

She was pleased with her appearance, a pale blue linen costume which set off her fair hair, a white boater with a blue ribbon, white gloves. She remembered Eunice Murray saying when she came to speak at Crannoch – and incidentally fired Maevy to take part in the campaign – 'You must always remember, ladies, you are representatives of a dignified body of women, a new breed, and dress accordingly.' (Hadn't she long ago, when she had worked in the Royal, thought of herself as a New Woman?) 'We must destroy the image of a crowd of ugly, badly-dressed women wielding gamps and shouting vociferously . . .'

When she had joined the 'Scottish Scattered', she had begun at the same time to take a renewed interest in clothes. Lizzie and her mother were her arbiters of taste. She took to discussing her costumes with them, and found their advice greatly helpful, Lizzie bemoaning only that she had to go around in 'bags' herself because of the coming baby.

She thoroughly enjoyed the meeting. Flora Drummond, with her tartan plaid, her diminutive stature but her tremendous personality and rousing words, convinced her even more of the justice of their cause. And where else could a woman of her age go unaccompanied? This was something for women, women in their own right, who were trying to make something of their lives and were determined on recognition.

She joined in the singing, went to the bazaar afterwards and bought some curios at the stall, and engaged in talk with some of the members from the Art School. She felt as smart as they looked, and left the hall full of enthusiasm. She had found something which would help to fill the gap in her life left by Charlie. Hadn't she vowed never to hang on to Ellie, to give her independence, and wasn't that what she herself was fighting for?

Girls of Ellie's age would thank her. Maybe, she thought, walking down Union Street towards Central Station, she would offer her services to the Scottish Federation of the NUWSS, the National Union of Women's Suffrage Societies, to give it its proper name. It embraced all the non-militant suffrage organizations, and through it she would meet other women in other towns and cities; maybe she would go to London and hear the great speakers there, even the Pankhursts. She was walking on air as she stepped into Gordon Street and then into the Central Station to catch the train back to Sholton, a New Woman.

When she chose a compartment and went in, Belle

Geddes was sitting there, smart in a black and white outfit, her black hair gleaming under a small white hat. There was no colour about her except for her red mouth, her cheeks were matt and pale, her eyes that odd silver-grey. They narrowed when they saw Maevy, presumably with pleasure, for she smiled.

'Good-evening, Mrs McNab. How are you?' She was composed. She showed no surprise.

'Very well, thank you.' Maevy hid hers. And her embarrassment. She could not turn and go out of the compartment. Since they were the only two occupants she had not got the excuse that it was crowded. She sat down, resigned. 'It's not often we meet like this.'

'We're both busy women.' Belle Geddes smiled. 'I saw you tonight at the meeting.'

'Did you?' That was a further surprise. 'I didn't see *you*. Are you a member?'

'Oh, yes. I have been practically since its inception. I'm with the WSPU. I find the Women's Freedom League a bit mealy-mouthed for me.'

'Do you?' She would not be drawn into an argument. 'You'll approve of the militant campaign in London, then?' She would, of course. Belle Geddes was used to getting her own way. She hoped Ellie would not lose her femininity when she became a doctor. Not that Dr Belle had, to give her her due. She was not so voluptuous in figure now, but her mouth had still a rich curve and her perfume was obtrusive in the confines of the compartment.

'It's the only way of bringing the question to the public notice. Women have been working for their suffrage for over sixty years. Even you, by becoming a nurse in the Royal, did your bit. But it didn't get us the vote. I know your brother-in-law preaches that the meek shall inherit the earth . . . well, eventually, perhaps, but some of us haven't time to wait for that.'

'Maybe not,' Maevy said. 'I've always wanted peace.'
The train was trundling through the suburbs of Glasgow,
and she thought how quickly she and this woman had got
down to talking about essentials. No feminine fripperies
here.

'Women have always wanted peace, Maevy.' She had
discarded her title. 'We're the peacemakers. But where
has it got us? I've been reading a lot on this subject. Kier
Hardie, for instance. He thought Burns gave him more
true socialism than Marx. Though there's not much time
left to read after surgeries and evening visits.'

'I know.' She felt strangely friendly towards her in this
lighted box now speeding past the winding wheels and
bings in the wastelands between Glasgow and Sholton.
'There isn't much time in a doctor's life.' Charlie relaxed
by playing the piano, she wanted to say, but could not
bring herself to use his name to this woman. The last time
they had been alone together was that terrible time when
Belle Geddes had called after Charlie's death and she had
been half-mad with grief. But her resentment had died
long ago. Maybe it was time to make amends. 'Maybe
you could recommend a book to me,' she said. 'I like
something to read at night in bed.'

'What I'm reading just now might surprise you.' Belle
smiled at Maevy. 'It's about slaves on the ships plying the
Atlantic. It makes gruesome reading, but you've to face
up to things, however bad.' '*I know*,' she had said, on
that terrible night when she had come to Braidholme,
'*that you can't stand the sight of me. I don't blame you
. . .*' 'They erected round them a barricade seven feet
high, with spiked nails at the top and two bolt-holes for
swivel guns. That was to keep them in order. There were
bare boards for them to sleep on in tiers, one for the men,
one for the boys and the lowest one, note that, for women
and children. No blankets, only ledges to keep them from
rolling off.'

'That's terrible,' Maevy said. And to hide her distress, 'It's not very pleasant night-time reading.' She looked at Belle Geddes. Her eyes seemed to have silver lights in them, her jet earrings swung as she shook her head.

'No, nor conducive to sleep, but then, for a long time, I've suffered from insomnia . . .' There was a silence. Six years ago I'd have said, 'Devil mend you,' Maevy thought. No longer. 'As they were brought on to the ship, the men were immediately fastened together two by two by handcuffs, and irons riveted on their legs. The women weren't ironed, but they were so closely packed that they had to lie on their sides . . .' She took a deep breath, looked at Maevy. 'There was a man called John Newton who had once been a captain on a slave ship and then became a clergyman. He described this packing of poor souls in quite a poetic way.' She smiled. ' "Like books on a shelf," he said. Pretty, isn't it?' She shrugged. 'Well, I'd better stop. Doctors sometimes forget other people haven't their stomachs . . .'

'I'm well able to stand it.'

'Yes, I haven't forgotten you were a nurse. The point of telling you this is an interesting one. In the middle of the last century the emancipation of slaves became a popular cause amongst wealthy, or at least educated, ladies who wanted to use their talents. But there was a fly in the ointment. They worked nobly raising funds, but what did they find in the end? That the emancipation was for Negro men only! In fact, if you think of it, those women who were working so hard for what they thought was a worthy cause, in the event, had it succeeded, would have had fewer rights than the Negro men! Ironical, isn't it?' She did not give Maevy time to reply. She leaned forward, her eyes bright. 'No, there's no other way. I admit they're smashing windows and firing pillar boxes in London, burning down or trying to burn down churches and houses, but the roughness of their treatment by the authorities and the police shows the fear in men's hearts.' She raised her hand to emphasize her point. 'These are on the whole well-brought-up women. They're being kicked and beaten, hatpins are being pushed into them by women, I regret to say, and the worst indignity of all, they're being forcibly fed in prisons because of their hunger strikes.'

Maevy shook her head. 'I've read of it. This Cat and Mouse Act is the most invidious thing of all.' She was fired by Belle's indignation.

'Yes, and it's well-named, too. To release them in a dangerous state of illness and then arrest them when they recover is no better than the treatment meted out to the slaves!'

'Yes, I agree. It makes your heart bleed. I can well appreciate how you feel, Belle, but we must work for the cause in the ways most appropriate to our various temperaments.'

She nodded. 'I accept that. I've great hopes of Asquith and his Reform Bill, but maybe I shouldn't get on to politics after my outburst about slavery.' She laughed.

'Man is a political animal, Charlie used to say.' She had mentioned his name without difficulty. She looked out of the window. The train was slowing down. 'Here's Sholton. My, that was a quick journey!' They smiled at each other as they gathered their things and stood up.

They were standing facing each other in the swaying train. Maevy touched Belle's arm shyly. 'I'm glad we've had this talk. We couldn't have got it more private, could we? Ever since . . . Charlie, I felt I couldn't speak freely to you.'

'You still blame me?' Her eyes were steady.

'No. It was simply the . . . irony of fate. He wouldn't want me to bear grudges.'

'He was . . .' The silver eyes suddenly swam in moisture. 'Go on,' she said, giving Maevy a gentle push, 'you first or we'll be carried on to Crannoch.'

286

When they were walking through the dark Sholton streets Maevy said, 'I found a quotation in one of Charlie's books. He'd marked it. That was to do with the irony of fate.'

'Oh, yes . . .' Belle Geddes was walking quickly, almost too quickly for Maevy.

'I'll show it to you sometime. Come and have a meal with Ellie and me. I've meant to ask Colin in for a bite for weeks. He's in sympathy with the Movement.' She laughed.

'And the young lassies in the village are in sympathy with him! They pack out his surgeries with imaginary ailments. Maybe I should have said "love" instead of "sympathy".'

'How about you? Have you fallen a victim to his charms?'

'He's just a boy. I'm thirty-four now. Past it.'

The darkness made it easier to say. 'What rubbish! Is there no one?'

'No one I want to marry. There's someone in Crannoch. We've been friends for a long time, some say more than friends, but you know how they talk in Sholton. Well, he . . . does me fine.' She had stopped at Maevy's garden gate. 'I'll say good-night, then.'

'Good night, Belle.'

She went straight to Charlie's study and looked up the lines she had been thinking about.

'"Fate has terrible power. You cannot escape by wealth or war. No fort will keep it out, no ships outrun it." Sophocles, *Antigone*,' it said, and in his small neat writing, 'Terrible power indeed.'

10

Ellie felt she had had a good day at Queen Margaret's College. Her enthusiasm for being there had not diminished although she was in her second year now and was attending classes in the Royal Infirmary. Her professor had pointed out to the students the advantages they shared compared with the early years of the medical school twenty years ago.

'Those worthy women,' he told them, 'when they got their tickets, found a note at the foot saying that the directors reserved the right to withdraw at any time permission to attend at the Infirmary. But they were made of stern stuff. They had fought plenty of opposition to get to Queen Margaret's. They gathered their tickets together and sent them to Dr Thomas, the Superintendent, saying they could not accept them on those terms as they had paid the full fee and had rights as perpetual students. The footnote was withdrawn. I see we have the same breed here today,' he smiled round the class as they clapped vociferously, 'and I'm sure you appreciate the facilities you now have when you consider what was extant in 1890. The dissecting room was in the old kitchen. In their third year medical jurisprudence and public health were taught in the dining-room of Dr Kennedy Dalziel's house in Bath Street. And he was always pleased to boast that his dining-room was licensed as a class-room of the University.'

Amid the laughter he said, 'Oh, there were plenty of men on your side, just as there are today in the Votes for Women cause, and perhaps the most important was Dr Henry Muirhead who left the bulk of his money to start this college. It's worth mentioning one of the clauses.' He lifted a piece of paper from his desk and read from it.

'"I do not wish clergymen to have anything to do with the management of the college, for creeds are the firmest fetters to intellectual progress, and a man who cannot break loose from such himself is not the best hand to help others."'

'No comment,' he said, breaking into the murmurs around him. 'Now ladies, to work, and good luck.' Ellie had metaphorically rolled up her sleeves. Oh, she was lucky to be here, to have had a father and mother who had encouraged her. She would make them proud of her.

On the way out she had met Iain Guthrie, a medical student and brother of a friend of hers at Queen Margaret's. 'They've let you into the Royal, have they? That'll send up the temperatures of the men patients.' And when she had laughed he had said, 'How about coming to the dance at the University Union on Saturday?' She had accepted. Life was good, life in fact was wonderful, and tonight would be good, too.

Mother had invited Belle Geddes and Colin Thomson to dinner, which pleased her. She had one or two questions to ask Belle if she could get her alone. She would understand the difficulties of a woman studying medicine since she had gone through it herself and at a more difficult time – a pioneer in fact, having graduated in 1900.

She was glad Mother had come round to having Belle Geddes in the house. It had been difficult for her to come to terms with the fact that she was with Father when he was killed. She could understand that. She herself felt that perhaps Dr Belle had encouraged father to try out a motor car. She was known as a forward-looking person who cared little for convention. She had shared her mother's bitterness, but however deep her own grief had been, she knew it could never have been as deep as her mother's.

It had been ironical that he should meet his death that way since there were now plenty of motor cars about. Some of the professors who came to Queen Margaret's drove them. Ernest had had a Napier for some time. Colin Thomson had a sturdy Austin 'Ascot' two-seater, and Belle had been seen in the village driving it. She might well have one of her own soon. She was that kind of woman.

She was on top of the tramcar swaying along Great Western Road now – the drivers were quite reckless on this stretch – having walked along by the Botanic Gardens to board it. She patted her bag full of books. In there, in her purse, was her latest letter from Kieran. She had glanced at it at breakfast this morning, but had decided to delay the pleasure and read it on the way home. All day it had lain there like a talisman as she listened more than dutifully to the various lecturers.

It was hardly a dull task. She was fired with enthusiasm, like every one of the female medical students. Some had found it a hard job to convince their families. She was lucky that her mother heartily approved, and they both knew it would have been Charlie's dearest wish.

It would soon be Christmas, she thought, looking at the glittering shop windows, first in St George's Cross, then Charing Cross, bracing herself as they swayed into Sauchiehall Street. The driver must be in a hurry to get home to his tea. Maybe she and Mother would come here on Saturday to do some Christmas shopping. This time there would be a gift to buy for Lizzie's coming baby. She was far on now. 'It's at this stage, Ellie,' she had said, 'when you'd go through fire and water to be able to wear decent-looking clothes again.'

She was so like Grandmother in her love of dress, or rather Grandmother when she was young. She remembered Lizzie telling her of their shopping expeditions to the old Colosseum. Now, because of the new Central

Station and the Caledonian Railway acquiring all the property on the west side of Jamaica Street, Mr Walter Wilson had set up magnificent premises in Sauchiehall Street, where Lizzie now shopped. There it was. She bent forward in her seat to see the long frontage of Tréron et Cie.

The strange thing about Lizzie's pregnancy was that as she bloomed Grandma had seemed to dwindle – that was the only word. She was thinner, her vitality had diminished, she had taken to spending more and more time in her own room, and when Ellie went to visit her there, she spoke more often about Ireland. 'I have a great longing for it at times,' she had said. Her eyes had a far-away look.

She had spoken to her mother about it. 'Do you think Grandma's all right? She's kind of . . . other-worldly at times.'

'She's seventy-seven, pet,' Maevy said, 'and she's had a hard life in many ways. It's only in the last few years or so that she's taken it easy.'

'But she talks about going back to Ireland.'

'Well, she'll go. If her body is maybe getting a bit feeble, you may be sure her will is as strong as ever.'

Now the tramcar was racing down Renfield Street which was like a rushing river with the homegoing crowds. She was later than she had meant to be, nevertheless. She jumped off the tramcar at the corner of Gordon Street and ran to the station. She had only four minutes, she saw by the clock. She ran through the station, a tall slim figure in her dark cape – she had persuaded Maevy to let her have a cape this winter. 'It would be warmer,' she had said, but she thought it lent an air of mystery. She also knew that the dark navy velour set off her fairness.

She went quickly along the length of the train, trying to find a compartment where she could get a seat; saw, by a stroke of luck, an empty corner one, and tumbled in. The

291

guard was at the open window preparing to wave his green flag.

'Don't leave it so late the next time, Miss,' he said officiously.

'Right-oh!' She charmed him with a smile and he smiled back, shaking his head, 'You young yins . . .'

'Dear Ellie,' she read, having settled down. She sank back in happy anticipation.

Thank you for your last interesting letter. You made me laugh with all your anecdotes about Queen Margaret's College. I'm sure I never had such a fine time at Yale. My memories of it are mostly of sport. I rowed a lot and I was supposed to be a fair swimmer, a bit of a water-baby *á la* Mr Kingsley.

I'm afraid I wouldn't be much good at that now, although I'm getting on famously and have thrown away my sticks. I manage to drive the motor to the station every morning and go up to New York to the business. Father tried to insist on a shorter day for me, but as he is now retired completely, I pay little heed to that.

If it weren't for his state of health I think I should have at last bought myself an establishment in the city. Although Mother looks forward to me coming home in the evening, she would be the last person to insist on it. She would dearly like to see me married.

She said to me one evening, 'Now that you no longer have any responsibility for Gaylord, you must feel free to leave home. You would have been away in any case had you been married.' She wants a lot of little Kierans round her, I know. I tease her and tell her she's a matriarch.

You must know, Ellie, that Lizzie occupied my mind and heart for many years, but Gaylord's death seems to have cured me of that obsession, and also the many talks you and I had together. In retrospect it seems foolish to me that I wasted so much time when I knew that Ernest was the only one she cared for, but the heart can't reason . . .

So now I am for the time being remaining at Wolf House but pleasing my mother by viewing properties nearer New York. I'm accepting invitations right, left and centre both in Wanapeake and New York – I suppose unmarried men, even those who limp, are always welcome. There have been a lot of balls, and in the spring, when my leg is completely healed, I intend to take up tennis. And I hope to come to Scotland.

But perhaps you won't have time for an elderly cousin? I have a picture of a young girl in a dark cape – it sounds very dashing – who rushes from lecture to lecture and to University dances with various young men in the kilt, or don't medical students wear them?

You're living in a wonderful time when women are beginning to acquire their freedom. I do admire your mother for taking up their cause, but she's always been a woman of strong character. My father has thought very highly of her ever since the first time she came with grandmother.

I said, 'a wonderful time', but I hope it isn't going to be marred by the world situation. Since I last wrote to you there's been the assassination of the Russian Premier, Italy has declared war on Turkey, there is a revolution in Central China, and as if you in Britain were reflecting this unrest, I see the Suffragettes have been rioting in Whitehall. It will be Scotland next. Also that Mr Churchill has been put into the Admiralty. Is there any significance in this?

All I know is that in our own export business things are topsy turvy. Workers are rising up all over the world, where we had good markets once we no longer have them, and in America there's a great fear of another war; as you may know, we have a lot of Isolationists.

It seems inconceivable that the powers that be should get themselves to such a stage. German militarism is being blamed. Fear and greed seem to me to be at the root of it. This time, if it comes, it won't seem as remote to us as the Boer War did. We are bound to be involved, and it will only take some incident to bring us in.

How did I get on to this subject? Perhaps because I feel I can talk to you about anything without fear or hindrance. There's a natural affinity between us. Do you feel it? Until I met you there had never been anyone to whom I could talk with such freedom. You helped me so much when you were here by your brightness and youthfulness.

Gaylord's death left me with a feeling of guilt as well as loss. I won't go into that again. You helped me to get back to normal. Now I think of him as an unfortunate but very dear young man who perhaps found what seemed to him to be the best remedy for his troubles.

There, too, I'm sure opinion will alter, and what is talked

about behind hushed doors will come out into the light of day. But that didn't come soon enough for Gaylord.

Uncle Patrick and Aunt Maria have taken up the threads of their life again with grim determination if very little joy. Sarah, mother tells me, has turned down Robert which is a great pity, but I can't interfere there. I haven't the same rapport with her as you had. The bright one is Ginny, but in such a sad house, her light is a little dimmed. And upstairs Great-Aunt Caroline refuses to die, which is the honest way of putting it. It can only get better at Claremont.

Is this a gloomy letter? I fear so. Next time I'll tell you all about the balls I've been to and the fine young ladies I've met and the new dances I've learnt. But meantime I must stop and hope we'll meet before long.

Give my love to everyone at Braidholme and the Hall. Probably your next news will be of Lizzie's new baby. I wish them every joy and happiness.

And I send my sincere love to you, my little comforter.
Kieran.

'Is that you, Ellie?' she heard her mother call from the kitchen as she shut the door.

'Yes, I'm a bit late. Had a busy day.' She went in. 'My first day at the Royal. Can you believe it?'

'Was it good?'

'Grand! I'll tell you later. What's up?' Susan and her mother were standing at the stove. Maevy had a spoon in her hand.

'Your mither thinks the soup's too *wersh*,' Susan said. Ellie *saw* her, as opposed to being aware of her over so many years. She was thinner, her hair was grey and scraped back from her gaunt face, she was an older woman than her mother and still working as hard as she had done when she first came to Braidholme.

'Let me taste.' She took the spoon from her mother, dipped it in the soup and sipped. 'Tomato takes a lot of salt. Why not put some sugar in it, Susan?'

'Sugar!' Susan said outraged. 'It's soup, not stewed apples!'

'It's a well-known fact that sugar is essential in tomato soup. You try it. That and some parsley should do the trick.'

'My, it's great what they teach them up at yon Queen Margaret's!' She addressed Maevy, not deigning to answer such nonsense. Ellie laughed.

'Are you having anyone in to help you tonight, Susan?'

'Aye, your mither's laid on a young lass frae the village, yin o' the Ritchie clan, name o' Dora. Her Ma wants her to go into service. A could have done fine with Tibby just to help me wi' the dishes.'

'Do Mrs Ritchie a favour, then. Dora's a smart lass. She wants experience.'

'Aye, a dare say, but a'd rather she didny get it in *ma* kitchen. Well, away you go the two o' ye and let me get on wi' the dinner. The folks will be here in half-an-hour.'

'She's looking older, mother,' Ellie said, as they stopped at the foot of the stairs.

'Yes, but she'll never admit to her age, says it's a secret between her and her Maker. I thought if young Dora could work in with her it would relieve her of some of the harder work. I can't bear the thought of life without Susan.' She smiled at Ellie. 'On you go and get ready. Have a bath. It will refresh you. I mind well that's what I looked forward to when I was a nurse.'

'I like to think I'm at the Royal, and you were, and Daddy . . .'

She touched Ellie's shoulder, her eyes tender. 'And so do I. And so would he.' She changed the touch to a brisk pat. 'I'm just going into the dining-room to see that the table's all right. I've never had Dr Belle here before. Women are far more critical than men. Colin Thomson wouldn't notice if you gave him his dinner on a tin plate.'

'Oh, that's not fair!' She laughed. 'All right. I'll hurry.' She went up the stairs two at a time, holding up her skirt.

Votes for Women should campaign for more comfortable clothes, get rid of stays, cut a foot off hems.

When she went downstairs later, refreshed and wearing her burgundy velvet with its touch of lace at the high collar and its regimental braiding, she found Colin Thomson and Belle Geddes already there. They were sipping sherry.

'I'm sorry,' she said, coming forward. 'Good-evening, Dr Belle,' she shook hands, 'good-evening, Dr Thomson. I was held up at the College today. Well, really at the Royal. I've started there.'

'Have you?' Belle Geddes looked interested.

'A sherry, Ellie,' Maevy brought it to her, 'after your hard day?' There was amusement in her eyes.

'You shouldn't encourage me, Mother. But I can do with this.' She could take a joke. 'I'm played out.'

'One of the world's workers,' Colin Thomson said. 'Poor thing! Are you sure you wouldn't rather go to bed?'

'You're pulling my leg. But you can't deny you both got here before me.'

'We had a small surgery, hadn't we, Belle? But we never count our chickens. We might be called out at any minute and miss your mother's lovely dinner.'

'Don't raise your hopes,' Maevy said, 'about the dinner, I mean. Susan's displeased with the soup.'

'Ah, well, her standards are so high that it won't make a great deal of difference. And I'd travel miles for her "aipple tairt".' He grinned, and turned to Ellie. 'Anyhow, you seem to be enjoying yourself at Queen Margaret's.'

'Oh, yes, it's wonderful! I wouldn't miss a minute of it for anything. I suppose it's quite different from the time you went, Dr Belle?'

Her silver eyes narrowed in a smile. Strange eyes . . . 'That makes me feel about a hundred. Maybe if you called me Belle it would help. As a matter of fact, my time there was comparatively easy. I think it was around 1891 when the students went up for their first professional examination at the University. I qualified much later, just before the Boer War. Sometimes I wish I'd gone out to South Africa.'

'I wanted to go, too,' Maevy said. 'But did you never think of staying in the academic field, even going on to take a chair like some of the women doctors now?'

'No, no,' she shook her head, 'that would have been unheard of in my time. Many of the girls intended to be medical missionaries. Though, strictly speaking, it *would* have been possible. Did you know that, Colin? The University is founded on the French pattern, I think, which means its chairs are open to women.' She laughed. 'But I think that was kept dark for a long time by the powers that be. There was a terrible fear in men's hearts,' she spoke in hushed tones, 'that we might best them at their own work. It's still there today.'

'Here, don't include me in your criticism!' He laughed. 'Just because I'm at a disadvantage amongst you ladies. I'm a strong supporter of women, always have been.' His eyes rested on Ellie and she saw for the first time – she was impressionable tonight – a comely young man with an open, laughing face, a strong body, decidedly attractive to the opposite sex. Had he a girl? she wondered.

'The only man I've ever known to have absolutely no prejudices against women, or prejudices in general,' Belle's face was sober, 'was your husband, Maevy.' She raised her glass slightly.

'Well, that's nice to hear.' Ellie saw her mother was touched, and embarrassed. She got up. 'We'd better not keep Susan waiting. We've got young Dora Ritchie from the village to serve and Susan will have put the fear of God in her by this time.'

It was a pleasant dinner, with good conversation. Mother should do this more often, Ellie thought. I could invite some friends at the weekends, and perhaps we could have a Christmas party. Lizzie won't want to be bothered. It was good to see her chatting away so easily with Belle Geddes. Of course they had Votes for Women in common. Time heals all wounds. Who said that? she thought. She must look it up in one of her father's books. She realized Colin was speaking to her.

'Do you get asked to the University dances, Ellie?'

'You mean by men?' she said to tease him.

'Or your professors . . .?'

'Aren't they men?'

He was not abashed. 'They say that's why they take on the job at Queen Margaret's.'

'What a thing to say! No, no professors as yet, but you never can tell. But since you mention it, I *am* going to a dance at the Union on Saturday.'

'I used to enjoy those.' His face was wistful. 'Somehow life seems to be all work nowadays.'

'You want me to feel sorry for you, that's what it is. Would you like my shoulder to cry on?'

'Now, that would be nice.' He had a fetching grin. 'No, I'm not complaining. I chose general practice because I like people and I wasn't clever enough to do anything else. I envy you all the same, with life before you, no responsibilities, plenty of comradeship . . . and then one day, you wake up, it's over and you have to settle into a routine.'

'Everything must be like that,' she said, 'even for the professors.' She added, greatly daring, 'What you need is a nice wife.'

'Ah, but I haven't met the right girl yet.' His brown eyes were merry, but there seemed to be something else in their depths.

When they were drinking their coffee, the young Dora came in looking important. She had a slip of paper in her hand. 'Susan says to tell you there's a call in for Dr Belle, she thinks. It's urgent. "Mrs Carter, 3, The Close",' she

298

read, and then, looking up, 'She's an owld targe, that yin. Aye complainin' to someyin or other. Ma says she fair deafens the folk at the Coperative wi' her moanin' . . .'

'Thank you, Dora,' Maevy said, and waited till the door had closed behind the girl before she put her hand up to her mouth. They were all laughing. 'Well, Susan has her work cut out . . .' Colin Thomson had got to his feet.

'I'll go, Belle. Dora's not far wrong. It will be something or nothing.'

'Are you sure? She's my patient.'

'No, no, take your time.' He turned to Maevy. 'It's been a grand evening. Thank you very much. And tell Susan the soup was fine.'

'I'll tell her.' She smiled. 'Come again, Colin. I haven't had folks in as often as I might. You're welcome any time.'

'I won't forget that.'

'See Colin to the door, Ellie.'

When he was putting on his coat and scarf in the hall he said, 'Do you ever stay on in Glasgow and have a meal?'

'No,' she said, surprised.

'Or go to the theatre or a music hall?'

'Rarely. Why?'

'I've a great desire to break out and paint the town red. I don't do an evening surgery on Thursdays. How about meeting me in town next Thursday? Maybe help me in my paintwork?' His eyes danced.

'Well . . . I like to work at nights, and mother – '

'Oh, come on, Ellie. Your mother's not going to deny you a bit of pleasure, that is, if *your're* willing?'

'Well, maybe . . . this Thursday perhaps.'

'But I haven't to make a habit of it, is that it? We'll see. Will you meet me in Glasgow?'

'Yes, that would be better. Where?'

'I thought Rogano's. Six o'clock? If you like seafood.'

'Rogano's?' She was impressed. Mother was wrong in her assumption that he would not know if he was eating off a tin plate.

11

It seemed like a sickness, beginning with the visit to Rogano's restaurant in Exchange Place. One minute she had been a laughing, high-spirited girl enjoying every minute of life, able to joke with everyone, and the next she was reduced to a trembling state of adoration, in which Colin's face, his laughing brown eyes, his disarming smile, were with her wherever she was, even in the dissecting room of the Royal Infirmary . . . a strange place to remember him.

The other girls wondered at her ability to perform the details associated with examining a cadaver, cutting out sections and the like, without fainting or even appearing upset as some of them did. 'Don't you feel absolutely sickened sometimes?' her companion at the dissecting table, Lily Armour, asked her.

'Sickened?' she said, surprised. 'No, not at all.'

'Sometimes I feel you're not with me,' Lily looked at her strangely, shaking her head, 'not with me at all.'

The truth of the matter was that it was love, first love, which had taken over her whole being. She walked on clouds, not on solid ground; sometimes the sight of the tracery of a tree in the Botanic Gardens moved her unbearably. Her mind was full of images of Colin.

'Are you going to be adventurous and have oysters?' he asked her when they were seated in Rogano's with an area of spotless napery between them.

'Oysters?' she said. 'Oh, I've never had those. Besides, they're far too expensive.'

'Never mind that. I've had a little windfall from an

elderly aunt who died recently. I'm inclined to celebrate, and with who else but you?'

'Why me?' She knew she was looking coy, a strange thing for her.

'Because I've been in love with you for years. I was just waiting for you to grow up.' He laughed at her. 'All those times when you used to come into the surgery I thought what a bobby-dazzler you'd become.'

'So you're not disappointed?' This wasn't Ellie McNab, medical student, this pouting miss.

'No, you've exceeded my wildest dreams.'

'Do you say that to all the girls you take out? I've heard you have a reputation for being a bit of a flirt.'

'Now, how would a rumour like that spread about, I wonder?' He looked pleased.

She had the oysters, but refused the champagne. It was one thing walking into cold water deliberately, but she wasn't going to *dive* in, for goodness' sake. She would go straight to the devil, she said, but she was persuaded to have some chilled white wine which, in spite of its coldness, set her on fire and loosened her tongue, or maybe it was the combination of the two.

'Oysters are an aphrodisiac, you know,' he said, smiling over a shell he held poised at his mouth. 'Yum-yum!' He swallowed the bivalve. 'Haven't you been told that at the Queen Margaret College for Women?' His eyes were bright with laughter.

'No, we're concentrating on much more serious things. Cutting up bits of old men and women, putting them under the microscope . . .'

He looked at her. 'I can't imagine you, Ellie. You look so . . . feminine. Belle Geddes, yes, she's harder than you in spite of her seductive ways, but I think of you as marrying young, living in a house like Braidholme with an adoring husband and children . . .' She stopped him.

'Oh, no, that's not my idea at all. I'm going to be a career woman.'

'Well, when you change your mind, let me know.' His eyes danced. It was always difficult to know whether he was joking or not. And was it perhaps that he did not approve of women doing medicine? There were some men like that.

'Are you jealous of women having careers?' she asked him.

'How could I be? I approve of what your mother's doing, don't I?'

'Lots of men approve generally, it's when it affects them that their hackles rise.'

'Have another oyster,' he said, 'that'll cure you.' She melted at his look.

He had too little spare time to pursue her, but he took advantage of her mother's invitation and began to call in at Braidholme between surgeries for tea. They always had it late to allow her mother and herself to get back from Glasgow, about five-thirty. It was a time they had both looked forward to, a sharing of their day's events together. Susan did not approve of Colin's visits. 'The doactor, Missus,' she would announce him, tight-lipped. The word 'again' quivered in the air.

And after this had happened more than a few times, she even voiced her displeasure, secure in her place in the family. 'You wad think someyin was no' weel in this house. *A* hevny seen ony signs o' it!'

Colin laughed merrily when she had gone. 'Am I taking too much advantage of your invitation to drop in, Mrs McNab? You did say . . .'

'Not at all, Colin,' Maevy said. 'Susan's Susan. We can do with a man about the house occasionally.'

'I thought it would be a change for Ellie.' His eyes sparkled. 'She's only seeing dead ones these days.'

She could still manage a reply despite her state. 'You're wrong, Colin. I'm a regular attender at the University dances on Saturday, with a partner.' She emphasized the last word.

'Oh, you don't want to bother with those callow youths! Someone mature like me is more suitable!' She thought she saw a slight frown between her mother's eyes.

'Do you like Colin?' Maevy asked her when he had gone. She was right. 'I don't flatter myself it's me he's coming to see.' Her mother's voice was sharp.

'Well, you can't *not* like Colin.' She dissembled. 'He's so . . . full of fun.'

'I've noticed that. And full of himself, too. What about this other lad, Iain Guthrie? Isn't your life getting a bit cluttered?'

'Oh, I'm just a dance partner to him. There's nothing in it. If you don't get asked to the Union dances your name's mud in Queen Margaret's.' Her mother frowned again.

'I thought you were there for more than that. Is it my imagination or are you slackening off with your work?'

'I don't think so.' She was stung. 'I come home every night and go upstairs as soon as I have my tea.'

'Except Thursdays. That seems to have become a regular occurrence.'

'Are you taking exception to that? It's nineteen hundred and eleven, for goodness' sake! Things have changed since your time. I'm studying medicine, don't forget. Other girls . . . well, you'd be surprised . . .'

'Ellie,' her mother stopped her, 'I don't want to know about other girls. And you know quite well I'm not taking exception to you going out occasionally. You need some fun. But don't forget, I have to be father and mother to you. You're our one ewe lamb. Charlie would expect me to do that.'

'I know, I know.' She got up. 'Well, I'd better get

upstairs and justify my existence. I'll see you at dinner.'
She went out of the room quickly because she was holding
back her tears. She and Mother had never rowed before
. . . She had enough insight as she unpacked her books
and spread them on the table to realize that perhaps she
was unduly sensitive to her mother's criticisms, and that
maybe she was suffering from a belated adolescence. Girls
generally went through that before nineteen.

Or was it love? Colin's face was there again in her
mind, his merry eyes, that particular look of his which
gave the impression that there was only her in the whole
world for him, that nothing or no one else counted. And
the way the laughter faded out of those brown eyes and
they became tender . . . she gave a shuddering sigh and
opened her Gray's *Anatomy*.

He stopped his motor car on the next Thursday at the
foot of the Sholtie Brae. Its border of dark trees made it
darker still. There were no houses near. 'If I come in with
you,' he said, turning off the engine, 'I have to speak to
your mother, and if we sit in the motor in the drive, I'm
sure she gets suspicious. All mothers with beautiful
daughters are suspicious.'

'Oh, Colin,' she laughed, 'she wouldn't be of you! She
knows you. You're a doctor.'

'Are doctors immune from her suspicions, then?'

'I don't know. She's bound to like you. Father was one.
I think she feels they're rather special.'

He put his arm round her. 'Do you think, then, she
wouldn't be cross if she could see us now?'

'I don't know.' She began to tremble. 'We don't . . .
discuss things like that. The only thing that would worry
her is if I neglected my work.'

He laughed and drew her close. 'Little Miss Innocent.
Do you really think that?'

'Yes . . .' She was not sure. 'We talked about it the other night.'

'Believe me,' he said, 'that's not what worries mothers, and you know it as well as I do. You're studying medicine. You've at least heard of the biological urge. It's in all men and all women. Some meet it sooner than others.' He sounded like a professor. 'In all cases it's very overwhelming when it occurs.' He drew her close, his voice changing. 'Do you feel it, Ellie?'

She could not control her trembling. I've never kissed any man except Kieran since I grew up, she thought. Not even Iain Guthrie. He was a shy lad. Colin, also, up to now, had been circumspect. Maybe her obvious innocence frightened them off. He had been a model escort, taking her home to Braidholme after their outings, accepting an invitation to come in and drink a cup of tea, taking his leave in front of Maevy.

'You're made to be loved, Ellie,' he said. 'You're so fresh and beautiful and vulnerable and your hair smells lemony,' she could have told him that it had been rinsed in their juice to keep it fair, 'and you're so slender . . . such a long slender back . . .' He drew a hand down it. There was still laughter in his voice, and she tried to laugh too, without the trembling showing.

'Don't talk such rubbish, Colin,' she said. 'You're always making fun of me.'

'Don't you realize,' his lips were against her face, tickling her as he spoke, 'that I'm not making fun of you? It's my way of hiding what I really feel. I don't want to frighten you. Every time I see you, you seem to be more desirable.' He took her face in his hand, turning it until their lips met. 'Tell me,' now he was speaking against her mouth, 'if you don't want this . . .'

She was surprised at the surge of feeling which went through her body. Impossible to control. 'Oh, I want it,' she said. He kissed her, and she thought, this is the first time I've been in a man's arms. I didn't think it would be like this, so commanding that it would make me so eager, that my body would rule my mind, wanting only to be loved. She was breathless when he released her.

'Have I frightened you, Ellie?' he said.

'No,' she shook her head. 'I think I've only frightened myself.'

'I'm twenty-eight,' his arm was now comfortably round her, his tone almost avuncular, 'I've known girls, any normal man has when he reaches my age. I've never met anyone who moved me so deeply as you. Sometimes I feel I should settle down, get married, rear a family.'

'I don't feel that,' she said. 'I want to be a doctor like my father and I should hate to settle down with any one person, shut up in a house . . .'

'Why are you so fierce, Ellie?'

'Because that's how I feel!' She could not understand herself. She was near to tears.

'Isn't that how you *felt*? Aren't you beginning to feel that what you've always aimed for might not be satisfying enough, might be a little . . . empty? Not many women doctors marry. Would you like to be like Belle Geddes?'

'I'll never be like Belle Geddes. We're different.'

'Yes, you're different.' He took her in his arms again. 'Think, Ellie. No one would want you to give up your studies, but think what it means, what you're consigning yourself to. You could be so happy, with me . . .'

'Not if I knew I'd let myself down, and my mother, and my father . . .' She stopped. *He* had known the satisfaction of work and marriage, the heady, unknown delights of it, the constant companionship. Would she always be a stranger to them, those secret nights? Mother had given up her nursing career for the sake of those joys. Ah, but she remembered, she had qualified first, had waited a long time before making up her mind. It had been a struggle. And she had gone to work in McGraths again. Even living with someone as perfect as Charlie, there had been something missing . . .

'You've confused me, Colin,' she said. 'Take me home.'

'Kiss me and forget about your confusion.'

She put her arms round his neck and kissed his mouth. At first she enjoyed the calmness of it, the lack of response on his part, but then she felt his lips move and his arms tighten and deep thrills went through her which were new and somehow sinful.

'Oh, you're a woman, Ellie,' he said, 'that's what you're meant for.'

'Take me home,' she said, coming out of his arms.

In bed that night she was sleepless. Had he or had he not asked her to marry him? And if he had, or did, would she accept? Could they come to some arrangement whereby they waited until she qualified as a doctor? Three years! How did people stand waiting so long? But supposing he agreed to wait, might they not go into practice together? Two doctors, man and wife. What would Belle Geddes think of it? What would her mother think of it? What would she herself think of it? She was not sure. She was too tired. She would have to think when she was rested, think and think again.

Meantime, she decided, she would not tell her mother. She was beginning to show just the slightest sign of impatience when Colin called. It could not be that she did not like him. No one could avoid liking Colin. For the time being, she would keep her feelings a secret. One thing she was sure about: nothing at this stage would make her give up seeing him. It was the most important happening in her life, in danger of eclipsing all her plans for her career, her wonderful medical career.

A last thought occurred to her. If he was truly interested in her welfare, wouldn't he have encouraged her to pursue her studies instead of hinting that she might give them up? Could there be the slightest feeling of envy in him, a dislike of women encroaching on his preserves? Not Colin, she thought.

She went to sleep remembering his merry eyes, and the strength of his arms round her.

12

Because Lizzie's confinement was imminent, Ernest had been leaving McGrath's office in York Street promptly at five o'clock. Maevy had encouraged him. 'I know she's never been better, but every wife likes that extra bit of attention when it's coming near her time. I know I did with Ellie.'

'I feel you're getting the heavy end of the stick,' he said. 'Dan's out more. There's all that correspondence today from the American office. They seem to be going ahead with the heavy vehicles there.'

'Yes, I'm envious of that. We're more conservative in Scotland. I hope I see those pantechnicons with "McGrath's Door-to-Door Removals" on them before I retire. It's my dream.'

'It's the war that's holding them up,' and seeing her startled face, 'I mean, "war, war, and rumours of war . . ." I don't know who said it. Europe's on the edge of it. We can't blind ourselves to that. Trouble worldwide, and yet here, except for a few scares about German spies, we go on our way regardless, even to the extent of having another Exhibition!'

She laughed. 'You must admit the Old-World Scottish Toonie's a rare sight!'

'Yes, if you can blind yourself to the rate Germany's Navy's increasing, and the unrest in the country, Trade Union squabbles, Suffragettes . . .'

'Don't say anything against the Suffragettes!'

'I'm not. You're simply reflecting the general state of unrest. I applaud it, but we can't blind ourselves to the feeling of uncertainty in the air. War's the greatest destroyer of progress, as well as people's lives.'

'Ah, but out of it there's good, too. Look at the advances in surgery because of the Boer War. Charlie often told me about those.' Her face softened. 'Well, you run away home to that lovely wife of yours, Ernest. If you have a Christmas baby we'll have extra cause for celebration.'

Lizze welcomed him with outstretched arms when he went into the drawing-room before dinner. There was no sign of strain on her face. 'Oh, there you are, Ernest! Come away to the fire and warm yourself.'

He kissed her before he sat down, looking into her face. 'Everything all right?'

'Yes, not a sign of anything.' She patted her swollen stomach. 'We have a shy little one here. I'll be glad when it decides to make its debut.'

'Think of Annabel and Kit's joy if they find a baby in their Christmas stocking.'

'It's what Jumping Jane will think of it.' She laughed. This was her name for the nurse because of her quick, jerky way of walking.

'It's Mrs Galbraith's presence she's objecting to.'

'I wish it had been Aunt Maevy instead of that woman Colin Thomson's engaged. All the way from Glasgow, too.'

'That den of iniquity? She's very well qualified, Colin says. All the best people in Glasgow have engaged her. He was right not to involve Aunt Maevy. She's on several committees for the Suffragettes, and she might not be available when we wanted her. She's addressing meetings now, much to her own surprise, I think, and you can't cancel those at the last minute, even for Lizzie Murray-Hyslop.'

'Well, I just hope it's over soon, otherwise there'll be fur and feathers flying upstairs between those two in the nursery. She arrived three days ago with all her paraphernalia and demanded a separate room for the delivery room, if you please! I would have been happier in our own room. It's familiar . . . and special to us.'

Ernest got down on his knees before her. He was full of love for her and admiration for the way she could be so light-hearted before such an ordeal. How did women go through with it? He remembered that night after the ball, the ecstasy when they had been lifted beyond themselves into a world of tremulous delight, a night to remember . . . and here was the result, he thought, putting his arms round her waist, which was difficult, and laying his head gently on her great stomach.

'Oh, my darling, what we men do to our women. There should be a law against it.'

'There would have to be a law against loving, then,' she said, cradling his head with her arms, 'and what would *this* woman do without it?'

He looked up at her. 'Is it worth it, Lizzie?'

'As a token of our love, yes, it's worth it. And I'm lucky. Just think if there was a token for every time. We'd have to build a bigger place than the Hall to house them all!'

'Oh, my Lizzie.' He lay against her, at one with the child in her womb, feeling like another child in the face of this female acceptance.

She moved about restlessly when they were in bed, and he put a pillow to her back. But that did not help and he cradled her in his arms for a long time before he fell into an uneasy sleep. He was wakened by her shaking him by the shoulder. 'Ernest, it's started.' Her voice was small.

'Oh, God,' he said, for the first second annoyed that he had been disturbed, then swept out of bed by his concern. 'Why didn't you tell me earlier?' He bent over her. 'Is it bad?'

'Bad enough to rouse Mrs Galbraith. "Galbraith" we've to call her. Did you ever . . .? You go and tell her and I'll be getting into my robe.'

'No, stay put, as far as you can.' He lit their bedside lamp, then hurriedly began to dress. 'Oh, my poor darling . . .' He knew he was jibbering.

'You've buttoned up your trousers wrongly. You'll frighten the life out of Jumping Jane and Galbraith. There, that's right. Oh!' He could see her face contract with pain. 'No . . .' this was as he started forward towards her, 'on you go!'

The next hour was a flurry of activity. Mrs Galbraith proved to be a heavy sleeper and had to be shaken awake by Jane. The room which she had chosen as the delivery room had to be opened up, a fire lit in it, and there was much scurrying of servants up and down stairs before Lizzie was led ceremoniously to it. She refused Ernest's desire to support her.

He knew by her face she did not like the change, but Mrs Galbraith had taken one look at their own bedroom on her arrival and declared it unsuitable for birthing. 'Too cluttered,' she had said. 'I would never get near the bed for all that furniture. All the best families in Glasgow prefer a special room.' They had managed all right with Annabel and Kit, but he thought it better not to point this out. The last thing he wanted to do was antagonize the woman. Lizzie's life was in her hands, and of course, Colin Thomson's.

'If you would have Dr Thomson alerted, sir,' she said, secure now in her sterile tower with her patient. His darling looked small, as far as that were possible considering her condition, and forlorn in her strange surroundings and the chilly atmosphere. Their own bedroom had absorbed into its walls for centuries the heat from thousands of fires.

He was glad of something to do. 'Get hot water bottles

and make my wife as comfortable as possible,' he said, 'and give her a cup of tea. She dearly likes a cup of tea from time to time.'

'We'll see to all that, Mr Murray-Hyslop,' she said, in a tone which indicated that she knew her own job better than he did.

He looked at the time on his watch as he went downstairs. Five o'clock. He would go himself to the doctor's house and warn him. None of the staff could drive the Napier and, besides, it would give him something to do.

He drove the short distance to Colin Thomson's house, trying to control his anxiety. He had gone through two births already (*I've* gone through, he thought, what nonsense), and all had been well. They had two lovely children. Look at the morning instead, he told himself. See the stirrings of light through the dark trees, feel life returning, to Sholton, all over the world, after the short death of sleep. He was surprised at his poetic turn of thought.

In the village street he heard and saw some men tramping along in a little group, their pose tired, heads dropping – miners returning from their shift. They looked up when he drew abreast of them and saluted respectfully. He was still an incomer, always would be. Their features, black with coaldust, made them scarcely discernible in the grey light.

Lizzie's grandfather had been a miner. He had an ancient memory of being taken by Kate as a child to visit the small cottage in Colliers Row, and the gentle-faced man who had been there. Kieran, his step-brother, had the same sweet mouth. Grandmother's life had been hard. She deserved all the comfort they could give her at the Hall. What would happen when Jonty came home for good? He might have other plans since he had been cut out of his father's firm by that man, Hamilton.

His ire was stirred. Thank God Hamilton was no longer

coming about with his lascivious eyes on Lizzie. They were well rid of him. And yet he had a sneaking sense of sympathy for him, alone in that big, ugly house further up the river, which could have lost its ugliness if he had had a wife and children. Oh, *he* was fortunate . . .

He had not told Maeve that Lizzie had gone into labour, but she was not deaf despite her years. She would guess by the early morning stir that something was amiss. He would go up to her room when he got back and reassure her, although everything was going to be all right. It was not Lizzie's first child. Colin had been cheerful when he had taken her for a last visit. 'She's a past master at it by this time, or should I say, "past mistress"?' He had laughed merrily. 'No, that hasn't got the right ring about it!'

He was just as cheerful this morning when he came down to his sitting-room, summoned by his housekeeper, Biddy. Lizzie had told him she had looked after Charlie before he and Aunt Maevy were married. That would account for the woman's anxious face when he showed up so early.

'Oh, is it wee Lizzie's time now, sir? Tell her Biddy was asking for her, will ye no'?' Her kindness relieved his anxiety somewhat. 'I'll tell her,' he promised.

Colin, also, made him feel a different man. 'That's good news, Ernest. She'll have the baby before midday, I'm willing to bet my boots. Have you had any breakfast?'

'No . . .'

'Would you care to join me? If you just take a seat while I dress?' The thought of inactivity was intolerable.

'No, no, thank you. I couldn't eat . . .'

'Come on, man.' Colin clapped him on the shoulder. 'You're an old hand at this game now.' But the other times there had been Aunt Maevy with her calmness, and Belle Geddes, efficient, cool . . . 'A good plate of bacon and eggs is just what you need.'

'No, thank you. I thought you might go back with me. I have my motor.'

'I have to shave, make myself presentable. Besides, I have a motor, too.' His eyes twinkled. 'Maybe not as grand as yours but it gets me about. No, I'll be with your wife within the hour. Nothing's going to happen in that time and she's in good hands. Mrs Galbraith has worked in some of the best houses in Glasgow.'

When he got back Cathy met him in the hall. 'Your breakfast is ready, sir. Madam says you've got to take it and not to come up to see her till you do.' She smiled at him. 'I have strict instructions.'

'People are plying me with breakfasts this morning. Has Lady Crawford had hers?'

'No, she decided to join you downstairs this morning, sir. She's had a cup of tea with madam.' She hesitated, and smiled. 'Don't worry, sir, I'm one of ten.'

'Are you, Cathy?' She was laughing at him, he, the cool one. Had he been as bad when Annabel and Kit were coming?

'Yes, and every one of us healthy, without the help of a doctor.' She went out. Obviously he was making a fool of himself. He made his way to the dining-room where, no doubt, Mrs Robertson had seen to a special breakfast for him, to keep his strength up. *His* strength . . . And grandmother was going to be there to set him an example in deportment. When he saw the straight figure at the table, he was not disappointed.

The rush in the early morning had made him forget an important fact: Jonty was due to arrive on the twelve o'clock train. He would have to go to the Central Station to meet him. That would take care of part of the afternoon, and indeed, he thought, comparatively cheerful after an excellent breakfast, he might have news of a new baby sister or brother.

Before that he was allowed in to see Lizzie who was having intermittent pain, but declared herself fairly comfortable. She looked a little overawed by Galbraith who rustled importantly about the room, but she asked him to bring in Annabel and Kit. 'Do you think that's wise, Mrs Murray-Hyslop?' the dragon asked disapprovingly.

'I haven't anything catching, Galbraith,' Lizzie said, and shot Ernest a triumphant glance. She was a marvel.

Annabel and Kit were led in, but failing to see much sense in the visit, wanted to be away again quickly. 'Let us know when our new brother or sister arrives,' Annabel said in a brisk tone, horrifying Galbraith who had no doubt some stories ready about babies being discovered under toadstools and such like.

Grandmother was in her room, quietly knitting. She was looking in from time to time. 'You'll be stopped before me,' she said to Ernest. 'Galbraith, I understand, has strong ideas about propriety.' Her eyes twinkled. He went off to meet Jonty with a comparatively light heart.

The afternoon passed pleasantly enough, which Ernest thought of as a relative term. He listened to tales about school from Jonty, ate a family tea with the children at Lizzie's request, and kept an eye on Grandmother as she would want to be kept up-to-date with the progress of the confinement.

But indeed there seemed to be very little progress. Colin Thomson called in the late afternoon to see Lizzie, then came downstairs and, with rather a forced smile, said he had lost his bet.

'You can never tell with confinements, worse luck,' he said. 'The . . . er . . . membranes had to be punctured. Your wife was a little slow there.'

'Will things quicken up now?' Ernest asked. 'It's over twelve hours now.'

'Oh, yes, I'm sure they will. I'll be looking in at

317

intervals. Don't you worry. You'll have a fine baby before the day is done.' His eyes were no longer merry.

Maevy came in straight from the office at six, and, after a brief word with Ernest, went upstairs. This was women's territory, he realized. He played a game of tiddlywinks with Jonty who looked disconsolate and almost disgruntled, as if Lizzie had deliberately gone into labour on the same day as he had arrived home for his Christmas holidays. Ernest took the bull by the horns.

'I daresay you've been told the facts of life at your school, Jonty.'

The boy blushed a painful red. 'I have a little, sir.'

'And don't call me "sir". Your mother is going through a very difficult time, a very painful time. Men tend to take it for granted. I want you to remember, if you ever marry, just what you're asking your wife to go through.' If possible, Jonty became redder. He looked close to tears, and Ernest could have bitten out his tongue. 'I'm sorry. Of course you're too young to know what I'm really getting at and you won't be marrying for ages. But the fact remains, this is territory we'll never travel, and we must appreciate always the courage of women and make sure we always give them our love and sympathy . . .' His voice trailed away. He had made a hash of it.

'Is Mother going to be all right?'

'Yes, of course. It's just a matter of time.'

At eight o'clock Colin arrived again, and this time when he came downstairs there was no pretence of a smile. Maevy and her mother were sitting in the drawing-room also.

'Well, how is she now, Colin?' Ernest jumped up.

'I'm afraid there are complications, sir . . .' Now *he* was at it.

'Is it a breech?' Maevy said clearly.

He looked round at her, surprised.

'Don't forget I was a midder nurse at the Royal,' she

said. Her face was calm. She was at her most Madonna-like.

'Yes,' he said.

'I thought so.'

'Even so, Mrs McNab,' – his chin went up – 'it wouldn't be right to discuss the case with you. All is going well. She's strong and healthy, as we know,' – his voice quickened – 'but I'm on my way to bring Belle . . .'

'Is there any danger?' Ernest heard his own voice in his ears. It seemed to have gone higher.

'No, no danger. But a second opinion is always useful. If you'll excuse me . . .'

'Could *I* go for her?' Ernest stopped him. 'Then you could stay with my wife?'

'Now, that's a good idea, if you would.' Ernest got the distinct impression that the young man had wanted to escape. He looked *trapped*.

'Right, I'll have her here in no time.'

Belle Geddes got up from her desk without a word when he told her. The surgery was empty, the place quiet.

'What can it be, Belle? She's so healthy. Nothing could go wrong with her, could it? I know she's over thirty but it isn't her first baby.'

'Anything can go wrong with any woman,' she said, as she put on her coat. 'I think I can guess what it is.'

'Maevy asked him if it was a breech.'

'Come along,' she said. 'I only hope too many cooks won't spoil the broth.'

The three of them could not eat although the dinner was served in its entirety by an impassive Redfern in the dining-room. Jonty had elected to be with the children in the nursery. Perhaps I frightened him, Ernest thought.

They went through the motions, with Maevy and her

mother carrying on a stilted conversation about generalities. Maevy was close-mouthed about Lizzie. Of course she could not give her own opinion. Nor could she meddle.

'As it happens you *could* have been with Lizzie,' he said, having to speak. 'We thought that your meetings might get in the way now that you've taken to the platform.' He tried to smile.

'Don't reproach yourself, Ernest,' she said. He had the impression that her mind was not on him, that she was in that sterile room upstairs.

Now he saw it, too late. Belle and Maevy were the perfect combination, both cool, both women. Colin Thomson was inclined to be taken by the latest ideas, and yet you could not blame the lad. He had wanted to lay on the best for Lizzie. He remembered vague rumours which hung about the village. Belle Geddes was 'the best wi' weans'. 'The new doactor', he would be 'the new doactor' until another one came, was inclined to be a bit of a *sprowser*, new-fangled, liked to be 'in wi' the nobs and him only a farmer's son when you thought o' it . . .' He got up suddenly and strode about the room.

'You're making us nervous,' Maeve said. 'Don't go creating a situation before we're sure there is one. If it's a breech as Maevy says, and thank God I've never had any experience of them, it can be managed. Plenty of women have them, Maevy, don't they?'

'What makes having a baby successful, Maevy?' he said, turning to her. 'Supposing you *have* this breech. What is a breech, for God's sake?'

'It's where the feet come first, instead of the head,' she said.

'I always thought they came that way.' She gave him a kind look, her Madonna-look, he thought. 'So what have you to watch?'

320

'Do you want to ask those questions, Ernest?' she said. 'Men don't usually . . .'

'Yes, I don't like floundering about in the dark . . .' It struck him that that was what this unborn child of Lizzie's and his was doing. What about his poor Lizzie at this very moment? It was too big a house to hear any screams or groans. Besides, Lizzie was not like that. She would bite her lip first until the blood came. 'So what have you to watch?' he said again.

'Oh, Ernest . . .' She looked embarrassed.

'Tell him,' her mother said. 'I want to know, too.'

'Well . . .' she hesitated, 'the baby is far out, as far as the umbilicus. It's wrapped in a warm, sterile towel. Knowing Mrs Galbraith, that would be done all right. After that, many midwives . . . or doctors . . . think there's an urgent need for a rapid delivery if the cord isn't pulsating . . .'

'Oh, my God!' He felt sick.

'Go on, Maevy.' He would like to look as cool as her mother.

'And is this *not* what should happen?'

'It depends on the doctor. Some take one view, others take a different one. *I* think you shouldn't panic. You might do the child an injury. Gently does it. A normal child can stand compression of the cord for ten minutes after it's delivered.'

'Which method will Colin use?'

'I don't know,' she said, 'nor do I know about Belle, come to that. You get a sixth sense when you're dealing with women in childbirth – what they can stand, what the baby can stand. The thing is to keep cool.'

'Well, Belle Geddes is cool.'

'Aye, *she's* cool.' She would say no more.

At half past nine Belle came downstairs. She stood at the door of the drawing-room. Her face looked very white to

321

him. He had never admired her looks. He knew some men did.

'Lizzie's come through,' she said. 'Don't forget, Ernest, he tried very hard.' He stood in the middle of the room, heard her voice. 'I'll say good-night.' There was silence behind him. Neither Maevy nor her mother spoke.

Colin Thomson had lost his merriness when he appeared. It was evident that a large part of his charm was caused by his merriness. His face looked . . . empty. He seemed to brace himself at the door for a second, then advanced with his hand outstretched. 'My deepest commiserations, Ernest,' he said. Ernest ignored his hand, not deliberately. He was listening intently. 'Your wife is going to be all right, but the baby . . . the cord wasn't pulsating . . . did everything I could . . . traction . . . I'm afraid it didn't live.'

Maevy was beside him. Her arm was round his shoulders. 'Bear up,' she said. And to Colin, 'Is she sleeping?'

'No . . .' He shook his head.

'Well, then . . .?'

'Yes, you go up and see her, Ernest. Comfort her. I want you to know that I did everything I could to save . . .' He pushed past this man who was blocking his way. *She* was alive at least, that was what really mattered to him. But what an emptiness there must be in her. He could not get up the stairs fast enough.

13

There were no celebrations at the Hall that Christmas. Lizzie did not get out of her bed for a fortnight, and Ellie and her mother had the children at Braidholme for their Christmas tea and many other times besides. And tried to amuse Jonty as well.

Annabel and Kit were too young for the loss of the baby to have made any effect on them, but Jonty seemed to be quiet, almost morose at times. He was at an introspective age, Ellie realized. It would have been better if he had been back at school.

Maevy was very busy at McGraths since she had told Ernest that he must put Lizzie first, although he showed up for a part of each day, the brunt of the work fell on her. The entertaining of the children was easy, Ellie thought, but Jonty was a different matter. She went on long walks with him – the weather was too inclement to do much cycling – and she encouraged him to talk. She told her mother it was like getting blood out of a stone.

'He's like his father,' Maeve said. 'He was withdrawn. I sometimes wonder how he would have developed had he lived. Would he have become more so? He hadn't the common touch. Now, Ernest is right with everybody, right with himself. And he's decisive. Lizzie is first in his thoughts just now, but when he feels he can leave her and come back to McGraths, he'll give it his full attention. He's right for Lizzie.'

Ellie tried once to draw Jonty out when they were trailing along the muddy towpath of the Sholtie. He liked the river. 'It's been a sad Christmas for you, Jonty. It's a pity you hadn't brought a friend home with you. Is there no one in the village of your own age?'

'Only village lads,' he said, dismissing them. It was not his fault, she thought, it was the fault of his father and his grandfather, even the villagers, for putting the Hall and its inmates on a pedestal.

'Your mother's had a bitter blow.' She tried again. 'You know how cheerful she usually is, how she plans so carefully for your holidays. She'll be sorry when you've gone that she wasn't well enough to spend more time with you. And Uncle Ernest,' she smiled, 'well, he just can't see past her . . .' The boy interrupted.

'Then why did he give her another baby, put her through all this?' His voice sounded strangled. When she looked at him his face had gone a dark red. He had found a stone and was kicking it along the path in front of him, viciously.

'You mustn't think that way, Jonty,' she said. 'You're old enough to understand, I'm old enough to say this to you. He didn't put her through anything. They love each other. It may seem unfair to you that the woman has to have the baby, even more unfair that it dies, but believe me, if Uncle Ernest could have borne it for her, he would. He's not unthinking, he's kind, devoted and you're lucky to have him as a stepfather.'

'Well, someone's to blame,' he said. 'Is it that doctor?' She was astonished. 'No one's to blame. It was . . . fate, or an act of God; whatever you like to believe.'

She told Maevy in the evening about their talk. 'I believe the silly lad is now going to blame Colin,' she said. 'Did you ever? He couldn't have been more attentive. You told me how many times he came to see Lizzie that day, and he engaged that fine nurse from Glasgow. He couldn't have done more, could he?' Maevy did not answer. '*Could* he?' she said again.

'I'm sure he couldn't have done more,' she said. Was

324

there some hidden meaning in her words? She was disturbed, more so when she thought how seldom she had seen Colin recently. Belle Geddes was going every day to the Hall. She had seen her there. She knew, of course, that he taken leave to go and visit a friend in Edinburgh for the Christmas week, but he would be back now, surely? So, why didn't he come to Braidholme? Her mind was in a whirl. She went upstairs and wrote to him and left the house. There was something she did not know . . .

Biddy answered the door to the cottage when she knocked. She did not show any surprise, but then she had always had a buttoned-up face. 'Come away in, Ellie. I'm busy in the kitchen.' She made no attempt to show her into the sitting-room but led the way to her own sanctum.

'I don't suppose the doctor's back, Biddy?' She spoke casually.

'Aye, he's back. Late last night.' She took up a wooden spoon and started pounding some butter and sugar against the wall of her baking bowl. She made small noises with the exertion. Susan did the same, she remembered. 'Pechs'. 'He's oot on his roons the noo, trying to catch up. I hope there's nothin' wrang w' yer ma.'

'Oh, no, I've brought an invitation for Dr Thomson, that's all. We're having a few friends in.' Biddy gave her what she called to herself 'the Sholton look – I can see through you like a window'. 'Will you give it to him?' Ellie went on.

'Aye, lave it there.' She pointed with her spoon to the dresser. 'An' you're comin' oot fur a doactor jist like your faither?'

'I hope so.'

'It must be awfully hard for a wumman.' The butter and sugar, Ellie saw, had been pounded into a pale cream.

'No, not really. Quite a lot of women study medicine nowadays. You have Doctor Geddes here.'

'Aye, but she's different.' Everybody said that of Belle Geddes, she thought.

Colin called the following evening in reply to her note. Maevy was not back from Glasgow, and he was on his rounds. It could only be a brief visit. He took her in his arms immediately. 'Oh, Ellie, the last week's been purgatory!' He kissed her so passionately that she could well believe him. Fire ran through her own body at his nearness. She had missed him, too. This was what had been wanting in her life this last week, this overwhelming sensation. She drew herself free to look at his face, the eyes she loved, the Sholtie Burn brownness of them with their light and shade, although there were dark circles under them. 'You must have been burning the midnight oil in Edinburgh,' she said.

'*Me* study?' He shook his head. 'No, I'm past that. It was a big enough struggle getting my finals. It was a different kind of oil. We had one party after another. The way they live in Edinburgh, Ellie, you have no idea. Folks in Glasgow get the notion it's stuck-up and stiff – well, I can tell you it's far from that. It makes Sholton seem like the Slough of Despond.'

'Thank you very much,' she said.

'Oh, I didn't mean that, you silly little girl.' He took her in his arms again and rocked her gently, his face against hers. 'You're the only bright star in it for me. I thought of you night and day, but getting away lets you see there are better places to live. Here they're small-minded and . . . critical.' She did not understand him.

'It's like that in all villages, Colin,' she said. 'Everybody knows everybody else's affairs. But if you're in trouble they rally round. Look at the kindness my mother has had since my father died.'

'Ah, but he was one in a million, as his patients are never done telling me! I'm not saying anything against your father, but the times patients have said to me when I'm actually attending them in their beds, 'Oh, it's no' the same since Dr Charlie went!' Well, it's not calculated to boost your ego, is it?'

She laughed against his shoulder, loving him. He was like a little boy. 'And you doing your best. You have to work here for a long time to get thought of like that, I'm afraid.' But she had to say it. 'Besides, my father *was* special.'

'I'm certainly not allowed to forget it, nor that Dr Belle Geddes is better than me.' His tone was so bitter that she drew away to look at him.

'What do you mean?' She had never seen his mouth like that before: peevish, the corners turned down.

'Your Uncle Ernest, for one, has been decidedly cool to me since their baby died.'

'You're imagining it. He's deeply grieved. They both are, but he'd never be like that.'

'Wouldn't he? You don't know the subtle ways he shows it. He's from a fine Glasgow family, isn't he, and his stepmother used to be his nurse, isn't that the way of it?'

'What does that matter?' she said, astonished.

'I'm a farmer's son. I don't have the social graces of Mr Murray-Hyslop. He's put me in my place and no two ways about it since I attended his wife. And he hasn't asked me to see her since . . . it happened.'

'But you were away in Edinburgh! Belle Geddes had to be called in. Oh, he wouldn't slight you like that without a reason . . .' She stopped, dismayed. 'What are you talking about, Colin?'

His face cleared. He laughed. His eyes were merry again. 'I don't know what I'm talking about. Just yapping on about nothing. All I know is I'm wasting time talking.' He kissed her and she pushed the conversation to the back of her mind.

He left before her mother came in. 'We'll start our Thursdays again,' he said, 'and maybe some Sundays we'll be able to have a run in my motor car up into the country. Oh, Ellie, you make everything worth while. I dreaded coming back . . .'

She went to see Lizzie regularly. Jonty had now gone back to school and the children's nurse had decided they had had enough of Christmas festivities and recalled them into her fold. Lizze was now up and going about her bedroom, looking more lovely than ever, Ellie thought. She had the tall girl's admiration for neat and smaller women.

'You have an ethereal look about you,' she said kissing her.

'Oh, I'll soon get rid of that! I'm resting to please Ernest. I'd come to terms quicker about losing the bairn if I was going about my own affairs. Up here I only have more time to think.'

'You had a bad time, Lizzie, and it was a great shock to your nervous system. All your plans, all your waiting time for nothing . . .'

'Nothing's for nothing. You'll find that out. Losing a baby is an experience I wouldn't like to go through again but it's taught me something. We take healthy babies too much for granted. I won't forget it, although I think we've stopped.' She smiled sadly. 'One loss is enough.'

'Colin's deeply distressed about it,' Ellie said.

'I'm sure he is. Ernest's a bit hard on him. He did all he could. You tell him from me that I bear him no ill-will.'

'I think he'd like to hear that from Ernest.'

'Maybe in his own time. It was an experience for Ernest as well. It takes you by the throat . . . Now we must stop being gloomy. Thank you for looking after Jonty. I felt badly about him, but a sick-room's no place for a young lad.'

'He'll be better at school. He's at an awkward age.'

'Yes, you're right. Ernest ought to have talks with him.' She smiled at Ellie. 'You know what I mean. That's not for mothers. But I was looking forward to seeing him on this holiday . . . he's growing so like Nigel.' Her eyes filled with tears. 'See, they're turning me into an invalid. It's high time I got back to my usual routine. The first thing is, I'm giving up this gloomy room and moving back to my own bed. I know it'll shock that woman, Galbraith, but I sleep far better close to my husband.'

'Why don't you give her the sack?'

'I have. She's going tomorrow.' She shook her head. 'It wasn't a good arrangement, that, Ellie. I'd have been better with your mother.'

She, too, was glad to get back to her usual routine, getting up at six in the morning to catch the early train to Glasgow and then the tramcar to Queen Margaret College. It had not been a good Christmas but it was behind her now, and there was Colin. She would see him every Thursday, and perhaps they would walk on Sundays, strolling along by the Sholtie, or going for runs in his motor. He would prefer that since he thought the Sholton folk were gossips. She would talk to him about all kinds of things, her work, perhaps their future. She could not foresee a future which did not contain him.

He was not the same. He was merry, but not consistently so, she soon found, and his eyes would not meet hers. And his lovemaking was rough when he stopped the motor in dark lanes. At first he apologized, and then he gave up apologizing and her love for him was so great that she told herself she did not mind.

She was a career woman. He was a doctor. They were both informed, advanced, different; if he kissed her breasts was that a sin? She was seeing breasts every day in the dissecting room, old ones, young ones. Had Charlie

329

kissed her mother's breasts before they married? She knew they had waited a long time. It must have been difficult, but nevertheless, she could not imagine him doing that. Not that he was priggish, simply that he had a respect for women, and an especial respect for his wife. It had been evident in everything he did or said.

But that was long ago. This was 1912. They were no longer living in Edwardian times, this was the age of progress and advancement for women as well as men. Besides, some girls told her of far worse things than just having their breasts kissed.

In March she sat her professional examination and was surprised that some of the questions seemed difficult. Halfway through the paper she panicked and thought she was going to faint. By the time she managed to gain control of herself she had lost a precious ten minutes. It was a scramble to get finished, and she knew she had skimped the remaining questions.

She told Colin (she dared not tell her mother), and he said he had always felt like that. 'They thought I was brainy at Glasgow High, but that was because there was no competition. It was a different matter when I got to University. I just scraped through my Finals.'

When she got her results, *she* had just scraped through. Both her anatomy and physiology professors saw her separately and said they were disappointed in her. She would really have to pull her socks up.

She chose an evening when she was not going out with Colin and she and her mother were sitting companionably at the fire. Maevy had said several times she really must go upstairs and freshen herself up before dinner. She looked tired. She had reached her half century now, and still did not spare herself, working every day at McGraths, going to Suffragette meetings several times each week. It enabled her to see Colin quite a lot. He had a capacity for dropping in when he knew her mother would not be there.

'I got poor results in my exams, Mother,' she said.

Maevy looked up from her book. 'Did you fail?'

'No, but I just scraped through.' Now that she had started she might as well tell her everything. 'I was warned by the professors. There was a letter . . .'

'Let me see it.'

She took it out of her handbag, handed it over without speaking. There was a great relief in her, as well as shame.

Her mother read it, sighed, then looked up. 'You haven't done yourself justice, Ellie. That's what I find hardest to take.'

'I panicked. I don't know what came over me.'

'Could it be that you hadn't worked hard enough and you couldn't answer the questions?'

'I *was* working hard! You don't always see me.'

'But Susan does. You should remember that. I know how often Colin Thomson comes here when I'm out.'

'He only drops in . . .'

'And forgets to go away. Is he courting you, Ellie? He hasn't said anything to me.'

'We don't talk about that . . .'

'Well, you should. You should know where you stand. He's monopolized you for over six months. You aren't working the way you did in your first year. Is he more important to you than your work?'

'I love him, Mother!' She could not stand any more of this. 'You don't understand!' She burst into tears, putting her hands to her face.

Maevy came and sat beside her. She put an arm round her. 'I'm not hounding you, at least I don't mean to. Why didn't you say, Ellie?'

'Well,' she sobbed, still with her hands to her face, 'we aren't courting . . . not in the way you mean it. There's

331

no talk of marriage. He knows my views. And he doesn't come here as often as he used to, officially, because he feels that the family blame him for Lizzie losing her baby.'

'No one ever said that.'

'No, you're all too polite. You know how polite and icy Ernest can be. He's made Lizzie change back to Belle Geddes and you don't ask him for dinner now.'

'I've been busy all winter. You know that.'

'You're always busy but it didn't stop you asking him before. Don't you like him?' She took her hands away from her face. Her tears had stopped.

'He's . . . yes, I like him.'

'You aren't very enthusiastic.'

'Look,' her mother put her hand on her arm, 'I'm not objecting to him. Dry your eyes.' She handed her a handkerchief. 'If Colin's keeping you off your work then that's a different matter. I don't want to influence you. You'll have to sit down and think about this on your own. You're a good worker. You have a flair for medicine. It's in your blood. We had high hopes of you.'

'Maybe if you had less high hopes it would be easier for me.'

'Do you think that?' Her mother's face was sad. 'Do I push you?'

'No, you don't push me, but it's there . . . oh, I don't know what to think! I ought to be happy, but everything's going wrong . . .' The tears ran down her cheeks again. She ran from the room. She thought her mother said, 'Ellie, come back . . .' but she did not want to hear her.

14

Travelling to London in the train with the other women, Belle wondered what she was doing there. Her mind was split in two. On the one hand, she believed that if she cared deeply enough about something she had to prove it, and surely she cared deeply enough about liberty and freedom for women.

'Deeply enough' was the operative term, she thought. The only time she had cared deeply without any qualification was for Charlie McNab. Maevy would never believe it if she told her that her own grief had been greater than hers, his wife. 'People shared your grief,' she would have said. 'You were surrounded by love and sympathy from all your friends and family. I had to grieve alone.'

Ah, well, it was a good thing she had found something to engage her leisure time, such as it was. The time she feared most was when she was alone in the rooms she had moved into once both parents were dead. She had not wanted the responsibility of a home, disliked domesticity. There her thoughts could run freely on that man who, unknown to him, had absorbed all her love: on his wryness, on his black eyes which had taken possession of her so completely without once touching her body.

And on the other hand? She looked around the compartment, listening to the noise, the laughter. What was this madcap scheme she was engaged in with these women, some of them professional like herself, certainly, but the others loud-mouthed and raucous, sincere enough, but giving the impression that they were only there for the jaunt?

Some of them had never been in London before. When volunteers had been asked for at the meeting in St Andrew's Hall there had been excited cries of assent. It was an expedition into unknown territory, a chance to see the metropolis, maybe see some of the well-known figures in the cause like the Pankhursts, the Pethick Lawrences, even the great Lloyd George and Keir Hardie, or that turncoat, Winston Churchill. They had gone into it the way some men went to war.

The politicians were to blame with their endless ploys and subterfuge. How long ago was it since Asquith had announced that a Reform Bill would be presented making franchise more democratic, with amendments for women's suffrage? And they were still waiting. No, she assured herself, there was no other way than this – militant aggression as some called it, demonstrations to show the country the injustices of the present system. Millions of women were depending on them, women who were tied to their homes with children and who could not join in the demonstrations themselves. It was something for the future. If you were happily married and building a home and family together, that was a stake in the future. She had none.

Rooms had been booked for them in various houses of sympathizers, and Belle was put up in a prim semi-detached in Fulham, with one of the loud-mouthed women whom she had listened to in the train. They had to share a bedroom, and she decided to put up with it with good grace. Were they not sisters under the skin?'

'Are ye a doactor, then?' her sleeping companion asked. 'Weel, a never! A wid hae thoct you wid hae plenty to dae without *this* caper.'

'I have,' she smiled, 'but I have a partner. He can managed without me for a day or two. It'll do him good.'

As a matter of fact Colin had been difficult since Christmas. She thought it must be because of the loss of

Lizzie Murray-Hyslop's baby. She had reassured him, knowing that he was deeply offended that Ernest had asked her to attend Lizzie in his place. Her private opinion was that Colin was ham-fisted. He was better behind his surgery desk charming his patients with that merry smile of his. He was too susceptible to women, not professional enough, and perhaps aware of his own deficiencies.

But he was a likeable lad, if without any great depth. It was a pity that Ellie McNab seemed to have fallen for him. She had met them on the towpath of the Sholtie when she was walking her dog, and the girl's eyes had made her feel uneasy. On, no, she had thought, smiling and saying, 'Good evening,' he's not good enough for Charlie's lass . . .

'Hae ye got yer stanes ready? They gied me a bag tae tie roon ma waist.' Her companion was unlacing her stays. Her underwear looked none too clean, but then she was not 'gaun tae the doactor's', which generally made some patients make an extra effort.

'I took a hammer,' she said, 'I thought I could hide it in my muff. Some have wrapped a flint in paper and tied a string round it so that they can drop it though the hole without hurting anyone.'

'Who's worried aboot hurtin' anybody? Is that no' how we're here?' Belle decided it would be better not to get involved in that discussion.

'How did you manage to get away from your home?' she asked.

'Ma man's no workin'. He was signed aff frae John Broon's last year wi' a bad back. He'll jist hae to take care o' the weans. Oh, it's gaun tae be a great tare!' She had now emerged through the neckline of a voluninous pink nightgown and plumped herself into bed. 'It's a treat tae stretch yerself, isn't it? Ma ankles are aw swelt up.'

Belle would dearly have liked to read but she did not

see any books at the woman's bedside. 'Do you want to put the gas out?' she said.

'Aye, am right tired, and we'll be at it aw day the morrow. Ma name's Daisy, Daisy McConachie. Whit's yours?'

'Belle Geddes.'

'Aye, that sounds like a doactor's name. Doactor Geddes. If a tak' poorly in the middle o' the nicht, am aw right wi' you, sure a am!' She gave a fat chuckle.

'Yes, I'll see you right,' Belle said, laughing. She and Daisy would get on fine.

It took all day to get organized. Belle chafed at the delay. They had to wait for the London organizer to arrive and drive them to their rendezvous, a row of fashionable shops in the Strand. She dropped them off half-a-mile from their chosen place, and told them to stroll along, looking as innocent as possible.

It was only an hour or so before closing time, and the street was busy with last-minute shoppers. As Belle looked at the beautiful goods behind the plate-glass windows, drapery, millinery and jewellery, her natural sense of order made her want to turn and run away. But it was a battle for the rights of women, she reminded herself. Soldiers going into battle had to overcome their personal feelings for the good of their cause.

She and Daisy were necessary cogs. The organizer had told them that when the commotion caused by their party made further attacks impossible, other ladies would be furthering the cause elsewhere. They would be driving up to fashionable shops, would be shown in as ostensible purchasers, before they too produced hammers and stones from their muffs and hurled them through the window.

The unreality of the situation she had got herself into overcame her. Her fingers trembled as she grasped the hammer concealed in her muff. She had always had a great fear of breakages, even in her own rooms. Mrs

Lawson, her landlady, had strict instructions not to touch her treasured pieces of Bell Pottery (she remembered someone telling her that Queen Margaret College had been the home of the famous Bell brothers), her Spode china, and not to polish her few fine pieces of furniture, especially her Chippendale mirror. But for her, Belle Geddes, to smash deliberately those beautiful vases of *cloisonné* ware behind that window! She closed her eyes against the thought.

She supposed Mrs Lawson regarded her as an old maid, but it was true that for lack of a husband you began to put too much emphasis on possessions. She thought of her excessive fears that her Dandy Dinmont, Jock, might be run over. She looked forward to his boisterous manly welcome every night, even to his weight on her bed – for want of the weight of a man – the thought crossed her mind. Of course there was still Hamish Black at Crannoch, but lately she had grown tired of him. She suspected he felt the same about her. There had been no real love there, just a need.

'Ur ye ready?' Daisy said in her ear.

'Aye, am ready,' she said.

She had suddenly an overwhelming desire to get the thing over and done with. She saw she was opposite an elegant dress shop with a black and white sign above it which said simply, 'Robert, Couturier'. In the window were a few dresses draped over elegant little pieces of furniture. Behind them hung a Chippendale mirror . . .

She took the hammer from her muff. Someone jostled her, and she said, politely, 'Sorry.' The man smiled, not seeing the hammer. This can't be me, she thought, general practitioner Belle Geddes, intent on behaving like a hooligan from the Glasgow slums with their brokendown closes stinking with filth . . . but there were women there, too, harassed, overworked, depending on her.

It was like blood lust, but, of course, it was the adrenalin

337

flowing. She knew if she put her finger on her wrist she would feel her pulse racing. She raised the hammer above her head, ran towards the plate glass window and smashed it, time and time again. She saw the Chippendale mirror sway then crash onto a stand, break into pieces.

The noise was terrific, whistles blowing, people screaming; there was a dancing, frock-coated man in the shop entrance, an elegant woman behind him, her hand to her mouth, her eyes staring . . . 'Rin!' It was Daisy's voice. 'Rin fur Christ's sake! Here's the bluidy police!' She gave Belle a vicious push, then darted ahead of her through the crowds like a centre forward at a Rangers and Celtic match.

She turned and raced in the opposite direction. She had seen the helmets of policemen bobbing amongst the crowds. She darted round the first corner she came to and ran full tilt into the arms of a burly Bobby who caught her before she could escape, twisting her arms behind her back.

'Thought you'd got away, did you?' There was another policeman there, a younger one. She felt a hard punch on her ribs.

'Stop that!' she shouted, shaking, but amazed at herself. 'You're assaulting me.'

'And what the 'ell do *you* think you were doing, Miss?' The burly policeman who was holding her had a voice with an unpleasant Cockney twang. Give me Daisy's 'Glesca talk' any day, she thought. Her hat had fallen off, and when she attempted to pick it up the younger policeman kicked it out of the way.

'I don't want a hatpin in my face, thank you. I advise you to come quietly.' She had thought at first he was the more pleasant of the two. 'If you don't, we'll drag you by the hair.' She saw his face, red, bursting with anger, pushed near hers, and she spat into it. She might as well be hung for a sheep as a lamb.

15

It was a lovely May morning. Diamond drops hung on the bushes, making the garden appear to tremble in the sunlight. The lawn shimmered. Maevy, breakfasting near the open window, saw that the wallflowers round the summer-house at the foot of the garden were a mass of colour. She could imagine their wet, velvety smell.

'Shame we both have to work today, Ellie.' They were going through the letters on their plates. 'This is one from Belle, I'm sure.' She had noticed the London stamp and another more ominous rubber one on the envelope. 'It will be from Holloway.'

'Mine is from Kieran. Read Belle's, Mother, and see what she's saying.'

'I'm almost afraid to open it.' She slit the envelope, glanced at the first few lines and shook her head. 'It's as I feared.'

'Go on, read it. You're only making it worse.'

'Yes.' The pain in her heart surprised her. She's done this for us . . . She pulled herself together and began to read.

Well, it's happened. I've been forcibly fed and it wasn't pleasant. I'm not surprised that even doctors have pronounced it a brutal thing to do. I think it was worse for me, if anything, understanding the mechanics of it, so to speak. But on the other hand I suffered less than some of the others. Mind over matter, or maybe I'm tough.

What I find even worse is the confinement in dark damp punishment cells, and the frog-marching. It's degrading. Because I've been on hunger strike I haven't been beaten but some have. We need Keir Hardie here to defend us . . .

Maevy looked up. 'Isn't that terrible? To treat an educated woman like that!'

'You mean that the ill-educated ones are more used to
being beaten?' She couldn't put a foot right with Ellie
these days. She went on reading.

But the surprising thing is the amount of laughter, because in
most cases we have powers of resilience which the authorities
hadn't counted on. We sing our songs, Ethel Smyth's 'March of
the Women', and other bawdier ones sometimes, 'Glesca yins'.
Some of the women who are artists do funny drawings to amuse
us, and the writers write humorous pieces and pass them around.
We model animals from the bread, childish stuff, but you'd be
surprised at the joy there is amongst us in spite of the conditions.

But it's liberty we miss, although it's liberty we're fighting for.
On a morning like this, seeing the sun above those high walls, I
wish I were a bird and could fly away back to Sholton. It's only
now that I realize I'm happy there with my quiet two rooms and
my dog and my work and my patients and my friends, like you.
Thank you for the parcels you send. We're only allowed one a
week.

I'm glad sometimes that my parents are dead. 'If only you'd
stayed at home with me,' mother once said. This was when I
qualified. Well, if we all did that, women would go on being
chattels, under-valued, unappreciated, unfulfilled. Knowing
your cause is just makes it possible to stand anything. And I'll
soon be home. Sholton is my home . . .

Maevy looked up at Ellie. 'It makes you humble, doesn't
it?'

'It makes me angry. How dare they treat women like
that! Frog-marching! Isn't there a painting I've seen somewhere of men walking round and round a prison yard? Like
caged animals. Bad enough for men, worse for women . . .'

'As bad for women as men, since it's equality we're
fighting for,' Maevy said, but Ellie ignored her.

'And forcing a tube down her throat! You and I should
go and throw a brick through the City Chambers windows
this very morning in protest.'

Maevy shook her head, smiling. 'I haven't the temperament for it and I doubt if you have. You certainly haven't
the time. Belle's fighting your battle for you. You can
best repay her by working hard and making sure you get
good results in your next exam.'

'You never miss a chance, do you?'

'That's no way to speak to your mother!' Now she was
angry.

'Well, don't nag! I *am* working. I do hardly anything
else but work.'

When you're not seeing Colin Thomson, Maevy
thought, but this time held her tongue. There was something wrong with her relationship with Ellie these days,
but she must not blame him. It could well be her own
fault. She said gently, 'I didn't mean to nag. I'm sorry.
What was Kieran saying?' The girl's face was sullen.
'Ellie?' she said.

'His leg is much improved. He can do without a stick
now. He's been busy buying an apartment in New York
and goes home each weekend to Wanapeake.' She was
terse.

'And Kate and James?'

'She's well and happy, as she always is.' *She* doesn't
nag. The unspoken comment was there. 'All the grandchildren are well. Uncle James is hoping to get out a little,
now that the weather's mild. They've had a cold spring
but it's hot now. Kieran might come here in the summer.'

'I hope he does. Well, give them my love when you
write. Do you have a regular correspondence with
Kieran?'

'If I have any time to spare. Besides,' she tossed her
head, 'I don't want to be a substitute for Lizzie.'

'What do you mean?'

'He adored her, maybe still does. They used to write to
each other. I've no intention of taking her place.'

'Oh, that's nonsense! If he did feel like that for Lizzie

341

it's all over now. He knows that. Lizzie and Ernest are the most devoted couple I've known. In a way the loss of that baby brought them closer. The only slight worry is that Jonty no longer has Crawfords to look forward to, but Ernest will help him when the time comes.'

'Well, it's nice to see somebody happy.' Ellie got up.

Somebody got out of their bed on the wrong side, Maevy thought, but she was learning sense. She did not say it.

Ellie met Colin in Glasgow that evening – it was Thursday – and once again they went to Rogano's. This time they did not have oysters and champagne. There had been no more mention of his windfall from his elderly aunt, and she teased him about it. 'Have you spent all your aunt's money, Colin?'

'What money?' He was studying the menu. 'I love the seafood here. I'm going to have prawns. What about you?'

'No, thanks, I'll have plaice and chips, thank you – very plebeian. I don't think I'm an exotic eater.'

'You have to live dangerously.' His brown eyes crinkled up.

'And *have* you spent all your windfall?' She loved teasing him. Thursdays were the bright spots in a week devoted to work. She enjoyed her classes, especially now that they were allowed to go into the medical and surgical wards in the Royal. She found herself drawn to surgery. Her hands were adroit, as Charlie's had been. There were nurses who still remembered him and spoke highly of him. One of the surgeons had said to her, 'Charlie McNab's daughter? We'll expect great things of you.'

Strangely enough, Colin showed little interest in her studies. When she tried to engage him in a medical conversation he said he was out to enjoy himself, that he got enough of it in the practice. And because her mother was critical of her these days, she took a perverse delight in not telling her how much she enjoyed surgery, although she knew it would have given her pleasure. She would surprise her with her examination results this time, she thought, and then she would have to apologize for her attitude.

'Mother had a letter from Belle Geddes this morning,' she said. 'She's been forcibly fed.'

'I'm not surprised.' He smiled up at the waitress who had appeared at his side. 'I'll take a prawn salad tonight, Maymie. Miss McNab will have your plaice. Tartare sauce?' His smile directed at Ellie now was that of a man in a role he liked.

'Yes, please.'

'And all the trimmings.' He gave the menu to the waitress. 'I'll leave it in your capable hands, Maymie.'

'I'll see everything's to your liking, doctor.' The woman smirked as she turned away.

'She's in a trance when she speaks to you,' Ellie said.

'Rubbish.' He looked pleased. And then, 'Belle was stupid to refuse to eat. It only antagonizes them. The sooner she's out of prison the better. I could do with her help in the practice.'

'She's fighting for her principles by every means in her power. I would have done the same.'

'Well, why aren't you a member of the WSPU?'

'Because I've got to get my Finals first. My mother would take a fit if I took up my time with that. It's bad enough going out with you.'

'I know she doesn't like me,' he said. The waiter came and poured some wine into the glass before him. 'Your usual, doctor.' He was smiling, deferential.

'Thank you.' He sipped, looked thoughtful, said, 'Yes, up to standard,' indicated Ellie's glass: 'Miss McNab.'

'You have a bee in your bonnet,' she said when the

man had gone. 'Ever since that business with Lizzie you've thought they're all against you.'

'I know they are. They've had to have me up at the Hall recently because the children developed chickenpox, but there was a decided coolness. I said to Ernest when I met him in the hall that I was rushed off my feet, and he didn't look at all sympathetic, just said why didn't I get someone else in Belle's place.'

'Well, why don't you?'

'I tried, didn't I, but I can't get anyone suitable. So I've just had to battle on. I can tell you, Ellie, it's all work and no play with me.'

'Aren't you allowed money for an assistant?'

'Yes, but if I can't find one, I should be allowed to pocket it, wouldn't you think?'

'I don't know about the ethics of it.' She would not say any more. She did not like the girl she was becoming recently – 'nebby', they would call it in the village: touchy with her mother this morning, and now Colin. Was it caused by working too hard, or frustration? She loved him, but he never talked about their future or marriage. 'This is the high spot of my week,' she said. 'I could scarcely sleep last night for thinking about it.'

His brown eyes became warm. 'Ellie . . . do you know what I was thinking in bed last night?'

'No . . .'

'That it's light longer now. Our dark lane is a thing of the past. Those cold winter nights when we snuggled together for warmth, gone . . .'

'It was so . . . hole-in-the-corner anyway,' she said. She was doing it again. 'Wouldn't you rather come home with me, sit in the garden, talk to mother?'

'If that's what you want.' His eyes emptied, became cold.

'No, but I thought this night we might. I was a bit short

with her this morning. We used to be . . . such good friends. Something's gone wrong.'

'You have the same feeling as I have. Something's happened to Sholton as far as I'm concerned. I feel like clearing out. Ellie . . .' He bent towards her then sat up again. The waitress was there with her panoply of silver dishes. She seemed to take an unconscionable time in laying them precisely on the table, placing serving spoons in the correct position, lifting the lids of the tureens to let the rich smells escape.

'There you are, doctor. I think you'll find everything to your satisfaction.' She went away, fussy and pleased, the white bow of her apron bobbing on her black-skirted backside.

'What were you going to say?' Ellie asked him. Was he going to propose to her, or at least suggest that they should become engaged? She had less than two years to go now, then perhaps they could start a practice on their own somewhere else . . .

'Supposing . . .' – he put his hand on hers – 'supposing I decided to go to Australia. Would you come with me?'

'Australia!' She'd been thinking of somewhere further into the country, or maybe the Ayrshire coast. It would be nice to live by the sea. 'When?'

'As soon as I get tickets. Next month.'

'Next month! You must be joking. I won't be qualified till 1914. I'm doing well this term. I can't possibly break up my career now.'

'You could take it up again in Australia.'

'How do you know that? I might have to go back to the beginning, sit examinations according to their regulations. Besides, I'm getting to know surgeons in the Royal. I would want to be near enough to Glasgow in case I decide to go in for that instead of general practice.'

'Surgery!' He withdrew his hand. 'You must be mad!'

'That's what Belle Geddes is having tubes stuck down

her throat for,' she waved her hands wildly, not caring about the other diners, 'so that people like me could have freedom to do medicine, to choose their speciality . . . !

'I never heard such nonsense! It seems to me that I come a very poor second in your calculations,' his mouth was bitter, 'like the rest of your family in Sholton, an also-ran. I'm surprised you can bring yourself to come out with me, a simple GP . . .'

She felt the tears rush to her eyes. 'I don't know what you're talking about, Colin. I don't understand you. You used to be in sympathy with women's efforts. I heard you once say you'd join the Men's League. You know I have to finish my course. Don't bother about the surgery – that was just a dream of mine – but nothing would make me give up at this stage.'

'Because of your mother,' he said. 'She comes first.'

'Because of myself. It's my career. My own career. Nobody's getting in the way of it, not even you . . .' She saw his closed face. 'Oh, Colin, I'm sorry, you know I love you, but if you love me you wouldn't ask me to go to Australia in a month!'

'I was asking you to marry me.'

'You didn't say that. But even so, I couldn't, not in a month. I'd become engaged, you could put it off for a year or so . . .' He held up his hand to stop her.

'At least I know where I stand.' He was quite calm. 'Eat your plaice. It's growing cold.'

In the lane, surrounded by May flourish in the trees and meadowsweet in the ditch and a lark singing above them, she wept in his arms, saying that she was tired, she hadn't meant half of what she had said, but surely he could see that it was important for her to take her Finals here when she was more than halfway towards them.

'Yes, I see it, Ellie.' He seemed quieter than usual, and

his lovemaking was quiet, too. He did not unbutton her blouse even when she put her body close to him and sighed. 'We'd better get home,' he said, 'we don't want to make your mother suspicious.'

16

On a quiet Saturday afternoon at the end of the month, when Maevy was sitting in the garden, she looked up and saw Belle Geddes coming through the garden gate. She was thinner. Her shirt-waist showed the slenderness of her body. The seductive curves were gone.

She got up hurriedly and went, half-running, to greet her. 'Belle, you're back! Oh, I *am* pleased to see you!' She would have liked to throw her arms round her but there was a remoteness in the woman's face which she now saw was thinner also, and that the skin was bad. She had always had a fine complexion.

'Yes, back.' The rich curving smile was still there. 'You're one of the first I wanted to see. I'm on my rounds, catching up, but I was passing by and saw you in the garden.'

'Come away and sit down. Have you time for a cup of tea?' She put her arm round her and led her towards the summer-house where the chairs were set out.

'No thanks. I've a list as long as your arm.'

'You look well, but thinner.'

'Ah, but I have a woman's satisfaction of taking a size smaller in clothes. There's nothing to beat that.'

'You're right.' She laughed. 'That's a comfortable chair.' And when she was seated, 'Was it bad?'

'Bad enough, but it's faded away like 'snaw aff a dyke' now that I'm back. And the friends I've made! Oh, Maevy, you'll have to go to London with me and meet them. Some of the best and kindest people. They taught me how to live, how to endure. Yes, I got more out of it than the authorities bargained for.'

'But that force feeding! I didn't sleep for thinking about it.'

'You've done the same in the wards, as I have. Now I know what it's like for the other person. A valuable experience . . .' She obviously did not want to dwell on it. 'How's Ellie?'

'Fine. She's upstairs in her room. She's worked very hard this year, almost defiantly.'

'Defiantly?' Belle raised her eyebrows.

'Yes, it's a strange word. What I mean is that I hope she's getting more joy out of it at Queen Margaret's than she appears to do at home. She seems to think I'm driving her, and that I'm against Colin Thomson. I'm not. But he avoids me, doesn't come to the house.'

'So their romance is still going on?'

'Yes, hotter than ever.' She laughed.

'The hotter it is, maybe the sooner it'll blow cool.' She paused. 'It's really him I came to see you about . . .'

'Oh.' She was immediately alarmed.

'You're right about him having a chip on his shoulder.'

'Since Lizzie's baby?'

Belle nodded. 'And then he had all the extra work when I was away. He's got it into his head that the whole village is against him . . . and particularly your family.'

'I'm sorry about that. It's largely in his imagination.'

'He started on about it first thing when I got back – I must stop these euphemisms, 'away', 'got back', and say 'in prison' – and how he wasn't appreciated. I said he was probably overworked, although I can't understand why he didn't get help, but now that I was back he'd find things easier. Colin's his own worst enemy.'

'Yes.' What was she leading up to?

'He dropped a bombshell. He tells me he's booked a ticket to go to Australia next month. He's clearing out.'

'Go to Australia!' She was astonished. Then terrified. 'Did you say *one* ticket?'

'That's what he said. Did you think . . . Ellie . . .?'

'Yes, for a moment, and then I thought, no, she wouldn't do that, not throw over all her work, but you never know with the young these days. They aren't as obedient as we were.' She smiled. 'My mother, Lady Crawford, no less, used to carry the clothes rope under her apron to make us jump!'

'I had to leave home to get my way, so I shouldn't be too surprised if Ellie does the same.'

'But, Australia? Not without talking about it! You're sure he said *one* ticket?'

'Yes, sure. I wouldn't ask her, Maevy. If she thinks you don't approve of him it might send her into his arms. The bubble's bound to burst soon. He's got to tell her.'

'He's seeing her tomorrow. They go for a run in his motor on Sundays, or take a walk.'

'If I were you, I'd not say a thing, but I thought I'd better warn you. Well, I must get on.' She got up.

Maevy got up too. 'Belle,' she said, laying her hand on her arm, 'I'm right glad to see you back. You've been sorely missed.'

'And I've missed this place. You have to go away to appreciate what you love.' Her eyes were full. She turned and went away, walking quickly over the lawn.

Sunday afternoon seemed endless. Saturday had passed quickly enough although in a doleful manner. She and Ellie had gone to see John who was now confined to bed. He still did not know the extent of his illness, or if he did, he was not going to name it.

He was querulous, complaining of the new young minister who was 'slapdash' as he put it, although he was filling the church more than John had ever done. It was better to go away from the service at the kirk content with yourself than feeling full of guilt with the old Reverend's castigations ringing in your ear.

'It's a lovely day, John,' she said when they were sitting in the stuffy bedroom. 'Would you like Ellie and me to help you out of bed and over to the chair at the window? It would do you good.'

'Nothing will do me good when I have an unquiet mind,' he said. 'Why has the Lord struck me down like this, I ask myself, his willing servant, when there is so much to be done? And Isobel!' He turned up his eyes. 'Well, the soul tries her best, but she just doesn't have the stamina or the inclination. I'd be better to go the way Charlie went, quickly and cleanly.'

'It wasn't very clean, Uncle, to be smashed up in a motor car!' Ellie said.

'Ellie . . .' Maevy looked at her. She must know, as she did, that this man was wasting away. There should be a subject in the medical curriculum called 'An Understanding of Death'. Maybe they were too busy teaching their students how to keep people alive.

She had gone out wearing a muslin dress of pale mauve and carrying a wide straw hat with violets in the brim. She looked so young and beautiful that Maevy could have wept. Had Colin come in instead of keeping his motor engine running in the drive she would have said to him, 'Treat her gently, please.' What would Ellie be like when she came back?

The clock seemed to tick away the afternoon slowly, too slowly. Susan always slept after lunch, not in her bed, but stiff and upright in her rocking chair by the kitchen fire, her hands clasped in her lap. I'll find her there one day with no life in her, Maevy thought . . . Susan had once said to her in a rare communicative mood, 'Although you're a fine nurse, Maevy, I couldn't be bothered with you or anybody else pooterin' roon me. A'd like to go sudden-like.'

It was five o'clock. She'd gone into the kitchen and

made the tea, given Susan, greatly mortified, a cup. 'A'll no hae ye waitin' on me,' she said, starting up out of her chair.

'Now, you just sit down.' Maevy pushed her back. 'We're old friends.' She smiled. 'You've known me since I was a wee lassie.' You've known it all, she thought, from the time I was in love with John Craigie, that poor soul dying in the manse, from that quarrel with Patrick and Terence and them landing up in the Sholtie, Charlie dying . . . 'If you can't take a cup of tea from a friend there's something far wrong.'

She thought of going to the evening service and hearing some of the Reverend Peter Kennedy's boisterous Christianity, but she was not in the mood. Besides, Ellie might be back any minute now. She could not bear not to be here.

Six o'clock came and went. She was in the drawing-room tidying the drawers of her desk for something to do, when she heard the door bang and then the rush of feet upstairs. She waited for a second or two, anguished, and then thought fiercely, I'm her mother. I don't care whether she thinks I'm meddling or not. I have to be with her.

She went upstairs and knocked on Ellie's door but there was no reply. She listened and heard the strangled sobbing, and then a single harsh cry which had escaped. It did not sound like Ellie, that young girl of hers and Charlie's. This was a woman in terrible distress. She went in.

She was lying across the bed where she had flung herself; the hat with the flowers lay on the floor. 'Go away,' she said, turning her head away. 'I don't want you here.'

'No, I can't go away.' She lay down on the bed beside her and took her in her arms. 'I'm your mother, Ellie. Don't shut me out. Tell me what it is.'

'No, you're glad . . .'

'Glad!' She was angry. 'Glad of anything that makes you like this! I've never heard such a thing! Oh, Ellie, let me comfort you.' She turned her gently round, and this time the girl crept into her arms, shaking with sobs. Maevy stroked her face. It was hot and wet with tears.

'Tell your Mammy,' she said, weeping herself.

'He's going to Australia . . . but he doesn't want me. He's starting a new life on his own . . .' Her voice rose with a dreadful high keening. 'My heart is broken . . . broken . . .'

She persuaded Ellie next morning to travel in the train to Glasgow with her. She had appeared at breakfast pale from weeping and her hair bedraggled. All her beauty had gone. 'I'll just stay at home today, Mother,' she said, sitting down at the breakfast table.

Susan came in with the tray of toast and marmalade, Ellie's favourite. She had 'gone off' porridge some time ago much to Susan's disgust. 'You need something to stick to your ribs, ma lass, and if ye dae withoot it, that's aw ye'll have. Ye'll be doon tae skin and bone.' Now she took a swift sideways glance at the girl, her drooping head. 'And whit's wrang wi' ma lady this fine mornin'? You look as if ye'd been dragged in by the cat.'

'Mind your own business,' Ellie said.

'It *is* ma business. A'm responsible for the vittles in this hoose and seein' that ye eat it.' She plumped down the toast and marmalade and swept out.

'If you stay at home you'll have Susan fussing about you all day. She's worried about you. Nothing passes her. She would hear you downstairs in the middle of the night, making tea. I heard you. Take my advice and go to your classes.'

'I couldn't concentrate. Life's over for me.' Her calmness was frightening. 'I told you last night. I can't contemplate work, anything, without Colin.'

353

'Try some righteous indignation, then, instead of saying what you can't do. He could have told you he was going.' She thought of the word 'jilted', but dared not use it.

'He told me, he asked me if I would go, but it was in a month, and I said I had my career . . . but I didn't think he meant it.'

'He evidently did. Well, there you are, then.' She was a sensible girl after all when it came to the pinch. 'Your career's waiting for you, and so will Colin be if you want it . . .'

'No, that's finished.' Her voice was dull. 'I told you last night, he's going alone. He wants to make a clean start in a new country.'

'Wait and see. But meantime if you get back to College and get on you'll be through all the sooner and then you'll be your own mistress, free to do what you like, make your own decisions. It's great what a bit of independence can do for a woman, and some money of your own jingling in your pocket.' Belle Geddes knew that.

She did not answer, sitting with her head in her hands, dejected, without hope. After a long time she said without any life in her voice, 'Yes, I'll go.' She poured herself some tea and took a slice of toast from the rack. 'Pass the butter, please.'

'Try some of Susan's ginger marmalade,' Maevy said, 'it's never been better.'

She went to the Hall a few days later when she felt Ellie was showing some semblance of normality, although she was a different girl, withdrawn and quiet. But she was working with a dogged determination which took her upstairs immediately she had finished tea. If she spent half the time weeping, at least the other half would be spent working.

Lizzie was out with Ernest at a ball in the City Chambers, and she found her mother seated at the window of

her own room upstairs. She welcomed Maevy almost
sadly. She's looking her age, Maevy thought. Her vitality's gone. 'Oh, Maevy, am I glad to see you! I was just
sitting here feeling sorry for myself.'

She kissed her and sat down beside her at the window.
'What were you thinking about, Mother? You looked
pensive.'

'The old days, I'm always thinking of the old days. Of
your father and me at Colliers Row. Do you remember
Patrick and Terence getting rolling drunk when they were
just boys?'

'Yes, I do. And Isobel and I listening to you and father
laughing in bed when the commotion was over. It was
only after I was married to Charlie that I knew what that
pleasure was.'

'There will never be another one like Charlie for you,
nor Kieran for me. You stick to that.' She sighed.
'Braidholme. A happy house. You all away but wee
Lizzie with us. The joy she brought us! She's always been
a good lass to me, but I'm beginning to feel . . . out of
things now.'

'But you had fine times here with Lord Crawford.
Remember your lovely retiral ball? That gorgeous gown
you wore, with gold orchids and the mink trimming . . .'

'And the table to match, although without the mink
trimming.' She still had some fun left in her. 'Yes, that
was a night. Nigel and Lizzie got engaged then. Now
they're both gone, father and son.'

'But there's Jonty.'

'Yes, there's Jonty. Growing up fast. I wonder if there
will be room for his old granny here if he . . .'

'It's yours, and he's only twelve! Old granny indeed!
You'll have me weeping bitter tears and singing a
Highland dirge. Besides, Braidholme is always there, the
door wide open.'

'Aye, you've always said that, Maevy. I'm getting

sentimental in my old age. But I have a terrible longing for Ireland these days. I was looking out on those fine gardens and instead I was seeing the purple Curlew Mountains and the glimmer of Lough Arrow. It's a green bible, Ireland. That's how I think of it.'

'Terence and Honor would love to have you for a visit. Why don't you think of going?'

'Would you come with me?' Her face was wistful. The beautiful blue eyes still dominated her face.

'I couldn't, Mother. We're very busy at McGraths and Ernest is booked to go to Arran for July with Lizzie and the family. I've got to take charge.' And there was Ellie. She would come to that. 'Remember Patrick and Maria used to take a house there?'

'Yes, and that wee one that died, Mary. It's always been the right place for folks of quality, Arran, or so they tell me. They meet their cronies, I suppose, and that makes them feel safe. It has no great appeal for me. Oh, well, if you can't manage, that's that. I was the one who encouraged you to work at McGraths.'

'There's another reason, Mother . . .'

'What is it?'

'Dr Colin is going to Australia. You know he's been courting Ellie for over a year . . . if you could call it courting.'

'Is she going with him?' She saw her mother's back straighten. She had always faced trouble like that.

'No, he's going alone, but she's heartbroken. He sprung it on her. He's been disenchanted with Sholton for some time.'

'And Sholton's been disenchanted with him. He's all front. Not good enough for Ellie. And Belle Geddes is a better doctor.'

'She's back. Did you know?'

'Yes, she came to see me for my arthritis. It's improved her, prison. Made her gentler.'

'Yes, I thought so too.'

'So what's to be done with the lass if she's breaking her heart? Will she go out to him later?'

'I doubt it. Her pride's been hurt. She won't forgive him for that. Mother . . . I've just had a notion while we were talking . . . Couldn't you persuade *her* to take you to Ireland?'

'Oh, I'm too old for Ellie!'

'Rubbish. You've always got on well with each other. Indeed, you've a way with the young ones. You might get her to talk it out. I've a feeling there's a lot she hasn't told me.'

'I never pry. You haven't learn that, Maevy. You've always been slow to learn. It's your stubborn bit. It's only when you don't pry that they confide in you.'

'I'm half-a-hundred and you're still treating me like a child, but I'll let it pass. Would you ask her? She's fond of Terence and Honor. It's just what she needs. New faces.' She became enthusiastic. 'It's just the answer. She'll be on holiday soon. There are those three fine girls. Moira's married and I think the other two are engaged, or have young men, so there would be plenty of young life. And perhaps young Terence would be home from Paris as well. And his father would take you to see all your old haunts. You could give him advice on his horses and all that . . . If I wrote and asked Honor, would you agree?'

'Would Ellie agree?'

'I think her pride would make her jump at the chance to be away from Sholton. And besides, if I told her that you long to be in Ireland and can't manage without her, that would do it.'

'You're a manipulator of the first degree.' There were tears in her eyes. 'But you're right about me longing for Ireland. Your father often talked about wanting to feel its

357

softness on his cheek. I've a notion I might find him there . . .'

Maevy put her arm round her. 'You'll find happiness. And you've always liked a jaunt.'

'Yes, so I have. I was a great one for a jaunt . . .'

17

'You're manipulating me,' she said, when her mother first mentioned her going to Ireland. She did not know it was the word her grandmother had used.

'I admit it was my idea, but she's afraid to go alone. She's old now, Ellie.'

'Don't get at me that way.'

'I'm not getting at you in any way. You're on holiday now. You've done well in your exams.'

'I couldn't care . . .'

'Oh, yes, you care or you wouldn't have done well. And you're hanging about the house with nothing to do. I told you to ask one of your College friends to stay but you haven't done it.'

'I don't like anyone. I like my own company.'

'Ellie,' she said, 'I know how you're feeling. I want to tell you something. I was once hopelessly in love with a man, not your father. When this man preferred someone else to me, I nearly died. That's why it took me so long to make up my mind about Charlie, or at least one of the reasons.'

She was roused out of her apthy. 'But I thought he'd always been the only one?'

'No. It's the lucky ones who know who the right one is first go. But maybe it makes you more appreciative in the long run. Certainly there was never anyone else in my life after I realized your father was the man for me.'

'I never suspected that.' She was curious. She had always been curious. Once when she had been saying, 'Why, Daddy?' for the umpteenth time, he had said that

was what would make her a good doctor. 'Was it somebody . . . local?'

'It was your Aunt Isobel's husband. Oh, I can see
you're shocked. You think of him as the Reverend, a bit
pompous, a dying man now, but he wasn't always like
that. In his youth he was handsome. When he visited our
house I secretly worshipped him. And when your Aunt
Isobel went to America with grandmother I was sure he
loved me. I was taking care of my father and almost every
night John visited us. I . . . shivered if he looked at me.'
Didn't *she* know that feeling? As if your insides were
drawing together. 'And then when we went to meet Isobel
and my mother at the docks she went into his arms.'

She could not find words. For the first time since that
terrible afternoon when Colin had told her, she felt
sorrow for others. Her mother, Aunt Isobel, Uncle John
. . . it was as if she had just met three strangers. But it
must be true. Mother had always been trusty, true,
sometimes splitting hairs in her truthfulness.

She held back the emotion her mother's story had
aroused in her. They would end up weeping in each
other's arms and she had done with weeping. 'I'll go and
see Grandma,' she said, 'and we can talk it over.'

They left for Ireland at the beginning of August, taking
the train to Stranraer and then the boat across the water.
It was a calm crossing.

'You're quiet, Grandma,' she said as they sat in the
saloon.

'I'm husbanding my strength.' Her face was calm under
the wide straw hat. Her red hair still waved on her brow.
'We've a long way to go yet.'

Her trained eye saw already the signs of fatigue on the
beautiful face. She's anaemic, she thought, and her heart's
bad. There's a tinge of blue in her lips. She knew Belle
had been visiting her, but she had given permission for

360

her to go. 'All medicine isn't in bottles,' she had said when Ellie had asked if her grandmother was well enough to travel.

She had got into the habit of dropping in at the end of the surgeries, not to consult Belle, but because she found her easier to talk to than her mother. She showed her her examination papers; they discussed the questions and how Ellie had answered them. Belle had interesting ideas.

'It's a curious fact,' she said, 'that having special medical schools for women has held back their progress instead of furthering it. St Andrew's University opened its doors to women from the very first. You're luckier than I was, of course, since they're gradually learning sense in Glasgow, too.'

She spoke of prison as if they had done her a favour. 'The women were wonderful,' she said. 'I discovered I was concentrating too much on myself, telling myself I was doing a worthwhile job tending the sick. But there's more to life than that. There are the big social questions of the day, the poverty of some opposed to the riches of others and what can be done about it, the reasons for war. You have to understand the reasons first . . . Here,' she opened a drawer in her desk, 'I had some of their poems copied. Sometimes when I get down I have a read of them.' She pushed the sheaf of papers across the table to Ellie. 'Take them.'

'But they're yours.'

'I have more. Keep them, Ellie. Maybe they'll help . . .'

And yet Colin Thomson's name was never mentioned between them. Belle had engaged an elderly bachelor who was efficent and already liked, and it seemed as if the water had closed over Colin's head as far as Sholton was concerned, and he had ever existed. But that did not stop the longing for him. Often she lay sleepless, reliving their lovemaking in the dark lane off the Sholtie Brae, and 'shivered'. That was the word her mother had used, a shivering delight. It helped if she thought of what she and Belle had talked about.

'You aren't a great talker yourself,' her grandmother said. 'Lizzie's a chatterbox. My, the good times we had with her at Braidholme before she went to live with Isobel and John.'

'It's strange that Uncle Terence is her father.'

'Yes, life's strange.' She smiled, shaking her head. 'I never knew any couple who did less with their lives than John and Isobel, and yet life surges round them!'

There was the long train journey from Dublin to Boyle and her grandmother slept some of the time. Ellie sat beside her looking out on the strange landscape of Ireland, greener than around Sholton, a fresher green, and the small white cottages huddled together in seemingly empty tracts of land. After the opulence of Dublin it looked like a poor country. But then they were torn with dissension. She must ask Uncle Terence about the Home Rule question, and pass on her findings to Belle.

Then suddenly, it seemed, they were on the last lap of their journey and her grandmother seemed to shed her years and her blue eyes became deeper. 'We're coming near Boyle, Ellie! Maybe we'll get a glimpse of the Abbey. My, that's a fine place for you to see. Oh, it's a grand place, Boyle, with a fine hotel. Terence and I stayed in it once and you'll never eat finer trout than you get there. You could fish for them out of the window. But just you wait. They'll be taking you jaunts all over the place . . .'

'The gift of the gab's got into you, Grandma,' she said, laughing, 'it must be in the air.'

The whole family were there to meet them on the station platform. She remembered them all coming to grandfather's funeral and Uncle Terence and Aunt Honor to Lizzie's wedding. There were the two beautiful cousins,

362

a strange young man and a litle boy of about two. When Ellie helped Grandma off the train she went straight into the arms of her son, while Honor enveloped *her* in a warm hug. She had just time to look at the dark cloudy hair, the Irishness of the features, the luscious mouth.

'Will you look at them!' Honor said. 'She's got eyes for no one but Terence. Sure and it's good to see you, Ellie! it seems no time since I saw you running about Braid-holme with your long plaits flying. You've grown into a beautiful young woman.' She felt herself grow beautiful with the words, shed her sadness.

'It's wonderful to see you, Aunt Honor, in your proper setting. It . . . becomes you.'

'Now, that's a rare like thing to say. And here are my three: Clare's nearest your age, now Mrs Aidan O'Brien, but that hasn't changed her.'

The girls embraced each other. 'I heard you were getting married,' Ellie said, and then, 'How like Grandma you are!' She was a beauty indeed, red-haired, with the same deep blue eyes.

'It's a fluke so it is since we're far out relations, but there's no one I'd rather be like and that's the truth. We were bowled over by her that time in her gold gown!'

'I'm Dymphna and not like your grandmother and the only old maid of the family.' The brown-haired girl put her arms round Ellie.

'You have to pay to speak to Dymphna,' Clare said, laughing. 'She's a lawyer now, practises in Sligo. She had to go far enough away in case she made some awful mistakes.'

'Oh, Clare!' The girl was as neat as a pin in her white serge skirt and mutton-sleeved blouse of white voile, a blue bow at the neck. 'Don't listen to her, Ellie. You understand. You're a career woman after my own heart. She's putting on airs because she's an old married woman of six months. But here's Moira, an old, *old* married woman indeed, with her husband and little Kevin – Mr and Mrs Bryan Vaughan.' Again Ellie was enveloped in warm hugs, even from the husband, Bryan, a shy young man with rimless glasses.

'Bryan's only here because we needed two motors,' Moira said, and then, 'Will you look at father with his mother, for goodness sake, billing and cooing like two lovebirds, and both smiling fit to bust!'

'Now, I won't have you mocking me, girls.' Her uncle came towards her, burly, red-faced, a younger edition of grandmother's brother in America, as if he had been charged to keep the line going. 'Well, you have to be congratulated, Ellie, to be sure!' He kissed her fondly. 'Acting as courier to this mother of mine. Did she lead you a fine song and dance?'

'No, she was very well-behaved.' She looked at her grandmother who seemed to have suffered an instant metamorphosis since stepping off the train. She was radiant, smiling, her eyes deeply blue.

'Now, are you sure she didn't try to get off with the captain of the boat? That's her favourite trick.'

'Maybe she did when I was sleeping,' Ellie said. She looked at her grandmother, bemused with the talk and the jollity. There must be something in this Irish air. 'Nor would it surprise me if she broke into an Irish jig!' The laughter made other people turn their heads, and Kevin, the little son of Moira and Bryan, burst into tears.

'Now then, now then,' his father said, lifting him into his arms, 'don't you go and spoil the party.' The boy buried his head in his father's shoulder, his sob silenced. 'He's a grand wee soul normally, just a bit bowled over.' He smiled at Maeve. 'Maybe we should get going, then. There's a fine tea waiting for you at Woodlea, Lady Crawford.'

Maeve took Terence's arm. 'Now we won't stand on ceremony, Bryan, or else I'll be forced to call you Mr

Vaughan and that wouldn't do at all. 'Grandmother' will do fine for me.' They all trooped to the motorcars, laughing and talking nineteen to the dozen.

Ellie's first sight of Woodlea was no surprise. Her grandmother had often described her old home to her, but it was a paler stone than she had imagined, and there were tubs of brilliant dahlias grouped round the stone gryphons at the foot of the stone steps. But otherwise the wide lawn was bare of flowers, unlike the garden at Braidholme where colour rioted from May till October.

Inside, the house looked like the people. There were dogs barking, servants rushing about or standing talking, totally unlike the quiet efficiency which was the rule at the Hall. Susan could not be counted. She was a law unto herself.

She was shown the downstairs rooms, the long drawing-room flooded with light, its worn chintz sofas, mostly sag-seated, redeemed by the fine pieces of Georgian furniture; she crossed the black and white tiled hall where the long-case clock stood – grandmother's father's regulator for his watch, she had been told often enough – and into the dining-room and Terence's study. Honor's was upstairs as she needed quiet for her writing.

She was introduced to Rory, the gardener, who happened to be in the kitchen, not the boy she had imagined but a robust, middle-aged man with side-whiskers, and Edna, the maid, a bustling, rosy-cheeked woman who seemed to be engaged in endless conversations with any one of the family who happened to be near her, or with the dogs for that matter.

'And did you mind to go into the chemist's and get me that stuff for me midge bites, Miss Dymphna? Sure an' they itch something awful. And, oh, there was a body phoning from your office. You have to phone back before five of the clock . . . here, Kevin, my lamb. come and see those wee chickens just hatched on the hob, will ye, and

I'm thinking there's a kitten or two besides snuggling at the fire. Oh, madam,' this to Maeve, 'what a fine thing it is to see you again! And what a fine upstanding lady you are still, in more ways than one, if you get me. Now why have you neglected your old home for so long and is this the young doctor herself?' All in one breath. 'My, your father would be proud of you! Sure enough he's likely looking down from heaven right at this minute and blessing the day you took up the doctoring. Now, don't you be for denying it!' Finger raised admonishingly. 'And are you getting married yet? Well there will be no trouble finding a good-looking young man to fall at *your* feet, I'll be thinking. What do you say, Mr McGrath?' For Terence was there, too. Indeed, the whole family had flooded into the kitchen. 'Now if you have the time, sor, why don't you set yourself the task of finding an Irishman for her?'

'Edna,' Honor said, 'do you think you could stop long enough to serve us tea? We're all parched for want of it, especially our visitors.'

'Aye, sure enough, Mrs McGrath. I'm forgetting my duties in the excitement of the moment, but it's not every day we have a deputation from Scotland.'

She got little time to grieve or indeed think about Colin. She had early absorbed at home the general belief that the Irish were 'easy-osy' if not downright indolent, but she soon found Woodlea to be a hive of activity.

The horses had to be exercised and ridden every day. There were constant trips to Boyle, or further afield to Sligo for food and necessities for the household, which generally included visits to friends who lived 'on the road' there. The Irish hospitality was more open and less critical than that of the douce Scots in Sholton. Ellie and her grandmother were welcomed as envoys from 'the far side' with a warmhearted enthusiasm. No one was ever too busy to sit down and talk. 'Ah, sure n' I've got all day to do it in,' would be the usual reply if Ellie protested that she was 'holding them up'. Back in Scotland, she realized, people often gave the impression of being 'held up'. Their eye was always fixed on the next objective. That must be why they made such good pioneers.

The evening meal seemed to be a gargantuan one. Dymphna was not there during the day, but she came straight from her lawyer's office in the evening and into the kitchen to help with the preparation. Ellie quickly found a place beside her. 'It's funny you being a lawyer and taking an interest in cooking as well,' she said once when she was cutting up a mountain of tomatoes from Rory's greenhouses for the salad. Susan would have banished her in no time – not that she had domestic leanings.

'To tell you the truth, I had quite a difficulty in making up my mind which to choose,' the girl said, 'then I met my darling Denis and he's a lawyer. The only way we could see each other was to study the same subjects, so we went to Dublin University together. We're looking for a house in Dublin – he works there – then we'll get married.'

'That's lovely for you,' she said.

'Have you found the right man, yet, Ellie?' Clare was there too, sitting at the big table drinking a cup of tea which Edna had provided. Tea ran like a fountain in Woodlea.

'Not yet.' She thought of saying, 'I did, but he got away,' but her grief was still too raw, and with it the shame of having been jilted. She only used that word to herself. There had been no ring, no definite promises, but she had acted as if there had been. She would remember the dark land and his eager fingers opening her blouse, sometimes hers on top of his, urging him on.

'Well, we'll soon remedy that. The balls haven't started yet, but there are plenty of parties going on in other houses, and Aidan has loads of lovely friends. I don't know how I managed to choose him from all the other grand young men around.'

'Because you were head over heels in love with him. That's why,' Dymphna said.

'Ah, but I didn't go off with him to Dublin like you did. God knows what you got up to there, eh, Edna?'

'Oh, don't bring Edna into it,' Dymphna said, 'she thinks I'm already consigned to hell-fire and damnation.'

'Did you ever hear such talk before your fine Scottish cousin!' Edna said from the sink. 'Goodness knows what she'll carry back with her! They'll think we're all heathens.' She staggered out of the kitchen with a loaded tray.

'Did your mother not object?' Ellie asked Dymphna.

'To me setting off with Denis? Sure and I don't know if she ever noticed! She's that wrapped up with her books that she hardly knows one of us from the other. Besides, she leaves it to father, and he classes us with the horses. "How are the girls and your horses doing, cushla?" she said to him one night at the dinner table. We've never let her forget it.'

'My mother can account for nearly every hour of my day,' Ellie said.

'Ah, but she hasn't a husband, don't you see?' Clare's piquant face was serious. 'Father often talked about him being an extraordinary man. She keeps in touch with him through you, especially since you're following in his footsteps.'

'Yes, that's so.' She thought kindly of her mother. Tonight she would sit down and write her a long letter.

The girls were as good as their word about taking her to parties. The tennis ones in the afternoon were a new experience for Ellie, which necessitated spending any spare time they had upstairs in the old nursery helping her to 'run up' a tennis costume of white serge. They were all 'dab hands' at 'running up' dresses, an operation whch Honor sometimes took part in as the chief 'dab hander'.

The dresses were like themselves, stitched in a hurry, the seams none too straight, the garments unfinished inside ('Sure and nobody will see that!'), and with trimmings stuck on not so much for effect as to cover deficiencies in sewing.

Aidan and Bryan produced old schoolfriends, business acquaintances, dashing young men who turned up at all the parties and dances and offered to escort Ellie if she were in need of a partner. She felt she was an object of curiosity rather than an attraction. Many of them were going back to Dublin University or into the Army. They had the same capacity for light-hearted enjoyment as the girls had, with no commitment.

Ireland was as class-ridden as Scotland, she soon decided. Although the girls fraternized freely with the servants at Woodlea, she would notice as they drove out to yet another party how sometimes in the twilight a donkey with its panniers laden with turf sods would be drawn back from the road by its owner, more often women than men. The women would be wrapped in rough shawls and they would stand respectfully as their motors whizzed by. The men would touch their forelocks. They all looked gaunt and ill-nourished.

'Don't think that's respect for us,' Clare once said as they drove past. 'It's the sight of the motor. They still think anything wth an engine is the work of the devil himself. They're heathens, most of them.'

What would Belle think of it all? Or her mother? If they thought people were deprived in Scotland, what would they say to the obvious gap between the rich and poor in Ireland?

She spoke to her uncle about it one day when she went to the stables with Maeve. Her grandmother made a daily visit, and seemed to like nothing better than to sit in a chair provided for her in the courtyard and watch the horses being fed and watered, or put through their paces for her. She looked relaxed and happy, as if she were at peace.

Ellie went along the stalls looking for Terence, and found him grooming Clare's horse, still kept there. 'Grandma's in her element,' she said to him, putting her hand on the warm chestnut flank. This passion for horses which they all shared was beyond her. It formed a large part of their conversation. She admired them but had no great urge to ride.

'It's the sight and smell and the sounds,' he said. 'Your grandfather worked as a groom in this very place. She used to steal out here to meet him, or have him saddle her horse. You can see why the memories are strong.'

'Do you think people always have this wish to go back to their roots, Uncle?' she asked him. She had developed a great fondness for him in the short time she had been here. Perhaps he was a father figure to her. Braidholme was a female stronghold.

'Yes, I think so. With me, I went back before I got so old and grey as this.' He laughed up at her as he brushed, handsome with his curly hair, an appealing man to women, she thought. 'The first time I came here I knew it was for me. Now that might have been something to do with your Aunt Honor, but the two together was a fatal combination.' He chuckled, intent on his task.

'And yet it's torn with dissension here.'

'Torn with dissension, is it?' He straightened himself, whacked the horse on its rump. 'There you are, my beauty. What a serious girl you are, Ellie.' He came round the horse towards her, smiling. 'Glasgow produces them like that. Come for a stroll with me.' He put his arm round her and led her towards the door. 'I like this time of day.' They passed Maeve talking to one of the grooms who was bent respectfully to listen to her. 'That's right,

Mother,' Terence said, 'you tell him what's going to win tomorrow . . .'

'Do you really think I'm serious?' Ellie said. She was not altogether pleased to be thought of as a blue-stocking.

'More so than our girls. It's a national characteristic. That's why I didn't fit in too well in Glasgow. I was never serious enough – like Patrick, for instance. But they're the folks who get on.' But they aren't always happy. She thought of Gaylord's death. 'Torn with dissension, is it?' he repeated. The air was mild, 'soft on the cheek', the trees black against a pale mauve sky. A lovely time, twilight, in Ireland, she thought, melancholy in spite of this uncle's talk about them all being so light-hearted. Honor understood. Her latest book *The Speaking Stones*, had captured it. She had read it, enthralled.

'You wouldn't think so,' she said, 'looking at this.'

'You're not far wrong, but being an incomer I've kept my opinions to myself. Every Irishman is a politician, but even I can see that the Irish are at the end of their tether over the Home Rule question. They've been kept waiting too long for a decision, just as the Trade Unionists have been kept waiting too long for their wages to increase, just as women like your mother have been kept waiting too long to be given a vote. They're beginning to see that slow-moving liberalism isn't enough.'

'I talk to Belle Geddes about this. Did mother tell you about her?'

'Yes. Being in prison would sort out her ideas a bit. She'll be beginning soon to wonder if it was worth it.'

'She'll never forget the women she met. They inspired her.'

'Well, that's something. It's a strange thing,' his eyes did not leave the fields, 'people who aren't in politics always think they could do much better. But it seems to me, an onlooker, that they could have kept the Irish happy with an Irish Parliament which would have been not much more than a glorified County Council. But not any more. Those in high places have missed their chance. We're fed up being ignored. Now, it's stalemate.' He turned to her. 'The Nationalists will never agree to excluding Ulster and Ulster will never be governed by the Pope, as we see it.' He had said we'.

She shook her head. 'I can't see what the fundamental objection in Parliament *is* to Irish Home Rule.'

'Nor could I at the begining, but I do now. If war comes, as it surely will any time now, they're afraid the Irish might range themselves on the German side.'

'And they would become a pawn?'

'A pawn it is. Great Britain's afraid it might lose the Irish market, or even Ireland itself, and find German naval bases interposed between their shores and the countries they need to draw from for food. You say dissension, Ellie. What I feel now is fear. I'm afraid for my daughters, and my son in Paris, my son in America, my son-in-law here. I'm afraid for my loved ones back in Scotland, especially for my mother if she's there, for every man who will be unwittingly drawn into this struggle – because make no mistake, it will be a worldwide one. There is a great fear of Germany . . .' He turned to look at the fields as if he did not want her to see his face.

She looked, too. They had lost their green and were a gentle grey, the sky a deeper mauve; sad, gentle colours. 'Grandma will have gone in now,' she said.

'No, she's here.' She heard Maeve's voice behind them, and turned, surprised. 'Oh, it's nice to see you two talking together!' She put an arm round each of them. 'But come away in now. It's the gloaming.'

'I know what it is,' Terence said, looking at her fondly. 'You want your evening tipple.'

'And isn't that why I came to Ireland at all for your fine Irish poteen . . .?' She smiled up at him.

If I ever have a son, Ellie thought, I hope he's as fond

of me. They walked towards the house. 'Oh, it's nice here,' she said, 'a lovely place to be in spite of its *throubles*.' She tried to say it the Irish way, laughing at herself.

And later, in bed, reading the poems Belle had given her, she had a sense of peace, a green peace since it was Ireland. The human spirit was abundantly there in its capacity to conquer . . .

> My heart is too much like the surging sea,
> Thinking of self it hollows with distress . . .

and in the triumphant ending . . .

> Whatever pangs, however hard the task,
> A strife, a consummation let me see.

18

Although the holiday for Ellie had been one of surprises, the totally different way of life shaking her out of her apathy and little by little pushing Colin from the forefront of her mind, two surprises still lay in wait for her on her last week.

Terence arrived from Paris with Giselle Barthe. He had said in a letter to his stepmother that he hoped to come that summer, but he was showing several of his paintings in an exhibition of modern work and had to be there to see the reaction. His arrival with Giselle, although not entirely unexpected, was greeted with the excitement which Ellie had grown to expect in this family, dogs barking, people and servants rushing about, Honor being summoned from her upstairs study and his father from the stables.

'And this is your Scottish cousin!' Ellie was brought forward almost as a *tour de force*. 'You didn't expect that!' He had already greeted Maeve with deference and the same charm as his father.

'Ellie McNab!'

She remembered the thin young lad and his sturdier brother, Robert. 'The last time I saw you was at Grand-father's funeral.'

'So it was. You were just a schoolgirl then.'

'But I was not.' This was Giselle, elegant, chic, her clothes definitely not 'run up'. She kissed Ellie on both cheeks. Her look was admiring. 'It's Leezie I know best, of course. She came to school in Versailles and visited us also in Normandy. Olivier and Marc, my brothers, they tease her and we laugh so much!'

So *soignée*, Ellie thought. The word, the only suitable

word, occurred to her. 'She's talked about France often to me,' she said. 'I think it was one of the happiest times in her life.'

'And here is Grandma,' Terence said, leading Giselle to Maeve who held out her arms.

'You bring back Paris to me. I visited your parents with Ellie's mother. You were just a wee girl running about that lovely house of yours. Monceau Park, was it?'

'You like it? Mama and I try to get father to move into a more avantgarde *quartier*, but, no, he will not do it. He says where we are is *comme il faut*.'

'That may be,' Maeve said. 'How is your mother?'

'She is in our house near Gisors at present. Father remains in town. Because of his work, you understand.' Ellie saw her grandmother's too limpid look. Wasn't Emily supposed to be a flirt, or was it her husband who had had a mistress? She must ask mother. It was something very French in any case.

'You must come to Paris sometime,' Terence said to Ellie. 'It's the place to be, I can tell you. I have an apartment with another student by the *Sacré Coeur*. On a clear day you can see the *Tour Eiffel* from it.'

'I went to its opening with you and your brothers, Giselle,' Maeve said.

'*L'Exposition* of 1889!' Giselle clapped her hands. 'I was only five years of age, but I remember it. And you too!'

'Well, of course,' Honor laughed. 'We have the world's best known traveller staying with us. Your Jules Verne had nothing on her, Giselle, America, Paris and Ireland. Goodness knows where next.'

'I think my travelling days are done.' Ellie, looking at her, saw the sadness in her eyes.

The last few days of their stay were a round of parties and visits, this time with the excuse of showing Giselle the countryside. Lough Arrow and Lough Keay enchanted her. But she was enchanting herself, Ellie thought, assured and with an extra sophistication which must only come from being French. Of course she was twenty-eight (she had done some mental arithmetic when the Eiffel Tower was under discussion), and two years older than Terence. He was in love with her, that was easy to see. He watched her adoringly. Was she in love with him or was she in love with the idea of being married? Time would tell.

Giselle, Clare and Ellie soon formed a threesome when Terence was busy sketching. He intended to do a painting of her father's favourite hunter while he was here. For the first time in her life Ellie knew the joy which could be had in the company of her own sex. The young women at Queen Margaret's were working too hard to be lighthearted.

A few days after Terence and Giselle's arrival, Honor put down her pen and declared they would all go on a picnic to Strandhill. 'It's where Terence and I plighted our troth,' she said, laughing.

'What is this plighting of the trot?' Giselle asked, adding to the laughter. Her almond-shaped eyes were entrancing, Ellie thought. Apparently so did Terence.

'It's what I would like you and me to do,' he said.

'You must explain, *chéri*.' They were not innocent eyes, but so what? Terence needed a sophisticated woman to bolster him in his career, and to keep those French models at bay.

'I will when we're alone,' he said. For a few minutes the feeling of loss was overpowering as she watched them. Why hadn't Colin written? Terence, naturally polite, or perhaps with the extra sensitivity of someone in love, had turned to her. Was it imagination or were his eyes sympathetic?

They went in a wagon which was kept in the stables

because only it would take all the company, their chairs, rugs, swimming costumes, towels and picnic baskets. Once packed in by Terence they rolled along the country lanes in fine style, Giselle, having to have every landmark explained to her.

Once, when Ellie looked at her uncle and aunt, she saw they were holding hands. She met Honor's eyes and they were wise and deep. 'It will come to you,' they seemed to be saying, but in the next moment Giselle's pronunciation was reducing them all to fits of laughter. "Coll*oo*ney". Is that right, Terence? Now try me with another of your names. "Ballysadare". Oh, yes, that is easy. I like Ballysadare. Like a dance, it sounds.'

They all went bathing except Maeve who was enthroned on a comfortable chair with a rug over her knees and a length of gauze produced by Honor to hold on her hat. She herself had a gypsy bandana tied round her dark hair. Ellie was not a swimmer, but Aidan, Clare's husband, much more dashing than Moira's, with a fine blond moustache, volunteered to hold her chin up while she floundered in the water. Giselle wore a very French swimming costume, black and white frills and a white frilled cap, and tripped prettily in and out of the shallows, taking care not to wet it too much.

Ellie flung herself down by her grandmother's chair after half-an-hour's lesson. 'I'll never make a swimmer,' she said, wrapping herself in one of the towels. 'But it was fun. She's fascinating, isn't she, Grandma?' Their eyes were on Giselle. Like a strange, exotic bird.'

'That's what we always said about her mother. See how she preens herself.'

'Terence is head over heels in love with her. Do you think she'd accept him if he proposed?'

'Oh yes, she's practical underneath. She knows she'd make an ideal wife for him. The preening is part of the courtship process.' She smiled. 'Frenchwomen are

377

interesting. They have little womanly wiles that Scottish girls never learn. They enjoy the pursuit of love. So do Frenchmen. I only hope that Terence isn't so utterly captivated rather than utterly in love that *he* changes. He'll be fêted in Paris. They adore painters. In Glasgow they'd think a man was a cissy if he painted pictures for a living. Oh, but Paris . . .'

She listened as Maeve told her about her French visit and the little *contretemps* between Emily and her husband, Charles. 'I think I helped about that duel – your mother will have told you – but I don't flatter myself that Emily took my advice. No one should ever give advice and expect it to be followed – ' Not many women of seventy-eight could talk so wisely, she thought.

'Do you mean advice about love, Grandma?'

'Most things. But certainly love.'

'You were very much in love with grandfather, weren't you?'

'Yes, he was my one true love. That's not to say Alastair didn't make a fine companion, and a good bedmate.' A good bedmate, Ellie thought. She was unique. 'But Kieran was part of me. I feel close to him here. Sometimes I feel his spirit . . .' She put her hand on her grandmother's knee affectionately.

'You've looked different since you came. So peaceful and happy.'

'That's true. And I've something to tell you. You know Honor has said I'm welcome here as long as I like? Well, then, I've made up my mind. I'm going to stay on for a bit at Woodlea. Could you manage to get home on your own?'

'Of course I could. But Grandma!' She was astonished. 'Are you sure? It's a bit sudden.'

'None the worse for that.'

'I'm wondering what Lizzie and Ernest will say. And mother.'

'They'll understand. Don't worry. And it will give Ernest and Lizzie some time on their own. You see, Ellie, it's not only the people here, it's the horses. I see Kieran every day when I watch them being groomed. I see him sitting on a stool with the horse's hoof on his knee and looking up when I appeared with that loving, gentle smile of his. "Your horse is ready for you, Miss Maeve." And knowing all the time that he'd held me in his arms the night before.' She smiled. 'I'm shocking you.'

'No, you're not.'

'High time if I am. It's the whole place. It's still real country here. They've given up the horses, given up real country life at the Hall. Before all those motors were rushing about, it was considered far away from Glasgow; now Lizzie and Ernest go to evening functions there two or three times a week. It's becoming 'an outlying district', and before we know it, houses like it will be turned into institutions or old people's homes. The era of the big house, unless it's buried in the country, is at an end. And maybe it'll last a wee bit longer in Ireland. If Woodlea sees me out I'll be happy.'

'Oh, don't talk like that, Grandma!' Ellie put her arms round here. 'You stay here and get refreshed. It's your home.'

'You're a good lass.' She looked her in the eye. 'Has it helped being here?'

'Did mother . . . tell you . . . about Colin?'

'Enough. But I only had to look at your face. I gave your mother advice long ago, nothing to do with love,' she smiled, 'and she took it. "Something outside yourself," I said. A husband and children claim you. You'll have something of your own when you're a doctor whether you're married or not. You'll be your own woman. And you'll meet someone who'll recognize that need in you and won't want you to give up everything for him . . .' She looked up. Honor was there, wrapped in a long white robe. She sat down beside them, smiling, pretending to shiver.

'You two look so happy together.' She began to rub her wet hair. 'Has Grandma told you we're keeping her for a little?'

'Yes. We'll all miss her at Sholton, but we'll know she's happy here.'

'And safer, perhaps.' She looked out to the sea, her hair in a dark mass round her face. 'I can feel the clouds gathering, even on a lovely day like this,' – her voice dropped – 'clouds of war.' Now it was even lower, 'Oh, the folly of it . . .' She turned to Ellie. 'Do you read Yeats?'

'No, I'm ashamed to say I haven't the time.'

'Then I'll give you a book of his poems as a parting gift.' She spoke in a low voice, looking towards the sea again:

> 'Turn if ye may, I call out to each one,
> From the grey ships and battles never won . . .'

The words were almost inaudible, 'They're never won, wars.'

The three of them were silent, looking at the pale blond strand, the blue sea rippling lacy-white as it stroked the sand, the bright colours of the bathers, the far-off sounds of their voices which seemed to die on the air sadly, as if they too felt it was the end of an era.

Honor stood up, her black hair flying in the wind which had sprung up. She put her hands to her mouth. 'Terence, bring them out now! It's getting cold!' Ellie saw her uncle's hand rise from the water.

19

'The strike's been on for a month now,' Ernest said to Maevy and Dan. It was February of the following year. 'The men are as determined as ever.'

'They have their women behind them this time,' Maevy nodded. 'They're well organized. Ellie was telling me she saw them walking down the Trongate on their way to the Panopticon for their Thursday treat. Councillor Lyon has been clever to bring the women into it.'

'That would please Belle Geddes,' Dan said.

'It pleases me.' Maevy was crisp. 'They've learnt at last that the wife is a very important factor in any strike, the backbone of her husband. He's telling these women that the present fight is for the purpose of giving them the same opportunities as the rest of us. The WSPU recognizes that these opportunities will only be got by giving us the vote.'

'That's *your* gas in a peep,' Ernest said, laughing.

'You're a thorough Scotsman now, Ernest.' Maevy laughed with him.

'I've always been that, even when I lived in America, and especially now, with Lizzie.' His face softened for a second and then he was saying, 'There are three thousand five hundred carters out on strike. It can't go on much longer or we'll be crippled. I've been approached. Are we willing to compromise on a two shilling increase?'

'They want *three* shillings,' Maevy said. 'They're still a penny behind the dock labourers. They want it up to 6d per day.'

'Nevertheless, a compromise seems fair enough for both sides. We're one of the three biggest contractors now and I've had a meeting with the other two, Bannister and Craig, and Naylor's. They're willing to accept.' He paused, and said casually, watching them both like hawks, 'There was talk of a merger in the future.' He stopped to let the words sink in.

'Never!' Dan Johnson said. 'My father would turn in his grave!'

'What do you say, Maevy?' Ernest looked at her.

'I think 'never' can become 'maybe' in time. I would put it to Patrick. He's always been the one for big ideas. A merger might be a possibility when we go in for longer hauls. The expense will be enormous to begin with on our resources.'

'You're still dreaming of your pantechnicons?'

'Yes, that will come. Look at the number of motor vehicles now on the road – forty thousand at the last count.'

'There's still the question of petrol or steam,' Dan said. 'The repairs on the petrol-driven vans are much too high and time-consuming.'

'They're fitting rubber tyres now on steamers. That increases their speed, makes them feasible and gets rid of your objection.' She looked at both of them. 'I've a bombshell to drop, of my own making.' She smiled. 'Don't look so worried, Dan. I saw a good piece of land the other day, going cheap . . .'

'What do we need . . .?' Dan Johnson interrupted.

'Go on, Maevy,' Ernest said.

'The price of land's going up all the time. Everything's getting dearer, including the cost of living which is the reason for the strike, as you both well know, *not* trade depression. It's because the workers are miserably poor compared with the owners who are extremely rich. Now that the carters have set an example and let their wives penetrate into that holy of holies, their working life, *they'll* help them to force the hand of the owners, just wait and see.'

'You're not on a platform now,' Dan grumbled.

Ernest said, 'I think you can say McGraths have always been fair. Ever since your mother and father started the business, Maevy, that's been our endeavour.'

'Fair enough, but we look after ourselves first.'

'So what's your bombshell?' Dan did not like this sort of talk. 'You said you saw a piece of land going cheap.'

'Yes, at Parkhead. I thought we might start a motor department. We have to look ahead, and the East End is the cheapest place to look.'

'A good place for labour.' Dan allowed himself to be judicial. 'Would this be a repair shop?'

'A repair shop, garaging, the lot. Long haul is going to give us the real profits eventually. We need room. You know how little we made last summer out of the lighter vans for holiday luggage traffic, but we decided to keep them on for prestige reasons.'

Dan smiled. It had been his decision. 'Any guid wife is one up on her neighbours if her trunk is delivered in a motor instead of an old horse and cart! Though sometimes I don't know what the world's coming to. The friend of man, the horse.'

'You wouldn't think so,' Maevy said, 'when you look at the poor trachled beasts you see about the Glasgow streets sometimes.'

Ernest took the initiative. 'We mustn't halt the march of progress,' he said. 'I'm all for Maevy's suggestion.' Maevy's plans did not go beyond long haulage at the moment: his went further than that. At least he'd sown the seed. The strike would see many contracting firms going to the wall, and there was no point in the remainder fighting amongst themselves. Far better to have a merger. But he was young enough to wait. It might not be in his time, but there were always younger ones coming along,

Jonty for instance. He had given Lizzie his promise that he would do what he could for Jonty when he was old enough. And there was Robert in America, in time Victoria and Abigail's sons. Keep a family connection . . .

'We'll leave you to do the negotiations with the other contractors,' Dan said, as if he was reading his mind. 'You're well in there. And I'll go and see the site at Parkhead.'

'And I'll get on with the work,' Maevy got up smiling. '*Someone* has to do it.'

The winter of 1912 and spring of 1913 had been a hard grind for Ellie, of her own choosing. Work was the best anodyne. In April she was feeling run down and tired and bothered by an irritable cough, and Maevy insisted she should see the doctor. She went reluctantly, but as always glad of an opportunity to have a chat with Belle. She called in on her way home from the College, when she knew that the surgery would be over.

Belle looked up from her desk with a smile, her silver-grey eyes seeming to miss nothing. 'Who's this peely-wally lass I'm seeing in front of me? Are you working too hard?'

'Yes, that's all. I'm here to please my mother.' She sat down. 'How about you? Are you still posting bottles of acid in the pillar boxes?'

'Did you read about it? No, not me. That was a servant, a member of the Domestic Workers' Union. She said it was quite simple. She just walked out of the house where she worked, wearing her cap and apron and did it. No one suspected her.' She smiled in admiration. 'No, I leave it to people like Jessie Stephen. I've done my bit. I'm going to Glasgow Green with your mother and addressing the crowds. I got a bottle thrown at me the other day.' She lifted the heavy dark hair on her brow to show a jagged scar. 'Done by a woman who shouted abuse at me although she was probably being beaten by her husband. It's a good thing there wasn't acid in it.'

'How terrible!' She was shocked at the violence. 'Mother didn't tell me.'

'Oh, she was all right. I seem to invite aggression, your mother calms it. But she's totally committed.'

'Thank goodness she isn't militant. There was that lot who set fire to the platforms at Shields Road Station.'

'Don't call them "that lot". They're fighting for *you*. It's a means to an end.'

'I know that, and I'm grateful. To you, too, Belle.' She remembered the poems. 'And the end always justifies the means?'

'Sometimes it has to. You ought to have learnt that in the dissecting room. How are your studies going?'

'Well. They get my whole attention.' She spoke grimly.

Belle could ask questions, her mother could not. 'Have you ever heard from Colin Thomson?'

'No.' She looked away. 'That part of my life's over.'

'Oh, I hope not! You're just a young thing. What age are you now, Ellie?'

'Twenty-one.'

'I'm thirty-six and it isn't over for me.'

'But you aren't married.'

'You're still young for twenty-one.' The silver-grey eyes rested on her coolly, and Ellie blushed. Of course, there was that young man at Crannoch, Hamish something or other. She was an attractive woman. Her mouth was not that of an old maid. She felt uncomfortable and blurted out:

'Well, are you going to give me a bottle or something for my peely-walliness?'

'No, some good advice. Did you find travelling hard this winter?'

'Oh, yes,' she was heartfelt about that, 'and next year,

my final one, will be worse. I'll be in the wards a lot and there will be midwifery.'

'Well, you're twenty-one. Leave home.'

'Leave home!' She was astonished.

'Why not? You've admitted it's going to be nearly impossible to travel next year, and that this year's been bad enough. That's why you're played out, ready to pick up any infection that's going and too tired for any social life.'

'But I would be leaving mother alone!'

'Your mother's a very busy woman. You would have been leaving her alone if you'd skipped off to Australia with Colin Thomson. It will be a wrench for her, but it will do you both good.'

'I never thought of it. But, yes, it's the answer. I'd like to. Will you speak to her, Belle?'

'Yes. I'll speak to her. Your mother and I see eye to eye in many things.'

She said, greatly daring, 'I would never have believed that the two of you would have become friendly.'

'No? Ah, but you see we have a great bond in common.'

'Votes for Women?'

'That.' She was turning over some papers on her desk, and she said it without raising her head, 'And we loved the same man. Now away you go and wash your hair and make yourself prettier than ever, and visit Lizzie Murray-Hyslop. She's someone who knows what life is about and where her priorities lie. She doesn't take life by the neck and wring it like you. She goes along nice and easy and . . . loving.'

'Ah, but she has Ernest.'

'Yes, I admit that makes a difference.' She got up and patted Ellie on the shoulder. 'Charlie would be proud of you.'

* * *

386

By the end of the month Ellie was sharing rooms in Hillhead with another student of Queen Margaret's, and as if fate had arranged to fill the gap, John Craigie died. He would have been pleased with the large turnout at his funeral, more than ever came to his services in the kirk.

Isobel was brave at first, and said she would soon find a 'wee place of her own', but as the weeks passed and she made no move, Maevy went to see her. 'When is the new man supposed to be moving into the manse, Isobel?' she asked her.

'Next month.' In the black dress she looked thinner than ever. 'I'm at my wit's end trying to find a place in Sholton. John did all my thinking for me. I don't seem able to spur myself to do anything.'

'Yes, I know what it's like.' She could not say to this frail creature that she had made a great mistake in letting her husband dominate her. 'But you *can* think, you know.' She smiled to take the sting out of her words.

'Oh, I don't know . . .'

'Do you remember, in the early days of McGraths, how clever you were at keeping the books in that office we had in Sholton? Everybody said how smart you were at figures.'

'That's a long time ago.'

'Yes, I know it is, but you still have the capacity.'

Isobel changed the subject. 'How is Ellie getting on at Hillhead?'

'Oh, fine. She and her friend, Jean, seem to hit it off well. Jean likes to cook and Ellie does the shopping . . .'

'I always enjoyed cooking, dainty things, but John liked heavy meals, dumplings in his mince, cabbage, potatoes. He said he owed it to the Lord to keep himself in good trim for Him.' But it had not been good enough, Maevy thought.

'Isobel,' she said, 'how would you like to come and stay at Braidholme?'

'Stay with you?'

'It's been known before. Two widowed sisters living together. Susan's getting on now. She could do with some help from you about the place, in the kitchen . . .' She trembled at the thought of that, but Isobel was like a mouse, she would not annoy her. 'And you were always good at helping John with his sermons and such like. You could help me with the talks I give, maybe copy them out for me. I have an awful hand.' She had been complimented on her calligraphy by the girls in the office.

'Oh, I'm good at that!' Isobel's face brightened, her frail body seemed to straighten and for a moment she was that delicate-looking pretty girl with flaxen hair, 'blind fair', Mother had called it. 'Sometimes – this is between you and me, Maevy – I wrote most of John's sermons. At his dictation. He got the ideas, but he couldn't be bothered framing them. I would write it out for him as I thought it should be and he'd say, "Yes, that's just as I put it." I never dared even hint . . .'

'Well, he put it over in the pulpit.'

'Yes, that was the bit he liked best.' Her eyes filled with tears. 'Poor John. I'll never be able to thank you enough, Maevy, all those things you did for him at the end, things I couldn't face . . .'

'I was a nurse long before I was in McGraths, don't forget. We each have our talents. You must begin to recognize your own.'

'Would you want me, Maevy?' She was crying softly, dabbing at her eyes. 'You've always been sort of . . . independent.'

'Of course I'd want you.' She put her hand on Isobel's knee. 'You're my sister. I love you.' The tears were running down her own cheeks, and she wiped them away. 'But that doesn't mean we're going to get into each other's hair. You'll have a nice room looking over the garden and you and I will eat together in the evening, and breakfast too if you're up as early as I am and you'll find plenty to do about the house when I'm in Glasgow. Just watch with Susan. She's touchy and not so well. She's missed Ellie . . .'

'Oh, Maevy.' She put her head in her hands, and Maevy got up and put her arms round her. 'There, there,' she said, holding her close, 'I know what a great gap it is for you without John. I thought I'd never live through it when I lost Charlie and here I am. You'll see.'

Isobel raised a tearful face. 'It's not that. It's just . . . oh, I'm that happy . . .' And when she had finally dried her tears, 'What do you think mother will say?'

'She'll be glad. I think she's settled at Woodlea. Ernest and Lizzie said, when they paid that visit with the clothes she wanted, that she didn't talk much about coming back to Sholton, at least before the summer. The winter's been against her.'

Yes, mother would be happy about Isobel, she thought, making her way back. Braidholme had always been a family home. That was how she would want it to be used.

20

It was the kind of morning Maeve liked. Although April, there was still a nip of frost. It lay like a pale haze with an occasional mica sparkle on the lawn, and caught in her nostrils as she stood by the open window.

Oh, to be riding on a morning like this, she thought, when your hands were cold on the reins but your blood was on fire, when your horse would catch your exhilaration as you put it to gallop so that its hooves barely touched the ground. She never managed to beat Kieran, despite her urging. 'It's the gentleness of the hands,' he'd said once, and didn't she know that all her married life with him, right up to the end. Oh, Alastair was all right, 'a good bedmate', she had said to that lass, Ellie, so hurt yet inside, but putting a brave face on it.

She had discovered the remedy, work, but you had to find it out for yourself. The fact that she had done that proved her mettle. Maevy, her mother had, she herself had. It was the only way.

Honor was already up in her study; Dymphna had long since left for Sligo for that law office of hers; Terence had gone even earlier to a horse fair in Mullaghmore. He would not be back till late. That was the nice thing about Woodlea. They left you alone, but always in the evening there was the coming together and the talk and the laughter and the feeling of being cherished. And sometimes in the afternoon Moira and little Kevin would come. Or that gem of a girl, Clare, now pregnant.

I've been a little selfish, she thought, downstairs now and putting rich Irish butter on her toast and then the bramble jelly which Edna made so thick that you could almost slice it, pouring herself a steaming cup of tea. Sure and to God it was worth staying on in Ireland for the sake of the tea.

She ate reflectively. Maybe she'd been a wee bit thoughtless sending Ellie home on her own last summer, but truth to tell, she had not felt up to the journey. For a time indeed, she could admit it now, she had had thoughts of death. Folks talked about its brushing wings, but she had felt them at times with all those aches and pains and queer-like pangs.

But a change had been as good as a rest, and where in the wide world would she find a more loving family than this, or a dearer son. It did her heart good to see him so happy after that awful business with Catherine, now thankfully buried as she was.

They wanted her to stay for good, but she would do the right thing. She would go back to the Hall soon and talk it out with Ernest and Lizzie. They had been very understanding when they had come to visit last October, Lizzie bringing those favourite dresses she had craved for, and her jewellery . . . Oh, she was a grand one with clothes, Lizzie, and Ernest so light and not making a fuss about things. 'You needed an Irish infusion, Grandma, I've never seen you look better. There's no need for a tug-of-war between Uncle Terence and us. Wait till the spirit moves you and wafts you over the Irish sea. If it doesn't, well, it will be our loss. But, remember, the Hall is your home. The children will miss you, too.'

Yes, there were the children, Annabel and Kit. She was needed there to see that that girl, Jane, did not come down too heavily on them. Every child needed a grandma's treats from time to time. And she did not want to miss Jonty's growing-up. He was coming to a difficult age, awkward and rebellious sometimes, although the Crawfords would never be awkward. They were born with grace in them – Alastair, Nigel and now the last of them, Jonty, who could be persuaded to open out if you just took it nice and easy with him. Thoroughbreds were all the same.

Then there was Maevy, that dear girl battling away at McGraths every day to keep them all in comfort, even luxury. She had had a bad time this winter with strikes and one thing and another, but she would see the carters all right. If she had a fault at all, she was inclined to come down too heavily on their side. But Ernest would strike a balance. He always did.

And Isobel, that frail child now left a widow. How was she faring? She might have known Maevy would do the right thing and take care of her. Maybe it would turn out that Isobel would be taking care of Maevy. She had seen before the metamorphosis in a woman after the death of a domineering husband.

And there was their pride and joy, their hope for the future. Ellie, well on the way to becoming a doctor now. Yes, that settled it, she thought, wiping her lips with her napkin. She would like another piece of toast with that jelly, but even at her age you had to think of your figure. Yes, that settled it. She had to be in Glasgow when the lass was getting her cap, and maybe give her a bit of support before that. She would go back to Sholton, and after Ellie became Dr McNab, she would see if Woodlea still claimed her as strongly as it had done when they'd set off together . . . was it eight months ago? How time flew when you became old.

The sun lay on the cobbles like a broad gold path, making them black and shining. That was where to walk. The frost was still sparkling on them where they were in shadow. She would go into the stables and see if the lads had started their grooming. They liked to have a crack while they were working. She had overheard Padraic say to Joseph, 'That auld yin knows all of the answers, doesn't she?'

Sean would never have spoken like that, dear Sean who

had carried letters between her and Kieran right up to when they ran way together. He had said he wouldn't stay at Woodlea after Kieran left. He had looked up to him like a saviour after the time he had saved him from that villain, Peters, who was beating him. As her father had done to Kieran . . . Don't go back, she told herself.

She came out of the stables with the smell of them in her nostrils. Nearly as good as this fresh air. She would sit down for a minute in the yard and watch the horses being led out for their exercise, then get away into the warm kitchen and let Edna give her a cup of tea. And maybe after that she would fix up for Seumas Byrne to take her in his jaunting car for a ride around Boyle. There were a few things she wanted to buy in Wynne's, and this was market day up at the top of Bridge Street. She always liked the stir there. And maybe after that a wee trip round Lough Gara or Lough Key. She would have to be visiting all those places if she was going away. Oh, but it was a great life . . .

Her chair had been placed in the lee of the low stone wall and Joseph had given her a horse blanket to put under her. 'And you be wrapping the end of it round your knees as well, my lady. It's nippy this morning. Winter's having a last fling, I'm thinking, before it lets the daisies through.' Now where would you find a Sholton man who'd talk like that?

The golden path had shifted. It did not lead to her chair, but no matter, one way was as good as another over these old cobbles. It was a pity she was carrying this heavy hap over her arm. It seemed to unbalance her, weigh her down on the one side. Her left foot slid away from her as the thought occurred to her, and although she tried to straighten, first forward and then back, she went down heavily on her side. Oh, the indignity of it! What a good thing those lads were still safely inside, and that Terence was away. He would give her such a telling-off for not taking care. She would pick herself up quickly and make for the seat and nobody would be any the wiser.

She moved, and the pain which shot through her was so excruciating that it sent a loud cry rushing past her lips. She heard a horse whinnying as if in sympathy, and then the two lads were at the stable door and bolting across the yard to her. 'In the name of God!' she heard Padraic shouting. 'What have you done to yourself?'

They were at her side. She saw Joseph's spud face, wrinkled even more than usual, hanging above her. 'Himself will kill us, sure enough, Padraic. Are we after trying to lift her, would you say? Would it be better . . .?'

'Stop yammering and get on with it!' she said. It was difficult to speak. The aftermath of the pain was still with her, penetrating every joint of her body. But when they tried to lift her, one on either side of her, the agony was so great that she made them stop. Sweat was pouring from her in spite of the cold. 'It's no good, Padraic. Run in to your mistress and tell her to get a doctor. I'd be better to lie here.'

Padraic went off like greased lightning, and Joseph knelt beside her, stroking her hand, his eyes staring terrified from his white face. 'Oh, Missus, my lady! This is a terrible thing to be sure! You're too auld to be gallivanting about, that's the truth of it. Oh, he'll kill us sure enough and you his own mother . . .' She drifted away into a limbo of pain.

21

Maevy looked up at Isobel from the letter she was
reading, her face concerned. Contrary to her expecta-
tions, far from Isobel staying in bed every morning, she
was up even before her and freshly groomed to preside
over breakfast; helping Susan in the kitchen, providing
the extra touches which Susan did not think of – a bowl
of flowers on the table, on cold mornings heating Maevy's
cushion in front of the fire. She found these little attentions strangely touching.

'You're going to get a shock, Isobel. Mother's had a
fall. She's broken her hip.'

'Oh, dear!' Isobel put her hand to her face. 'Is it bad?'

'Bad enough. It happened in the stable yard. They've
had to put her in plaster.'

'Oh, poor mother! This is terrible! And her so happy
there. Do you think we should go over right away,
Maevy?'

'Terence doesn't think so. I'll read it to you.' She took
up the letter, peered a little. She would have to get
reading glasses soon. Mother had not needed them until
she was past sixty.

I didn't tell you girls right away, knowing it would only alarm
you. It happened when I was at Mullaghmore at a horse fair,
but Honor was in the house and she quickly got the doctor.

Mother liked to go out every morning to see the stable lads at
work and we never stopped her, indeed there was no need to
when it gave her so much pleasure. We had a late frost, and you
know what the cobbles can be like . . .

The doctor says her constitution is strong, and already she's
beginning to get over the shock of it and talking about writing

to all of you to say she's all right, so you can expect a letter from her soon.

She's not short of company with all the family popping in and out, and Edna sitting down to have a crack with her every time she brings up her food. I've curtailed my trips and Honor makes a point of stopping her work every now and then and looking in.

Maybe you'd go up to the Hall and tell them. She frets about Lizzie being upset, apart from the rest of you. I'll keep you informed . . .

She looked up. 'That's most of it. Isn't it a crying shame? It'll take away all the good of her stay there. Mother never liked inaction.' She said, looking into space, 'I remember her long ago when we were all having a sail on the Clyde and her walking up and down the deck so sprightly with Terence while the rest of us were sitting. Yes, it's the inaction that will . . .' she stopped herself in time, horrified at what she had so nearly said.

'There's no danger apart from that, is there?' Isobel had never been silly.

'That *is* the danger. But I'm sure the doctor is good there, although sometimes I think they think more of their vets in Ireland. He'll get her downstairs as soon as possible – there's no reason why she shouldn't rest on a couch during the day – and he'll make her do a few exercises, I hope.' She sighed. 'I wish more could be done for fractures. If Charlie were here he'd have all kinds of suggestions.'

'Yes, he was always ahead of his time, Charlie. He would have been a great man if he'd lived.'

'He was a great man when he died,' Maevy said, and then seeing the lack of envy on her sister's face, 'and so was your John.' Truthfulness made her add, 'in his own way.'

Lizzie and Ernest looked up surprised, when the two sisters were shown into the sitting-room that evening by

Jessie, the maid. Lizzie's immediate impression was how well Aunt Isobel was looking since Uncle John had died, or rather, since she had gone to live with Maevy. 'Now, this is lovely!' She jumped up, followed more leisurely by Ernest. 'Look who's here, Kit and Annabel!' The children were sitting on two stools with books in their hands. 'Ernest's giving them a reading lesson.' They were kissed and cuddled and their books admired until Ernest broke in and asked when he was going to be noticed.

'You must stay for dinner,' he said. 'It's not often I get the chance of dining with three beautiful ladies.'

'I'm afraid we can't,' Maevy said. 'Susan's cooking a roast, and the smell from the kitchen was so powerful that it wafted us to your very door.'

'I put rosemary in the pan,' Isobel said, 'that's why.' She led the children back to their stools, looking pointedly at her sister. Lizzie saw the look.

'I can just hear Susan,' she said, hiding her anxiety. It couldn't be anything to do with Grandma, could it? '"Whit outlandish thing is this, Missus Craigie? Rosemary!"' It was a good imitation. '"Ur ye tryin' to pooson us aw?"'

'You ought to be on the stage, Lizzie.' Maevy looked amused. 'You've always been a great mimic.' Surely if it was something awful which had brought her, Lizzie thought, she would have burst right out with it.

'Don't put wicked ideas in her head,' Ernest said. 'She has enough already. Well, if you aren't going to stay, may I give you a glass of sherry?'

'Yes, please,' Isobel said without hesitation. 'Tell them, Maevy. Lizzie's anxious to know.'

'We had a letter from Terence this morning. I couldn't find you in the office today, Ernest.'

'I was at Kilmarnock seeing . . . go on.' Lizzie's heart became contracted, there was a dull, fearful kind of pain in it.

'It's Grandma, isn't it?' She had known from the

397

beginning. Her aunts always stood on ceremony in their visiting. 'Don't tell me she's ill?' She tried to smile, to be calm.

'Thanks, Ernest.' Maevy had accepted a sherry. 'She's fallen, I'm sorry to tell you. Now, don't distress yourself so much, Lizzie. I know how fond you are of her. We all are. It was a week ago. Terence didn't want to alarm us once he knew there was no danger.'

'Has she broken anything?' Ernest said from the side table.

'Yes, I'm afraid she has. Her hip.'

'Oh, poor Grandma!' Images rushed to Lizzie's mind: she and Grandma choosing clothes at the Colosseum, walking round the store queening it – 'Good morning, Mrs McGrath.' That was long ago before Nigel's father. Afternoon teas in Buchanan Street, with those blue eyes like jewels under her veil: 'A little more hot water, please,' to the waitress. She charmed everybody. 'What will it mean?'

'She'll be confined to bed to begin with. She's in plaster. But her health's good, and possibly in another week or so they'll carry her downstairs during the day, to a couch.'

'Shouldn't we go right away, my love?' Lizzie appealed to Ernest.

'Perhaps. Let's sit down sensibly and talk about it now we know the worst.' He dispensed drinks to Isobel and Lizzie, said to the children, 'I want you to go upstairs now, please. Jane will be waiting with your tea.'

'But we like it here!' Kit pouted. 'We can make a mess . . .'

'Do as Daddy says.' Lizzie spoke sternly. 'But first I'll help you to clear up your toys, and those books. That's right, Annabel,' – Annabel was more biddable – 'you're a clever girl. Now you can take your brother by the hand and say good-night to your great-aunts.' She hugged them. 'I'll come up and see you in your beds later.'

398

When she had shut the door on them she sighed, 'I'd spoil them, I know.' She sat down beside Maevy. 'You just can't think of Grandma unable to move. What do you think? Should we go over?'

'Terence doesn't seem to think so.'

'I agree with him,' Ernest said. 'It would only alarm her. He would have said if she were in any danger. There are letters, and in a few weeks we can pay visits, in turns . . .'

'If we waited,' Lizzie appealed to Maevy, 'we wouldn't regret it, I mean, there isn't any real danger with a broken hip, is there?' She'd been a good nurse, Aunt Maevy. Look how she'd helped through the children's births, so calm and cool. Not like Colin Thomson . . .

'Just the obvious one. People's bodies are meant to be used. Parts don't work so well when they aren't, but that would apply to you and me as well. And especially someone like Mother who is active by nature . . .' Lizzie knew she could not press her.

'It's a cold house, Woodlea.' She remembered the black and white tiled hall with the roaring fire of logs and the draughts playing round her ankles. The Hall was in a hollow, well sheltered by trees, and she and Ernest spent a fortune on heating, with fires in every room. Aunt Honor was not domesticated. She sat at her writing desk wrapped in a weird variety of shawls, doors were left open if not windows; they were the type of family who brought the outdoors in with them and seemed sometimes not to know the difference.

'Oh, she would have fared for better here!' she burst out. 'That lovely warm room of hers and the eiderdowns and hot-water bottles, and I got her such nice fluffy bed-jackets with satin ribbons which she adored, and I would never let her downstairs until all the rooms were properly aired and warmed; but there she wanders about as she likes with Terence away a lot and Honor shut up there, not unkind, they love her very much, but the difference is that they didn't change their way of life for her whereas we did . . .' She felt the tears running down her face.

Ernest came to her and put his arms round her. Dear Ernest. He understood. 'Don't pay too much attention to what my Lizzie's saying,' she could hear the smile in his voice. 'She's upset at the thought of her beloved grandmother.'

The aunts understood it was the suffering. 'I'm sorry.' She took the handkerchief which Ernest held out. 'I didn't mean half of that, or if I did I exaggerated. I know it was Grandma's choice to go to Woodlea. It's her home. It gives her something she can't get here.' She took a sip of sherry and smiled around. 'That's my exhibition over.'

'We must make plans,' Ernest said, 'to spread our visits. Maevy and I can't be away at the same time, so supposing you and Isobel go first? We have Kieran coming this summer. We'd go before that. And there's Ellie.'

'And letters,' Isobel said, 'plenty of letters.'

'You write wonderful ones,' Lizzie said. 'And presents. I'll go to Glasgow tomorrow and see what I can find for her: something beautiful like a fringed shawl, and those lovely chocolates you can buy from that Continental man in Sauchiehall Street. Grandma likes the dark bitter ones. And books . . .' She was talking gaily again, she heard her own voice, but her heart was still aching. She could not understand it. Grandmother was old now. Most elderly people had some sort of setback sometime or other because of their age. They became frailer . . .

She said to Ernest in bed later, 'Did I make an awful fool of myself with the aunts? My tongue runs away with me when I'm upset, and that weeping, when they were so calm! I'm ashamed of myself.'

'I'm sure you didn't make a fool of yourself. I know you, and so do they. Did you notice how sensible Aunt

Isobel was, by the way? Few comments, but those to the point. They know how much you're attached to your grandmother. You lived with her as a little girl and you've always confided in her.'

'And yet, isn't it strange? Aunt Isobel was my mother for so long and sometimes now I can hardly believe it.'

'It's the early years that count. But it's my guess you'll draw closer to her now that her husband is dead. He restricted her emotionally.'

'Why are you so clever, my darling?' She got up on one elbow to look at him. Her low-cut nightgown slid off one shoulder. She did not adjust it.

He smiled at her. 'Now don't put on the pouting little ninny with me because you know I can see through you. You're the clever one, and the intuitive one. Do you know what I think?' He pulled her down so that she lay on his chest, her head under his chin.

'What do you think?' she mumbled at his throat, laughing.

'This is serious. Behave yourself!' He tapped her bottom. 'Those years of constriction, living in the manse, made you go to the opposite extreme later on. Oh, I don't mean you threw your cap over the windmill – at least, not as far as I know – but you needed colour and gaiety in your life. You were deprived, just as your aunt was deprived. But I know that my Lizzie is a deeply caring, loving woman who knows how to use her head as well as her body and her heart. It's my secret.' He raised her face and kissed her mouth.

'Just as it's my secret that you are the most passionate lover a woman could ever wish for although you pretend to be so cool.'

He made love to her with his light kisses and his lean body until he had to drop the lightness. He groaned once or twice.

'Yes, I know your secret,' she said.

401

'What is it?' His tone was light again, but his body was not still.

'You're afraid of your emotions, although unlike mine they weren't nipped in the bud. It's only with me you can release them.'

He took her in his arms, silent for once. Usually after lovemaking she slept deeply and peacefully, but this time her thoughts were full of Maeve lying in bed in far-off Ireland, stiff and immobile while that busy household went on round her, trapped in a bedroom which was not warm enough, where she probably did not have enough scented bath salts or perfume. Yes, that was another thing. She must put some in the parcel tomorrow from her favourite parfumier in Buchanan Street.

And as well as deputations of visitors from Scotland, Uncle Patrick might visit Ireland when he heard about her accident, and certainly Aunt Kate. One thing about Woodlea, she thought, the British Army itself could march in the front door and they would get a good welcome, a warm sup of tea or something stronger, if my father had anything to do with it. It was that kind of house.

22

Ellie was finishing a letter to Kieran. She had thought her
mother had looked tired when she had visited her that
weekend, and had said she would take on the task of the
weekly report on Grandma's condition.

She's downstairs now and being thoroughly spoiled, although
Lizzie thinks she would have been better off with her. I only
wish I could go oftener to see her, but my studies are demanding,
as you can guess. I must get a good pass. I've a feeling my skills,
such as they are, are going to be needed.

You're far away from war clouds, Kieran, but here – there is
a strong feeling of what I can only call impending doom. I went
with mother to hear Earl Roberts speaking at the University,
and came home full of foreboding.

I wish you could have been there. Everyone in the hall had
their faces lifted to him as if they were listening to a prophet.

Hearing him brought back my father to me. He thought
Roberts had prolonged the Boer War. I said this to mother, and
she said, 'Well, you know Charlie wasn't committed to the idea
of war, long or short. He never believed that out of evil came
good. But I think sometimes they're necessary.' I said that didn't
excuse the prisoners' camps set up by Kitchener, and she
laughed at me and said, 'Your moral indignation does you
credit.' Am I a prig, do you think?

He told us that war was coming to Europe, that 'Britain alone
stands still, repeating the old watchwords, recklessly trusting to
worn-out systems.'

My father was never taken in by rally cries or slogans, but he
went because he felt he was needed. And yet isn't it ironical that
it wasn't in the War he lost his life but in a motor accident at
home . . .

We stood up and cheered with the rest when the old man had
finished. I said to mother that he was like an old oak in the wind
and she whispered back, 'Aye, but not as good as Mrs Pankhurst!' She's a caution . . .

It was late September before Kieran came to Scotland, but he was now installed in the Hall. Kate had intended to come also, with the intention of visiting Maeve as well, but at the last moment James had one of his bronchitic attacks.

'They're frightening while they last,' Kieran told Lizzie and Ernest at dinner the first night. 'She didn't dare set off. All summer she's wanted to go to Ireland, but it seems that's the worst time for him. We're beginning to think it's the humidity of the Hudson Valley. They're talking about coming back to Scotland.'

'That would be a big move for them,' Ernest said.

'You did it once or twice and it's suited you all right.' He raised his glass to Lizzie. He was able to say that in all sincerity and without envy. That long-lasting love of his for her had died slowly, to be replaced by a cousinly caring. It gave him pleasure to see them together.

His mother and father had known, but they had never raised any objection to the idea of cousins marrying. They had none of the prejudices of Uncle Patrick, who had once said to him that he would rather die than see Sarah marrying Robert. Prejudices made you old before your time, he had thought, looking at his uncle's stern mouth. Thank God his mother had never been like that. She was an example for living.

But although his love for Lizzie was dead, it did not prevent him admiring her sitting opposite him in her white lace dress, low cut, with her copper hair piled high. She was grandmother when she was young but on a smaller scale, a desirable woman in her prime and obviously in love with her husband, which was right and proper. The glances which she and Ernest exchanged made him feel *de trop*, although he was sure they were unintentional.

'And you'll be looking forward to seeing Ellie,' Lizzie said. 'We would have asked her here tonight but she's too busy during the week. She works at her studies like a Trojan. Aunt Maevy thinks she's trying for a First.'

'Is it partly a justification for Colin Thomson?' he asked.

'Do you know about him?' She looked surprised.

'Yes, I do.' He smiled at her because she was a joy to look at, and it was pleasant to admire without desiring. 'We've always exchanged letters. There's something about me which induces young women to give me their confidences.' He teased her. 'Remember you did the same?'

'Well, what if I did!' Her eyes flashed. 'You're wicked to remind me before Ernest! What is it about your half-brother?' She appealed to Ernest. 'Is it something in his temperament?'

'Goodness only knows. It was the same with Gaylord.' He looked at Kieran. 'Sorry. Do you prefer not to speak of it?'

'No, no. It's over now. Just as I've decided to throw away my sticks, and my guilt at the same time, and keep only the good memories. But I sometimes think Uncle Patrick hasn't.'

'There he's unfortunate. He can neither forgive nor forget.'

'Who is it he has to forgive?' Lizzie asked.

'Fate, or God, if you like.'

'Aunt Maria is the best wife for him,' he told her, 'but the best tonic is young Ginny. He adores her. Needless to say, she can twist him round her little finger. She's sixteen now and bringing a lot of her friends about the place. Claremont is a happier house because of her.'

'And what about Sarah?'

'She's a confirmed old maid now. Full of good works and like an aunt to her sister. Robert has a young lady now. Edith Barnes – Edie, she's called. I don't know what

Sarah feels about that, but she's too like her father for you ever to know.'

'He was *my* father for a short time.' Lizzie shook her head unbelievingly. 'I was too young to remember. But he should never have stopped Sarah from marrying Robert, or she should have done what Grandmother did, run away.'

'Ah, but she's not Grandmother,' Ernest said.

'How is she?' Kieran asked. 'I'm charged by my mother to visit her before I go back, and indeed she may well be there before me. She's torn at the moment, but she worries about her a great deal in spite of the cheerful letters Grandma sends from Ireland.'

'That's her principal occupation,' Lizzie said. 'And receiving visitors. Ernest and I have gone twice and so have Aunt Maevy and Aunt Isobel, Ellie once. As has half Roscommon County. She's downstairs all day now, but unable to walk much. The plaster's off, but it's left her a cripple. Can you imagine, our grandmother a cripple?' Kieran saw her eyes fill with tears.

'Maybe Ellie and I could pay her a visit while I'm here?'

'Well, you could ask her on Sunday. We're having a hen party here for you. The ladies from Braidholme. We call them the Distaff Side. They're all involved in Votes for Women.'

'Not Aunt Isobel?'

'Yes, Aunt Isobel, believe it or not. She helps to prepare Aunt Maevy's speeches and attends meetings in Glasgow Green like her bodyguard. Ellie's too busy to go to many. She's at the Royal most of the time now, coming up to her last year. Then there's Dr Geddes in the village. She's another member of the party. She was even locked up in Holloway Prison for two months for smashing shop windows in London.'

'Well, well!' Kieran looked at them, rolling his eyes. 'I can see I have to visit Scotland to see action!'

The dinner party on Sunday was just as pleasant, with all the ease which families experience when there are no outsiders. Ellie was staying the night at Braidholme so that she would not have to rush away. She looked different, Kieran thought. Her new slenderness made her look taller, and her hair was dressed in a severe fashion, pulled back from her face in a low knot. The dress itself was a dull green marocain, and she wore no jewellery except a simple string of pearls. She gave him the impression of a girl who had put away her femininity for the time being.

She relaxed soon, however, aided by Ernest's teasing, and he saw she still had the same sense of fun which he remembered. 'I'll soon be afraid to speak to you,' he told her, 'Dr McNab, no less.'

'Oh, I'm not there yet.' Her eyes were still laughing at one of Ernest's sallies. 'Not till next March.'

'Is it all work and no play?' he asked her. 'I was hoping you'd let me take you to the King's Theatre or a sail down the Clyde at least. Mother said I mustn't miss that.'

'Evenings are out except Sundays,' she said. The laughter died.

'Well, then, a breath of fresh air won't go amiss. What do you say, Aunt Isobel?' He turned to her. 'Wouldn't you say that a sail down the Clyde would do Ellie a lot of good?'

'I would indeed. I should think she'd be glad to get the smell of sickness out of her nose.'

'Thanks very much.' He looked triumphantly at Ellie. His mother would be pleased to hear about the change in her weakly sister. Lizzie was right in that expression she had used, the distaff side. Women together were a formidable force.

* * *

The following Saturday he and Ellie set off for a sail down the Clyde to Rothesay. Aunt Maria had told him not to miss that, nor the joys of Ettrick Bay. 'You've changed, Ellie,' he said to her, when they were leaning on the rail of the steamer. It was the end of the season and the boat was half empty. The band sounded melancholy, and the man who had come round with the velvet collecting bag had shaken it sadly as if he did not expect much. His face brightened at the sight of Kieran's two half-crowns.

'In what way?' She did not look at him.

'You've grown up. You're more serious, too serious . . .' he burst out, 'and your dress sense's completely gone. You're dressing like an old woman.'

She turned to him, her eyes blazing. 'What an impudent thing to say! It takes an American to be really rude. Oh, I daresay all the women have to do *there* is dress to please men, but *here*, at least amongst the people I know, there are more important things – study, votes for women . . .' – she paused for breath – '. . . Mother and Ernest are constantly involved in Trade Union problems, and everyone knows we're rushing towards war. Don't you *think* in America?'

'You should get angry more often,' he said. 'It makes your eyes flash instead of looking like a cold fish. And if you try really hard your hair might come tumbling down, which would be a great improvement . . .' She stared at him, transfixed, then turned away, a look of disgust on her face.

'Ach, you!' she said, 'I don't know why I bother!'

He put his hand through her arm. 'I was teasing you, Ellie. I'm sorry. I wanted to . . . ruffle you up. But I have to think about labour problems in our business, too, and we think and talk a lot about the war. Don't you remember the long talk we had with Father when we had tea together after the accident . . .' – he still did not say it easily – '. . . with Gaylord?'

408

He saw her face soften. The wind had whipped some stray wisps of hair about her face, and she looked absurdly young, fourteen years younger than me, he remembered. No, it was impossible.

She turned and because of the background of the shipyards there seemed to be a gantry growing out of the top of her head. If I say that, he thought, she'll jump off the ship and swim for John Brown's. But her anger was gone. 'Yes, those were nice times, in spite of that terrible tragedy, or maybe because of it. It brought us closer.'

'You helped me so much. I owe my recovery to you. I don't mean my injury. That was only physical.'

'I can tell you now,' she said, 'I admired you at the time. Though,' she spoke with mock asperity, 'I can't say the same now. "Dressing like an old woman" indeed!'

'I'm sorry, but you *have* changed. It wouldn't have mattered what I said. You're quieter now, except for that cloudburst. But I know why. It's Colin, isn't it?' She did not speak. 'Ellie,' he drew his hand away and put it round her shoulders, 'you helped me about Gaylord. Let me help you about Colin.'

'There's no need,' she said. 'I don't love him any more. I don't like . . . men. Maybe that's why I dress like an old woman. It was the humiliation. He took way my belief in myself as a woman. He . . . spurned me.' She laughed. 'Now, isn't that an old-fashioned word to use and me a courtesy member of the Scottish Branch of the Women's Social and Political Union.'

'Not if it's true. Tell me, has anyone ever asked you out since then, I mean, a man . . .?'

'Oh, yes.' She shrugged. 'There are plenty of men at the Royal.'

'Well, isn't that proof enough for you?'

'I don't count them as men. They're workmates.'

'Would you count *me* if I asked you out? Not just a sail down the Clyde.'

'You're my cousin.'

'But still "a man for aw that and aw that",' he quoted, laughing.

'More like an uncle,' she said.

He hugged her closely against him. 'Well, will you do what your old uncle asks you and put on your prettiest dress and let your hair hang loose and wear earrings?'

'I don't . . . go in for earrings.'

'That's a pity, because my mother asked me to give you a pair from America, turquoises. They're in my pocket now. She said she thought they would suit your fair beauty.'

'Oh, that's kind. No, don't show me them now. Yes,' she turned to him, her eyes soft, 'I'd do what you say, to please Aunt Kate.'

'I've got tickets for the King's Theatre for tonight,' he said.

'Oh, I couldn't! That would be wasting too much time . . . Well,' she put her finger to her lower lip, 'I *could* work all day tomorrow. All right,' she said, smiling brilliantly at him. 'I'm a bought woman. For the sake of the earrings . . .'

He thought she looked beautiful in the dress which, it so happened, nearly matched the earrings, and although her hair was not hanging loose she had let little ringlets escape which glinted on her neck. Nor was the dress low-cut, but the upper part of the bodice was of fine voile, the half-revealed flesh being more seductive than had it been fully exposed. He told her she was lovely in the cab going down Elmbank Street, and after that they talked of other things, safe things. He did not notice the play although she said, being a Glaswegian, that it was very well done and they were seeing it before it went to London because it was well known that they were the most critical of audiences. When he left her at the door of her lodgings at

Dowanside Street, he hugged her. 'Dear wee cousin,' he said. He was suddenly afraid of his feelings.

She was shy. 'I'd ask you in, but Jean'll be in bed.'

'Oh, no. I wouldn't want to spoil your good name. Thank you for coming, Ellie.' He went away, smiling stupidly, he thought, for someone of his age.

Ernest was sitting up having a last brandy. 'Come and join me, Kieran,' he said when he went in. 'Lizzie's gone up. I said I would wait for you.'

'There was no need.'

'It's a pleasure. Did you have a nice time?'

'Very. It's a fine theatre. I couldn't tell you a word about the play.'

'Couldn't you hear? Some say the acoustics . . .'

'They couldn't have been better. I was too busy thinking about Ellie.'

Ernest got up and poured him a brandy, handed it over and sat down again. 'Thinking about Ellie?' he said conversationally.

'You're a cool chap,' Kieran said. 'I wonder what Lizzie sees in you.'

'Wonder away, then. You'll never know.'

'Do you think I'm too old for her?'

'Lizzie?' Now he was being mischievous.

'You know damn well I don't mean Lizzie, but I don't mind telling you now that I was in love with her for years.'

'Tell me something I *don't* know.'

'Ah, but you always know everything. You were that kind of brother, superior, knowing. Ernest, tell me what I should do. I've fallen in love with another cousin and this one's fourteen years younger than me! She probably wouldn't look at me in a month of Sundays. Oh, Ernest, if you could have seen her tonight . . .' Ernest listened sympathetically, silently, for a long time, getting up occasionally to top up their glasses.

* * *

411

Next morning the telegram came from Terence when they were at breakfast.

'Mother has pneumonia. Sinking. Come at once.'

Ernest got up, grim-faced. 'I'll drive round and see Maevy at once. Terence will have sent her one, too.'

Kieran was surprised at Lizzie's calmness, as if she had borrowed it from Ernest. 'I'll go upstairs and get our valises packed. Could you drive to Crannoch and get the tickets, Kieran? Aunt Maevy and Aunt Isobel, Ellie – she will want to be there – Ernest and I. That's five.'

'Six,' he said. 'There's me.'

At Crannoch Post Office he sent telegrams to Wolf House and Claremont saying they were on their way to Ireland. Some of the calmness had infected him. This was too important an event for hysteria. It was as if the image of the dying woman with all her beauty and dignity was strong in their minds.

23

She knew she was dying when they carried her upstairs again. The leg was useless – she had long since accepted that – but she had got quite used to queening it on the sofa with the family *breenjing* in and out most of the day to see her, and that nice minister from Boyle, and the special visits of Ernest and Lizzie, Maevy and Isobel, and that dear lass, Ellie . . .

But there had been a wet miserable day when wee Kevin had been left to sit on the sofa beside her and coughed all the time. 'You ought to get that lad a good cough mixture from the chemist's, Moira,' she had said. 'Tell him to make you one up specially. They all have their own tried and trusted remedies and they're often better than getting a line from the doctor.'

'I'll do that, Grandma,' she had said, 'first thing in the morning. I told him to put his hand up when he coughed, and turn away from you.'

'Oh, he did that all right, he was as good as gold . . .'

She fought for a few days against the feeling that there was something wrong, and not only with the leg. Maybe she should read the Bible for a bit, and tell them in the kitchen that she wanted quiet because it had become an effort to speak much with that tightness in her chest. She had asked Terence, when she was first carried down, to put the Bible near her, that it gave a good impression.

'To tell you the truth,' she had said to him, laughing, 'old Mooly Murdoch, your father-in-law, no less, put me off it, God rest his soul.' Now she took it up and looked for the bits she liked best.

'But the greatest of these is charity.'

Charlie had said it was a bad translation, that it meant 'love'. Oh, she knew all about love. The Bible slipped from her fingers. Making love with Alastair on her sixty-second birthday, for instance. What would old Mooly have said about that?

But Alastair was gone, like so many from her life, starting with that dear lad, John, drowned at six in the Sholtie. Would she ever forget the face of that man of hers with tears streaking the coal dust and the dead lad in his arms? Like one of those paintings you sometimes saw in great churches, only it was Mary with the Lord, sometimes a gey big Lord for her knees. 'Pietas', they were called. That had been *her* Pieta, hers and Kieran's.

All gone. Catherine with her voluntary work for the Temperance Union and her man quietly drinking himself to death because she did not like him in bed, and in the end taking her own life because of him carrying on with Maria's maid. No, it was the letters from Ethel Mavor that had done it. She had died, too, poor soul, of some wasting disease. That seemed harsh justice, considering she had sent the letters for love of Terence, even if it were thwarted love. And what had happened to Flora Paterson, Flora Napier she became, and that child growing up in faraway Melrose, most likely Terence's? He'd be a young man now. It would serve no purpose to know.

And Charlie. She had grieved deeply about Charlie, that king of men who lived on in his daughter. Maevy was too stoical. She should have wept more. She had encouraged Terence to weep when Catherine died, but she could not do it for herself. Now she and Isobel had found some kind of goal in working for Votes for Women. That was love of a kind, too.

But, all the same, Maevy's stoicism had made Ellie copy her when the young doctor had upped and gone off to Australia. Or did it build character rather than too much weeping? It was difficult to tell. So many things that were not settled in her mind, questions she had pondered over, so little time.

Alastair had been a good partner there, not so intuitive as Kieran, but always willing to apply his mind to a problem, and tease it like a dog shaking a rat. 'Intellectual discussions', he had called them. Ah, well, he had had the grand education at Eton, like Nigel, like Jonty who was having it now. She would not see what happened to Jonty . . . that brought it home, sure enough.

Somehow she was no longer on the sofa downstairs, like Elizabeth Barrett Browning, Honor had often said. She was in that airy bedroom, sometimes too airy if Edna forgot to shut the window, and Honor never noticed when she sat down to talk.

'What about your writing, Honor?' she said. 'I don't want you to . . .'

'To the devil with my writing,' she said, 'you come first.'

She liked that. A strange lass, Honor, but the right one for Terence.

Terence sat with her in the evenings and talked, or listened to her talking. She was like a well which kept on filling up the more she talked. 'It's as if my life was pouring out of me,' she said, 'everything that's happened to me isn't in the past, it's here and now. Are you fed up listening, Terence?'

'Fed up? Not a chance. I had to listen to you when I was a wee lad, so I'm into the swing of it. Do you remember that rope you kept hidden under your apron when you chased us over the fields?'

'But I never used it. It was my sign of authority. Your father couldn't bear to punish you. He was too gentle . . .' he was the one she could not think about yet. It hurt too much, the thought, or was it the joy that soon . . . no, she would not say that to Terence. It would only distress him.

'What's wrong with me, Terence,' she said, 'apart from this old hip? No beating about the bush or I'll bring out the rope.'

'A touch on your chest, the doctor says.' He looked away.

'A touch of what? Come on, now.'

'Pneumonia.' He had the voice he had used long ago when he was confessing to some misdeed, but when he turned, his face was running with tears.

'What's all this?' she said. '*A'm* no' greetin'.' The Scottish way of speaking came to her from the past. It was mostly Irish with her now, the speech of her childhood.

'I'm just a big babby when it comes to it.' He took out his handkerchief and wiped his eyes. 'Have a rest now.'

'What does the doctor say?' She put a hand on his arm. 'The truth, now.'

'It's not severe, just a touch and that's the God's truth. But . . .'

'But we have to bear in mind that I'm not so young now, is that it?'

'Something of that nature.' The old Terence looked out of his eyes, as handsome as the devil.

'It's not funny growing old. I want to say that when I'm not rambling. Oh, I know I ramble at times, but I'm clear-headed the now. I'm proud, vain, and not for want of being told. No man took more pleasure in my looks than I did myself. I don't think that was so wicked, do you?'

'I'd say it was downright healthy.'

'Maybe it's easier for a plain woman to grow old. They melt into the background better. Or one who didn't like the pleasures . . . the pleasures . . .' Terence wasn't there any more, or she wasn't with him. It was the same thing.

So much love, so many loving days too, not only here in Ireland or in Scotland, but in far-off America. That time they had all gone for a sail on the *Mary Powell* and

416

got off for a picnic at a place with the strange name of Poughkeepsie. Sitting at the side of that great, broad river, with the childen playing on the bank and the girls busy laying the tablecloth, she had said, 'Today I am happy.' She saw their smiling faces, Isobel, Kate and Caroline, the boys turning at the sound of her voice, waving in the sunlight; a day without tomorrow, she had thought, and had known she would remember it.

And there was the day of Maevy's and Charlie's wedding, back in Scotland. Oh, the time that girl had wasted while she got everything sorted out, and the compassion of Charlie while he waited! Any love which was a real love had to have compassion in it. She had never known the other kind, thank God.

The bedroom was never clear now, the furniture seemed to advance out of the shadows and retreat. The doctor came in and out through the shadows like a wee fairy man from the bogs, sounding her, poulticing her and giving her strange-like concoctions to drink which made her vomit.

'Doctor Doherty,' she said, 'I want to keep my dignity if you please, and I cannot do with your purges nor your medicines that make me *bock* over the sheets.' He looked amazed.

'Lady Crawford!' he said. Oh, he had to go away and change his ideas about ladies!

There was a dark woman with a sweet face bending over her. The dark hair had a streak of white in it. 'Don't you know me, Mother?' she said. 'It's Kate.'

'Kate? How did you get here?'

'By boat.' She was smiling.

'Did Terence send for you? I'm not having any fuss when it's just a touch of . . . a touch on my chest.'

'I give you my word of honour he didn't send for me, or if he did, the letter's with James. I was coming with Kieran but James had one of his bad turns . . .'

417

'Kieran's dead.'

'Not *your* Kieran, Mother, mine. He's visiting Ernest and Lizzie in Scotland.'

'Oh, *that* Kieran? Didn't he get shot?' There was something about that poor lad Gaylord in her mind but she could not get the hang of it. Long ago there had been that other shooting over Emily Barthe, a duel . . . 'She said I was very much *du monde*,' she said.

'Who did?' Kate was stroking her brow, softly. A lovely woman. Everything you could wish for in a daughter. Never one troublesome moment in her whole life. If there was a fault in her, that was it.

'Emily. Your step-daughter.' She felt her mind clear, her voice like a bell. 'Had you forgotten that Charles and her lover had a duel?'

Kate for some reason was weeping. 'You'll never cease to surprise me. Fancy remembering that.'

'It was a grand time. Exciting. And the Eiffel Tower in the background. We went to its inauguration. To *l'Exposition Universelle*. All those French voices. *Le Premier coup de canon*. Charles said I was a natural linguist. *Une ascension dans la Tour* . . .' she heard her own voice speaking those strange words with no trouble. She had had a flair . . .

There was a time when her body seemed to be on fire and she was being sponged down by a nurse, but the nurse turned out to be Maevy. With Kieran's hands. 'You should be at the Royal,' she said, enjoying the pleasure.

'I don't work there now, Mother. I'm in McGraths.'

'And what does Charlie say to that?'

'He's dead, Mother, a long time ago, but he wouldn't object.'

'Something of your own, that's it, something of your own. I worked there too, Maevy, started it. It's a great thing for a woman to find herself with something away from her man, and you know me, there was no one who cared more about her man.'

'Nor me,' Maevy said. 'We're two of a kind. That's right, Ellie, put some more hot water in.' There was an assistant nurse beside her with fair hair like Ellie, or *was* it her? She tried to smile but she was too tired . . .

Sometimes it was men. Ernest with his light hands and that quirk at the side of his mouth. Oh, he was debonair, Ernest, light and yet strong underneath, the right choice for Lizzie. She needed lightness and frills and frivolity after that dreary manse upbringing. No wonder she liked clothes. 'Has Lizzie got any new dresses for the winter?' she asked him. If you had said to Ernest, 'Is the Lord God coming up the Sholtie Brae?' he would have said without turning a hair, 'I'll go and see.'

'I think she's brought one or two to show you,' he said. 'I'll go and get her.' Why were they all here, she thought. Was it a family reunion, like her retiral party, only it was being held at Woodlea because of her useless leg?

Lizzie came in wearing a burgundy costume with a skirt so tight you could see the shape of her legs through it. She whirled round. 'It's called a hobble skirt, Grandma. The very devil to walk in but Ernest likes it.'

'Very much *du monde*,' she pronounced, pursing her lips judiciously the way she used to do at the Colosseum.

'Emily.' Lizzie knew at once because she had been at school there, at her expense, although she had never told her. She sat down at the bedside and her expensive perfume floated about them seductively, but then, Lizzie *was* seductive.

'You can give me a mannequin show every day, like Mr Walter Wilson used to lay on for us. Oh, the joy of it! Do you remember the Colosseum that Christmas we took tea in their new salon?'

'Yes, but it was Aunt Maevy you had tea with. I was with Robert, being shown the dancing horse.'

'The dancing horse?' That sounded magical. But she did not want to think of horses yet because that made her think of Kieran and she was keeping that for later.

She knew that Lizzie slipped away and that the doctor and Maevy were there, swift and silent, and that there was a great deal of pain all over her body. 'It's no fun growing old,' she said, and Dr Doherty put his red face close to hers and said, 'You never spoke a truer word, Lady Crawford.' He must be thinking of someone else. She was Mrs McGrath, formerly Major Muldoon's daughter of Woodlea in the County of Roscommon.

You couldn't dream of anything decent when you had all this pain. Patrick was there and he was no trouble, sitting silently beside her holding her hand. Poor Patrick. He suffered so much over one thing or another. Maybe it would be easier for him at the end because of that.

'You tell him to let himself go a little,' she said to Maria. How had she got in? 'Life's difficult enough without making it any harder for yourself.'

'I always try to do my best, Mother,' she said.

'Well, try doing your worst for a change,' and then since that was maybe a bit nippy, she said, 'You were my support when your father died, Patrick. Once you washed the kitchen floor. Just a boy. I'll never forget that. Nor how you were such a good father to Lizzie for as long as Bessie . . . lasted.' She shouldn't have said that with Maria there, but you couldn't think of everything.

Once when she opened her eyes a frail girl with fair hair was sitting beside her. 'Isobel,' she said, 'you've hardly changed after all those years.'

'Oh, I've changed a lot, Mother,' she said. She was so light when she bent to give her a kiss, like a shadow.

'Maybe your voice is different, more . . . positive. Do you like living with Maevy?'

'Yes, I take care of her.' More than her voice had

changed. 'She's a hard worker, but I manage to lighten her load a little. And I write out her speeches.'

'For McGraths?' It would be for the board meetings.

'No, for Votes for Women.'

'Oh,' she nodded, trying to look wise, 'there's no saying where that will reach.'

'You were a pioneer, Mother, in that direction. I realize that now. I'm trying to do my bit.' Yes, there was no doubt about it. John's dying had done her a lot of good.

Lizzie's perfume helped a lot, and the sweet-smelling lotions, because there were bad times in pneumonia or whatever it was a touch of, horrible times. But Maevy was the best nurse who ever lived, efficient, cool, making you feel the same. She dampened by some means or other that terrible fire in her chest, but the next trial was that the room kept fading. And the people. They did not make a sound, as if the wind from the Curlew Mountains wafted them in and out. Sometimes there were two or three at a time emerging from the shadows, touching her hand, saying, 'Mother,' then going away again; sometimes there was only one.

This time it was Terence, or was he there more than the others? He had always been a Mammy's boy, and his hands were Kieran's, firm and gentle on her. 'Your father's hands, Terence,' she said, 'on me, or on a horse . . .' She was sorry her voice sounded rough. The fire in her chest must have singed it. 'Those morning rides with the frost in the air just about this time . . . of the year. I know it's October by the smell. Is old Mick burning the leaves?'

'Yes, he is, Mother,' he said.

'He always beat me on those rides, your father, how-ever hard I tried. It was the hands, so gentle, so sure. That's why you're good with horses. You take it off him. Alastair was different, kind, but he hadn't that extra bit, the gentleness with the sureness. When he and I were together we were two people . . .'

'I know,' he said, 'I know. I've found with Honor what you found with father. It's a rare gift . . .' – he coughed – . . . from Someone.' Old Mooly had put him off it too, or at least the saying of it.

The room was fading again. So were the faces round her. She had thought there was only Terence. Honor, Maevy, Isobel, Kate, Patrick, Maria, Ellie, a sea of faces. And Kate's Kieran. Had he been with the other children on that picnic in that place with the strange name, Poughkeepsie? When she had sat watching them playing at the river; such a happy day, she had thought, *a day without tomorrow* . . .

She gathered her strength to ask him, and then it did not matter. A thought had struck her, a clear thought like an imprisoned crystal drop in a glass. *This* was tomorrow. Tomorrow was today. It was like a radiance surrounding her, the certainty of it, the wonder of it. Why were they weeping when she was so happy?

24

Ellie graduated in May, 1914, with a proud Maevy, Isobel, Lizzie and Ernest all there to wish her well. It was difficult to believe it was all over, after those long years of study. Except for the short, swift stab of excitement when she walked up to be capped, the principal feeling was one of anti-climax. 'Dr McNab'. It was like wearing her father's clothes.

She seemed to be the only woman there without an escort. Jean had her young man, many of her fellow-students had fiancés, brothers. Ernest had left for the office taking Lizzie and Isobel with him. They were going back to Sholton to see to the celebration dinner at the Hall.

She thought of Colin Thomson in far-off Australia, perhaps somewhere else. He had never written. Had she been right in putting her career first? There had been dark times which no one knew about, when she had longed to be 'ordinary', to be a wife, a lover, wanted anything rather than the sterile life of study. But now there was Kieran. 'My patience is not inexhaustible,' he had written in his last letter.

They did not speak much on the train going home to Sholton. Her mother looked tremulous, as if she could not trust herself. Ellie squeezed her arm. 'Do you remember we heard Earl Roberts warning us last May about the prospect of war, Mother?' she said. Maevy nodded.

'Then I was so busy and I forgot about it, especially

423

with Lloyd George busy convincing us that it wouldn't happen.'

'Oh, him! He's a great seducer with words.'

'I was thinking today, at the ceremony, that if it does I'll do what father did, go wherever I'm needed. Never mind the moral implications.' She smiled.

She had never seen her mother's face dissolve like that before. It was running with tears. A young man sitting opposite them looked at her strangely, then kindly turned away and gazed out of the window.

She registered for the degree course in surgery the next day.

'Dearest Kieran . . .' She was writing to him in her room in Hillhead. She had not gone home to live at Braidholme. Although Jean had left and was working in general practice in Coatbridge, she had decided to keep her independence. It was handier here for the University, and for the Royal Infirmary where she was working as a clinical assistant to a surgeon who had known her father.

It was a great day but not the end of the road as I'm going on to do surgery. But the pressure's off a little. If the war doesn't come I'll maybe cast dull care away a little and go to some concerts in St Andrew's Hall. I've developed an interest in music.

As you see I'm still at Dowanside Street. Braidholme now is like a branch of the WSPU with Belle Geddes popping in every evening to keep them up to scratch.

But I'm looking forward to seeing you at Giselle's and Terence's wedding. The invitation came today. She hopes it will be a great family gathering, after the last sad one at Woodlea.

No one here has got over Grandma's death yet. She's left such a gap in our lives, and we all compensate by working or playing harder than ever. It marked for me the beginning of a great change in the world, as if the old one was heaving under us and was about to throw us into some unknown holocaust. Maybe it's as well she isn't here to see it. I say 'unknown', but in my heart of hearts I know what it is. Its long nails are tearing at everything I hold dear – most of all, peace. I've absorbed so much from father. I'm his daughter rather than mother's. Her enthusiasm for Votes for Women will turn to recruiting women for the war effort as soon as it is declared.

Am I a pessimist, do you think? I wouldn't write like this to anyone else. You're my mentor, my dear cousin. To others I'm Dr Elspeth McNab, cool and resourceful in the wards, but 'aye ready for a tare' – and if you don't know what that is I'll show you when we meet in Paris on the 28th June . . .'

For the most part, Ellie thought, looking around, it seemed to be a young person's wedding. Usually weddings and funerals winkled out all the old ones from their corners, but here there were the young, smart Parisian friends of Giselle and her twin brother, and the more Bohemian ones of Terence. The only older people were the bride's and bridegroom's parents, and her mother.

Aunt Isobel had decided to stay at home 'to look after Braidholme and Susan', her own words; Aunt Kate could not leave Kieran's father, and Aunt Maria and Uncle Patrick had decided against the long journey. Perhaps Aunt Maria was beginning to resemble her mother who had always hated the sea voyage.

But as representatives from America, Kieran had escorted Sarah and Ginny, and from Ireland there were the three girls with their husbands, the six of them intent on seeing 'gay Paree'. Dymphna had now married her Denis. Lizzie and Ernest had brought Jonty, now, at fourteen, even more like Nigel in his elegance.

The star of the wedding guests, apart from strong competition from the lively Clare, was young Ginny, Ellie thought, now seventeen and reminding her of Lizzie at the same age. Mother always said Lizzie took after Grandma. She'd never die out. That particular gene was much too strong. Her eyes were drawn again and again to Ginny's bright face, the abundant red-gold hair, the air of owning the world, a very particular thing to be blessed with.

She found herself at a quiet corner table with Kieran. If he had organized it he had done it adroitly, as well as the glasses of champagne and the two plates of wedding cake, recently cut with great aplomb by Terence and Giselle. There had been much laughter and applause. The champagne seemed to be flowing without stop from some hidden fountain in this elegant home of the Barthes.

'Don't they make a wonderful couple?' she said. 'They're so suited. I expect Giselle will became one of those smart young matrons with a weekly *salon* for the great and famous. And we'll boast back home about her and her wonderful painter cousin when his works are selling at enormous prices. Uncle Terence and Aunt Honor are so proud of him.'

'And did you see Emily fluttering round Giselle, arranging her veil as if she had created a wonderful picture herself? She'll boast about Giselle's establishment, Terence's paintings, perhaps their babies. Maybe she'll even give up her lovers.'

She pretended to be shocked. 'What a thing to say!'

'I'm not criticizing, only making a general observation.' She had forgotten how sweet his mouth was. 'In any case it's *quid pro quo*. Charles is reported to have a little love nest on the Left Bank. It was discarded temporarily during a spot of bother – you must have heard the Great Duel Story and how Grandma intervened – but I imagine a few twigs soon put the love-nest to rights again.'

'You're becoming a cynic in your old age.' She laughed, feeling at ease with him, as she always did. Maybe it was enough.

'That was an unkind cut.' His eyes smiled at her. 'I'm still only fourteen years older than you.' He took her hands. 'Have you thought about what I said in my last letter, and the one before that and the one before that?'

'Yes, often. Did you see the papers today?'

'The murder of the Archduke?'

'Yes. I've decided.'

She was ashamed when she saw how his eyes changed, the love in them. 'You're going to marry me? You've kept me waiting for so long, Ellie. I want you so much . . .'

'I . . . think I love you.' Of course she loved him. It was as natural as daylight, wasn't it? 'But the War comes first. I have to wait and see . . .'

'But there's no need to wait! I've plenty of money. It's time you and I were married. Past time. Is it because of your studies?'

She grasped at the straw. 'Yes. I want to be like father, do surgery.' She saw the despair in his face. 'The War's coming. I can't see beyond that. The Naval Reserves have been called up – '

'You don't want to marry me.' He interrupted her. Oh, it was difficult . . .

'I've got to do this. The thought has been with me for a long time. It's something to do with my mother who wanted to go last time and my father who didn't but went, and a justification of myself, my mother's belief in me, Belle's, and so many others. I wouldn't be right with myself otherwise. After that I'll see . . .'

'Just see?' The sweetness went out of his mouth. His eyes were full of hurt.

'I've been trained for this, Kieran.' She had to justify herself. 'My whole life has been shaped towards it. I couldn't just be a married woman sitting at home . . . you understand, don't you?'

'I understand your dilemma. And how you've made your choice.'

'It doesn't mean I'm not fond of you. But how can I even *contemplate* a peaceable married existence in the middle of. . . what's ahead of us, ahead of the whole world especially going to America where I'd just bury my head in the sand?'

'Your mind's made up.' His voice was bleak.

'That's how I am.' Her heart ached for him. 'But after that . . .'

'You'll . . . see?' She heard the bitterness in his voice, but she was fighting a battle for women, wasn't she, not only for herself, just as mother had been doing for so long. They were in the vanguard. Some day it would be different. Men would fully recognize women's rights to fulfil themselves in every way, there would be better arrangements made . . . for eating their cake and having it . . . The truth is, she thought, your love, affection, fondness for Kieran, call it what you will, isn't overwhelming. There was something lacking, something which would drown everything but her need. It might come. But until it did or she found it elsewhere, her need to take part in the War came first. There was certainty.

'Kieran,' she said, suddenly full of tenderness towards him. She put out her hand.

'Am I interrupting anything?' It was Ernest. None of the Frenchmen were any smarter than he in his grey morning coat, the immaculate grey silk cravat, the diamond pin. 'Shall I go away?'

Kieran got up. 'Don't be an ass. Ellie's been telling me that she wants to go and fight the Kaiser single-handed.'

'Well, why don't we join her? All the best people will be there.' He was as insouciant as ever, she thought, and as astute. If he had seen anything in their faces there was to be no comment. 'Meantime I've been sent to gather you in for speechifying. There's a long list of people and most of it will be in French, but my talented wife will translate for us. Come along!'

She sat with Kieran listening to the eulogies to Giselle and Terence who looked well enough content without them. Why did the tears flood her eyes, making her use her handkerchief discreetly? The bride might well lead the bridegroom a song and dance occasionally – the bright mascara-red eyes under the virginal veil promised that – but it would be worth it. Everybody must be true to their own nature. And try to have no regrets.

The future would be exciting and she would be a part of it. Good as well as evil came out of wars. There would be advances in medicine, better communictions, opportunites for travel, barriers would be broken.

But it was not so much the opportunities as the will, she told herself, thinking of Grandma who had always taken her courage in both hands from that first time when she had eloped from Ireland to a strange Scottish village which had become their home. Each place she had lived in she had imbued with her personality, but in the end she had chosen to die in the home she came from. Where would *she* die, now that she had made her choice?

'Do you understand most of it?' Kieran was saying. He was bending his head towards her and a swift pang went through her at the sight of his kind eyes, the sweet mouth. Wasn't he the reincarnation of the man who Grandma had run away with, and whom she had always loved? Was she making a terrible mistake?

'In a way. Look, your sister's on her feet.' She admired Emily the way you would admire a strange bird in an Amazonian forest. She was wearing a brilliant peacock dress and a hat of feathers to match, the veil of which covered her heavily maquillaged features. Her lips were scarlet through it, her eyes sparkled in competition with the diamond brooch at her throat. She fluttered her hands, the scarlet nails gleamed.

'Dear friends,' she smiled around them, she was more French than the French, 'I'm deputizing for my husband, Charles, because in spite of living with me for all those years,' her laughter tinkled and, taking their cue, the dear friends tinkled also, 'his English is very poor. But I couldn't let this occasion go without a few words about the one person whom we all wish had been here today.' Her voice changed. She spoke softly.

'We all loved her, loved her for her beauty and grace, her wonderful vitality. We all listened to her wise counsel. She was part of our life and now she is gone.' There was silence in the elegant room with its white panelled walls and glittering sconces.

'When she came here with her daughter, Maevy . . .' she searched and, having found her, waved elegantly, '. . . dear Maevy . . . in the year of the Paris *Exposition*, I and my family were captivated by her.' She looked at her husband and said, '*Souviens-toi*?'

'*Comment*?' The dark-haired, white-skinned man seemed to wake up from a reverie.

'Lady Crawford, *chéri*.' His wife showed the slightest sign of impatience. '*Grand-mère*.'

'Ah, yes, of course; Lady Crawford!' He kissed his hand in the air. '*De bon courage*.' He searched. '*Et très du monde*.' He looked round the room satisfied.

It was a second before the guests applauded. Ellie was smiling as she did so. Her tears were gone.